SOLOMON'S CARPET

AND

SOLOMON'S SUBMARINE:

THE COMPLETE ADVENTURES

OF JOHN SOLOMON, VOLUME 6

H . BEDFORD-JONES

SOLOMON'S CARPET
AND
SOLOMON'S SUBMARINE
THE ADVENTURES OF
JOHN SOLOMON, VOLUME 6

H. BEDFORD-JONES

COVER BY
JOHN A. COUGHLIN

STEEGER BOOKS • 2021

SOLOMON'S CARPET

IN ORDER rightly to reconstruct the thread of things, it must be remembered that murder was incidental to the real crime. Also, it is necessary to take cognizance of three men who played a rather important part in this hitherto hidden drama of Chicago—even though, to the world at large, each of them might seem insignificant.

If one walks from Van Buren Street to Randolph, on State Street, a very interesting store will be passed. More strictly speaking, it is an auction room, where each afternoon is devoted to auction sales. The greater part of its business is done by private sale, however, and limousines are always standing at its door.

In the windows one may see an amazing collection of choice Oriental rugs, old furniture, Capo di Monte, Sheffield, and other *objets d'art,* yet more being on display inside. The store is a permanent institution, and has been conducted by more than one owner, but always in the same fashion. At the period when John Solomon was settled in Chicago, the owner and auctioneer was one Lucius Bogard.

The name might be odd, but not so the owner. Bogard was a handsome man of nine-and-twenty, and emphatically a gentleman. He lived in bachelor apartments in East End Avenue, on the South Side, by the lake.

Bogard wore a neatly-clipped beard, his face was rather florid but powerful. He was a connoisseur in all that the term implies; he catered to the wealthiest families of the Middle West; his was the final word in all discussions of art, rugs, and antiques. He had travelled extensively before taking over the auction rooms; an apparently unimportant item, this.

Let us now pass to Harrison Street, near the post office. Here, in a superb suite of offices, worked a man named Harvey Lind. He was of remote Scandinavian descent, and had come to Chicago from Wisconsin, unheralded of fame, two years previously. Being a yellow-haired young giant with a jaw like a rocky cliff, and blue eyes like ice, Lind had not wasted his two years.

He was now private secretary to Herbert Stuart Everingham, head of the oldest and wealthiest brokerage firm in Chicago—which is saying a good deal. Lind was twenty-four. Knowing that he could go no higher in his present line of work, and being not at all content to remain where he was, Harvey Lind was gradually but firmly building foundations for his future.

Returning to Adams Street, and entering the Gas Building, one might gain the upper floors and come to an office in the corner overlooking Adams Street and Michigan Boulevard. The dingy roof of the Art Institute and the dingier lake front, with the uncompleted and sooty "city-beautiful" project, lay spread out below in prospect vile. On the door of this office was—and is—an inscription to the following effect:

JOHN SOLOMON
Entrance by Appointment Only
KEEP OUT!

Supposing that one had an appointment—which included a key to open the curious lock on the door, John Solomon refusing to have his rooms cleaned except in his presence—the visitor would find himself in an odd place.

The outer room seemed blank, until one observed that the four walls were solidly lined with sectional cabinets, each section of which seemed to be separately locked. The inner room had two large windows, fronting on Michigan and on Adams, and, except for a huge, built-in safe and John Solomon, was almost empty.

Solomon's Carpet

Solomon was a pudgy little man with a perfectly blank face and wide, innocent blue eyes. His right leg was gone at the knee, and had been replaced by an artificial limb which at times served him poorly. Whenever in his office, he always wore carpet slippers and a battered tarboosh—a variety of fez. He smoked incessantly at a vilely ancient clay pipe. He had an easy-chair, a smoking set, and a small table. Two straight chairs and a rather tattered but beautiful Ispahan rug completed his furnishings.

Within the great, built-in safe could be seen a dozen brass-bound, heavily-clamped wooden boxes. Each box, if opened, would be found to contain a great number of small, red morocco notebooks; each notebook was numbered, and each was closely written from cover to cover in many languages, but chiefly in Arabic.

It will be seen that Lucius Bogard was a most interesting man; that Harvey Lind was a most promising man; and that John Solomon was a most eccentric man. Each of the three was engaged in a wholly diverse occupation, and each was devoted to his own pursuits; yet the paths of these three men had been long destined to cross and cross again.

In such fashion did fate set the stage for the involved affair which came to be known in police annals as the case of Solomon's Carpet—although as usual with the police, the name was quite wrongly bestowed.

THE INNER sanctum of Herbert Stuart Everingham's office was luxurious. He was a man who loved magnificent things, who knew them passing well, and who paid as high for them as the average wealthy dilettante does. Some said that he paid higher.

The walls were silver-leafed, the furniture was antique rosewood and very uncomfortable, and the floor was covered by a handsome Serapi carpet—a real Serapi, be it noted, and not the factory-made Smyrna product which fills the rug shops to-day.

Everingham's home on the North Shore housed a superb collection of Oriental rugs. The broker himself was on the "private-sale" list of Lucius Bogard. Often, however, Everingham would drop into Bogard's auction sales when something good was on the tapis; the auctioneer was absolutely fair and aboveboard in his sales, but could often favour a good customer and personal friend such as Everingham.

On a bright morning in early spring, the broker sat at his desk. After trimming a fat Havana with appreciative care, he pressed the call button for his private secretary. Lind's own private office was just outside the sanctum. An instant later, Lind entered and at the first glance saw that his employer was perfectly content with the world.

Being a man of forty-five, Everingham was a slave to custom. He subscribed to the opera, but never attended; and, as Lind knew, he never smoked one of his fifty-cent Havanas before noon unless he was remarkably pleased with himself. He was keen-eyed, heavily built, and his mind had begun to turn from the making of money to the spending of it. The only distinction between him and hundreds of other brokers was his name.

"Sit down, Harve," he said affably, swinging his desk chair around. "I had a stroke of luck yesterday—dropped into Bogard's. What do you think I found?"

Lind grinned cheerfully. He had a superb contempt for rugs and *objets d'art,* expressed this contempt openly, and never truckled to any man. That was one reason why the broker trusted him implicitly.

"What is it now? Rags or rotten wood?"

Everingham chuckled in delight and shoved a cigar across the desk.

"Rags, my young Philistine! Rags! I told you yesterday about that magnificent Chinese piece Bogard just received from a French collector who had gone broke through the war. Remember? The Imperial Dragon rug, at least four hundred years old?"

Lind nodded, level-eyed. The broker chuckled again.

"I dropped in to the sale yesterday and found several agents and collectors. Old Joe Hardinge was there, too. Sure enough, Bogard tipped me off that the Chinese rug had been asked for. Well, Harve, I backed 'em all off the map except Joe—he bid me up to fourteen thousand and then quit, cussing mad! I got the rug for fourteen thousand—and dirt cheap at the price!"

He ended in a gurgle of laughter.

"Huh!" grunted Lind imperturbably. "I'd like to see the thing. Bet it's a fake. How much is it really worth?"

"Well"—and Everingham, chuckled again—"Bogard refused an offer of twenty thousand at private sale, two days ago. He couldn't help himself at auction, though."

"Maybe he did give you something soft," admitted Lind grudgingly. "But you watch out for that same Lucius Bogard. He's a—"

"He's what?" demanded the broker, as Lind paused.

"He's a personal friend of yours, and I don't talk about him," snapped the private secretary firmly, though his quick smile relieved the words.

"Bully for you, Harve!" approved Everingham, nodding. "All the same, he can't put over anything raw on me. I know too much about rugs. If you'll come up to dinner to-night, you'll see the rug. Bogard is going to bring it up, and I want his advice as to placing it."

"Thank you, sir," responded Lind, with an affectation of servile humility which he knew always irritated his employer. "I'm sure it's very kind if you, sir—"

"Drop that, confound you! See here, do you know a good detective?"

"Not personally, I'm glad to say. But there are agencies—"

"Oh, curse agencies!" Everingham laid his cigar on an ash tray, and for a moment drummed with his fingers on his blotter. "Harve, did you ever tell a soul about those burglar alarms of mine? The ones that Thimms installed when I built my house last year?"

"Not guilty," responded Lind, with a frown. The other sat silent for a moment.

Lind wondered what was up. Thimms was an inconspicuous old Dane, an electrical worker of high ability who specialized in burglar alarms. His inventions safeguarded the greatest house in Chicago, yet Thimms dwelt and worked alone in his laboratory. Lind, Everingham, and Thimms were the only ones who had seen the plans of the complicated alarms which had been installed in the broker's residence.

"The whole alarm system has been destroyed," said Everingham at last. "I found it out last night, when I tested them, quite by accident."

"Eh?" Lind sat up suddenly. "Anything missing? Was it—"

"No, nothing was missing," frowned the broker. "The hidden switch had been smashed, that's all. No other harm done."

"That looks queer," commented Lind, staring. "No, I haven't even mentioned Thimms to a soul."

"Oh, I'm not suspecting any one, Harve. But I want to put a first-class sleuth on the job and find out what it means. Turn your desk over to Hopkins and find me one."

Lind sat in thought for a moment.

"I know of one already," he stated, looking up. It was this habit of knowing the unexpected which had helped to place him where he now was. "But I don't think he'll come to see you."

"Eh? Why not? Who the devil is he?"

"Well, you know that I have a friend on *The Times*—Jack Brune, the financial reporter? Brune was telling me yesterday that the Mains murder case had been solved by a queer little chap named Solomon, who has an office in the Gas Building. It's not for publication, you know; the police grabbed the publicity. This man Solomon merely turned up, gave the name of the murderer, told where to find him and the proofs—and it was done. Why not try him? Brune says he doesn't work for pay—"

"Bosh! No man works without pay," snorted the broker. "Send for him."

Lind retired, hiding a discreet smile, for he had not told all that Jack Brune had said about John Solomon. In five minutes he returned to the sanctum, grinning openly.

"I 'phoned him. He said that you could come to him if you wanted him, and that he was sending a key to his office. I made an appointment for eleven."

Herbert Stuart Everingham gasped—then chuckled anew at the memory of his precious Chinese rug, and picked up his cigar. He liked men who could give him orders.

"All right. Tell that lazy chauffeur of mine to be here. You'll go with me."

Lind turned to leave. He stepped back with a bow as the door opened and the broker's daughter swept breezily into the sanctum.

Diana Everingham, at twenty, dipped very lightly into the

society where her mother, at forty odd, swam heavily and with
distinction. She was not a tall girl, but neither was she short.
Being as athletically inclined as any girl can be without incurring
the taint of "masculine," she was possessed of a perfect figure
externally and an equally perfect mental poise.

For lack of interest in society, she spent the better part of
her time in Associated Charities work; this, it may be added,
to her mother's disgust and her father's concealed but ardent
admiration.

"Good morning, Harve!" she exclaimed. "Daddy, there's to
be a bazaar for the benefit of the fresh-air schools, and I want
something to auction off—"

Lind departed to his own office, and began mechanically to
sort out the mail on his desk. But behind his high brow, behind
his graven mask of a face, his mind was picturing the fresh
features of Diana Everingham.

Waves of netted black hair, ardent black eyes beneath brows
that might have been pencilled but were not, delicately carven
nostrils and lips, and rounded, uptilted chin—he pictured her as
he had done since his first sight of her, a year previously.

Five minutes later, a messenger boy was sent in from the outer
offices, bearing a brass key and a receipt, which Lind signed.
Then, taking the key, he returned to the sanctum, was admitted,
and held up the bit of brass.

"Here's your key," he smiled. "Solomon seems—"

"Keep it," snapped Everingham. "Turn over your desk to
Hopkins, Harve. What do you know about this charity bazaar,
huh?"

Lind glanced at the girl, his blue eyes suddenly warmed and
lifened.

"All the morning paper told," he rejoined easily. "To be held
in the Blackstone ballroom next week, to be patronized by society, and to swindle said society for the sake of poor children. It
was a splendid idea of yours, Miss Everingham. I visited one of

those fresh-air schools last week, and they're doing great work, great work!"

He checked himself abruptly, not caring to present his inner self to the vision of Herbert Stuart Everingham. The latter grunted.

"Harve, we've framed up something. Sis, here, is going to Bogard's and buy a rug, on condition that Bogard will auction it at the bazaar. You go along and keep her from exceeding the limit. Don't let her get swindled—"

"I know more about rugs than you ever will," broke in the girl, laughing. "And I think Harve knows more about them than either of us."

"Not I," disclaimed Lind quickly. "Rags are rags. I'd sooner spend my money on other things."

"Fresh-air schools, for example?" queried the girl, her head on one side as she eyed him for the effect of her shot.

Lind glanced at her and frowned, masking his surprise excellently. He had made a modest ten-dollar contribution certainly—but who could have blabbed about it?

"Well, trot along," sighed the broker, as a telegram was sent in. "Get back with the car by ten-fifty, Harve. And whatever the rug comes to, charge it."

Lind got his hat from the closet and departed with Diana through the outer offices. Not until they had gained the waiting car in the street below, and were moving, did either of them speak. It was the girl who broke silence.

"Well, sir? You did not expect that your sins would find you out, eh?"

"What sins? I've so many that I've lost track of 'em all."

"The ten dollars you contributed—oh, you needn't lie to me, Harvey Lind! I know all about it, even if you did refuse to give your name. And I know about that life membership in the Scribes Club, too. You're getting on, young man!"

Lind grinned, but made no reply. He had long since learned that his greatest shield and weapon combined was silence. He

was sorry that Diana had learned of his impulsive act in contrib-
uting to the fresh-air school fund—but how had she learned of
the other?

A life membership in a club composed of writers, artists,
newspaper men and others, costing five hundred dollars, does
not come out of a fifty-per-week salary. He guessed at the
thought behind her words, and it worried him.

"Well," she added sharply, "what have you to say about it?"

"This." The gravity in his face sobered her, turned her laughing
eyes to pools of liquid blackness. "I mean to get on in the world,
Diana Everingham. I mean to do big things—not to make
money, but to *do* things— To get on in the world, a man must
have friends higher than himself; then he must raise himself
above them. Get me?"

She nodded, a keen breathlessness in her face. Harvey Lind
could be forceful when he chose; he could make his words
command attention, but he could at times display an astonishing knowledge of men and things, and a more astonishing
softness. The girl had long since guessed that his hard sternness
was but a chosen mask.

"I had a few hundred dollars saved up," he went on quietly.
"Last week I was offered a membership in the Scribes, through
my friend Brune, of *The Times*. I invested those savings in a life
membership—invested, remember. I'll meet brainy men, active
men, men of influence in all walks of life. They'll keep my brain
wide awake; I'll make them give me occasional lifts, and I'll
eventually make that membership pay a thousand per cent. Now
do you understand?"

"Yes," she returned quietly, watching his vibrant face. "Yes.
Harve, how soon do you leave my father's office?"

The shot told, for his eyelids narrowed. Then he smiled.

"When I am offered a better position, Diana. I am not seeking it."

She nodded again. Harvey Lind was not the type of man who

had to seek work; the work sought him, and found him as well. And so they came to the shop of Bogard.

Lind accompanied the girl inside, and waited passively while she talked with Lucius Bogard, for he really knew nothing about rugs, and cared less. He was conscious that he knew enough about Bogard to dislike him, however.

The man's very gentility, his carefully cultivated tact and taste and conversational ability irritated the more abrupt Lind. Yet Bogard was famous for these very things. More than one aspiring orator frequented the auction rooms merely to hear Bogard talk, to jot down Bogard's mannerisms. His auctions were absolutely "square," as all men agreed, but it was his way of auctioneering that sold the goods.

Watching him, Lind caught an unmistakable eagerness in Bogard's handsome face, a look of zealous enthusiasm for the girl he talked with rather than for the rugs he displayed. With his blue eyes turned to ice again, Lind walked to the front of the store and gazed out on the street, immobile, until Diana had finished her business and was ready to depart.

"Confound it!" he thought. "What chance have I? This fellow Bogard is a gentleman, and I'm a nobody. He makes thousands a month at his game, and I have nothing. He's handsome and affable and smooth, and I talk and look the farmer I am. But, by Godfrey—he'll have to fight!"

All of which was not only cryptic, but was somewhat unjust to himself.

The visit left him silent and hard and cold, and while he rode to the Associated Charities headquarters with Diana he spoke not at all. She eyed him with a twinkle of feminine intuition, and left him with a clear "Until to-night, Harve."

Lind rode back to get his employer, and reached the kerb where Everingham was standing at ten-forty-nine. Without loss of time, they sped to the Gas Building, and sped aloft to Solomon's floor. Upon reaching the oddly inscribed door of the office, Lind inserted the key in the lock and they entered the outer room.

"Come in, gentlemen," sounded a wheezy voice. "Werry 'appy I am to see you."

At the door of the other room appeared John Solomon, clay pipe and all, and he met them with a hearty handshake. The broker was visibly taken aback at his aspect; but Lind, having heard of the little man through Brune, knew what to expect.

Everingham sank into a chair, glancing at the carpet. He emitted a startled gasp.

"Good heavens, man! Where did you get this fifteenth-century Ispahan?"

Instantly all was forgotten in the absorbing passion of the rug lover. He fell to his knees and examined the knotting, the selvage, the wool; he cried inarticulate things and raved in ecstasy, while Solomon chuckled and Lind looked on coldly.

"No, sir; not for sale," returned Solomon apologetically to the fire of offers and questions. "It was give to me by a werry dear friend, just like that. Now, Mr. Everingham, sir, you wanted to see me about them 'ere burglar alarms? Werry good, sir."

Everingham stared up, and then rose suddenly with a sharp look at Lind. But the secretary was gazing at the complacent Solomon in puzzled amazement. Was this queer little person a thought reader?

CHAPTER III

"HARVE, DID you mention to Mr. Solomon the object of our visit?"

"Certainly not, sir."

What with the Ispahan rug and Solomon's remark, Herbert Stuart Everingham relapsed into speechless amazement. But not so his secretary.

Lind was quietly amused. His two years of city life, and his earlier years spent on the farm and in working his way to an education, had given him a keen perception of men and the values of men. He weighed John Solomon carefully, and found him no fool.

The pudgy little Cockney, with a wisp of grey hair sticking from beneath his tarboosh, with his blank expressionless face, did not appear formidable, yet the complacent surety of his bearing, the lurking twinkle in his wide blue eyes, fascinated Lind. The secretary smiled, and bit at the cigar which Everingham had given him an hour earlier.

"Out with it, Mr. Solomon! That's a vile pipe you're smoking. How did you know what we came about?"

"Guessed it, sir," confessed the pudgy little man solemnly. "Yes, sir, just like that. Three other men in this 'ere town 'as complained of the werry same thing. Each of 'em was a collector, sir, a connoisseur o' rugs and such-like. You're werry well known as the same, Mr. Everingham, so I guessed as 'ow you 'ad the same trouble. It ain't every man as is a connoisseur, as the old gent said when 'e picked out 'is third."

This touch of subtle flattery mollified and yet irritated the broker, who disliked to be flattered.

"You're dead right, however you came at it," he admitted, staring at Solomon. "Are you a detective?"

"No, sir."

"Well, what are you, then? English, by your accent."

"Yes, sir. Now about this 'ere business, sir. Might I be so bold as to 'ave a look at your 'ouse?"

"Certainly. Then you'll take the job in hand?"

"Yes, sir. Werry interesting work it is, sir."

"Very good. Get to the bottom of this, and you can name your own price. I can't afford to have my house open to burglars and cracksmen. Charge expenses to me."

"Thank you, sir. But I 'ave one thing to ask, if I might make so bold. I ain't so young as I was, sir, and if I 'ad a brisk young gent to be 'elping of me, like Mr. Lind, there, it would be a mortal sight easier, sir."

"Eh? Oh, nonsense! I can't spare Lind—"

"Well, sir, you can spare 'im better than you can spare them jewels of Mrs. Everingham's, and them rugs of yours and the rest."

The broker bent a sudden keen gaze upon the speaker.

Even Lind was puzzled and rather startled by Solomon's words and imperturbable air.

"What do you mean? Do you think my place is seriously menaced?"

Solomon carefully knocked out his pipe. Then, looking up, he spoke earnestly:

"Mr. Everingham, you 'ave rugs in your 'ouse what's worth a hundred and fifty thousand dollars. Now, sir, I'll tell you this. If so be as you don't give me a free 'and you'll lose every blessed rug you 'ave. Yes, sir, just like that."

"Confound it, man, what do you mean?" exploded the puzzled broker.

"I can't say, sir, not yet. It's a mortal 'ard nut to crack, and it ain't to be cracked with a 'ammer, I says. Now you let Mr. Lind 'elp me, and you give me a free 'and or I'll 'ave nothing to do with you, sir. Just like that."

With this ultimatum he hauled forth a knife and a plug of seaman's tobacco, and in absolute absorption began to whittle the tobacco into his palm. Everingham watched him for a moment, then rose with a helpless snort.

"Confound you, go ahead! Lind, the thing is in your hands. Hopkins will take your desk for the present, and if you can drop in every day, do so. Now I've fooled away enough time this morning—give me results, and I'm willing to pay."

Everingham stalked forth and the outer door slammed behind him. Lind, who remained, calmly puffed at his Havana and eyed Solomon. The Cockney tamped down his pipe, struck a match, sighed, and glanced up through the blue smoke he created.

"A werry fine gentleman, in 'is way, Mr. Lind. Werry fine young lady, too."

Lind's blue eyes contracted slightly.

"Don't try to come any fly detective work over me, Solomon," he said evenly. "I'm here on business, not to discuss my employer's family."

The little man chuckled, seeming not at all abashed. His eyes widened very perceptibly as they rested on Lind.

"I like you fine, Mr. Lind, I do that! But business is business, and werry bad business it sometimes is, sir, as the Good Book says. Just one minute, sir."

He went to the big safe, which stood open, and extracted a box. Unlocking this, he drew out a notebook. From the notebook he took several folded papers, and returned to his easy-chair. It was all done in a very matter-of-fact way, and the secretary had no hint of what was coming.

"Now, Mr. Lind, just look over this 'ere paper, if you'll be so good."

Lind took the paper. Not by the twitch of a muscle did he betray the amazement which swept over him—for the paper held a complete outline of the ingenious burglar-alarm system installed in the new mansion of Herbert Stuart Everingham! And, as Lind knew, that system had been known only to himself, to Everingham, and to Thimms, its builder.

"Where'd you get this?" he asked quietly. "Only three men knew of it."

"I 'ad it from the builder, sir—Mr. Thimms is 'is name. You see, I 'appened to learn of 'ow three other big men in this town 'ad 'ad their burglar alarms broken up. One was Larsen, the publisher; one was Garvel, the banker, and one was that 'ere financier 'Ardinge. All 'ad werry fine collections of rugs, sir. So I got me data on other big collectors, expecting this werry thing to 'appen. And it's 'appened."

Lind merely nodded his comprehension, for his quick brain was beginning to pierce the supposed magic of Solomon. He knew Larsen, Garvel, and Hardinge well. All three were extremely wealthy, moved in Everingham's social set, and frequented the auction rooms of Lucius Bogard in their common rivalry for priceless rugs. Thus the reasoning of the pudgy Cockney had been quite simple—but what lay behind it all?

"Who are you, John Solomon?" asked Lind curiously. Solomon gave him direct reply:

"A crime detector, sir. That's me business, so to speak, or me 'obby if you likes it that way better. But now to business, Mr. Lind."

He then proceeded to set before Lind an extremely surprising state of affairs. Including Everingham, all four of the rug collectors named possessed stately mansions on the North Side, between the river and Evanston. All four residences had been guarded by electrical burglar devices built by the Dane, Thimms. All four of these protective agencies were secret, and all four had been rendered useless within the past three weeks—yet nothing had been stolen. There seemed to be no motive attached.

Out of the vast wealth in jewels and collections which the deadened alarms had left at the mercy of cracksmen, nothing had vanished. The destruction of these alarms had not been accident, for in each house the whole system had been destroyed at the controlling switch—though each switch control had been hidden. In each case the thing had only been discovered by chance, and how long the alarms might have been out of order was unknown.

All of which, as Solomon pointed out, went to show some set and very definite motive; but what that motive was no one could say. Hardinge had reported the matter to the police, in his own case, but the police had afforded him no satisfaction. Solomon was impressed by the fact that all four men were rug collectors, or else some member of their immediate family was one. In any case, this was a common bond, and the only possible clue that offered.

"But, see here," asked Lind finally, "how were the plans of those burglar alarms known? A builder named Thimms installed all four of them, and no two were alike. Each system was known only to Thimms, the owner of the house, and possibly someone who could be trusted—as Mr. Everingham trusted me. But Thimms is a Dane, a steady fellow, and he can be trusted absolutely—"

"No man can be trusted what tips 'is elbow," said Solomon sagely. "I know Mr. Thimms, I do that. I made 'is acquaintance, just like that, and 'e 'ad a drink with me, and there you are—all shipshape and proper, sir. Bless 'im, 'e don't know as I got them plans from 'im! No more 'e don't know as the burglars got 'em— if burglars they was. 'E don't know it, I say. 'E was drunk. You remember that 'ere fact, sir."

"But someone got the plans. I see." Lind nodded slowly. "What's on the programme?"

"Go to lunch." Solomon shut up his wall safe as he spoke,

discarded slippers and tarboosh for street attire, and was ready. "After some wittles, we'll know each other better, sir, I 'opes."

Lind smiled to himself as he followed. He guessed shrewdly enough that this respectful attitude of John Solomon was no more than a mask, and he was right. But Harvey Lind made one great mistake. He quite forgot the one fact that Solomon had cautioned him to remember.

They crossed the street to the Pullman Building and ascended to the Tip Top Inn for luncheon. Lind was surprised to see that not only did Solomon nod to Morgan, the head waiter, as to an old acquaintance, but that the grinning Morgan had a table reserved for them in the window overlooking the lake. Also the luncheon was ordered and ready for them.

The descendant of Vikings was still more surprised by what followed. John Solomon talked of himself, not only with freedom, but with the evident intention of letting Lind absorb a complete knowledge of his business. And this proved to be detective work after a fashion new to Lind.

"I ain't a 'tec, mind," explained Solomon gravely. "I'm a crime detector, which is werry different, Mr. Lind. Now, 'ow does them 'ere 'tecs work in storybooks? Why, they wait till a crime is gone an' done, then they 'unt down the criminal till 'e either 'fesses up an' pops out 'is brains, or till 'e ups an' goes to jail.

"That's all werry fine in storybooks, sir, but it don't work in real life, I says. Let the bobbies handle the crime, I says, but John Solomon, 'e'll do summat more."

Thus it was that Lind heard something of Solomon's private history. The little man had been in Chicago only a year. Previously to that, he had spent almost the whole of his life abroad in odd corners of the earth; and, to judge by his dark hints, he had been engaged in some very queer business.

In the course of his life he had encountered directly or indirectly a great percentage of master-criminals, and had apparently been in a position to learn everything there was to learn about them. He did not bother with the small fry, but had now established himself in Chicago to search out these masterminds, many of whom had crowded into America on the outbreak of the European War.

"Plain robbery or murder ain't in their line, sir," he vouchsafed. "It's money as they want, and mortal big money. I ain't interested in plain crooks 'cause why, there ain't nothin' interesting about 'em. But it's them that works in mysterious ways, as the Good Book says, that I'm giving me time to."

As he listened, Lind discovered that Solomon's entire system of work was, at least to him, extremely novel, and the little Cockney impressed him deeply. Here were no "old-sleuth" methods, no gumshoes, no magnifying glass, no elaborate theories or deductions. Here, so far as Lind could see, was—simply the blank visage of John Solomon.

Of course, the Cockney detective had a method; but it was entirely his own, and seemed to be founded on instinct plus an amazing knowledge of criminal methods plus an unerringly keen brain. His grasp of detail was marvellous.

Regarding the case in hand, Solomon only ventured that it was "werry queer," and that it looked interesting. When they had finished luncheon and had returned to the office across the street, however, Lind began to discover on what the methods of the little Cockney were based.

As has been mentioned previously, the outer room of Solomon's offices was lined from floor to ceiling with cabinets. Solomon unlocked one section and displayed the contents to the gaze of Lind, who nodded carelessly.

"Bertillon system—got all the crooks listed, eh?"

"No, sir," and Solomon chuckled. "Nothin' like that, sir. You take a better look, Mr. Lind."

From the cabinet Lind took at random one of the portfolios with which it was crammed. To his astonishment, he found that it contained photographs and an intimate history of a socially prominent Chicagoan—and the details of that intimate history drew from him a startled ejaculation:

"Great Scott. Solomon! This man is no criminal—"

"Mebbe 'e is, and, again, mebbe 'e ain't, sir," came the answer. "Most o' these 'ere listed folks ain't criminals, so to speak."

The little man drew a patient sigh, and explained. He was not interested in the underworld, and knew nothing about it. But he knew a great deal about the world of finance; he had at his fingers' ends a mass of detail about the most ingenious criminals—the masters of criminal art. Most of these he knew personally, in fact.

In the cabinets which lined his outer office were dossiers covering the most important people in Chicago, through all branches of life and work. Solomon's prime idea was to deal with the master-criminal from a standpoint of brains. The Cockney prided himself on his foresight, his ability to look ahead, to plan ahead, to think ahead. And he had this very curious ability to the *n*th degree.

Lind discovered these things gradually, as he pierced through the veil of the Cockney's mannerisms; and the farther he pierced, the more he liked John Solomon as an individual.

"Now, sir"—and Solomon lighted his ancient clay pipe with an air of huge self-satisfaction—"I may say as you know a mortal lot about me, Mr. Lind, and there ain't many men what Id trust this far."

Lind nodded gravely.

"Thanks—I understand. You needn't worry about me, Solomon, for I'll keep a close tongue regarding you. But what on earth do you intend doing with all this information on Chicago citizens?"

"It comes in 'andy, Mr. Lind." Solomon chuckled wheezily and waved his pipe at the encircling cabinets.

"In this 'ere room, Mr. Lind, I 'ave fifty thousand people listed, covering them as it may come in 'andy to know. That's 'ow I come to learn the priwate weakness o' that there man Thimms, sir."

"But—good heavens, man!" exclaimed Lind. "You say you've

only been here a year, and yet you have this amazing amount
of—"

"Oh, I'as me 'elpers, sir," said the other diffidently. "I've rented
a 'ouse near Lincoln Park, where me friends stay, but this is me
priwate office, so to speak. By the way, Mr. Lind, 'ave you any
enemies 'ere in town?"

"A few," laughed Lind, thinking that the little man intended
to look up some of them in this astonishing cabinet of Chicago
residents. "Why?"

"I mean in the office, sir."

"Oh!" Lind frowned thoughtfully. "No one unless it's
Hopkins, the chief clerk. I was promoted over his head to my
present job. He didn't like it, but hasn't said much one way or
another. Why?"

"Well, sir, since you telephoned me this morning I've been
an' found out a mortal lot about you." And Solomon sucked at
his pipe noisily, his blue eyes fastened on Lind. "I'm afraid as
'ow you're a-going to get a werry 'ard jolt one o' these days, sir. I
can't say just 'ow, 'cause why, I don't know; but I'm afraid, just like
that. If it comes, then you never mind what 'appens, but come
straight to me. Mind that, sir."

Lind studied him, still frowning. What did the man mean?
Was this some furtive warning, as it seemed, or was it a wild
guess? He had not been quite sure whether John Solomon was
a man to be liked or a man to be feared; but now, looking into
those wide blue eyes, he came to sudden decision in the matter.

"You're a queer fish, Solomon, but I like you. Yes—if any trouble arises, which I don't in the least anticipate, I'll come to you.
Now let's get down to cases on this burglar-alarm job. What
can I do to help you?"

Solomon instructed him to return to the office for the afternoon; but on each and every afternoon following to attend
Bogard's auction sales and report back to the Gas Building by
telephone. They would visit the Everingham residence together

in a day or so. And aside from this John Solomon seemed content to bide with folded hands.

Under this arrangement, Lind could spend his mornings with Everingham and his afternoons at the auction rooms. But Solomon warned him that he might be summoned any moment, and to hold himself in readiness. Further, the Cockney gave him the absolute use of an automobile and chauffeur, stating that the car was waiting below.

Solomon took him to the window and pointed it out—a black limousine, parked on the other side of Michigan Boulevard. Lind protesting, Solomon said that while working with him, Lind must accept the gifts of Providence, and that the chauffeur had already been made acquainted with his new master.

This Lind found to be true when he descended to the street alone. He walked out to the kerb, and saw the black limousine move instantly. The car swept around and slowed up for him; the chauffeur was a coffee-coloured person who seemed to speak perfect English. Poor Lind returned to the brokerage offices in a jumbled state of mind.

He had learned a great deal about John Solomon, but he had learned nothing at all about the destruction of the Everingham burglar alarms.

Relieving Hopkins at the private secretary's desk, Lind recalled the covert warning of Solomon, and eyed the man narrowly. Hopkins was a pale silent fellow who knew his duties to a dot. His face was saturnine and unwholesome, and his nose was pointed. Lind had no great liking for the chief clerk, but had found no animosity in his bearing.

Upon reporting to Everingham what had taken place, Lind was instructed to put himself absolutely at the disposal of the Cockney. When he left the office, he found to his surprise that the black limousine was awaiting him, and questioned the chauffeur.

"Solomon effendi—"The chauffeur checked himself suddenly. "Mr. Solomon told me to obey you in all things, sir. You are to use this car as your own. Mr. Solomon pays the garage bills himself. Thank you, I do not receive tips."

So Lind shrugged his shoulders and entered driving home to his lodgings on North Dearborn in state. Solomon must be pretty well off, he considered, and must have really taken a fancy to him.

When Lind had finished dressing for dinner, he descended and found his landlady, a decent German woman who cleared a good profit from her lodgers, standing in the hall and eyeing the limousine which was awaiting Lind at the kerb.

"Good evening, Mrs. Krause," he cried gaily. "Do you like my new car?"

She flung him a smiling nod and withdrew in some embarrassment. Lind passed on in blissful ignorance of how those jesting words were to be flung in his teeth later with a wholly different meaning.

Arrived at his destination, he found Everingham waiting at the *porte-cochère*, sent the chauffeur to the servants' quarters, and explained to the broker how the car had been lent to him. Everingham chuckled and led him inside.

The dinner-party consisted only of Lind, Lucius Bogard, and the family. Diana was seated between the two guests, and with malice aforethought Lind left Bogard to the mercies of plump Mrs. Everingham, monopolizing Diana himself. Consumed with eagerness to display his new rug and get it placed, Everingham hurried the dinner along as much as he could in decency. The affair of the burglar alarms was, of course, not brought up in the presence of Bogard and the servants.

"Congratulations, Mr. Lind!" exclaimed Bogard, during a lull in the conversation. He looked very handsome, very distinguished, in evening dress. His neat Vandyke was becoming, for he had a strong chin beneath it. "I hear that you are now a life member of the Scribes. That is an honour worthy of you, sir."

If there was aught beneath the words, Lind could not detect it. Bogard had always been very cordial with him, though Lind felt that it was the cordiality of the merchant to the possible customer and little more than a mask.

"Thank you," he rejoined quietly. "It is an honour, even though an expensive one. But I am to be still further honoured in the near future, as Mr. Everingham has ordered me to attend your sales until I learn to appreciate rugs."

Everingham, who had thus backed up Solomon's instructions, led the general laugh. Lind's grand contempt for rugs was well known even to Bogard, and the importer promised cordially that Lind should receive the desired education in antiques. With this the topic passed, the dinner was ended, and all adjourned to the reception rooms, where the rug had meantime been unpacked.

Herbert Stuart Everingham had built a house to suit himself. It was placed a hundred feet back from the North Shore Drive. While not large, the grounds were thickly planted with trees and shrubs. To the left of the entrance was the *porte-cochère;* from the entry hall opened four large rooms which upon occasion could be converted into one huge ballroom. There was little likelihood of this ever being done, however, for Everingham refused to have his collections disturbed.

His rug collection was distributed over the entire house; but in the four large rooms were placed those of especial rarity—and price. The first of the four rooms contained three fairsized rugs, two very old Feraghans, and one choice Tabriz. In the second room was a magnificent Royal Ispahan of silk, done in rich browns—a carpet of almost incalculable worth which had once hung in the shah's palace as a wall covering.

In the third room were four smaller rugs—one Shiraz and three antique Saruks. In the fourth room was a single priceless Keshan. This last was the "gold room," the walls and ornate ceiling being gold-leafed, and here Bogard ordered the Chinese rug fetched, the Keshan carpet being removed temporarily.

Even to the tyro's eye of Lind, that Chinese rug was a marvel. In size it was sixteen by twenty-four feet, and was a blend of the rarest blues, fawns, and yellows, picked out with white. In the centre was the five-clawed Imperial Dragon rising from the conventionalized ocean rainbow pattern, and the entire dragon was done with scales of blue and white. The rug was very heavy, and its soft colours fitted the "gold room" as a jewel fits its setting.

"I hope," said Bogard casually, "that you have protection against thieves, Everingham."

"Ample," nodded the broker reassuringly, with a quiet look at Lind. "Then, in your opinion, this rug was made for the emperor himself? I'm glad Joe Hardinge got sore and quit bidding. Whew, that man did cuss!"

Frowning to himself, Lind turned away and sought Diana. Impossible that thieves could ever carry away a rug so heavy and so large; yet more impossible that, having stolen it, they could ever dispose of it. As he trod across one corner that was upturned, he noticed a little tag of cloth stamped into the selvage, bearing Chinese characters. It was a tiny thing, and Lind thought nothing of it at the time, save that Bogard must have neglected to remove it.

After that, he spent a very pleasant hour with Diana Everingham.

CHAPTER IV

"**L** ET'S SEE if I've me inwentory right, Mr. Lind."
A week had passed—a barren, fruitless week for
Lind. Solomon had visited the Everingham mansion, but had
discovered nothing, save that the collection of rugs was marvellous.

He had listed those rugs, for some occult reason of his own,
and was now having Lind check them over. At the head of the
list were the rugs contained in the four reception rooms—the
finest of the collection. Certain changes having been made in
their arrangement since the addition of the dragon rug, the list
now read as follows:

> Room 1. One Tabriz, two Feraghans.
> Room 2. One Royal Ispahan, silk.
> Room 3. One Keshan palace carpet.
> Room 4. Imperial Dragon rug.

Lind verified this list, then left Solomon's office on his daily
visit to the auctions.

Despite himself, Lind was now learning a good deal about art
in general and rugs in particular. He attended the auction rooms
every afternoon, and could not help absorbing from Bogard
information that was both accurate and rather interesting.

On this particular afternoon, Bogard met him with the usual
cheery smile and courteous greeting, even pausing in his sale to
shake hands with Lind.

"Glad to see you so regular, Mr. L." For Bogard invariably greeted his customers by initial only, through tactful policy. "All well with you, I trust?"

"Quite, thanks," smiled Lind, forcing an amiability which he was far from feeling. "Is that a Saruk you're selling?"

"No, it's a Keshan—but you're learning fast! Good work! Are you all through at sixty-five—five—five— Thank you, ma'am—seventy. Seventy I have! Seventy-eventy-eventy, seventy I am bid for this blue-bordered Keshan, this imperial gem from Persia! Seventy dollars, ladies and gentlemen, would not buy an ordinary Mahal; it would not cover the duty on this rug! But I sell on commission only—thank you, seventy-five. Eighty, do I hear? I am bid seventy-five—gone at seventy-five!"

"And gone at a good profit, too," muttered a voice behind Lind, yet rather in amusement than criticism. Lind turned and nodded to Hardinge, a broker and friend of Everingham, whom he knew personally. Hardinge also collected rugs, and often dropped in at the auction rooms.

"We have here," went on Bogard, turning to the rug stand under the glare of strong lights, "a wonderful hall runner. Please notice this piece, ladies and gentlemen. Size twelve by three—yes, ma'am, a very fine specimen of Kurdish weaving!"

The auctioneer caressed the soft rich pile of the rug as though he hated to see it put up before the rude gaze of the public. Then he struck into his usual informative discussion which preceded the bids.

"Notice the blue background of this rug, please—notice how in places it is much lighter than others. A sure sign of the genuine Oriental rug! Picture to yourselves how strand by strand this rug was woven on the loom—knot by knot, inch by inch! I would say that two years at least were consumed in weaving this piece, ladies and gentlemen. It holds about three hundred knots to the square inch.

"Here, you see, the colour of the blue ground is very uneven—perhaps the stock of wool gave out, perhaps one of the children

was at work and selected the wrong shade. It is easy to see that
the whole family worked on this rug—the father or mother
here, at this beautifully designed end; the old and shaky-fin-
gered grandfather here, where the pattern is badly matched;
the children here where the figures are uneven and poorly
constructed—"

And so the "patter" ran, all of it dominated by the florid,
handsome personality of the speaker. Bogard had character, and
could make his personality felt strongly, but with each passing
day Lind had felt a growing aversion for the man. And he felt
that this aversion was fully returned by Bogard, though the
auctioneer was invariably courteous.

In all that week Lind had seen nothing untoward happen at
the auctions. That Solomon had sent him here to gain knowledge of rugs, as the Cockney insisted, seemed very improbable
to Lind; yet he had gained nothing else.

He had learned to appreciate Bogard's tactful handling of
customers, and the keen though subtle teamwork between
auctioneer and assistants, but in all this was nothing crooked.
Surely Solomon did not suspect Bogard of burglarizing, he
reflected. That was too far-fetched altogether. Lind never
suspected that Solomon might actually have desired him to get
a thorough knowledge of Oriental rugs.

Then, like a bolt from the blue, came the first of that terrible
sequence of events which so nearly wrecked Harvey Lind on
the shoals of circumstance.

"We now come to this Meer Saraband," Bogard was declaim-
ing. "Observe the wonderful ivory ground, the heavy pile, the
sheen of the rug! Notice the blue weft thread, the distinctive
mark of the Meer. Easily three hundred knots to the square inch,
every one of which is done by hand—please start this wonderful
production of the desert caravans—"

"Mr. Lind! Mr. Everingham wants you at the phone."

Lind started, finding one of the assistants at his shoulder. In
some wonder at the summons, he followed to the telephone desk

in front of the store. As he did so, he noticed a small and shab-
bily clad man who was entering. The fellow seemed much out of
place, being plainly a street loafer; and Lind only remarked him
because of his general aspect and because of a livid birthmark
splotch decorating the man's right cheek. Then he sat down to
the desk and spoke into the telephone.

"Hello—that you, Harve?" came the crisp voice of the broker.
"Come right over, will you? Yes, get here on the jump."

Thinking the affair one of office routine, and expecting to be
called upon to find some mislaid papers, Lind smiled a little and
departed to the black limousine. This was still as entirely at his
service as though he owned it.

Ten minutes later, he entered the Everingham offices, and
Hopkins smilingly bade him proceed to the sanctum. There
was sly triumph in that smile, but Lind passed on and found
the broker alone.

"Sit down, Harve," Everingham picked up a cigar, chewed it,
and laid it down again. "Here's a letter—came in on the afternoon mail. Look it over."

Lind took the paper handed him. It was typewritten, was
addressed to Everingham personally, and was unsigned:

> Dear Sir: This friendly note is to inform you that you are
> served by a scoundrel and traitor. Your private secretary joins
> clubs, uses limousines openly, and spends money like water.
> He sold the secret of your burglar alarms to a gang of cracks-
> men, and he gets money in other ways. If you want to know
> how, look in the upper right-hand drawer of his desk. He has
> his eyes on your daughter, also. Get rid of him.

The venomous cowardice, the absolute falsehood of it, sent
Lind into a cold, heartsick passion; but he only laughed slightly
and looked at the broker.

"This is a nice business," he said evenly. "Have you looked in
my desk yet?"

"I am a gentleman, Harve," said Everingham, his eyes very
keen, "and I do not take stock in anonymous letters. Before we

take this up, here's another matter. The electrician and builder
Thimms, died this morning from heart-failure; an hour before
that, I had telephoned him and he stated positively that he had
never mentioned those alarms to a soul. Have you and Solomon
arrived anywhere?"

With an effort, Lind wrenched his mind away from that
venomous letter. He had not told the broker about Thimms'
fatal weakness, and now a sudden swift anger drove the thought
from him.

"Then you suspect me?" he demanded harshly. "We were the
only other ones who knew—you suspect me, eh?"

"No, I don't—and, you'd better keep cool, Harve," cautioned
the other crisply. "How did this letter writer know about those
alarms? What's Solomon doing?"

"I don't know." Lind's voice was taut, keen intense; his mind
was wholly engaged with that letter. "We've put a detective on
the job to guard the place at night, and Solomon hasn't told me
a thing so far."

"All right." Everingham nodded, and took up his cigar anew.
"How about this damned cowardly letter, Harve? Have you any
idea of the author?"

Lind looked at him steadily, his blue eyes narrowed like jets of
flame. Then the closing words came to his mind and he flashed
to his feet.

"Yes! I'll bet a dollar to a doughnut that Bogard had a hand
in it—"

Everingham chuckled, and his hard eyes twinkled with
hidden amusement.

"Harve, you be careful. Don't talk like that outside this room.
It's all bosh about Bogard, and you know it. So you deny all those
damnfool charges, eh? All of 'em!"

Lind caught that amused twinkle, but his instinctive caution
was swept away.

"No, I don't deny them. One is true—the last one." He met

the broker's hard gaze very squarely. Then Everingham took the cigar from his mouth, held it up, and inspected it carefully.

"As far as Diana is concerned, I've known that for a long time," he said calmly. "I hope to glory you get her, too! She's floated around with a lot of these half-bred millionaires and second generation products; I'd hate to see her marry any of 'em, and I guess you'll beat the bunch as a square, hard-throttled man, Harve!"

Lind stared, incredulous. Everingham's words caught him unawares, and when he saw that they were spoken in earnest, he forgot all else.

"You mean it?" he demanded hoarsely. "You mean it?"

The broker leaned forward over the desk.

"Harve, if you get her to say 'Yes,' I'll—I'll give you that Chinese dragon rug for a wedding present."

"You will—*not!*"

Their hands met in a firm grip. Then Everingham, looking somewhat embarrassed, rose to his feet.

"Let's go see what's in your desk drawer, Harve. It's a rotten old trick. Then we'll get to work and see who's trying to kill your character, eh?"

Together they went to the private secretary's office, but Lind moved as in a dream. The anonymous letter did not greatly bother him, though he was intensely gratified over the manner in which Everingham received its calumnies; but the broker's attitude toward his frankly confessed hopes left Lind stunned, unbelieving, yet feeling as though a swift exhilarating wave had surged up with his soul riding its crest.

Examining Lind's desk, they found that the upper right-hand drawer was, as usual, locked. Lind took out his key ring, opened the drawer—and then watched with a return of his cold anger as Everingham scooped up a dozen slips of paper. They were broker's notices of transactions and statements of closed accounts.

"An old trick, Harve—a rotten old trick!" said Everingham

quietly. "You're in mighty bad with some one, old man. According to these, you bought five hundred T. & O. on the tenth,
the day we started that stiff bull movement. On the fifteenth,
another five hundred. Here's one for last month, the thirtieth—a
thousand C. & C. I. on margin. That was the day you wrote out
that secret agreement with the C. & C. I. people. Harve, there's
something damnably ingenious about all this! Must have been
someone in the offices, too."

Lind saw one thing predominate over all: Everingham
trusted him. Another man would have at least suspected him,
for here was damning evidence that he had played traitor to his
employer; but the broker had calmly swept it aside.

"It's good of you, Everingham," said Lind, a trifle thickly. For
almost the first time in his life, he knew real embarrassment.
"It's good of you—everything. The whole thing. I don't know
what to say—"

"Forget it!" snapped the other, and turned to the harshly
ringing telephone, catching up the receiver. "Yes, Hopkins. No,
I won't see any one. I'm busy with Lind. I don't care—tell 'em to
go to the devil if you like."

He rang off abruptly and whirled about in his chair. The
anonymous letter and notices of transactions he placed on his
desk under a glass paperweight.

"Now, Harve, we'll call up Bunker & Grove, since all these
receipts are from their office. Bunker will talk to *me*, I guess."

He called up the other brokerage firm while Lind waited,
his first anger now settled into calm. Who was behind this
"plant"? He suspected Bogard, from the reference in the letter
to Diana, but admitted to himself that the suspicion was unjust
in the extreme.

More likely, he thought, it was someone in the office—
perhaps Hopkins. Yet Hopkins could know nothing of the
burglar alarms. Neither had Hopkins been trusted with the
secret of those stock transactions, which had lain between Lind
and Everingham alone.

The broker hung up the receiver angrily. It seemed that Bunker Grove had written instructions from Lind to send all notices of transactions and also to send all money to an address at North Clark Street; at this address Lind had himself presumably been found.

"But I never wrote such orders!" cried the astounded Lind. "I've never been at that address—don't even know where it is—"

Everingham smiled grimly.

"Lind, you have a slick enemy. Someone has forged your signature and has done it remarkably well if Bunker & Grove were deceived. That fellow, whoever he is, has been impersonating you. Your orders stated that all notices of transactions were to be sent by messenger boys—so that Bunker & Grove's regular messengers would not recognize the deception."

Lind nodded, white-lipped. Who had done this thing? Everingham continued evenly:

"These deals have been put through presumably by you, on the same days when I gave you confidential letters or instructions. Whoever did the job has pulled down a wad of money, Harve."

"But we've got the crook," exploded Lind, leaning forward eagerly. "Send to that address, get my forged letters, and we'll nab the fellow—"

Everingham smiled.

"We'll get after this the first thing in the morning, old fellow. I can't quite see the crook's game, though. This anonymous letter would evidently bring the thing to light on investigation, and that would clear you—No, by Jove!" The broker sat up in quick excitement and his fist banged down.

"Harve, someone hates you like the devil hates holy water! He hates you so damned much that he's over-reached himself! Now forget this, Harve; leave it alone till the morning, and trust the details to me. By the way, what's Solomon doing?"

"Nothing that I know of," returned Lind wearily.

"Tell him I'm tired of his foolery. I'm going to have those burglar alarms repaired to-morrow, whether he likes it or not.

You get down first thing in the morning, and we'll go after this anonymous writer and smash him. Personally, I think it's Hopkins. Eh?"

Lind met the other's gaze squarely, his face inscrutable.

"If we broke anyone on suspicion only," he countered, "it would be a raw deal, Everingham. It seems to me that there are enough clues in this letter to make us certain."

"Good boy!" Everingham chuckled and stretched out a Havana. "Keep your poise and count on me to back you. Good night and good luck, son."

Another handshake, and Lind emerged.

So unexpected, so sudden, so sincere had been the attitude of Everingham that he felt deeply stirred. That venomous letter had only done him good, after all! It had brought him squarely out before Everingham, man to man—and the result left Lind in a state of wild inward exultation. He even cared nothing whether or not Hopkins had written that letter. He rather felt sorry for Hopkins.

It occurred to him that he might go to Solomon, but felt in no mood to relate the matter to the little Cockney, nor did it seem urgent. Also the afternoon was growing late. So Lind dismissed his chauffeur and black limousine for the evening and went to the Scribes Club.

There he dined with Jack Brune and other newspaper men, played a few games of Kelly pool, and departed without naming his destination.

Knowing that Diana and Mrs. Everingham were to occupy a theatre box that evening, he went to the same theatre, getting a balcony seat from which he could steal an occasional look at Diana.

Unfortunately to himself, he tore up his seat check on leaving. This was close to eleven o'clock.

Lind walked home to his lodgings, which were on North Dearborn near Lincoln Park. He reached there at eleven-forty-five. As he entered, he met his German landlady, who happened to be nursing a sick lodger that night. And so the strings of fate were interwound on the cogs.

At eleven-five, that night, Herbert Stuart Everingham was murdered.

L IND USUALLY took breakfast at a small German delicatessen shop in the neighbourhood of his lodgings, on North Clark Street. He was out early the next morning, bought a paper, and settled down to his table without foreboding. He never used the black limousine in going to work.

Opening the paper, Lind was horrified and astounded to read of the murder of Diana's father. To one who knew the man, it had come about in dramatic fashion; even the news accounts could not overshadow that.

> Mr. Everingham had not gone with his family to the theatre, but had remained at home. At eleven-five the butler heard him cry out sharply from the famous gold room.
>
> Upon investigation, the butler found his master lying stretched upon a Chinese rug, the finest of the Everingham collection. The rug was much disturbed, indicating a struggle of some kind. Mr. Everingham was quite dead, having been stabbed through the jugular.
>
> At present the motive for the murder is unknown, and the police admit that the mystery is of peculiar character.
>
> Their belief is that Mr. Everingham surprised a thief immediately upon the latter's entry, and that the criminal stabbed him in order to avoid arrest.
>
> A private detective guarding the grounds had been knocked senseless and bound, and cannot tell who struck him down. He knows that the blow came almost exactly at eleven o'clock, having just glanced at his watch.

The murderer had entered the gold room by one of the French windows. The ground outside bore traces of a heavy object having been dragged, obliterating the footprints completely. As nothing had been taken from the house, this was no doubt done purposely, and the track was not made by a bag of loot.

A man dropped into one of the three vacant chairs at Lind's table. Lind paid no attention. Everingham murdered! It was astounding, incredible.

"I see as 'ow you've 'eard the news, sir—" Lind positively jumped. His eyes lifted to meet the calm stare of John Solomon. Yet so horrified was he by the news that he even forgot to ask how this man had ferreted him out.

"Good God, it's unbelievable!" he cried hoarsely. "Is it true, Solomon?"

"Yes, sir, I'm werry sorry to say as it's true. Eat your wittles, sir."

The waitress brought Lind's order, and he forced himself to eat mechanically. Bitterly enough he told Solomon about the anonymous letter of the previous afternoon. No sooner had he done so than the Cockney's face paled.

"Dang it, why didn't you come to me wi' that?" cried Solomon, staring at him. "Dang it! Now you've been and done it for fair! What 'appened at Bogard's?"

"Nothing," returned the wondering Lind. "A little bum who looked as though he had just stepped out of Hinky Dink's saloon came in as I was leaving—must have dropped in to get warm. As to that letter—"

"Wait!" For a moment Solomon gazed across the table, his rotund face agitated. Then he drew forth his clay pipe.

"Mr. Lind," he said solemnly, "I'm werry sorry to say as you've put your foot in it, just like that. What was the man like?"

"The bum? Oh, he was small, sharp-featured, with a birthmark on his right cheek. What's wrong? Surely you didn't care to know that?"

Solomon positively snorted his disgust.

"No, sir. It don't matter now. Could we have a look at that 'ere Everingham place? Me car is outside."

Lind nodded, and finished his coffee. When he had paid for his meal, they left the shop to find the black limousine waiting at the curb. While they bowled north, Solomon made Lind go over everything he had done and said on the previous afternoon and evening. The secretary could see no reason for it, but Solomon would answer no questions.

"Them as asks questions gets less'n they asks, I says. I see trouble ahead for you, sir; but never you mind what. 'Cause why, I can't help it now."

"Could you have helped it last night?" demanded Lind half-angrily. "I suppose you'll make me responsible for Mr. Everingham's murder next."

"No, sir, not me, sir," came the enigmatic answer. Solomon would say no more.

They reached the house to find Mrs. Everingham prostrated and Diana in charge of affairs. Lind could not but admire the girl's quiet efficiency, even in her bitter distress. Pale and hollow-eyed, she received them in the first of the four reception rooms. Her father's body lay in the gold room, closed off and guarded by a policeman.

"Diana, this is my friend, Mr. Solomon," said Lind. "He is a private investigator who enjoyed your father's confidence to a considerable extent."

She extended a hand to Solomon, who bowed over it with more grace than Lind had given him credit for.

"Can I be of any service to you?" went on the secretary. "We would like to look at the gold room, if possible, after which I'll get back to the office and take charge of things there. If I can help you out in any way, Diana, please command me."

"Thank you, Harve," she said quietly. "I think you can do nothing, but I may call you up at the office later. Things are sure to turn up. Oh, it's dreadful—we have just found that the burglar-alarm system was broken—"

"I know," nodded Lind. "Your father discovered that over a week ago, and put the investigation in our hands. Mr. Solomon is still working on the case."

She looked at Solomon in startled wonder, then turned away, her eyes brimming with sudden tears.

"Excuse me, please," she said chokingly moving toward the door. "I—I can't talk about it now, Harve."

They waited in silence until she had gone. Then Solomon beckoned to Lind and walked toward the gold room.

"We'll 'ave a look, sir," he said calmly, "though I 'aven't much 'ope."

Upon reaching the gold room and being halted by the policeman, Lind stated that he was Mr. Everingham's private secretary, and requested to look at the scene of the crime, promising that they would disturb nothing.

"It don't matter much, sir," returned the officer with a nod, unlocking the door. "The detective ain't found nothing so far, and there ain't any footprints outside."

"No fingerprints on the window?" queried Lind.

"Nary sign, sir."

All three paused on the threshold of the magnificent room. On the sofa lay the murdered man's body, covered with a sheet. A chair was overturned, and the wonderful dragon rug was wrinkle in wild confusion, but that was all.

As the officer went on to remark, "The dicks hadn't picked up a thing." The wound in Everingham's throat had apparently been made with a knife—just beyond a turned-up edge of the rug was a black congealed pool of blood.

Solomon pulled out his pipe and began to suck at it noisily, his wide blue eyes roving about the room. Leaving the officer, he walked over to the French windows and gazed out at the gardens, and here Lind followed a moment later. The gold room was in a rear angle of the house, and gave directly on a section of the gardens thirty feet in width; beyond this was the winding cement driveway, while the *porte-cochère* was far to the front of the mansion.

"You'd best wait in 'ere, sir, while I 'ave a look outside," said Solomon.

Unlatching the French window before him, he stepped out to the tiled but unaided platform beyond. Lind observed that the trail of the murderer was plain to see, for some heavy object had been dragged out to the driveway, leaving a swath of broken bushes and shrubs behind.

"I suppose the newspaper account was correct?" asked Lind, turning to rejoin the policeman.

"Yes, sir, but they got another fact out o' the butler this mornin'. Seems he heard a car drive up just before the murder, an' heard it go off while he was lookin' around for Mr. Everingham."

"A car, eh?" Lind frowned. "How about the iron gates at the street end? Had they been left open?"

"I dunno. Looks to me like a bad business all around."

Lind stared down at the dishevelled dragon rug. One side was turned back as if to free it of any danger of contact with the pool of blood. Lind's first stupefied horror had passed by this time, but he could not look again at that sheeted figure on the sofa.

Then, still gazing down at the yellow-blue-white reverse portion of the rug, his eyes narrowed swiftly. His brain leaped back to the first occasion on which he had seen this rug, when first it had been placed here. He remembered that a corner of it had then been turned back also—the same corner, bearing the parti-coloured moon symbol which the dragon was swallowing. On that corner had been a tiny tag stamped into the reverse side, bearing a Chinese dealer's mark, perhaps.

Now, however, he saw nothing of the tag. Lind stooped forward and went to his knees, examining the fabric, but could find no marks of any kind to show that such a tag had been there. Then he rose quickly, smiling at himself.

Of course, Everingham had seen the thing and had removed it! Lind turned away, in some irritation at his own action. Everingham had removed the tag, carefully, fearful of the slightest blemish or mark on his treasure.

Despite himself, Lind had learned enough about rugs to appreciate the beauty of this marvellous texture at his feet. It shimmered in the early-morning sunlight like silk, in its rich colouring and deep-yellow background. Every inch of the thing, as Lind knew, had been slowly knotted by hand, hundreds of knots tied by patient fingers to the glory of the gods and the emperor. It had taken years for the making, and, like all Oriental rugs, had no duplicate. The pattern might be duplicated, true, but each rug would have individualities of colour or texture or weaving which would place it apart from all others.

Solomon re-entered the room, still sucking at his pipe, and Lind turned away from the rug.

"Thank you werry much, officer," said the Cockney. "I think, Mr. Lind, as 'ow we'd best be gettin' down-town, if so be you're ready."

Lind nodded to the policeman and they left. The butler, haggard of face, escorted them to the door, and Lind turned to him with a word.

"You heard a car drive up last night, I understand? Just before the murder?"

"Yes, Mr. Lind—I—I thought it was the ladies returning, sir. As I came downstairs to answer Mr. Everingham's call I heard the car drive away. I thought nothing of it until this morning sir."

The man was in a pitiable state of collapse, and Lind bothered him with no more questions. No sooner were they in the black limousine, however, and passing the high iron gates that guarded the street end of the driveway, than Solomon held out his hand.

"Look at this 'ere, Mr. Lind. It was a-stickin' at the edge of the cement driveway, at the end o' that there trail."

Lind gazed down at a shred of wool—a shred consisting of a tiny tuft of yellow hairs. Puzzled, his eyes came up to the innocent stare of the Cockney, then returned to that little shred of yellow wool. Suddenly a gleam of fire shot into his gaze.

"Why—isn't it a bit of that rug, Solomon? That Chinese rug, you know—it has a deep-yellow background of exactly that shade!"

"Werry singular, sir. I 'ad thought the same meself."

Puzzled, lost betwixt surmise and bewilderment, Lind looked into that pudgy blank face and wondered.

"But—see here, Solomon! That rug couldn't have been dragged out? It wasn't that which left the track to the driveway?"

Even before the Cockney shook his head, Lind realized that this surmise could not be a fact. The rug had shown no signs of such treatment. The very fact that Everingham, when murdered, had fallen on the rug went to prove that it had not been moved from the room.

"I found two more bits o' them 'ere woollen tufts on bushes," said Solomon, and began to tamp tobacco into his pipe. He was undoubtedly perplexed. "But when I 'ad a look at that rug, sir, I didn't see no places where the wool 'ad been pulled out, like. I'm danged if I know what to think!"

"There couldn't have been two rugs?"

"Mr. Everingham only 'ad that one Chinese rug, sir."

Lind told him about the missing tag, but Solomon made no comment whatever, although the blue eyes widened a trifle. The Cockney carefully inserted the bits of wool in an envelope and sealed it.

"It may come in wallyble some day, sir. In fact, I may say as 'ow them 'ere bits o' Chinese wool is a-goin' to 'ang a man, just like that."

"Eh?" Lind started. "What do you mean? You have a clue?"

"No sir. I knows nothing and I says nothing."

"What the devil do you mean, then? How will that wool hang anyone?"

"I'm danged if I know, sir—but I'm a-gamblin' on Prowidence, just like that. Prowidence is a werry mysterious thing, as the old gent said when 'e was took up for double bigamy. But 'ere we are at me office—good luck to you, sir! I'll see you later."

The limousine had halted at the Gas Building, and Solomon clambered to the pavement. He spoke to the chauffeur for a moment, then the car went on with Lind to the brokerage offices.

These were closed, of course. Everingham's partner was out of the city, and Lind found the pallid-faced Hopkins in charge. The clerks had been sent away as they came, but it was only a trifle after nine o'clock. Lind caught the sound of voices from the inner offices, and turned to Hopkins in surprise.

"Who's inside there, Hopkins?"

"The chief of police," rejoined the chief clerk rather curtly. "Didn't you see his machine outside?"

"Didn't notice it. How long has he been here?"

"Half an hour. I was just opening up when he arrived. The chief of the detective bureau is in there also."

Lind nodded. Besides Hopkins, only the telephone exchange operator was in the offices. Doubtless the police had come to investigate the dead broker's personal effects in the hope of finding some clue to the murder; it seemed that the department must have been badly stirred up by the newspapers, since the chief himself was in charge of operations.

Hanging up his hat and coat, and donning his silk office coat, Lind walked on through his own office to the sanctum. He was personally responsible for things here, and had no intention of allowing the police to rummage at will without keeping an eye on affairs. He walked into the sanctum and closed the door.

"Who's this? What're you doing here?" demanded one of the two officers who faced him. Lind recognized the chief of police even without the gold star.

"I'm Harvey Lind, chief," he said coming forward, "Mr. Everingham's private secretary. I was at the house, and came down to take charge of things here. Have you found anything that'll be of service to you?"

The attitude of the two men startled him. The detective head was staring at him from across an open desk drawer; the chiefs heavy, bulldog visage was drawn into an aspect of threatening ferocity.

"You're Harvey Lind?" demanded the latter, swinging around in Everingham's desk chair and clenching his teeth on a cigar.

"Of course I am," frowned Lind, wondering what all this meant.

"Set down—we want a word with you."

Lind, angered by the tone, drew up a chair, and his blue eyes flamed over the desk at the chief.

"See here, chief," he said quietly, "you can begin right here and now to use a different manner when you're talking to me. Don't try any bulldozing—cut it out. I'm here to give you all the help in my power, and I'll do it."

The detective, who looked very much like any business man of the Loop, had risen and was scrutinizing Lind keenly, but the chief's menacing visage did not change. To Lind, these two men seemed like indomitable, dehumanized man-hunters—which was exactly what they were. But his eyes met those of the chief unflinchingly, with a cold poise which seemed to surprise the other.

"You're a cool one all right!" said the chief bluntly. "So you're willin' to help us, eh?"

"Exactly," snapped Lind.

"Well, then, s'pose you come across with a confession of Everingham's murder, and save us all trouble. Come on, now; we got the goods on you as it stands, so loosen up. Mac, move your chair over by the door—we got a slick bird here."

CHAPTER VI

L IND STARED at the chief, thunderstruck, yet angered.

"What is this—a joke or a bluff?" he broke out coldly.

"Neither. We got you, that's all." The chiefs eyes narrowed, and his heavy chin jerked up as he puffed a cloud of cigar smoke from one corner of his mouth. He was the picture of power, of relentless mastery, and of ease.

"But—what on earth do you mean?" queried Lind. "Surely you know better than that, chief! No one but a fool—"

"Now see here, we got the stuff on you. I'm tellin' you facts, Lind, and I'm givin' you a chance to talk right here before you get the irons on." The heavy face shoved forward, and the chief's huge fist thumped down on the desk. "You killed Everingham, you murderer! We know it; we got the proofs. Now cough up the story."

Lind sat motionless, holding down the cold rage and colder fear that surged up within his breast. He knew enough to be able to see that this arch-bluffer was not bluffing now. Yet what could they hold against him? What possible kind of evidence could they ever hope to bring against him—provided that the police had picked him out as a scapegoat? Or was it another attempt of his anonymous enemy?

He felt fear in that moment; not physical fear, but fear of the imagination. He visualized how the newspapers would seize on the accusation, how they would ruin his whole future, innocent or guilty, with news articles and stories and pictures of him. He saw himself held up to scorn before Diana Everingham, and winced.

The chief caught that flash of fear in his eyes, and smiled cruelly. But Lind, whose gaze had never flickered from that of the chief, in his turn saw the smile. He pulled himself together. He must find what lay behind this, he must fight as he had never fought before, he must smash this damnable accusation before it ever got to the public ear!

"Chief, you're barking up the wrong tree," he said evenly, holding himself well under control. "If you have anything on me, I don't know what it is. Now don't try to bully me, because you can't do it, but in common fairness go over the thing with me. I know perfectly well what my legal rights are; I don't have to say a word to you, and you've no right to quiz me—just the same, I'll talk. I've nothing to conceal, and I am willing to go over the situation frankly with you. I'm a lot more interested than you are in finding Mr. Everingham's murderer."

Before the chief could answer, there came a knock on the door. The chief of detectives turned at a nod from his superior, and flung the door open, to reveal the face of Hopkins, apologetic and pallid, with John Solomon behind him.

"This gentleman insisted that you would receive him," said the chief clerk nervously.

"Yes, sir, werry 'appy I am to see you all," and Solomon calmly shoved Hopkins aside and stepped in, with a bland gaze at the scowling chief.

"What you buttin' in here for?" demanded the latter. "We got this case cinched, Solomon."

"Thankee, sir," nodded the Cockney. "If you'll be so good, sir, I'll just sit down to rest me bad leg for a bit. I may 'ave a word to say, sir, if you don't mind."

He paid no attention to Lind, but seated himself. The chief glared at him for a moment, then gave a jerk of his head.

"Set down, then! You're a fly dick, but you got the right dope in that Mains case, anyhow. This here Lind is the feller that murdered Everingham, and we got him dead to rights."

"Yes, sir, werry good work, says I," answered Solomon, drawing out his pipe.

Lind brought his gaze back to the chief as the latter turned to him, leaning over the desk. Solomon sat near the door unobserved.

"You're a good bluffer," said the chief slowly. "Sure you want to go over things, eh? Sure you don't want to confess right now, eh?"

"You heard what I said," retorted Lind smoothly. "I've nothing to hide."

"All right. Where were you at eleven o'clock last night?"

"Walking home, on North Dearborn."

"Oh, you were! Alone?"

"Yes. I had been to the theatre and wanted the fresh air."

The chief sneered openly.

"Let's have your theatre check."

"I haven't it," answered Lind, a little pallor creeping to his cheeks as he perceived whither this was tending. Yet the horrible absurdity of it made him want to rise and scream out what injustice was being inflicted on him. "I tore it up as I left the theatre. But I've no doubt that if you advertised for people who were in the front balcony row you'd find one or two men who might remember seeing me—"

"Egotistical cuss, ain't you?" broke in the chief, with heavy irony. "That don't go down, Lind. They said you left the theatre a little before eleven?"

"Yes—about a quarter to eleven. I walked home to where I live, near Lincoln Park, and I took my time about it. I think I got home about eleven-forty-five."

"I know you did," said the other. "I told you we had the dope on you."

He glared across the table with an open brutality that sick-

ened Lind. Then he took up a paper from the desk and held it
up facing Lind; it was the anonymous letter.

"Ever see that before?"

"Yes."

"When?"

"Yesterday afternoon," snapped Lind angrily. "Mr. Everingham called me in and we went over the dirty slander together. It
was to have gone to the post-office people to-day, to be traced,
if possible."

"Sounds likely," grunted the other. "I'm going to tell you
something, Lind. You were in here for an hour with Everingham
yesterday and Everingham refused to see some people because
he was rakin' you over the coals. Ain't that right?"

"No. He refused to see anyone because he was trying—"

"All right. He refused, anyhow. I s'pose he found these broker's
accounts in your desk, eh? Playing the market, eh?"

"Not at all." And Lind forced a smile to his lips, knowing
this for the best form of irritation. "We found from Bunker &
Grove that those stocks had been purchased by messenger, on
my forged order. On the dates in question Mr. Everingham had
been putting through some confidential stock transactions of
which only he and I were aware. Whoever bought those stocks
in my name cleaned up a pretty penny."

"Uh-huh!" The chiefs features expressed open disbelief "It was
a slick dodge to use a messenger boy, huh? I—"

"Beggin' your pardon, sir," and Solomon came forward, his
blue eyes very wide. "If you'd 'ave the kindness to call up that 'ere
messenger service, it might be as you'd find out summat. And
I'd call that man 'Opkins in 'ere, sir, if I was you."

The chief looked up quickly, but Solomon's face was quite
blank.

"Call him in? What do you mean?"

"Just to 'ave 'im 'andy, sir, in case o' need. While 'e's in 'ere, that
there 'tec might 'ave a look around Mr. 'Opkins' office with me.

I 'ave a notion, sir, that we might find summat. There's allus a chance, as the old gent said when 'e buried 'is third."

The chief nodded to the detective. Hopkins entered, plainly nervous, and looked none too much relieved when asked to sit down and wait. Solomon and the detective went into the outer offices, and the police chief took up the telephone.

Connecting with the messenger service, he requested that they send over the boys who had taken the Bunker & Grove messages on the dates shown by the notices, and that the records for those dates be sent over also. The chief then called up Bunker & Grove and requested that they send over the orders purporting to have come from Lind. This done, he swung around to Lind.

"Lind, these papers are proof positive that you had a scrap with Everingham yesterday and that you were caught in a bad mess. Also, you knew that his burglar alarms were out of order. What you got to say about that, hey? I s'pose you didn't put somebody wise, hey?"

Lind merely shook his head, waiting for the end, his eyes steady and his lips clenched in self-repression. From the outer offices, through the half-closed door, came the click of a type-writer, but he did not heed the fact.

He perceived at last with what damnable certitude this net of circumstance was enmeshing him. The little things, so harmless in themselves, all tended the same way. The very absurdity of it horrified him. Yet, had he not received warning? He was reminded of that warning by the next flat accusation.

"You sold the secret of them burglar alarms, Lind! Didn't you?"

"No," said Lind suddenly, remembering the one thing which Solomon had bade him keep in mind. "No. The murderer could have gotten those plans from Thimms, the builder—"

"Come out of it! Thimms was a straight man, and you're blacking him now that he's dead, Lind! Thimms made a specialty of carrying such things in his head, and he was trusted by the richest guys in this town. Get that?"

"Yes, but Thimms drank. He—"

"Aw, come out of it, you dub! What if he did? He wasn't giving away what he could have sold to crooks—like you did! Where'd you get your money, Lind? See here, we've looked you up this morning, my man. You've a life membership, in the Scribes Club, you've been blowing money right and left, and you own a big limousine. You admitted as much to your landlady on one occasion. We've got her for one witness, and we've got more. We—"

"That limousine affair can be disproved by Solomon," began Lind slowly, trying vainly to make his mind arrange the charges in sequence. "And as to Thimms—"

"Hold on, that don't matter," broke in the other savagely. "Where was that car last night?"

"I can't say, having dismissed the chauffeur early. Probably Solomon—"

"Huh! It was someone in a car who killed Everingham, though! And it was you, Lind—you. That car was seen and a guy took its number, and you was seen—"

"You lie!" said Lind quietly and smiled.

For an instant he thought the furious chief would leap at him and tensed his muscles for a row. But the policeman, seeing that his final bluff had failed, was making no such error. Instead, he leaned across the desk with a venomous look that struck Lind like a blow.

"You'll sorrow for that word! Call me a liar, eh? Where's the knife you killed Everingham with, eh?"

Still Lind was smiling, his face like a graven mask and giving no hint of the desperate thoughts surging through his brain. That smile drove the chiefs simulated fury into something approaching reality.

"You can't put that stuff over on me, you boob," he exclaimed, his voice tense. "You confess and you'll save us money convicting you and you may get off lighter by doing it—"

"I said you were a liar," returned Lind, his face pale, but his blue eyes like the sun-glint in ice. "You're a fool also, chief. Take this anonymous letter, for example. I can show you exactly where and how that burglar-alarm system was given away to thugs—"

"You can do that?" demanded the other swiftly.

"Yes—or Solomon can do it. Now go slow on the matter of those stock notices for another thing, until the messenger boys get up here. They'll tell you quick enough that I wasn't the man who received them, and you know I'd have been a damn fool to let anyone else handle the matter—"

Lind broke off and turned as the chief's eyes shot up over his shoulder. The chief clerk was stepping to the door.

"Stop, there!" cracked out the chief, and his voice was like a whip. "Where you goin'?"

"I—I had some accounts to make up," said Hopkins shakily.

"Go back and sit down!"

Hopkins obeyed. Lind smiled again as the chief settled down and faced him.

"Now, Lind, that talk is all smooth enough, sure! But it don't matter what you can prove now. The facts are that yesterday afternoon you got into a mess with Everingham, that Everingham was killed last night, and that—"

"Who set you on my track, chief?" asked Lind quietly. And the shot told.

The chief puffed at his cigar without answering for a moment. Then his grim eyes flickered to Hopkins and back to Lind again—and that glance was enough. Lind understood now.

Before either man could break silence, however, there came steps from behind Lind, and he turned. Entering the room were three very dirty and frightened boys in messenger uniform, who stared at the chief with widening eyes. Behind them came in Solomon, who closed the door as the chief of detectives entered. The stage was set.

"Come over here, kids," said the chief, beckoning the three boys. They came to the desk with feet hesitant, and before them the chief spread out the Bunker & Grove notices of transactions, which bore the address on North Clark Street to which they had been sent by Bunker & Grove to the false Lind.

"Maybe you kids remember takin' messages over to Bunker & Grove's, in the Commerce Building, and takin' back messages to this North Clark address. How about it?"

After some urging, he extricated from two of the youngsters that they could not remember, though their record books verified the fact. The third boy, however, was quite positive that he remembered.

"Good work, kid!" said the chief approvingly. "You went to North Clark Street then, and your book was signed by Mr. Harvey Lind, remember? Well, you see if Mr. Lind is in this room. Pick the right man and you get a dollar."

Eyes shining, the boy turned. A cry broke from him, and he pointed at Hopkins.

"That's him, chief! He didn't give me no tip, an' I spotted his face fer the next time. Do I get the iron man, chief?"

"Here it is—now clear out of here, all three of you! Mac, take their names down, will you!"

Lind was dimly aware that they were leaving, but he was watching Hopkins. The chief clerk had shrunk back into the corner, his face ashen pale, his eyes fastened on the chief.

At this juncture the detective re-entered, bringing the forged orders which had arrived from Bunker & Grove. Lind glanced at the papers with a frowning nod. His signature had been excellently counterfeited.

"I suppose this is your work also, Hopkins?" Lind tossed the orders on the desk. "You did it well enough, I will say. No wonder it fooled Bunker & Grove. As I said, chief, those orders are forged."

The head of the police nodded and chewed his cigar for a moment. Lind waited for the outcome of this affair, conscious that it had temporarily over-shadowed the murder charge. Hopkins, he thought, was in a bad way. It was evident that the same thought had come to the chief clerk, whose features were ghastly.

"I guess this shows you up, Hopkins," asserted the chief of police.

"No, sir; don't say that!" burst out Hopkins, who, to the surprise of Lind, seemed suddenly imbued with the courage of a cornered rat. "Don't say that, for God's sake! I haven't done anything wrong; I signed the books in Lind's name because he asked me to. He said he was putting through a private deal for Mr. Everingham—doing it in his own name—he told me to use his signature on the orders, too—"

Hopkins lied desperately in that moment, but he also did it well—so well that the chief looked back to Lind with hard-glinting eyes. Then another voice broke suddenly upon them—a voice that was apologetic and a trifle wheezy.

"Beggin' your pardon, sir," said Solomon, "but I'd be mortal glad to ask Mr. 'Opkins a few things, if so be as you don't mind."

The chief, shifting his cigar in his mouth, eyed him keenly and then grinned.

"Solomon, you've pulled some queer stunts in this here burg! Now go ahead and let's see what's goin' to happen."

"Thank you, sir; thank you werry kindly. May I be so bold as to ask the loan o' that 'ere anonymous letter, sir?"

The chief reached it across the desk. Solomon took it and inspected it for a moment. The others watched him with curious fascination, but in Lind's heart was a wild sweep of hope.

"Werry good," said the little Cockney, nodding as if to himself. "Mr. 'Opkins, do you know anything about this 'ere letter, sir?"

That mild blue eye, that apologetic tone, brought Hopkins forward with more firmness than he had yet displayed. He took the letter from Solomon, read it with growing surprise depicted on his sallow face, and then handed it back.

"No, I never saw it before. I—I hope it isn't true, Lind."

"It's me as you're a-dealing with, sir," Solomon rebuked him mildly. "Just a minute, Mr. 'Opkins, beggin' your pardon. Was you in the office night before last?"

"Eh?" Hopkins frowned, then nodded. "Why, yes. I figure up the pay checks for the firm each week, you know."

"Was anyone else 'ere, sir—"

"No. I was working overtime that night."

"Thank you werry much, sir." Solomon paused, then turned to the chief and handed back the anonymous letter. "You might be pleased to know, sir, as that 'ere letter was wrote night before last on Mr. 'Opkins's typewriter by Mr. 'Opkins 'imself."

THE CHIEF sat back in his chair, seemingly content to wait and watch. Solomon looked around, one hand in his capacious coat pocket, with the solemnity of a blue-eyed owl, and with as much facial expression.

Lind, like the others, was watching Hopkins. Solomon's final words had dealt the chief clerk a hard blow, as his increasing pallor showed, but he was still game.

"What makes you say that?" he cried out, his voice rising shriller with every word. "Why are you all trying to fasten things on me? I can't stand it! I won't stand it, I tell you!"

"Then sit down, sir," said the Cockney quietly. "I knows that letter was wrote on your typewriter, 'cause why, that 'ere machine has a letter 'e' what jumps out o' place, just like that. It was wrote night before last, 'cause why, it was wrote with a clean black ribbon, and night before last you told the telephone girl as 'ow you was a-goin' to put a new ribbon on that 'ere machine to make up them pay checks with. And what's more, you done it, sir."

There was no need to say more. Hopkins, appalled by these almost incredible proofs of his guilt, drew back with his face livid, and attempted no defence. To the others the truth of Solomon's words was at once substantiated.

Lind was not surprised, for he had seen how events were tending. Now, however, he looked at Solomon, wondering if that strange little man could clear up the further mysteries of the letter.

"Did you find this out just now, John?"

"Yes, sir; I 'adn't no chance to do it before. But I suspected summat, I did that! So I says as 'ow I'd give you a 'elping 'and, sir. A 'elping 'and is a werry good thing in its place, says I, if so be as a man knows where its place is—"

"Let me handle this, Solomon." The chief leaned forward, frowning. "If Hopkins wrote this letter, how could he have known things that were confidential between Lind and Everingham? Such as the burglar alarms and stock deals?"

"Just like this, sir." Solomon drew from his pocket a disc and a few feet of broken-off wire. "This 'ere thing was in 'is desk drawer, sir. I 'ad to clean bust the lock to find it," he added apologetically.

"Dictograph, eh?" The chief took the disc and wire and put them in his pocket. "Uh-huh. That establishes the case pretty well. What do you want to do with him—"

"Beggin' your pardon, sir, I ain't through yet," interrupted Solomon. Under his wide blue eyes the chiefs frowning look passed into a nod of assent.

"Go ahead."

Solomon turned to the shrinking horrified chief clerk.

"Mr. 'Opkins, I'm werry sorry to see you in this 'ere 'ole, I am that. I 'opes as 'ow someone 'as been and put you up to writin' that there letter, sir?"

Hopkins started slightly.

"No, they didn't," he broke out, with a burst of self-abnegation that both disgusted and surprised Lind, so sudden was the change. "I'll tell it all—I was sore because Lind had been made private secretary in my place. I only meant to queer him with Mr. Everingham, and I thought I'd get the job then. I never thought that there'd be murder—oh, I can't go on with it! I confess, I confess—for God's sake don't send me to jail, Lind! Let me go, and I swear that I'll never—"

"Shut up!" snapped the chief. Hopkins, sobbing against the wall, his face in his hands, obeyed quickly—almost too quickly, thought Lind. "Solomon, are you done?"

"Not yet, sir. Now, Mr. 'Opkins, I'd like to know werry much indeed just where you 'appened to meet up wi' that 'ere chap as 'as a birthmark on 'is right cheek?"

Lind started, and stared at the Cockney. But Hopkins, lifting his tear-stained cheeks in wild amazement, shrieked out suddenly. The detective watching, gripped him.

"Who told you? You devil—you devil! Who told you?"

"Tell us where you met 'im," urged Solomon. "Tell us, sir, and you goes out o' this room a free man."

At that Hopkins straightened up and flung off the mask. He had been a good actor, thought Lind, a very good actor; now, as he peered at Solomon with all the cunning of a rat in his ratlike, sallow face, he made no further effort at pretence.

"You mean it?" he demanded hoarsely, "You'll let me go free?"

"Yes, sir, just like that."

For a moment Hopkins stared into those fathomless wide blue eyes. Then he drew himself erect with a sudden jaunty air.

"All right," he said abruptly. "I'll tell; I've got the money to blow with, and I'll blow! I don't know the man's name, but I met him the other night at a Greek restaurant on Dearborn, just outside the Loop, where I usually get my supper. We got to talking, and had a few drinks. He seemed a good sort. He said that he knew Lind and hated him, and by and by we—"

"He said he knew me?" demanded Lind in amazement. "Are you sure?"

"You bet I am!" sneered Hopkins, with a desperate defiance. "I'd been listening over that dictograph for a long time, and I had already cleaned up a good bit in stocks through forging your name. So this fellow and I framed up the deal together, and night before last I wrote the letter. That's all."

"Not yet, sir," objected Solomon. "Who put that 'ere man on your track?"

"Who?" snarled Hopkins. "Didn't I tell you I met him? No one put him on my track, you fathead! Now do I go or not?"

"If you'll type out that 'ere confession and sign it, Mr. 'Opkins, you can go. And a werry good job when you're gone, I says!"

"Take him in the other office, Mac, and witness that confession," directed the chief. The head detective and Hopkins passed out together, and Lind drew a long breath.

"John," he said, smiling a little, "I can only say thank you for this, but I'll never forget it."

"Werry good, sir." And Solomon brought out his pipe with a great sigh. "So that 'ere 'as finished Mr. 'Opkins."

"But it ain't finished *me,* not by a long shot!" put in the chief quietly. "I ain't got hangin' evidence on Lind for Everingham's murder, I'll admit, but I can hold him as a suspect and I'm goin' to do it."

"But on what grounds?" exclaimed Lind, dismayed. "Surely you can't believe—"

"Where's your alibi?" demanded the chief. "The newspapers are hollerin' for action, and I'm goin' to give it to 'em."

"Beggin' your pardon, sir," said Solomon, holding a match to his pipe, "but you ain't a-going to do nothing of the kind."

"Hey? Why not?"

Lind, urged by the impulse to argue things out to the end and show this bull-necked policeman herein he was a fool, repressed himself. Solomon was working for him, he realized, and so implicit was his faith in the little man that he refrained from saying anything.

His pipe well alight, Solomon looked calmly at the chief.

"You can't bring out no cause for the crime, sir. That's one werry good reason, as the old gent said when 'e engaged a new 'ousemaid as 'ad a pretty face. But there's others."

He puffed at his pipe, and then resumed;

"Werry sorry I am to say it, but the last bit o' Mr. 'Opkins's letter brings in a werry fine young lady, if you'll note."

The chief picked up that letter, and frowned. He gave Lind

a quick glance, then fastened his attention on Solomon with a nod of assent.

"Now, sir, you 'eard what Mr. 'Opkins said about that 'ere dictograph. Mr. Lind, did you and Mr. Everingham ever discuss that 'ere young lady in this room?"

"Not—not until yesterday afternoon," said Lind, hesitant to drag Diana into this miry affair. "That letter brought up the subject, and Mr. Everingham was kind enough to favour my suit for his daughter's hand."

This drew a quick look of surprise from the chief, but Solomon only nodded.

"And by that, sir, Mr. 'Opkins couldn't 'ave known previously as 'ow Mr. Lind favoured the young lady in question. That showed me werry clear as Mr. 'Opkins 'ad been put up to this 'ere job—"

"Ah—you mean the man with the birthmark?" broke in the chief quickly. "Who is he?"

"No one as you've ever 'eard of, sir, and don't rightly know 'is present name meself. Now sir, I've been and talked a mortal lot, and talking ain't always good for the 'ealth, I says. Are you a-going to let Mr. Lind go wi' me?"

"Eh? Certainly not!" snapped the chief. Solomon nodded.

"Werry good, sir. Then you'll never find the man what murdered Mr. Everingham, mind that, sir."

With this Solomon rose, caught up his hat, and started toward the door.

"Hold on there!" The chief leaped up, an angry flush suffusing his face. "Who d'you think you're talkin' to, Solomon? I'm tired o' this foolin'! Do you know who killed Everingham?"

Solomon turned, his face very blank.

"Yes, sir."

The chief stared at him.

"Who was it?"

"I 'aven't me proofs, sir," returned Solomon quietly. "If so

be as you let Mr. Lind go wi' me, sir, just like that, then I'll put
the murderer in your 'ands inside of a month. Mind this, sir,"
he added, with a solemnity which was impressive, "it ain't only
murder what's goin' on—it's more, I don't rightly know meself.
But if so be as you let Mr. Lind go wi' me, I'll answer for 'im, and
I'll answer for that 'ere murderer."

"I've got to have action inside of a month," objected the chief,
weakening obviously. "We can't wait—"

"Announce that if you don't get that 'ere murderer in a month,
sir, you'll resign, just like that. Werry good plan, sir, if I do say it
as shouldn't. I'll promise you the murderer—"

"And how the devil do I know you'll get him?"

Solomon's eyes widened.

"I'll send you a certified cheque for 'alf a million, sir, and you
can be cashin' of it a month from to-day if I fails, sir."

Tense silence settled on the room, and the chief's heavy
breathing sounded loud. Lind sat motionless, wondering
whether Solomon were crazy, but by the keen calculation in
the policeman's eyes he saw that the chief at least was taking the
little Cockney with great seriousness.

Then he realized what it meant, and drew in his breath
sharply. Solomon was simply staking a cool half-million that
he could apprehend Everingham's murderer within a month.
The chief would announce that unless he caught the murderer
in that time he would resign his office.

With Solomon's cheque in his pocket, he could resign cheerfully; if Solomon succeeded in turning over to him the murderer,
he would be able to silence effectually both his critics and the
newspapers, and uphold the efficiency of the department. But
Lind conjectured shrewdly that the chief would much prefer the
half-million and resignation, and he was proven right.

"No strings to it?" inquired the chief thickly.

"No, sir. 'Alf a million dollars or the criminal, sir, and you
know werry well as 'ow I 'ave the money, sir."

"Sure I know it," muttered the chief, sudden beads of perspiration on his brow. "It's a bargain, Solomon! When do I get the certified cheque?"

"I'll send it to your office in an hour, sir. And now, Mr. Lind, if you'll be so good, we might be steppin' along."

Lind looked at the chief, and rose smiling. After all, this bluffing, bullying chief of police had been reduced to the level of mere man by the simple formula of the dollar sign; yet that was a magnificent bribe, a bribe worthy this man who virtually ruled the second largest city in the country but who was ruled in turn by politics.

Also, Lind observed that there was no question in the chief's mind of Solomon's ability to turn over that amount of money. The little Cockney seemed to be well known and trusted.

"I'd better take charge of things here, John," said Lind, accepting the situation without further comment. "I can get things straightened up, and the place will be in shape when Mr. Everingham's partner returns to-morrow—"

"You'll come wi' me, sir," broke in Solomon. "We'll go to me office, then we'll 'ave lunch, and then you can come back 'ere if so be as you wants to."

The door opened, and the chief of detectives entered.

"I suppose you'll want to keep this, Mr. Lind," he said, holding out the signed confession which Hopkins had written.

"Come on, Mac; we'll get out." The chief rose, picked up his hat, and strode to the door, slamming it behind them.

"I'd better be here this afternoon, John," explained Lind, getting his hat and coat from his own office. "You know, Diana promised to call up if I could do anything for her."

They left the building together, found the black limousine waiting, and got into the car. On their way to the Gas Building neither man spoke. Solomon seemed very much absorbed in watching the streets, and Lind was straightening things out in his own mind. But he was soon to find that he had not plumbed the depths of John Solomon.

Upon reaching their destination, Solomon told the chauffeur

to accompany them to his office. Once seated in his easy chair, the Cockney wrote out a cheque for five hundred thousand dollars, payable to Cash, and showed it to Lind. Then he turned to the chauffeur.

"Take this to me bank, Ali. Get it certified, then 'and it to the chief of police in person. Be werry sure as you don't give it to no one else."

"It is done, effendi."

The chauffeur turned and departed. Lind stared at Solomon in blank consternation.

"John, are you crazy? You made that cheque payable to Cash; don't you know that nigger can cash it and skip? Good heavens, man—"

Solomon chuckled wheezily.

"Don't you worry, sir. 'E ain't no nigger."

"What? He's not?"

"No, sir. 'E's an Arab, and a werry good friend to 'ave. That 'ere man 'as been wi' me nigh on to ten year, sir, and 'e loves me like a brother, 'e does that. Don't you worry about 'im, sir."

"But—an Arab? Are all your men Arabs?"

"Yes, sir."

Lind sat back, silenced. Solomon filled and lighted his pipe, then went into the outer room. After a moment he came back and went to his big safe. From the safe he took one of his brass-bound boxes, and from the box drew out a red notebook. After running over this, he took a large photograph from beneath his arm and held it out to Lind. "You might 'ave a look at this, sir."

The picture was evidently an enlargement. It showed a small, sharp-featured man clad in frock coat and silk hat—quite irreproachably garbed, in fact. Lind frowned in remembrance, trying to place that face. And suddenly it came to him.

"Why—it's the double of that fellow with the birthmark on his cheek!" he exclaimed, looking up quickly. "Say, John, I want to know what all this means. Why did that man tell Hopkins that he knew me and hated me?"

"I don't know meself," returned Solomon. "I'd like werry much to know what it all means, sir."

"But this photograph?" queried the puzzled Lind. "Who is it?"

"The same man as worked 'Opkins, sir."

"The same? Impossible! That fellow had a birthmark!"

"Yes, sir. Just cast your eye on this 'ere, Mr. Lind."

Solomon held out his notebook. There, written in small but very legible writing, was the following entry:

> *Dubois, John Francis.*—Born Marseilles. Age thirty-six. French parents. Lived five years in England. Broke jail Liverpool. Turned up in Cairo, posing as English nobleman. Exposed. Convicted of murder, escaped. Last heard of at Smyrna—Assumes disguise of birthmark, right cheek. Fluent linguist. Has never seen J.S. Expert cracksman.

Then at last Lind understood. The man of the birthmark, whom he had seen in Bogard's auction rooms, who had inspired Hopkins—was this same Dubois!

"But why on earth did he claim to know me, John?"

"To get 'Opkins's attention, sir. Bless 'im, 'e don't know you, nor you 'im! Nor do the police know 'im. But I do, sir, just like that. Now, if so be as you're ready to lunch, Mr. Lind—"

"One thing." Lind tossed the notebook to the desk, whence Solomon retrieved it. "You told the chief that you knew who killed Mr. Everingham. Do you know?"

"Yes, sir," replied Solomon, closing his safe. "This 'ere Dubois done it."

"Then, since you know him, why not put the police after him and end all this?"

Solomon chuckled wheezily.

"I 'as me 'opes, sir, just like that. But we 'as a mortal long way to go, sir, as the old gent said when 'e married 'is fourth. This 'ere thing ain't rightly started yet, mind that! Now, Mr. Lind, if so be as you're ready—"

Lind followed him, hopelessly bewildered.

CHAPTER VIII

LIND WAS weary of talking. Since Solomon had met
him in the delicatessen that morning it seemed that he had
been talking perpetually. Consequently, he resigned himself to
silence during lunch, having learned enough to make him digest
the situation with care.

The great fact that overshadowed all others was—John Francis Dubois.

During their luncheon at the "Tip Top," Solomon volunteered a few more scraps of information concerning this man,
whom he had apparently known of old. Dubois was not only a
criminal, but he was an accomplished and clever criminal, whose
crimes had of late years been confined to the Levant. Now, it
seemed, he was in Chicago.

For disguise, Dubois either adopted ragged garb and a disfiguring birthmark, or else dressed immaculately and posed as "a
somebody" from Europe. He was the more dangerous from
being well educated and from having a keen appreciation of art.

Solomon's opinion was that Dubois had calmly driven up to
the Everingham residence in an automobile and entered the
gold room; that the broker had caught him, and that Dubois had
stabbed Everingham to avoid discovery. Then he had departed—

"—and 'e dragged that 'ere dragon rug after 'im," asserted
Solomon gloomily.

At this, Lind laughed openly. The thing was rankly impossible. Only an immensely strong man could have carried that heavy rug ten feet; Dubois could not have dragged it out, then have carried it back and replaced it. Besides, this was disproven by the absence of any footprints. Dubois had gone out to his car and driven off.

Yet he had left behind him those tell-tale bits of yellow wool, which must have come from the Chinese rug. Solomon had matched them with the rug, and had found them not only absolutely identical in hue, but also in length. It was rankly improbable that any two ancient Chinese rugs would have pile of exactly the same shade and length, and the wool which Solomon had found in two places was of the same yellow colour, denoting that the body of the rug must have been of that colour also. None the less, the dragon rug still reposed in the gold room, untorn and seemingly untouched.

Even more remarkable than the way in which Dubois had thus covered his trail and yet had left a clue was, to Lind's mind, the fact that Dubois had claimed to know him and had thus instigated Hopkins to his shameful task.

Even Solomon admitted that this claim seemed preposterous, not only because Lind did not know the man, but because Dubois had been last seen in Smyrna, six months previously, and thus could not have been in Chicago any great length of time.

As the two men sat in silence over their coffee, Solomon suddenly drove into his pocket and produced a red notebook. Thumbing this over in his matter-of-fact way, he finally reached his objective and passed the book to Lind, who was astonished to find before him a very complete summary of Lucius Bogard's life and history. He inspected it with interest.

Bogard was thirty-two and had gone from an Eastern university to Naples ten years previously. At that time his father had been concerned in some scandal and had suicided. Bogard, thrown on his own resources, had drifted about the Near East for three years and had finally returned to America.

Coming to Chicago, he had turned his talents to good purpose and had established himself under the wing of one

Travers, then owner of the auction rooms. Bogard's ability had raised him in two years to the level of an importer; Travers had retired from business; Bogard had remained as auctioneer and owner, and had prospered.

Such was the brief sketch of his history, and Solomon knew no more of him, save that he had agents in Constantinople, Smyrna, and elsewhere, who sent him Oriental goods to sell. Bogard claimed to sell all goods on commission only; this, Solomon knew for a lie, in part, as Bogard personally imported a large share of the things he sold.

"But where do you drag him into this thing?" queried Lind, puzzled.

"A man as ain't straight in one thing, sir, ain't straight in other things, I says, just like that. You seen Dubois in 'is store. 'Ow did 'Opkins know as you liked Miss Everingham? 'Count o' Dubois. 'Ow did Dubois know? 'Count o' Bogard, I says. Who'd steal a wallyble rug? Bogard or Dubois."

The little man rose and beckoned for his hat. Lind stared up at him blankly.

"But—you think there's some connection between Bogard and Dubois, then? And you think Dubois murdered Everingham—good heavens, man! It can't be possible!"

"All right, sir. We'll see, just like that. You'd better be a-going back to that 'ere office, Mr. Lind, 'cause why, Miss Everingham might be a-callin' up."

Thus abruptly dismissed, Lind took his way to his own office, in the black limousine which was again at his disposal. And, once in the lonely reminiscent quarters, where now the telephone girl alone remained at work, Lind passed on through his own office and began putting Everingham's sanctum in order—it had been sadly disturbed that morning. Then he sat down to await Diana's promised message, but his thoughts were not on the girl. He knew that this day had effected a crisis in his life, and sinister thoughts gripped him.

Was Everingham's murderer reaching out to him? Lind

thought not. Dubois was the murderer, according to Solomon. And Solomon had expressly told the chief of police that Everingham's murder had been incidental to some larger crime as yet unknown, that it had not been a deliberately planned murder.

Were this theory correct, Lind saw that his own implication in the crime had not been schemed by Dubois, but had been pure circumstance. The scheme had lain in sending the letter and planting the brokerage receipts in hope that Lind would thereby lose his position. Dubois had done this, of course, but behind Dubois had been—who?

To put two and two together was easy. Lind had never liked Lucius Bogard. He had seen that Bogard was more than interested in Diana Everingham. He had a shrewd suspicion that Bogard, behind the eternal affability of the auctioneer, disliked him intensely. He sent his thoughts groping—groping after Lucius Bogard.

Solomon suspected Bogard of trying to steal back the very rugs he had sold to Everingham. This Lind could hardly credit, nor would there be point to such a theft. That Imperial Dragon rug, for example, could never be disposed of if it were stolen, as all the rug world would be on the lookout for it.

Yet between Bogard and Dubois existed some connection, quite aside from that suggested by Hopkins and the letter. Lind had seen Dubois entering the auction rooms. Both Bogard and Dubois had spent years in the Levant—one as an adventurer and fortune hunter, the other as a criminal. Could Bogard be acting as a "fence" for this master thief—

"No, but I wouldn't be surprised if Bogard had hired Dubois to get rid of me as an obstacle in his projected love affair!" thought Lind grimly. "Perhaps Bogard told more than he intended, and Dubois planned a fine robbery. Dubois could have learned of those burglar alarms from Thimms, could have entered the house as a plumber or electrician—yes, even as a guest—and could have smashed them. He could have done that with Garvel's house too, and Larsen's and Hardinge's. Then he came back last

night to make his get-away with the dragon rug, and Everingham caught him—"

From this rather plausible train of reasoning he turned to
the telephone and called up Solomon. With the Cockney on
the wire, Lind excitedly outlined his theory, only to be brutally
interrupted.

"Don't you go a-botherin' your 'ead wi' things as you don't
know nothing about, sir," wheezed Solomon.

"But doesn't it seem likely—"

"No, it don't," came the irritable reply.

"How about those other places?" persisted Lind hotly. "You
told me that the alarms were smashed at the homes of Hardinge,
Garvel, Larsen—"

"Them 'ere gents ain't 'ired me, sir," answered the other. "They
sticks to the police, and werry glad I am. Now, Mr. Lind, just
you trust to me, sir. This 'ere is Friday, ain't it?"

"It is," retorted Lind curtly.

"When does Mr. Everingham's partner come back, sir?"

"To-night or to-morrow. Why?"

"Would you be willin', sir, to take up a job 'elping me? If so
be as you would then rest up over Sunday, see Mr. Everingham
buried all ship-shape and proper, and turn up 'ere at me office
Monday mornin', just like that."

"Eh? Are you in earnest?" exclaimed the surprised Lind.

"Werry much so, Mr. Lind. I'll even go so far as to offer you a
hundred a week, sir. We gets on werry well together, sir. When
so be as two men gets on well together, it don't pay to let go in a
'urry, says I; it ain't a thing as 'appens werry often, I says. You'll
see some werry queer goings-on, sir, and you—"

"Wait a moment," said Lind. "Hold the phone."

He rested the receiver on the desk, and glanced around; Solomon's offer had staggered him for more reasons than one.

The little Cockney must be wealthy; to that the certified
cheque, the limousine, and this salary offer all testified. So far

as money was concerned the offer was a large upward step, but Lind was not thinking solely of money.

Two years previously he had deliberately set out to climb via the route of a secretaryship. He knew whither that route led—through offices, private offices and sanctums, to the managerial chair. Lind had set that chair as his goal, and was now well along the road. Should he abandon it or not? There was another and unexpected crisis.

Turning suddenly, he caught up the receiver.

"Hello, John. Is this position permanent or temporary?"

"I 'opes it'll last, sir," came a wheezy chuckle.

"How long can I have to think it over?"

"A matter of 'alf an hour, sir."

"Then I'll call you."

Lind drew a cigar from his pocket and lighted it, frowning. He faced his crisis squarely.

He was no detective, and realized it—nor did he want to be a detective. Yet Solomon himself was not one, at least nominally. Reflecting, Lind could not remember that Solomon had said a word about being on any other "case" at present. As a detective, the little Cockney was in one sense a disappointment; in another sense he was a joke.

Ah, but was he, after all, either of these things? On remembering how close he himself had come that same morning to a felon's cell, Lind found sweat starting on his brow. Who but Solomon could have gained him clearance? Who but Solomon could have imagined so grotesque a bribe—a bribe to cheat justice, but a bribe whose very spirit was of justice itself? And who but Solomon could have ferreted out John Francis Dubois—and Hopkins?

Arriving thus far in his meditations, Lind was interrupted by a persistent hammering at the outer office door. He answered the call, to find the boy who brought to the office force their early editions of the afternoon papers. Lind took the sheets, tossed the boy a coin, and retired to the sanctum again to sit and stare at the type which stood out before him. So, then, the chief had taken Solomon seriously that morning!

"Police Head Jabs Critics!" read the scarehead, and under this was a scathing pronunciamento issued by the chief of police. Lind, knowing that the chief could little more than write his own name, admired the secretarial genius which had evolved this article.

After hauling his critics and the newspapers over the coals, the chief stated that all the energies of the department would be given to apprehending the murderer of Herbert Stuart Everingham, and that, were the murderer not in jail within a month, he, the chief, would resign his position. To all appearance it was a frank, brutal, fearless challenge to Chicago at large. But Lind, knowing of that huge certified cheque which by now must be reposing in the chiefs pocket, smiled as he read.

"Well, I must choose," he muttered, flinging aside the papers. "What future does this work of Solomon's hold out to me? Hm!"

After all, the proffered opening might be far ahead of anything he could look to for some time to come, quite aside from the doubled salary. And even as he had joined the Scribe's Club for other reasons than the pursuit of happiness, now Lind reflected on the aid he might find in Solomon's employ.

Nor was this a self-centred, cold-blooded reflection as at first might seem. True, Harvey Lind was possessed of a savage determination to get on in the world, but in no sense was he inclined to be unscrupulous in his getting on. When he found that he could secure a thing that might weigh to his advantage, he secured it and used it, but legitimately.

He never gambled on a chance opening, because he knew that he could not afford to lose. For the same reason, in a material way, he never gambled in the stock market or elsewhere. He hewed squarely to the line, and was content to know that the line never doubled backward, never lost a foot of ground by any wasted axework.

So, to Lind, it was no easy matter to abandon the sort of work

which he had chosen. As the confidant of Everingham, he had
known with some intimacy his employer's friends—all of them
men like Hardinge or Garvel, influential in the business world
of Chicago. Now that Everingham was dead, Lind knew that he
could obtain a step upward from any of these men, or he might
remain in the office for Everingham's partner.

Then he thought of John Solomon's office. In that office he
would doubtless be thrown in contact with a fund of valuable
information, especially as regarded Chicago and Chicagoans,
and he would certainly see an interesting side of life. But Lind
was thinking of something else—of the pudgy, blue-eyed, lonely
little man who had men to serve him, but none to aid him.

Lind pitied Solomon. He liked the man, and just why Solomon impressed him as lonely he could not tell. Perhaps it was
the tales of the colourful East which Solomon had related;
perhaps it was the helpless, apologetic air habitually worn by
the Cockney; perhaps it was nothing but Solomon's wooden leg
and wide-eyed stare. Yet the impression was there.

"That's why he wants me, too," thought Lind suddenly. "Else
why should he offer me a hundred a week salary? I can't be worth
that to him—or can I? Perhaps I can, after all. He has to have
someone whom he can trust, of course; someone with decent
intelligence and average ability. No, I don't think that he's trying
to buy my friendship by any means. I think he likes me—and
I'm quite sure that I like him. We'd get on well. And then I'd
like to be in on this murder solution—I owe it to Everingham!"

Lind recollected his last conversation with the dead broker.
He felt a hot wave of anger sweep through him at thought
of Dubois. Were Solomon's supposition true, there was the
murderer of Everingham! But—was Solomon's theory accurate?
It was hardly a theory, in fact; it was a statement of belief, no
more. It had no background of evidence except for the confession of Hopkins.

Drawing out that signed paper, Lind read it over. Hopkins
had written his tale in full; although he had not known Dubois

by name, he had included a full description of "the man with the birthmark," and the confession was very complete.

"Well, this is now a closed incident," thought Lind, refolding it. "Only, it may react on the future of things. Solomon was dead right—there's more to this than a murder! Somebody's behind Dubois. It may or may not be Bogard; whoever it is, and whatever is going on, the affair looks to me like a pretty cunning piece of work."

Should he accept Solomon's offer—or refuse it? Lind weighed one thing after another, yet all the while there persistently stuck in his mind's eye that pudgy figure with the mild blue eyes. He felt as if the very pudgy calmness of that figure concealed tragedy—the tragedy of loneliness.

Abruptly the telephone rang, and the exchange girl informed him that Miss Everingham was on the wire. Another instant and Lind heard her voice.

"Hello, Diana! I was expecting you to call—or hoping, rather. How is your mother?"

"She's sleeping at last, Harve. I think she'll get over the shock safely. You're taking care of things at the office?"

"Yes. I can leave any time now. If I can be of any help at the house, or if there's anything that I can do in the shape of errands, let me know."

"Thank you, Harve," came the answer, and his heart was sore for the sadness of her voice, "but both Mr. Hardinge and Mr. Bogard are here, and are helping me take care of all—all arrangements."

"Oh," said Lind mechanically, "that's very good. Is there nothing I can do?"

"I don't know of anything, Harve. You're getting the office into shape, and that's enough for anyone. Things here are being taken care of very well."

Lind's face tightened. So Bogard had stepped in, eh?

"I want to see you, Diana," he said almost harshly, then paused. He had meant to tell her abruptly that he was about to take service with Solomon; second thought advised him that she had better not be told at this moment.

"Yes, Harve? Anything special?"

"In a way, yes." A thought flashed into Lind's mind and sent swift excitement surging through him. "It's business, Diana—business that you must join me in! If I send for you about eleven Monday morning will you come down-town and meet me at an office in the Gas Building?"

"I suppose I could," she hesitated slightly. "Of course, if it's important—"

"It is! I'm going to sit down now and write you a letter which will explain pretty fully what I can't say over the phone. You'll get it to-morrow morning. I'll send a car for you Monday, then—say ten-forty-five. Agreed?"

"Very well. Good-bye."

He hung up the receiver and turned staring at the window with a flame of purpose in his blue eyes. Then, excitement strong upon him, he whirled again to the telephone and called up Solomon. He had come to the parting of the roads, and had decided.

"Hello—this you, John? Lind speaking. About that offer of yours, I'll accept it on one condition."

"Yes, sir?" wheezed Solomon's phlegmatic voice. "Let's 'ave it, sir."

"It's this," responded Lind rapidly, as the hastily-visioned plan assumed clearer form in his brain. "You know Miss Everingham. Well, I'm going to write her a letter and tell her exactly what happened this morning. Naturally I'll leave out all the passing references to herself that popped up. She'll meet us at your office Monday morning at eleven. We'll go over the whole thing, and take her in as a partner on this mystery—"

"I don't 'old by no womenfolks, sir," broke in Solomon, with mild objection. "They ain't werry logical, so to speak."

"Nonsense! Miss Everingham has a better head than I. She's no fool, and you know it! Naturally, we'd have to omit any reference to Bogard until we get the goods on him—he's a family friend. But to have her as consultant will help us, John. Anyhow, I want her to know exactly what I'm doing in leaving her father's firm."

"Oh, I see!" To Lind's irritation, the Cockney chuckled at this. "Well, sir, you 'ave it your own way, just like that. But send me over that 'ere confession of 'Opkins's by messenger right off, sir. It's safer in me own 'ands, as the old gent said when 'e caught the butler kissin' of the 'ousemaid."

"Then you agree to my proposal?"

"Yes, sir. Werry good, says I. Monday mornin' at eleven, sir."

"Bully for you!" exclaimed Lind, and rang off.

Knowing Diana Everingham as he did, Lind thought it likely that she would be glad to join them. Yet it would be a grim task for her to assist in hounding down her father's murderer. Moreover, she could not be told of the implied connection between Bogard and Dubois. Bogard was a friend of the family and a highly probable suitor for Diana's hand, which in itself closed Lind's lips until he could produce definite proof of what he now only vaguely suspected.

Nor could Lind tell her of the sentence in Hopkins's letter which referred to her. The thing was too personal. It would inevitably bring into the open his own feelings towards Diana, and from this Lind shrank, at the present juncture. Although those encouraging words of the dead broker still burned in his mind, he must forget them yet awhile.

As he had always faced them, Harvey Lind now faced frankly and clearly the facts surrounding his supreme ambition—for such he knew it to be. He knew that Mrs. Everingham, now a wealthy widow, did not like him because she had instinctively divined his attitude toward Diana. He knew that she considered him as a mere wage-earner, a salaried employee whose annual hire was less than she donated each season to the opera funds.

To Lind her likes and dislikes mattered nothing, except as they might influence Diana. And Diana, he knew, was not apt to be influenced by any such considerations—if she loved a man. There was the rub!

A deep frown crept into Lind's strong face as he stared at the window and once more mentally contrasted himself with Lucius Bogard. Diana had other suitors in plenty, but he swept them aside without a thought.

"There are just two real men sitting in this game," he reflected, quite without egotism, and with a calm sense of values. "I am one and Bogard one—I'll give him that credit. He's got everything—and what have I?"

His frown deepened. Lind was not a college man. He knew that he lacked much of Bogard's culture, polish, *savoir-faire*. Yet, through his confidential position with Everingham, he had been brought into contact with such men as Hardinge and Garvel—men of wealth and business position. In such meetings he had made himself known and felt. He was not a nonentity.

"I'll ask her some day," he muttered, rising and passing out to his own office. "If that job with Solomon is permanent, the salary will be enough. She doesn't give a whoop for money—I know that. Yes, I'll ask her. But I'll have to whip Bogard first, that's sure!"

He sat down at his typewriter, and began to write his letter to Diana.

CHAPTER IX

MONDAY MORNING.

The final act of the tragedy was over. Herbert Stuart Everingham had been laid to rest on the preceding day, while the Press and the public discussed the funeral baked meats of gossip, speculation, and morbid interest. The chief of police's "self challenge," as it was called, was the chief theme of editorials and kerb conversation alike.

Lind, watching at the funeral, with Jack Brune at his side, had observed Lucius Bogard lending respectful assistance to the two bereaved women who were now left alone in the world. Lind had not desired to urge his attentions upon them at the time.

"Looks to me," observed the reporter, "as if Bogard took a mighty keen interest in the orphan yonder."

There was cutting irony in that last word, which did not escape Lind.

"Mrs. Everingham isn't a bad sort, Jack," he returned softly.

"Neither was King Charles the First, but they cut off his head. Say, Harve, have you any inside dope on that murder?"

"Nothing."

"I heard last night that you'd resigned your job."

"Yes. Got another one. Never mind that now."

Lind had not seen his friend since the funeral, and thus had made no further explanation of his plans and his new position with Solomon.

Now, seated in Solomon's office, while the Cockney puffed

placidly at his clay pipe and stared at the lake front, Lind was awaiting the coming of Diana Everingham.

How she had received his letter he did not know. He had heard nothing from her and was in some doubt as to what her attitude would be. The black limousine had been sent for her half an hour previously.

A noise at the door. Solomon hastily laid aside his pipe and turned on an electric fan; the windows were open, and the warm spring air sweetened the room instantly. Lind, springing up, reached the outer office and met the girl who was just entering.

She had flung back her heavy veil, and greeted him with the shadow of her old cheery smile. But the depths of her blue-black eyes were very sad. A sudden maturity, a new womanliness, seemed to have come upon her.

"Good morning, Harve! I want to thank you for those flowers—"

"No thanks, please," he said, and nodded toward the inner office. "Mr. Solomon is waiting for us. You remember him—the gentleman who came to the house with me on Friday morning? And you got my letter all right?"

"Yes." Her eyes, which had wandered toward the inner office, came back to him swiftly. "Harve, I couldn't believe it! Did they really try to make you out a—a—"

"A murderer," he finished gravely. "Yes. But it was too thin, Diana; they couldn't do it. Now come along and get acquainted with the queerest man in Chicago—and I'll bet a cooky you like him!"

He ushered her into the corner room, where Solomon received her with a pudgy bow that was surprisingly graceful. Lind had already noted that the little Cockney could display a deal of agility when he so wished.

"Now, sir, and miss," declared Solomon gravely, "there ain't nothing like gettin' a bad business over with, I says, so we'll start right in."

He did so accordingly. The girl's eyes were fastened on him

in slow wonder, which changed to a growing keenness as she perceived the fine brain at work behind that pudgy countenance and that china-blue stare. Lind, watching her in his turn, was inwardly both amused and gratified to see that she was not deceived by the superficial appearance of the little man.

Solomon went into his somewhat intricate task of explanation in a slow methodical manner which left no point uncovered—save the theoretical agency of Bogard.

The letter and the crafty villainy of Hopkins, the bargain with the chief of police, and finally the mysterious deviltry of John Francis Dubois were cleared off point by point. Here and there Diana put in curt incisive questions which seemed to please Solomon immensely.

This probing into her father's murder was by no means a pleasant task, but she forced herself to it with a concentration which deepened as Solomon brought out the underlying mystery of the whole affair. When he had finished, she leaned back in her chair with a frowning nod of comprehension.

"It's queer, certainly," she commented. "Nothing was stolen from the house, and I know the Chinese rug was unharmed, because I examined it carefully after getting Harve's letter on Saturday. You're sure that those tufts of wool you found outside the house had come from that very rug?"

"Werry sure, miss."

"And why do you connect Dubois with this—aside from the confession of Hopkins?"

"That's 'is old trick, miss, stabbin' of a man in the throat, like. Then there ain't many crooks in this 'ere town as would 'ave the nerve to tackle a big job like that."

She was silent for a moment, then made a little gesture of despair.

"Well, what do you want of me? What can I do, Harve?"

"You can help us track down this man," said Lind quickly, eagerly. "As I wrote you, I'm now in Solomon's employ, and we're going to bring your father's murderer to justice, Diana. I want the help of your brain and your ability. I want you to chip in with us, if you will. There's no telling where or how you may be able to give us assistance—"

"I want to know one thing," she broke in suddenly. "Why should this man Dubois hate you, Harve, when you've never even seen him?"

For they had not told her of that chance meeting in Bogard's store.

Lind glanced at Solomon. He still inclined to his theory that Bogard had set Dubois to work with Hopkins, but that did not imply that Bogard was connected with the attempted robbery. The auctioneer might simply have told Dubois too much, and the criminal might then have utilized his knowledge in the attempted theft, ending with murder.

"Why, miss, that's summat as we don't rightly know," wheezed Solomon in answer to the girl's query. "We thinks as 'ow Mr. Lind 'as some enemy or mebbe some friend what's interesting 'imself, just like that. Friends is werry good things to 'ave while they keeps their distance, as the old gent said when 'e found the gardener kissin' the new 'ousemaid."

Diana smiled slightly, but her eyes remained grave.

"Then, Harve," she said slowly, "someone is trying to knife you in the back. That is evident. I don't think that Mr. Solomon—"

"Make it John, miss," broke in the Cockney apologetically. "I've been called John all me life, and it comes more natural-like."

"All right," she nodded quietly—and somewhat to Lind's surprise. "I was going to say, John, that to connect Dubois with this—this crime seems rather far-fetched. But it's quite plain that for some reason he was working against Harve. Now, what am I to do?"

"Then you'll help?" exclaimed Lind.

"Of course. I'm waiting to learn if I can be of any use to you."

Solomon cleared his throat.

"You can do this, miss. You can go 'ome and wait, just like that. When so be as we're ready, we'll call you in."

Diana frowned slightly.

"But—"

"See here, Diana," and Lind leaned forward earnestly, sensing her unspoken objection and sensing Solomon's purport. "We don't know where this trail will lead or what will come up. Now that I know you're with me, I'll call on you quick enough when we need you. But for the present—do as John says.

"You're in no shape for such work, after what you've just been through, and you'd be wise to gain rest and to recover from the shock that has come to us all alike. Then, when we want you, we'll find you ready and able to give us double the help you would otherwise. Don't you see?"

"Very well, then," she nodded, and rose. "You may count on me to do whatever I can. Good-bye for the present."

Lind took her to the elevator, and returned to find Solomon tamping down his pipe reflectively. Having been in some doubt as to the nature of his own work, Lind was relieved to find that Solomon had some very definite instructions for him.

The little Cockney proved to be very much disturbed, in fact. Not Everingham's alone, but the homes of three other men had been tampered with. All these places housed valuable collections of Oriental rugs. All of them had been equipped with Thimms's electric alarms. The secret of these alarms had doubtless been gained from the builder in the same fashion—by means of too much liquor. And Thimms was dead and could not speak.

The other three men had reported the matter to the police and had at once had their alarms repaired. Solomon, it seemed, had learned this through police channels. None of the residences had been burglarized, yet this general menace seemed to point to some deeply laid scheme connected with Oriental rugs. Further, the whole thing had occurred within the past month.

This point would serve to implicate Dubois, who, according to Solomon, could have been in the United States little over two or three months. Also, in his previous career, Dubois had had a nasty habit of using a knife.

"But what could lie behind it all? What object?" asked Lind.

"I don't know, sir. But it's summat mortal big."

Solomon's orders were concise and brief.

Dubois was to be found and watched. Lind might encounter him at the Greek restaurant mentioned by Hopkins, or he might see him again at Bogard's. Also, that same afternoon, Lind was to visit the auction rooms and contrive a look over the basement of the place. Solomon had a curiosity to know what that basement was like.

"But find that 'ere Dubois inside o' three days, or we'll 'ave more devilment," concluded the Cockney.

"You know Jack Brune, *The Times* reporter?" asked Lind slowly. "He'd prove of help to me, and I needn't tell him anything except that I must find Dubois. How about it?"

Solomon nodded gravely, his mild blue eyes quite inscrutable.

"Werry good, sir. Two young 'eads is better than one old one, says I."

Lind departed to the Scribes Club with a suspicion that John Solomon had been poking fun at him in that last remark.

As Brune usually lunched at the club, and it was now close to noon, Lind was confident of his friend at once. He decided to tell Brune that he was in the employ of Solomon, that the Cockney wanted to locate Dubois, and that he was bound not to reveal more than this. If Solomon wanted Brune to know more, he could himself tell him.

There was nothing imposing about the Scribes Club, either on the exterior or the interior. It was meant not to be imposing but homelike. Occupying a position on Dearborn, near Madison, it was located centrally within the Loop and was easy of access from any quarter. The club proper occupied the upper five floors of the building.

Seeking Brune, Lind left the elevator at the third and office floor. Passing to the taproom, he scanned the card tables. Here he found a dozen men of the poseur type, who invariably gravitated to the taproom and the tables adjacent.

"Anyone seen Jack Brune?" called out Lind.

"Went to Elgin half an hour ago," answered one, glancing up. "Dynamite plot or something in the watch factory—said he'd be back to-night with a big story. Sit in?"

Lind declined, and sought the street. Since his friend was for the moment unavailable, he determined to lunch at the Greek restaurant, keep an eye out for Dubois, and then go to Bogard's auction for the afternoon.

He knew the restaurant quite well himself, having lunched there occasionally about a year before. Its habitues were chiefly Greeks, one of two tables being given over to "misfits" in the Chicago scheme of things—an aged Belgian sculptor, a Portugese commission merchant, the head house detective from Field's, one or two others of like types.

Lind entered and took a chair at the first table, where the Belgian was sitting, and a quick glance showed him that Dubois was not in the place. Knowing the old Belgian for a sturdy, thoroughly honest cosmopolite, Lind ventured a few cautious inquiries, and unexpectedly struck pay dirt.

Yes, the sculptor had seen that small man with the birthmark, had seen him many times. The small man spoke delicious French, and had travelled. No, not for the last two or three days; not since the preceding Thursday, to be exact—ah, yes, a very charming fellow, if one overlooked his clothes. No, the Belgian knew not where the other lived.

That was something, at all events, thought Lind. After lingering an hour, he finished his wine and departed. He was quite certain that Dubois had not appeared, for the man's face was stamped on his memory as clear and sharp as a cameo.

Then, quite unconscious of how the storm clouds were being driven upon him by the winds of hatred and driving fate, Lind sought the auction rooms of Lucius Bogard. He was not using the black limousine to-day, and felt rather glad to be afoot.

At Bogard's, Lind found the auctioneer still absent at lunch, and was received by the solemn but extremely crafty assistant—

an Americanized Armenian who commonly went by the name of David and who knew the stock as well as Bogard himself.

"I suppose Mr. Bogard will be back pretty soon?" inquired Lind.

"Oh, yes—it's nearly time for the sale now. We have one or two people waiting."

"Any objection to my looking around in the back room and downstairs?"

As he said this, Lind thought that David looked at him a trifle curiously. But the little dark man only shrugged his shoulders and glanced toward the street again.

"Certainly, Mr. Lind—everything is at your service. Anything you pick out, of course, we'll be very glad to put up."

Lind nodded and walked on down the store. He passed the rows of chairs with rugs thrown over them, where already a few early bidders were sitting, and came to the rug stand just beyond. Here Bogard usually took his place when auctioning, and the stand on which the rugs were displayed was cunningly arranged beneath powerful electric lights.

With a smiling word to the book-keeper at her desk, Lind passed on into the mammoth back room—a huge place where the larger rugs were stored on tierlike shelves around the walls, with old furniture, marbles, and every manner of bric-a-brac disposed at the sides, leaving the centre of the room clear for the display of room-sized rugs.

Lind had no great interest in these things, having seen them before. He turned to the stairway leading down cellar. At the head of this, working over a table, was a man who looked up at him with a nod of greeting—a rug weaver, repairing odd pieces for Bogard or his customers, and by his looks an Armenian or Turk.

Feeling an uncomfortable sense of running a gauntlet of guards, Lind turned down the basement stairs and so came to a series of rather damp rooms, in the first of which two packers were at work crating a table. These paid him no attention, and he went on, finding the whole basement well lighted by electric bulbs placed at intervals.

There was nothing in the basement rooms which would justify Solomon's curiosity, decided Lind. Parts of spindle and four-poster beds, in natural wood fresh from the factory—freshly made reproductions of old chairs and tables—packing cases and boxes—and little more. Bogard made no secret of the fact that he sold these reproductions, and even that he made them himself.

Lind strolled over to where one of the packers was painting an address on a stout iron-bound packing case. Quite without any intent, he glanced down, and idly noted the name because of its very oddness. At the same moment he caught a faint odour of sulphuric acid.

JEREMIAH V. GILLAM
No.—, Fourth Avenue, New York City

The man who was writing suddenly looked up with a scowl.

"Whaddye want?" he demanded gruffly.

"Civility," said Lind quietly. "Do I get it?"

The packer glared at him, but under the swift, cold ice of Lind's blue eyes his gaze shifted abruptly. Grunting something unintelligible, he turned and strode off. At this instant Lind caught the voice of David from the top of the stairs:

"Mr. Lind! Mr. Lind! Mr. Bogard wants you."

"Coming, thanks," sang out Lind, and turned to the stairs.

He found Bogard awaiting him at the head of the stairs—and, to his surprise, Bogard's face was flushed with anger. Also there was none of the wonted civility and smooth suavity in the tone with which the importer spoke:

"Mr. Lind, are you acquainted with a Mr. John Solomon?"

"Why, yes," responded Lind, on his guard at once. For a moment Bogard met his gaze steadily, and in the man's dark eyes Lind read a repressed anger as clearly as he had read it in

Bogard's flushed face. But the other, evidently checking himself, forced a smile.

"A Mr. Solomon just called up and asked me to give you a message. Said he wanted to see you at once, and that you'd find him in a back room at the Honkytonk Saloon on South State Street. Is it a joke of some kind, do you think?"

"Sounds like it." And Lind frowned. "Much obliged, though. Guess I'll look into it. I suppose you didn't mind my looking around the basement?"

"Bless you, my dear fellow, of course not!" And now Bogard had regained his habitual manner quite completely. "See you later, I hope?"

Lind assented and strode off.

Inwardly he was wondering what had caused Bogard to lose his perfect poise for a fleeting moment. Lind had read hatred in the man's face—hatred and suspicion. But what could have caused those emotions? His trip down to the basement?

Lind strode up Adams to State and turned south. He knew where the Honkytonk Saloon was—a place of no good reputation, located in the evil district just beyond the Loop. He was too puzzled over Bogard to waste much wonder on such a summons, more especially as he gave little wonder to anything that John Solomon might do.

It was very plain that for one brief moment the hatred that lay latent between himself and Lucius Bogard had almost come to the surface. Bogard's effort to restrain himself had been all too obvious to Lind's eye.

"And what was that sulphuric acid I caught a whiff of?" he reflected. "It seemed to come from that workman—yet there was nothing of the kind in sight, and no indication of any acid carboys. Well, maybe they use it to age furniture or something."

In that instant Lind was closer to the heart of things than he knew—but the instant passed unsuspected.

After a brisk, twenty-minute walk, he came to his destination. The "Honkytonk" was flanked by "shows" more flamboyant than virtuous, and it advertised the "largest beer in the city," with some truth. A little cluster of ragged, bloated specimens hung outside the door and loudly begged Lind to "buy a drink" as he entered.

He passed inside with an angry resolve to let Solomon understand flatly how he felt at being summoned to such a place. The long bar-room was almost empty, and Lind went directly to the bar-tender.

"Any one named Solomon here?" he inquired.

"Back room," responded the other, with a flick of his towel. "Take the passage and first room on your right."

Thanking him, Lind crossed to the dark passage at the rear end of the place. A number of doors were in view on either side the passage, and Lind turned the handle of the first on his right.

As he entered, he had one brief glimpse of a face—a face that stood out in his memory like a cameo, except that now the birthmark had disappeared. Then something struck him under the ear, and be knew no more.

CHAPTER X

"SLUGGED?"

"Slugged."

"By you?"

"By me."

Lind laughed quietly.

"What are you so merry about?" said Dubois, a sudden snarl in his voice.

"About what I shall do to you when I get my hands on you, murderer!"

Dubois stared at him for a moment, then turned and left the room, cursing.

Harvey Lind lay back on his couch, and his smile turned to a grimace of pain as his head touched the covers. Handcuffs were on his wrists, irons on his ankles.

He closed his eyes. From the moment when he had entered that back room of the saloon, he had known nothing until he wakened to the jolting of an automobile. Then he had been half-carried into a house, and so brought—here.

Dubois had aroused him—Dubois, impeccably dressed from boutonnière to spats, the small weasel-like features clean-shaven, and set in gentle melancholy. Lind's three curt speeches had stripped the man of his pose, however, and had sent him forth snarling.

Now, as Lind thought back over what had happened, he began to reconstruct the trend of things with grim certainty.

Someone—and no doubt it was the vanished Hopkins—had tipped off Dubois that Lind and Solomon were on his trail; possibly Hopkins had sent a letter either to Bogard or Dubois.

That letter must have come in this morning's mail, explaining why Lucius Bogard had been so long absent at lunch—with Dubois. There they had cooked up this pretty little plot, which had succeeded. This theory also explained the indubitable anger of Bogard on finding that Lind was prowling around the basement of his auction rooms.

"The devil of it is that there's no evidence!" thought Lind. "Bogard merely gave me a telephone message. Even if I got away, I'd have nothing on *him*. Damn it!"

With this mild and entirely natural expletive, Lind forced himself to sit up again despite his swimming head. From the Honkytonk Saloon he had been carried—somewhere. His irons were not particularly uncomfortable, save as they hobbled any movement, and he was extremely curious as to the location of his prison chamber.

Prison though it undoubtedly was, he discovered that he was confined in gilded luxury. He was in a very large, high-ceilinged room, fitted with a Napoleon couch, an old-fashioned bed of carved walnut, and several small chairs of carved teakwood. Lind noted that these chairs were of genuine teak and very heavy, and then dismissed the detail.

A table of antique design, with marble top, stood in one corner. The walls were bare of pictures.

"Seems to be a miscellaneous collection of old furniture, and of a mighty good sort," he reflected. "By the general look of things, I might be in one of the formerly high-class houses, either on the North or South Side, where the ruins of aristocracy have given place to the inroads of boarding houses, publicans, and sinners. Hm!"

Moving with slow and shuffling step, he crossed the large room to the door. This was locked, and he turned to eye the windows.

Of these there were two, each quite large, and each protected by an outer grillwork of heavy iron. Both were set in the same wall. Beyond the fact that the room seemed to be situated on the ground floor, Lind could make out nothing, as a blank brick wall rose three feet from the windows, shutting out all view. He could see nothing but that wall of red bricks, and whether it were a house or a surrounding wall he could not tell. He found the windows nailed fast in place.

"A hero of romance would smash the glass and file through that grille," thought Lind, in grim humour. "But I'm human, and I'm well ironed. Hm! Must be pretty near evening, to judge from the fading light."

He had been trapped shortly after noon, and had no notion of how long be might have lain in the Honkytonk Saloon. At any rate, he did not think the automobile ride had taken him far; he thought he could remember the rattling bang of the elevated road, which might mean that he had been carried to the North Side, across the Loop.

His disappearance would arouse Solomon, of course; but Lind did not comfort himself with any false hopes of rescue. Solomon would never be able to trace him, and Bogard would certainly not give the Honkytonk Saloon as a clue.

"At least I've established a connection between Bogard and Dubois, to my own satisfaction," he muttered. "Rather to my sorrow. What in thunder did they do it for?"

Sitting on his couch and resting his aching head in his hands, he went over the theory which he had evolved. That Hopkins had written to Dubois seemed far-fetched, but was at least plausible. Then Bogard and Dubois had gotten together and had struck. But why? What reason lay beneath it?

"Bogard certainly set Dubois and Hopkins on my trail," be thought. "The whole business started before Everingham was killed. That could mean but one thing—Bogard wanted me out of the way, eh? And the answer to that is Diana."

It was rapidly growing dark. As Lind reached this point in his bitter musings, he heard the door of his room unlocked, a switch was turned, and the room flooded with electric light. Dubois stood in the doorway, urbane and polished.

"Mr. Lind, will you accompany me to dinner? When we have dined, you may be glad to hear my explanation of certain things. Allow me to warn you that you are constantly watched and that anything in the nature of force would involve your instant death."

"You don't propose to starve me, then?" said Lind, rising. "And these irons?"

"Must remain, I regret to say." Dubois bowed mockingly.

So, then, there was to be an explanation! Lind shuffled forward, and Dubois ushered him into a long, dark passage-way. In that moment Lind was strongly tempted to smash his ironed wrists into the cunning, smiling weasel face of Dubois, but a dark figure in the passage moved slightly and gave him proof that his captor had spoken truly. Dubois was not taking chances with his prisoner.

The passage ended in a dining-room, wainscoted in oak, where a table glittered with candles and silver. Two silent servants moved about, and from their features Lind determined that they were Armenian or Turk. He took the chair held back for him, and Dubois seated himself across the table. The room was lighted only by candles.

"We may talk as we dine," said Dubois, who played his role of gentleman uncommonly well. "I have long wanted to meet you, Mr. Lind."

"I may return the compliment," said Lind dryly, though the recollection that he sat at meat with Everingham's murderer sent his heart pulsing savagely. "Why did you make a tool of Hopkins? At Bogard's instigation?"

Dubois laughed, his shifty eyes appraising Lind openly.

"Yes. You are a very good-looking young man, eh? I suspect Bogard rather loses his head when the jealous mood is on him. Had I been in his place, now, I would not have bothered poor

Hopkins—the man was inefficient and hated you too much to be tactful, as shown by his bungling. Had he taken more care in preparing his proofs of your stock transactions, for example, you might now be in jail. But no matter. Any more questions?"

Though his face betrayed no sign of it, Lind was filled with amazement as he looked across the table at Dubois. Here was frankness with a vengeance! And he understood that hint about Hopkins, who had hated him. Dubois, not hating him at all, was a crafty and inhuman machine of evil, unutterably dangerous.

"Yes," nodded Lind quietly. "Several things might be made clear to me."

He paused and tasted the excellent soup that had been set before him, his irons allowing him to eat with little discomfort. He was trying to adapt himself to the mood of this cool frank scoundrel across the table. So Bogard's jealousy was really behind all this!

"For instance, how was this coup of yours planned today? And why? I imagine that Hopkins wrote you a letter explaining what he had confessed?"

Dubois laughed softly.

"You give him too much credit, my friend. What time did Miss Everingham leave the Gas Building? Was it not eleven-forty?"

"Just about." And Lind frowned, startled. "Why?"

"At eleven fifty-five she had reached home. At twelve Bogard called her up. She told enough to warn us that you were dangerous, so we put you out of the way. Rather neat, eh, what? Now try this roast lamb, Mr. Lind. You'll find it really excellent, I think."

The astounded Lind obeyed.

Of course they should have warned Diana to say nothing to any one, especially to Bogard. Lind had been quite blind to that danger. The girl trusted Bogard absolutely, and, while she had probably said nothing direct, still she must have given Bogard enough of a hint to scare him thoroughly.

"Why the devil didn't you kill me outright?"' Lind broke out abruptly.

"Ah, now we approach the heart of things!" Dubois glanced swiftly at him. "You see, I have a question or two to ask you myself, later. But for the present I am content to answer."

"Then tell me how you hid your tracks after murdering Mr. Everingham."

Lind's eyes were like ice, but for a full moment Dubois looked steadily at him.

"Ah! You tell me a good deal in those words, Mr. Lind. So you do not know what it was that I dragged after me? That, I admit, was an idea of Bogard's."

Lind quivered suddenly. The murderer had confessed—had admitted his guilt! The last doubt was shredded away now; the whole sickening thing stood out plainly in all its mocking horror. Bogard and Dubois had done that thing; or at least Bogard had knowledge of it.

And with that crime on his soul, Bogard had played the hypocrite, had tenderly assisted the stricken women, was still posing as their friend and confidant!

"God!" muttered Lind hoarsely, then controlled himself with an effort. "No, we were puzzled by that. What was it?"

Dubois smiled at him.

"That, my friend, is one of the things which I cannot tell you. Now pray forget this unpleasant discourse and do justice to the salad which is about to appear. It is, I assure you, a supreme triumph, that salad. An invention of my own, by the way."

Lind forced himself into compliance. For a space he had been heartsick, dazed by the devilish coolness with which Dubois spoke of the murder as if it had been no more than a passing incident unworthy of comment. But he was not long in regaining control of himself as he swung back to poise again.

Degenerate undoubtedly though Dubois was, a criminal of high poses who enjoyed his own very lack of conscience and his own devilry, yet the man's manner held something terrible.

Lind not being in the least afraid of him, could not quite put a name to that thing, that aura which girded Dubois. It was as though the man were quite without heart, were strong in the confidence of his own crafty powers that he could laugh amusedly at all the virtue in the world, as a weasel might laugh at the clucking of hens.

Regarding Bogard, Lind was gradually getting things straightened out in his own mind, and was assigning relative place to these two arch-conspirators. Bogard had very probably formed some infernally cunning and lucrative scheme in which Dubois was aiding him. Lind's conception of the importer was rapidly changing.

He had hitherto regarded Bogard somewhat at his face value, as a connoisseur, a plausible fellow, a gentleman of sorts. True, he had heartily disliked the man, but he had not believed that Bogard could have had any agency in the murder of Everingham. Now, however, Bogard had been convicted by the words of Dubois.

"What an infernal devil Bogard is!" exclaimed Lind, only half-aware that he was speaking aloud, but not caring greatly. "And does he think that he could enjoy his stakes even did he win them? What is he playing for, Dubois?"

"For Miss Everingham, and for a good pot of money," came the cool answer. Then Dubois smiled thinly. "You are a little wrong, Mr. Lind—merely ignorant, perhaps. Bogard will win his stakes, and will enjoy them through life. Men of that sort always do. He is lucky in having no more conscience than have I myself, and the memory of a few little peccadillos—pouf! Nothing at all."

"Was it you or Bogard who discovered that the secret of the burglar alarms could be gained from Thimms?"

"Bogard—that was done early in the game, an accidental discovery, in fact. It saved us a great deal of trouble, though unfortunately it could not prevent an incidental death. But the salad, my friend? Was it not superb?"

"It was the acme of excellence," said Lind quietly.

"Incidental" he was thinking. That was the same word Solomon had used! The Cockney had declared the murder to be incidental, and now Dubois had proved that declaration to have been correct.

So the weird dinner passed. Lind would have thought his captor demented had not Dubois been so palpably sane. Never had Lind encountered a man in whom wickedness was so frank, cool, nerveless; but Dubois gave him an explanation of that over the mousse that followed the salad.

"I am tired of pretence, Mr. Lind," he said, with a little sigh of comfort. "That is Bogard's game, but it is mine only when necessary. It relieves me, at times, to speak quite frankly with one in whom lies no danger."

"Then you don't consider me dangerous?" said Lind, unsmiling.

Dubois shrugged his shoulders.

"Not at present. To continue my policy of frankness, I don't think you'll be dangerous either now or in future—though not for the world would I want the fact to spoil your enjoyment of this really beautiful meal."

A very faint accent had crept into the smooth voice—a slight slurring of "though" to "zough," of "this" to "zis." Lind tightly conjectured that it was a dangerous signal, even though Dubois seemed anything but dangerous, holding his cigarette to the match which one of the servants had struck.

"Coffee now," he ordered, nodding. "Then leave us. We must be alone, but let one stay always on guard in the passage."

As the two servants bowed, Lind gazed at Dubois in well-assumed calmness.

"Do you intend to kill me?"

The Frenchman raised his eyebrows.

"Really I do not know. So far as I myself am concerned, you are a charming fellow, Mr. Lind. I hope that your death does not become necessary. In fact, it will give me great pleasure to set you free in ten minutes from now, if—"

Dubois paused as coffee was set before them—Lind leaned forward eagerly, his blue eyes suddenly aflame.

"If—?" he questioned.

"If," resumed the other, watching the two servants go, "if you will answer three little questions and answer them truly upon your honour."

Lind only smiled slightly and reached his bound hands for the sugar.

"Ask them," he said curtly, nodding thanks for the cigar Dubois shoved at him.

He was not fool enough to imagine that he could buy freedom with any ordinary information, and like a flash his guard was up. Perhaps he read the thought in the mind of Dubois, perhaps it was sheer intuition—but he knew that those three questions were to concern his present employer.

"First"—and Dubois sipped lazily at his coffee—"is this man Solomon an Englishman who used to be in Port Said? Second, what information does he possess about me, if any? Third, and most important, were you alone helping him, or has he other men at work? Now, my friend, tell me these things and you go free."

Lind caught that faint trace of accent again, and it warned him that Dubois was putting no idle queries. The first two questions seemed unimportant enough, doubtless a mere blind for the third.

Remembering the Arab chauffeur, Ali, and what Solomon had said about having a few of his men somewhere within reach, Lind was not slow to guess the motives of Dubois. The Frenchman, who had lived for years in the East, probably knew something about Solomon's activities in that quarter of the world; this precious firm of Bogard & Dubois must be extremely anxious to know just to what extent Solomon was engaged against them.

Lind lighted his cigar a trifle clumsily, and eyed his captor.

"I shan't answer those questions, Mr. Dubois."

The Frenchman smiled thinly, and his furtive eyes narrowed.

"You are quite determined, my dear Mr. Lind?" he asked. "Very well. I am sorry, however, for your sake. Now I must ask you to return to you room—take the cigar, by all means!—as I must go to a conference with our mutual friend Bogard. If you desire a valet to help you with your clothes, address the guard in the passage outside your door."

"I am to be held a prisoner, then?" said Lind quietly.

"For to-night, yes. In the morning I fancy that we must proceed to sterner measures in order to make you answer those questions. You see, we are very curious to hear more about your little friend Solomon, who has evidently told you my name at least."

With a sudden cruelty snarling through his suave smile, Dubois bowed slightly and preceded Lind along the passage from the dining-room. He flung open the door of Lind's room and snapped on the lights. The window curtains were already drawn.

"Au revoir," he said ironically. "In the morning!"

"Pleasant dreams of murdered men to you." And Lind smiled as the door slammed.

The American flung himself on his couch-bed and puffed at his cigar in no pleasant frame of mind. He was in the power of Bogard and Dubois, men who wanted certain information about John Solomon and who would not be scrupulous about obtaining it.

Dubois had himself hinted as much—"sterner measures" could mean but one thing. And Lind's long jaw set like a rock at the prospect. He would never betray Solomon, that was quite certain; even though the Cockney had been checkmated thus far, the evident fear of Dubois and Bogard showed that they regarded Solomon as a potent enemy.

"Well, I guess they've got me, all right," he muttered aloud, staring at the closed door, "but they'll have a job to get anything out of me! And if I ever pull out of this cursed place alive I'm going to look up Lucius Bogard and give him such an impression of my feelings that he'll be in bed for a week! I'd like to get that sneaking hound under my hands for about ten minutes and—"

Something like a wheezy sigh seemed to escape from nowhere in particular.

"And I'd like werry much to see 'im there, sir," said the strangely familiar voice, in cautious tones. "If you'll be so kind as to turn out them 'ere lights, why, mebbe we'd 'ave a bit o' talk together, Mr. Lind."

CHAPTER XI

LIND, DAZED by the sound of that voice, shuffled
across the room and switched off the lights. On his return
he bumped into a pudgy panting figure which seized his hands
with a low word of delight.

A cold breath on his face, and he looked at the dark window,
understanding. Solomon explained hurriedly how this seeming
miracle had been effected.

Two of his men had followed Lind that day, shadowing
him closely, for Solomon appeared to have foreseen some such
move as had taken place. The two Arabs had seen Lind enter
the "Honkytonk," later had seen him bundled out of the side
entrance into a waiting taxicab, and had followed.

"Then you simply used me as bait, eh?" said Lind, half-angrily.
"Well, all I can say is that—"

"Don't you say it, sir," chuckled Solomon. "I come 'ere meself
after dark, put me men to filin' away that there ironwork, cut a
'ole in the glass, and waited. Werry good job it was that I didn't
come in, else that 'ere Dubois would ha' caught me when he
come back from dinner. Now what's 'appened?"

With a great sigh of amazed relief, Lind seated himself on
the couch and related his story, sparing no details.

"'Old on!" exclaimed Solomon quickly. "You smelled sulphuric
acid, and there wasn't no sign 'o tanks, so to speak?"

"No tanks or carboys, either," returned Lind. "Nothing at all."

"Werry good, sir. Now give me that 'ere New York address

98

again. We'll inwestigate that 'ere Mr. Jeremiah V. Gillam just like that."

Lind proceeded, in some wonder, and Solomon seemed to be lost in thought, for he said nothing at the end of the tale.

"Well?" demanded the American sharply. "I'd like to get rid of these irons, John. Then get in a police call and raid this place."

"You're a werry impetuous young man, sir," sighed Solomon wheezily. "The man what's in a 'urry don't never get to 'is end, as the Good Book says. No, sir! I'll have them irons off you in a jiffy, just like that, but we'll call in no bobbies, sir."

"Good heavens, man, why not?" exclaimed Lind. "We'd catch Dubois when he got back and he's confessed to murdering Everingham, and once we had him he'd loosen up and squeal on Bogard to save himself—"

"Beggin' your pardon, sir, but 'e wouldn't do nothin' of the kind. 'E ain't that sort, as you ought to know, sir. 'Sides, it's Bogard as we want most of all. Dang it, I want to smoke, and a man can't enjoy 'is bit o' baccy in the dark."

"Suppose you get these irons off, and smoke later," said Lind crisply.

"Werry good, sir. Let's 'ave your 'ands, Mr. Lind. There ain't many patterns of 'andcuffs, and I 'appen to 'ave keys to most on 'em."

Silenced by this evidence of forethought, Lind held out his hands. There came a faint jingle of keys while Solomon fumbled at his wrists; after a moment the handcuffs loosened with a sharp click, then the Cockney knelt and released the ankle irons.

"About them 'ere police, sir," he said, as Lind stretched himself with a breath of vast relief, "we ain't got no ewidence against Mr. Bogard, not yet. None as'll stand in court, so to speak. But I 'opes, sir, to 'ave some werry quick, if so be as you'll do just what I tell you."

Lind realized that the little man spoke truth regarding Bogard, and he felt a new surge of confidence in the slow but certain methods of John Solomon.

"Give your orders, John," he said quietly. "By the way, where are we?"

"Dearborn Street, sir, two doors from your own boarding 'ouse. Now, if you'll be so good as to call in that 'ere guard from the passage and 'it 'im over the 'ead with a chair, we can turn on the lights and enjoy a bit o' smoke. I likes to 'ave me pipe at work, and it'd be mortal dangerous wi' that chap at the keyhole, so to speak."

Now Lind knew very well that Solomon never gave an order without some very definite but obscure purpose behind it, and therefore asked no questions. The chance was given him to repay the slugging which he had himself received that day, and he crossed to the door with a grim smile.

He picked up one of the small teak-wood chairs and swung it up, his iron muscles making light of its great weight. Then he knocked stoutly at the door.

"Come in, you guard! Come in and see what's wrong with my lights?"

From without came a grunt, followed by a heavy step. A bolt was shot back, and as the door opened Lind glimpsed the dim figure of the guard outside, vague against a faint glow of light that filled the passage.

"What you want?"

"My lights went out," said Lind, with entire truth. "See if you can make the switch work."

The man grunted again and entered. Lind brought down the chair without any compunction whatever, and under that dull thud the guard fell limply. Lind shut the door and switched on the light.

"Hope I didn't kill him," he said calmly.

He had not done so. The guard, who was one of the foreigners serving Dubois, lay breathing stertorously, blood running from his scalp. Solomon crossed the room with the same irons which so lately Lind had worn.

"Good idea," nodded the American, clicking them on the

man's wrists and ankles. With his handkerchief he extempo-
rised a gag, and found a heavy automatic revolver in the guard's
pocket.

"Now what?" he said, looking at Solomon.

"Sit down and 'ave a smoke, just like that."

And the little Cockney seated himself comfortably, shredding
tobacco into his old clay pipe. When it was filled to his satisfaction, he drew a match from his pocket, and, with unnecessary
noise, thought Lind, scratched it across his shoe.

With that, Lind was treated to an excellent sample of the
intricate but carefully planned methods of his present employer.
Immediately upon the scratch of the match, there was a noise at
the window; the shade was run up, and into the room climbed
first the chauffeur, Ali, and after him another and blacker man,
both grinning widely at Lind. Solomon puffed at his pipe in
huge enjoyment, then flung Ali a sharp order, presumably in
Arabic.

"Now, Mr. Lind," he said calmly, as the two Arabs slipped
from the room into the passage, "when me men 'ave taken care o'
them 'ere precious Armenian servants, we'll 'ave a look around."

"What do you expect to find, then?" asked Lind, in helpless
bewilderment.

"I 'ave me 'opes, sir, just like that, as the old gent said when 'e
kissed the 'ousekeeper. You mark me words, Mr. Lind, them 'ere
bits o' yellow wool that I found outside Mr. Everingham's house
is a-goin' to 'ang Dubois."

"But how, man? Why don't you loosen up with some real
information? What do you suspect is back of all this?"

"I don't know, sir. What's more, I don't suspect, neither. If so
be as we don't find nothing 'ere, why, we'll inwestigate that 'ere
Jeremiah V. Gillam."

"And you're not going to bag Dubois when he comes back
from meeting Bogard?"

"That all depends, sir, just like that."

Than this John Solomon would say nothing more, but sat

and puffed away, blinking at the electric lights and eyeing Lind with his mild inscrutable gaze. At their feet lay the Armenian, still unconscious.

Solomon was just knocking out his pipe when Ali glided into the room, saluted, and pattered out something in his own tongue. The Cockney rose.

"All them 'ere serwants is tied up, Mr. Lind, so come along."

Of what Solomon hoped to find Lind had not the faintest idea, but accompanied the little man through the passage into the dining room. There, under guard of the second Arab, sat the two men who had served dinner, bound and trussed to chairs. Solomon paid them no attention, but passed on into the next room, an electric flash lamp in hand.

The house, as Lind had conjectured, proved to be an old residence which had formerly been quite pretentious and was filled with dusty furniture now long out of date. The high-ceilinged rooms proved quite bare of any interest, however, and Solomon led the way upstairs.

The bedroom, which was evidently occupied by Dubois, contained nothing beyond a few clothes, and with a grunt of contempt Solomon passed on. The search was quite barren of any result, and Solomon, sighing a little, adjusted his wooden leg more comfortably and sought the basement.

This, too, was bare and all too plainly unused, the flash lamp evoking nothing but cobwebs from the dark corners. Lind ventured no comment; and Solomon, his blue eyes widened a trifle, returned whence they had come. Not until they stood in Lind's prison chamber again did the little Cockney speak.

"Now, sir, we'd best be goin'."

"Eh?" Lind stared at him. "Do you mean you're going to let Dubois go?"

"Yes, sir, just like that, but one o' me men will be watchin' of 'im, sir. I'm a-goin' to catch the midnight train for New York and 'unt up that 'ere man Gillam. Now, Mr. Lind, if you'll come along, we'll be going 'ome, where I'll 'ave a werry big surprise waitin' for you.'"

Lind, looking into those fathomless blue eyes, felt his anger fall away from him, and he laughed.

"John, you are a queer piece," he exclaimed. "But I wish you'd tell me what's the game that Bogard is playing."

"I wish I knowed that meself, sir," nodded Solomon gravely, and would say no more.

Leaving the servants of Dubois bound fast, and accompanied by the two Arabs, Lind and Solomon walked to the front door, quietly left the house, and stood at the kerb. As if in obedience to some invisible signal, the black limousine came whirring down on them out of the night, and in thirty seconds was bearing them away.

The car ran into Lincoln Park, and Lind recollected that Solomon had once spoken of having rented a house somewhere in the vicinity of the park, to which they must now be going. As to the surprise which Solomon had promised he gave it no thought.

Why had Dubois been left free and unhampered, even though he might be shadowed? Surely the man would take alarm when he reached home! With his first heat of anger passing into calm, however, Lind realized that Solomon had been right in two respects. Dubois was no man to turn State's evidence, nor did Lind have conclusive proof as to Bogard's share in the criminal work that was going on, whatever it was.

True, Bogard had sent him to the "Honkytonk" that day, but could easily deny having done so. Were Lind to appear on the stand and relate to a courtroom the things that Dubois had told him, and the suspicions that Dubois had confirmed that evening at dinner, the result would be disaster.

Dubois would promptly deny the whole thing, and no motive could be shown for Bogard's alleged connection.

Assault could be proven against Dubois, of course, but that was a little thing compared to what they were after. Dubois must hang, and Bogard must—what? Of what was Bogard guilty, except a possible complicity in the death of Everingham?

"Not a thing, so far," thought Lind gloomily, rubbing his sore but unbroken head. "We can't fasten a thing to him, but we have the word of Dubois that the scoundrel is playing for a big stake. Well, I'll gamble that he won't touch Diana Evering-ham, at least."

Was Solomon sincere in protesting that he had neither knowledge nor suspicion of Bogard's game?

This thought troubled Lind. It seemed incredible that the Cockney should have formulated no theory; yet, on the other hand, what theory could possibly have been formed? Dubois, in committing the murder, might have been attempting a robbery of some nature, although nothing had been stolen from the house.

What made the whole thing conflict was the Chinese rug. According to all the evidence, Dubois had dragged that rug after him when he left, thus obliterating his tracks and at the same time leaving the tell-tale bits of wool which Solomon had found.

Yet the rug now reposed in the Everingham house—nay, Everingham had fallen upon it when he was murdered!

Lind knew enough about rugs to realize perfectly that there could be no two Oriental rugs exactly alike to the last detail. Did the dragon rug have an exact duplicate, one would be quite as valuable as the other. But it had none. It was a relic of olden time, an almost priceless piece of art, toned down in colour by great age and long usage.

Therefore why should it be stolen—if Dubois had been after it? There was the question. These precious bits of hand weav-ing could not be sold again anywhere in the United States—the mere fact of their theft would be advertised abroad and every collector in the world would be watching for them, every museum would be cautious in its buying. The thief could not market such stolen wares as these.

This fact seemed effectually to remove the rugs as an objective of Dubois. To offset this was the wrecking of the burglar-alarm systems in the houses of three other rug collectors.

"The whole thing is a blind maze," groaned Lind inwardly. "One supposition looms up, and another knocks it out; then a third pops up to— Oh, shucks! I give it up. None of the blamed rugs has been stolen, anyhow."

And this fact was the final stumbling-block. The only crime so far committed was the murder of Herbert Stuart Everingham.

"'Ere we be, sir, all shipshape and proper."

The limousine had halted, having turned into one of the streets that ends at the park line, and was standing before a small dark house. Lind glanced at the clock before him and found that it was exactly seven-thirty— As in a dream, he climbed out after Solomon, noting idly that another automobile stood before the house.

Seven-thirty! Then that must have been an early dinner with Dubois. Still, little time had passed since the arrival of Solomon, in his prison, and the search of the house had been a rapid one. Silent, he followed Solomon up the steps at the dark door, where the little Cockney touched the button of an electric bell.

The door swung open, and Lind entered into a perfectly bare ball, while another Arab bowed to Solomon and slammed the door. Lind heard a few words exchanged in that unknown tongue, then Solomon touched his elbow and opened a door on the right.

Lind found himself standing in a very small room, bare of everything save chairs, a desk, and a thick rug on the floor. At a gesture from Solomon, he seated himself, while Ali entered and solemnly proceeded to divest Solomon of his boots, exchanging for them a pair of large carpet slippers. Lind had already observed that the little man paid as much attention to his artificial as to his natural limb in this respect.

"There!" grunted Solomon, sitting down to his desk and donning a pair of thick spectacles. "Ali!"

"Yes, effendi."

"I go away to-night. Until I return, Mr. Lind is master 'ere."

"Yes, effendi."

Solomon was sorting papers and jotting down memoranda at a furious rate.

"Are you actually going to New York to look up that Gillam address?" asked Lind.

"Yes, sir. And 'ere's some werry positive orders for you, Mr. Lind. You stay right in this 'ere 'ouse, understand? I'm a-going to give you some work to do. There—them 'ere papers is straight.

"Come along, Mr. Lind—I 'aven't werry much time to be wasting. Ali is a-going to your lodgings and fetch your clothes. Come along, sir."

Wondering what was going to transpire next at the bidding of this man of wonders, Lind followed out into the bare hall and passed to the door opposite.

Entering, he found himself in a room such as he had dreamed of but had never seen.

The room, a fairly large one, was carpeted with a tremendously thick Kurdish Shiraz carpet of soft blues and yellows. About the walls were hung vari-coloured kilims and Bagdad tapestries, against which was banked a wonderful collection of Oriental arms—spears, yataghans, shields, Arab guns, and others too numerous to be detailed in his mind at the time, though he observed that more than one glittered with gold and gems.

Low, pearl-mounted tables stood about the room, with no chairs, but several small Oriental couches. The place was lighted by electric bulbs half-hidden in small lanterns which Lind later found to be made of carved ivory cunningly jointed and fitted.

"Set down, Mr. Lind." And Solomon gave him the example by sinking on a couch. "Ali, you can fetch in them 'ere wisitors."

Lind, who had already settled comfortably into the soft embrace of the nearest lounge, sprang to his feet again, a cry of surprise on his lips. For Ali had opened another door, bowing low, and into the room was coming Diana Everingham, with Jack Brune close behind her!

"Good evening, sir and miss," said Solomon, rising with a little bow and sinking back again. "If you'll be so good as to sit down, I'll 'ave a word to say."

CHAPTER XII

L IND SHOOK hands with Diana, who seemed quite as
surprised as he himself was, then gripped the hand of Jack
Brune—a square-jawed, alert young man who beamed cheer-
ily at the world from behind enormous, black-rimmed glasses.

"What's up?" demanded Brune, smiling.

"Search me," responded Lind. "Miss Everingham, may I—"

"Oh, I've known Mr. Brune for the past ten minutes," she
laughed. "We've been talking about—quite a number of things
haven't we? Well, Mr. Solomon, since you seem to have sent for
us on an urgent matter, and since you seem to have enlisted Mr.
Brune in your detective work, we're here."

"And werry 'appy I am to see you, sir and miss," declared
Solomon.

Lind said nothing, for he was beginning to understand things
quite clearly now, and knew that Solomon abhorred questions.

So Brune had been enlisted, eh? Therefore Solomon and the
reporter must have been working together that afternoon—no,
for Brune had gone to Elgin on a story. Still, Solomon might
have caught him immediately on his return, might have enlisted
him, and might have then come to release Lind. This was a very
accurate guess, as Lind found later. He was coming to admire
more and more the way in which Solomon looked ahead and
mapped out every detail of things—and then made the details
dovetail.

"You've told me an astonishing mess of stuff," said Brune,

with his placid smile. "I hope there's a rattling good yarn in this Dubois fellow, John, because I'm due on the city desk right now. What proof have you that he—er—"

He paused, with a sidelong glance at the girl. Solomon nodded.

"Yes, 'e went and killed Mr. Everingham—beggin' your pardon, miss. That's werry certain, cause why, 'e owned up to it to-night while a-talkin' with Mr. Lind."

Diana went white, and a startled ejaculation broke from Jack Brune.

"You've arrested him?"

"No, sir." Solomon began to fill his pipe, then told briefly and succinctly all that had happened to Lind during the afternoon, omitting only one thing—the name of Bogard. He took a step in that direction, however, by explaining what Diana did not as yet know, that behind Dubois was another and greater scoundrel.

"Who?" demanded Diana and Brune, almost in the same breath.

"Beggin' your pardon, miss, I ain't a-going to tell, not till I comes back from New York."

"And when will that be?" asked Lind.

"When I've inwestigated a party there," said Solomon cautiously, for he had not mentioned the name of Gillam, which would have drawn Bogard into the discussion.

Diana looked at Lind, and in her star-bright eyes he beheld a swift fear.

"Didn't they hurt you, Harve? If you were knocked down and—and handcuffed, and all that, hadn't you better see a doctor at once?"

"No, I'm all right," smiled Lind, and Brune chimed in, with a quick laugh:

"He's a bone-headed old farmer, anyhow, Miss Everingham. By the way, may I ask when you'll return to your Associated Charities work—"

"'Ere, 'ere!" interrupted Solomon testily, while Lind was still smiling at the dominant news instinct of his friend. "Mr. Brune, I'd be werry pleased if you'd keep quite still, sir, just like that. I 'ave summat to say, and mortal little time to say it. Now, miss, I called you 'ere to-night 'cause I need your 'elp."

Diana nodded, gravely inspecting the pudgy Cockney.

"Of course—John. So I supposed."

"Werry good, miss. First on, Mr. Lind 'as got to stay right in this 'ere 'ouse till I gets back. Mind that! 'E mustn't stir outside, Miss. It was all your fault as 'e was in trouble today."

"What!" The girl's eyes leaped into startled protest. "Mine?"

"Yes, miss," continued Solomon, taking no heed of Lind's frown. "You said something to Mr. Bogard this mornin', and Mr. Bogard 'e passed it on. All hinnocent 'e was, o' course, but the man what's be'ind Dubois found as Mr. Lind was working wi' me, and jugged Mr. Lind."

Giving Diana no time for protest or for questions which might embarrass this cleverly constructed story, Solomon warned her against trusting anyone in future. Thus, having travelled in a circle after his wonted fashion, he bit suddenly to the heart of things:

"Miss, could you fetch that 'ere dragon rug 'ere—say day after to-morrow?"

Diana, surprised, considered him for a silent moment.

"I think so," she said finally. "I could have it rolled up and put in my car. You don't want me to explain what we're doing to mother?"

"No, miss, that I don't. Not to no one."

"Then I'll tell her I may be able to sell it. She has hated the thing ever since father was killed. She asked Mr. Bogard if he could sell it again, and he said that he'd look around for a buyer."

"Hm!" Solomon grunted, and began to puff at his pipe. He reflected for a moment, then nodded as if to himself, and looked at the girl with the suspicion of a twinkle in his eye.

"I'll change that 'ere request, miss. This is Monday night, ain't

it? Well, could you bring that rug and come 'ere and 'ave dinner
wi' me on Thursday night, miss? Better yet, send that rug over 'ere
on Thursday morning. Then you come for dinner, seven o'clock
sharp, and bring Mr. Bogard with you."

Diana studied him once more.

"Am I to consider that a social invitation," she asked slowly,
"or one of business? You see, I could not—"

"Oh, business, miss!" broke in Solomon hastily. "I'm a-going
to buy that 'ere rug right this blessed minute."

And, while the others watched in blank surprise, he drew
forth fountain pen and cheque-book and wrote rapidly. Then
he held out the cheque to the girl, chuckling a little.

"Fourteen thousand, miss—just what Mr. Everingham paid.
Is it enough?"

"Why, certainly," she faltered, gazing at the cheque.

"Thank you, miss. Then you'll deliver the rug Thursday morning, and you'll be 'ere Thursday night at seven sharp—with Mr.
Bogard?"

"Since it's a matter of business, yes," she nodded quietly. "Of
course, I can't answer for Mr. Bogard, you know."

"Never mind that, miss; 'e'll come right enough. You might
tell 'im as I want 'is adwice on some rugs, just like that."

Lind inspected the little man, level-eyed, inwardly wondering
what on earth John Solomon could be driving at.

"We'll 'ave a quiet little dinner," mused Solomon as if to
himself. "You and 'im and me and Mr. Lind and Mr. Brune—
just like that. A werry 'appy party, as the old gent said when 'e
buried 'is third."

Would Bogard come? Lind pondered that question, and his
quick brain suddenly awoke to admiration of the strategy of
Solomon.

Dubois had admitted that both he and Bogard were mystified
and apprehensive of what Solomon was doing in this matter.
Bogard, on receiving the invitation to come to Solomon's house

for dinner, in company with Diana Everingham, would leap at the chance to pump the Cockney personally.

But why did Solomon issue that invitation—and spend fourteen thousand dollars on a rug that he surely did not want?

Solomon rose to his feet.

"Mr. Lind, I'll say good-bye to you 'ere and now, sir—and to you, miss. Mr. Brune is a-going downtown wi' me in me limousine, and I'm a-going to catch me train. Mr. Lind, you might see Miss Everingham 'ome in me other car, which same is out in front. Ali!"

The Arab appeared at the door, and handed Lind his own light overcoat and cap—showing that his belongings had been fetched from his boarding house.

"If you'll come wi' me, Mr. Brune, I'll get me things on and we'll 'ave a bit of a talk before leaving. Good-bye, sir and miss, and may you both 'ave sweet dreams."

"See you to-morrow, Harve," flung back Brune, and had gone.

"All ready, Diana?" asked Lind, smiling at the girl.

She nodded, and Ali ushered them through the bare hall to the front door. On the steps she paused.

"I'd much sooner walk, Harve—really! Tell that chauffeur to come and pick you up at the house, and we'll walk, if your head doesn't hurt—"

Lind nodded. The chauffeur, also an Arab, received his instructions with a wide grin of assent, and Lind swung off at the side of the girl.

For a little way they walked in silence, and Lind flung from his mind all thought of Solomon and the mystery hanging over them. In the clear starlight, he had glimpses of Diana's face— the delicately carven lines of brow and nose and mouth, posed like a gem against the setting of her black mourning—and her nearness, a trace of perfume, the splendid poise of her mind, all these things swelled the heart in him with love.

"Harve, do you know who is behind this man Dubois?" she asked suddenly.

"Yes," he said, compelling himself to cold sanity.

"And you won't tell me?"

"I can't, Diana—not till John has the clear-cut proof. Dubois was the actual murderer. The other man was merely an accessory, and probably did not expect the crime to be committed."

"Is it someone I might know about?"

"I can't say, Diana."

"You're an odd man, Harve," she said softly, after a little silence. "Do you know, that night before—before it happened, father was speaking of you."

"Yes?" Lind recalled his last conversation with Everingham, and trembled. But he was resolved not to yield to the temptation—yet. Time enough when he had brought Bogard down.

"Yes. He told us then about that letter—the one Hopkins wrote. Father was angry, though he did not suspect Hopkins then, of course. I had never heard him speak of you with such liking. Mother rather took exception to it, in fact."

Things were getting pretty close to home, thought Lind. He wondered if Everingham had mentioned the one thing which had so closely concerned Diana, in that letter.

"Yes," he said. "Your mother does not like me—no use beating about the bush as regards that fact. And from her point of view she's right. She doesn't approve of your charity work and such things. She has her heart set on your social climbing, Diana, and I don't blame her. Why, girl, you have the world at your feet!"

She laughed, not very merrily. But if she had probed to the faint bitterness that underlay his effort to be just, he could not tell. He had adroitly shifted the subject.

"Yes, Harve, that's all very well—from mother's viewpoint. She does it for my best interests naturally, as she thinks. Oh, dear! I wish that poor father had never made any money at all, that we could have just lived our lives out and worked—"

She broke off, gazing straight ahead at the street lights, her rather pale features set hard. Lind laughed a trifle unsteadily.

This was one of the rare occasions when he was not quite certain how far his self-control might extend.

"You're wrong, Diana, though you may not know it. You couldn't exist as a poor girl. You couldn't live without your limousines and necessary luxuries. You've been brought up to things like Oriental rugs, and if you didn't have them, your cultured soul would be starved. Of course you don't think so—you've never tried."

"No, I don't think so," she said, glancing in some wonder at the harsh rugged lines of his face. "Why do you attack me in that way, Harve? Do you think I'm a pampered little rich girl, then?"

"No, thank God! If I did, I wouldn't be walking here beside you." Lind, knowing that his diatribe had been true in a small sense, but unjust in a much larger sense, felt ashamed of the outbreak. "But you couldn't live on fifty a week, Diana."

"Why not? If I weren't able to buy fine things, I wouldn't want them, that's all. I don't live for luxuries, Harve. I happen to be able to afford them, so I have them."

Lind felt his heart hammering at his ribs, and paused. He knew this girl far too well to suspect that she was leading him on. He knew her simple directness, and he knew that she had not proposed this walk home in order to draw him out.

Nay, why should she? What could she want of a penniless man, who had neither position nor influence? The thought drove him on.

"You may be right, Diana," he said, not without bitterness. "But could you—"

"Yes?" she said, looking at him again as he paused.

"Did Brune tell you what Solomon wanted him for?" he asked abruptly—far too abruptly—savagely forcing his mind back to other things.

"No. He did not know himself. But what did you start to ask me, Harve?"

And with that Lind abandoned the effort.

"Could you be content to spend your life with a man who was

a bare wage-earner, who had no wealth or social position, and with whom you would be forced to count pennies and gauge living expenses by his salary? That was what I meant by my attack, as you called it. I wondered if you could face life in that fashion."

He stared straight ahead, frightened now lest she take his words in the same personal sense in which they had sprung to his lips, and he dared not look at her.

"Unless I could do just that, Harve," he heard her saying quietly, "why would such a man want me?"

To that question was but one answer—and his big jaw clenched hard, shutting back the words that came so hot from his heart.

"Not now," he told himself, fighting down the temptation. "What if she loves Bogard? What if we strike her heart by dragging him into jail?"

Pondering this new and disturbing suggestion, he walked on in silence for a space. He had no definite idea that Diana loved Lucius Bogard, nor did he have any definite information to the contrary.

From Dubois, however, he did know that Bogard was determined to win Diana. And for all the girl's stalwart frankness and steady poise, Lind saw very distinctly how she could be dazzled by this unscrupulous, polished, infinitely cunning man who was a master of the art of reading human nature and moulding it to his will.

"She wouldn't be the first clear-headed girl to be taken in by an artful scoundrel," he thought. "A man like Bogard is confoundedly dangerous."

Then he turned to the girl as she broke the silence, and his nerves jumped to her words in startled surmise.

"Harve, what do you think of Lucius Bogard?"

He stared at her profile, wondering if she had read his thoughts in that moment. But she was not looking at him.

"I don't wish to discuss him," said he, finality in his tone.

"You bring him to dinner at John's house Thursday night and see what happens."

"What will happen then?" she demanded quickly.

"I don't know." And Lind smiled grimly. "I'm not sure that John knows, either, but he usually gambles on a sure thing, I've found."

"Doesn't he want to ask Mr. Bogard about some rugs?"

"So he said—and I expect his questions will be interesting. But really, Diana, you know just as much about it as I do. Well, here we are. I shan't see you before our dinner-party?"

"I'm afraid not, Harve. Thank you so much for coming with me. Good night."

"Good night, Diana," he said softly, and turned away from the gates.

The automobile was waiting, and, as Lind climbed in, the car began to move at once. He was swept back to Solomon's house at high speed, and it seemed very much as though Solomon was afraid to allow him abroad.

"Probably Dubois will have private detectives and all kinds of spies looking me up," thought Lind, with a grimace. "So I have to stay housed until Solomon gets back and springs something on Bogard. Confound it, I wish I knew what he expects to spring!"

But when he thought of the words which had passed between himself and Diana Everingham that night, and of her question which he had left unanswered, he smiled a little and straightway forgot all else.

WHEN LIND returned to Solomon's house after parting with Diana that evening, Ali met him at the door
and handed him a note. Opening it, Lind perceived the fine,
copperplate writing of the little Cockney:

> "MR. LIND: You once spoke of a tag on the Imperial Dragon
> rug. Try to remember what that tag was like.
> "Inclosed find list of chief rugs in Everingham collection.
> Compare with list Mr. Brune will bring you. Sizes important.
>   "JOHN SOLOMON."

Being unable to glean anything from these instructions, and
having a very clear memory of the tiny tag with Chinese characters, Lind put the note and list of rugs in his pocket and went
to bed in the room Ali assigned him.

The following day, Tuesday, passed monotonously for Lind,
who was not accustomed to being confined to quarters. Ali fore-
stalled his every wish, but when Lind tried to find out something
about Solomon's activities, the Arab only grinned and laid claim
to a vast fund of ignorance.

Lind was free of the house, however, and found it to be an
amazingly rich place. Except for the bedrooms, the bare hall,
and the little office-like room off the hall, all the rooms were
furnished in magnificent Oriental splendour.

The carpets and rugs were, even to his eye, worth a fortune.
There was an astonishing collection of weapons, many being
mounted with gems; in the dining-room hung two large mosque

lamps of solid gold, and over the buffet was displayed a scimitar whose hilt was a solid blaze of diamonds.

"Great Scott!" thought Lind, staring up at this as he sat at breakfast. "Have I struck an Arabian Nights dream, or what? And here in Chicago—why, it's preposterous!"

So it was. Even more preposterous was the thought of pudgy John Solomon, in tarboosh and carpet slippers, surrounding himself with this magnificence which kings might have envied. Yet Lind had to accept it as a fact. If Solomon loved these things and could afford to have them, surely it was no one's business but the little man's.

On Tuesday afternoon, Lind was agreeably aroused from a languid perusal of the evening papers by the arrival of Jack Brune.

"Whew, but you sure are housed in luxury!" exclaimed the reporter, flinging himself on one of the divans in the reception room. "Bring on the houris and the dancing girls. Say, Harve, you've been having a great little streak of adventure, you and your friend Dubois."

"Did John tell you about the yarn?" asked Lind.

"Sure. Our little blue-eyed friend left orders last night that have kept me on the jump this afternoon. He told me the whole story about Bogard and all."

"Oh, he did?" Lind eyed his friend hopefully. "Well, what about Bogard? I'm dead anxious to know what kind of a game that fellow is playing."

"What—don't you know?"

"No; what is it?"

"Blessed if I know, either," grinned Brune placidly. "John wouldn't loosen up worth a darn as to what was going on. All that I know is that behind Everingham's murder was some sort of crime—and a mighty big sort."

Lind found that Solomon had promised the reporter not only a scoop, but the biggest sensation of the year, and that

Brune accordingly had managed to be relieved from his financial reporting.

"It's a blind mystery to me," sighed Lind. "You see, Jack, we know that Dubois committed the murder, though we haven't legal proof. Dubois is a high-class thief, and therefore he was in Everingham's house to steal. Bogard's connection with the affair makes it plausible that Dubois was after the rugs—but common sense prohibits that theory."

"Sure," nodded Brune, rubbing at his black-rimmed spectacles. "The minute one of those rugs was stolen, people would be watching for it all over the world. Say, what did Dubois drag out after him to hide his tracks?"

"Solomon says that it was Everingham's Chinese dragon rug—but the rug was not stolen. Jack, cut out this talk. It's enough to drive a fellow mad! We can't make head nor tail of the business till Solomon comes back Thursday, so drop it."

"Willingly," laughed Brune, and began fishing papers from his pocket. "Did John give you a list of rugs, Harve?"

"Yes—got it right here."

"Let's see it."

"Uh-huh." Lind drew Solomon's note and inclosure from his pocket and handed them to Brune.

The reporter pored over them in silence, evidently puzzled anew. Lind watched, wondering what new source of mystery had cropped up. Presently Brune emitted a grunt and glanced at Lind.

"Harve, I'm blessed if I can fathom John Solomon! He wanted this stuff for some purpose, of course, but it's past me."

Brune explained that before catching his midnight train Solomon had instructed him to get a list of the rugs imported by Bogard for the past six months.

"You see, Harve, all rug importations to Chicago are sent here in bond. I went over to the appraisers' stores, at Fifth and Harrison, and found that all such importations are carefully kept track of. The values of the rugs are not open to the public, for obvious reasons; but the dates and descriptions are. Here's the list of rugs Bogard imported in the past six months, until the war broke up the importing end of it."

He handed Lind a long list, on which appeared the date of arrival, the port of shipment, the name, and the size of each rug imported. This applied only to the more valuable rugs, as the smaller and ordinary pieces came in by bale and were not listed separately.

"Hm!" mused Lind, scanning the list. "He gets most of 'em from Constantinople, some from Smyrna, and an occasional lot from Alexandria. Well, what about it?"

"Search me, Harve. In his note to you, John says to compare Everingham's rugs with this list, the size being important. Here's the list of Everingham's collection."

Lind took the latter, and found it to be identical with that which Solomon had made after Everingham had employed him in the matter of the burglar alarms. The only change was that the size of the rugs had been added, the list reading as follows:

> Room 1. One Tabriz, 7 × 4.
>   Two Feraghans, 4 × 6 and 5 × 6 ½.
> Room 2. One Royal Ispahan, silk, 14 × 26' 8".
> Room 3. One Keshan palace carpet, 19' 4" × 37' 11".
> Room 4. Imperial Dragon rug, 16 × 24' 2".

"I don't see what object John has in making the comparison," said Lind slowly, "but you may be sure he has one. You don't suppose Bogard has been evading the customs in any way, Jack?"

"Couldn't be done—I thought of that. You see, rugs are appraised for duty by a committee of three: Bogard appoints one, the customs people appoint one, and these two choose a third. This committee examines and classifies the imports. No, it isn't a question of that kind, Harve."

Lind shrugged his shoulders.

"Well, let's get down to business on this comparison. You read down your list, sizes only."

Brune took the list which he had made at the appraisers' stores, and began to read the sizes as indicated. Lind halted him suddenly.

"Hold on—fourteen by twenty-six, eight! That's the size of this Royal Ispahan, Jack. How is it classified there?"

"Nothing here about Ispahan. That's a Smyrna rug, imported from Smyrna five months ago."

"That's funny! Well, check it and go ahead."

Within ten minutes the comparison was finished. Lind found that each of the choice Everingham pieces was duplicated in size by a Smyrna rug. The only exception was the Imperial Dragon rug. A modern Chinese rug of the same size had been imported, this time from Shanghai, only six weeks previously.

"What does the blamed thing mean?" queried the puzzled Brune. "Are these Smyrna rugs the same ones that Everingham bought from Bogard?"

"No, of course not, Jack. These Smyrna rugs were imported since he bought his rugs."

"But how about the sizes being exactly similar?"

"That doesn't signify anything," said Lind who was himself puzzled. "You see, an Oriental rug is all handwork—every thread is knotted by hand, and the looms run to certain sizes in certain localities. For instance, Feraghans are usually about the same size and Giordiz rugs will run about alike—"

"Sure. But these Smyrna rugs are just the size of those rugs of Everingham's, and there are no others of the same sizes except the Tabriz. We found half a dozen seven by fours, if you remember. That's a common size, eh?"

"Yes," nodded Lind.

"Are two rugs ever alike in design and colour?"

"No, not if they're genuine," and Lind smiled as he vaunted his lately acquired knowledge of textiles. "The general pattern of all Senna or Saraband rugs is similar, for example, but the design and colouring always differ. That's the distinction of handwork, Jack. These rugs of Everingham's are old ones, but you could go to Bogard and buy even a cheap new Mosul rug and could be absolutely certain that you'd never strike another in the world of exactly the same size, colouring, and design.

"It's like the grain in wood, Jack. Oak and cherry and mahogany are all different, just like Senna and Tabriz and Keshan rugs are different. Two pieces, or a dozen pieces, of quarter-sawed oak will have the same general pattern of grain, but you'll never on earth find two pieces grained and coloured absolutely alike. Get me?"

The reporter nodded.

"Yes, I see. That's a mighty good simile, too. Well, the deeper I get in this affair, Harve, the more of a headache I get. There's only one thing sure."

"What's that?

"Behind the murder of Everingham lies some damned intricate, involved, and utterly mysterious kind of crime, and I'm not going to bother my head about it. You turn those lists over to John. I'm going down to work."

"Coming in to-morrow?" asked Lind. "It's blamed lonesome here."

"Sorry, old man, but I have to work to-morrow on our yearly financial issue for next Sunday—it's a big thing and the copy has to be in by Thursday morning sure. I'll get here for dinner Thursday night, and here's hoping that something loosens up!"

When his friend had departed, Lind went over those lists once more, but failed to extract any further information from them. Bogard had imported rugs the exact size of those owned by Everingham, all of them Smyrna rugs—a fact which might mean anything, as there are no individual rugs produced in Smyrna, the term being a trade name. Also, Bogard had imported from Shanghai one modern Chinese rug, of the same size as the Imperial Dragon rug owned by Everingham.

"There's no clue here, that's sure!" sighed Lind, and gave himself over to waiting.

Wednesday was broken in its monotony by a brief telephone

conversation with Diana, who called up to say that Bogard was coming with her the following evening. She also promised that the dragon rug would be sent over in the morning, as Solomon had requested, and said that her mother was glad to be rid of the thing because of its associations.

"Mr. Bogard was disappointed that I had sold it," she went on, "and even offered me a thousand dollars above the price Mr. Solomon paid. Of course I couldn't do that—"

"I thought you said the other night," broke in Lind, "that Bogard had not encouraged its sale?"

"I suppose he changed his mind or found a customer."

"Does he know that I'm to be here?"

"No, I fancy not. I forgot to mention it—"

"Then be careful to forget it, Diana. Don't tell him."

"But that wouldn't be—"

"Yes, it would," laughed Lind, but with earnestness in his tone. "You just trust to me in this, Diana."

"All right, then. Good-bye!"

Lind pondered over this conversation, finding therein some food for thought. Of course, as Diana had said, Bogard might have found a customer for that rug. But to Lind it appeared very much as though Bogard had not wanted it sold to John Solomon.

"Say, it's getting hot!" he thought excitedly. "Solomon didn't buy that rug for sentimental reasons, not by a blame sight! I'll bet something is going to drop on Mr. Lucius Bogard to-morrow night! Bogard and Dubois are afraid of John, and Bogard is coming here to see what he can see—"

Having a fair knowledge of the ways of John Solomon, Lind made a shrewd guess that the little Cockney was preparing to draw the net at his dinner-party. But how? Why was it important that Lind should remember the tag he had observed on the dragon rug that evening when he had first seen it? And where did Jeremiah V. Gillam, of New York, enter into the scheme of things?

Solomon had professed ignorance, but Solomon had a habit of professing ignorance when it suited him to do so. Behind the murder of Everingham lay a mystery. Dubois was the murderer, of course, the mystery lay in the motive for the murder and in Bogard's connection therewith. Not only had Solomon to solve Bogard's schemes, but he had to obtain the proof which would hang Dubois and jail Bogard—for what? What had Bogard done, after all?

Thus Lind, running once more into a blank wall, gave up the problem in disgust.

Thursday broke with a drizzling, misty rain that drove in from across the lake and washed Chicago into cleanly discomfort. Lind had just finished breakfasting beneath the two gold mosque lamps when the Imperial Dragon rug arrived from Diana.

Two of the Arabs carried it into the reception room and laid it there in place of the thick Kurdish Shiraz—by the orders of Solomon, as Ali explained. The thing was certainly a magnificent creation, yet as Lind gazed at it he felt a little thrill of repulsion. It was on this rug that Everingham had fallen, murdered; it was this thing, to judge by Solomon's scattered hints, which had caused the broker's death. And how were those tiny tufts of wool, presumably snagged from this rug, to bring about the hanging of Everingham's murderer—as Solomon had also hinted?

Lind looked very carefully for the little tag with the Chinese characters, but made sure, as he had previously done, that it was not on the rug. Nor was there any sign of any such tag having been clamped into the rug.

The morning wore away slowly, so slowly that Lind's nerves began to buckle under the strain of impotent waiting. Then, as he was sitting at luncheon, came relief. Ali summoned him to the telephone with word that Solomon effendi wished to speak with him.

CHAPTER XIV

"**M**R. LIND?"

"Hello, John!" cried Lind in eager delight. "How'd the trip come out?"

"Werry good, sir; werry good, indeed," wheezed Solomon's voice. "Is that 'ere rug on 'and, sir?"

"Yes, it's here. Ali put it in the reception room. Where are you—at the Gas Building?"

"Yes, sir. That 'ere Mr. Gillam turned out to be a werry wallyble person, sir, I'm 'appy to say. Any news from Mr. B.?"

"Diana called up to say that he'd be here to-night. Say, have you got the goods on him? Come on, John, give me a tip!"

"Werry 'appy to say I 'ave, Mr. Lind, just like that. But I can't say no more, 'cause why, I ain't got time. I'm a-going to be werry busy this afternoon. Dang it, that 'ere Dubois 'as gone and vanished!"

"I told you to grab him when you had a chance," exulted Lind. "Bogard hasn't vanished, too, I hope?"

"No chance o' that, sir. 'E don't know as I'm a-going to bust 'im wide open, just like that. But I've got to find that Dubois mortal quick. Goodbye, sir."

Solomon rang off abruptly, and Lind hung up with an exclamation of impatience. Then he settled down to wait until evening.

So Solomon had actually made ready to close his net on Bogard! That was big news, indeed. Just why Gillam had been pronounced "valuable," Lind could not see, nor did he care greatly. The great thing was that with the evening all the mystery would be cleared away.

"The disappearance of Dubois seemed to worry him," reflected Lind. "If he has over-reached himself there, it'll be a bad thing. I knew that we should have bagged the murderer there at his house when we had such a good chance. Still, John may have had good reasons for acting as he did—he doesn't make mistakes, as a rule."

Lind observed that Ali and the other Arab servants were exceedingly busy that afternoon, and several very bulky and mysterious packages were left at the house. The lower rooms were swept and garnished, and later, with obvious pride, Ali beckoned Lind to the dining-room. There the American found a service of massive silver being unpacked; the service was evidently very old, was highly chased, and one of its features was a set of extremely heavy wine goblets.

Each goblet was wrought in the shape of a cunningly devised bunch of grapes, resting on a large and solid silver stand, with a great ruby set in this base. Examining one of the unwieldy but beautiful things, Lind perceived that it must be of very ancient workmanship. Evidently Solomon was bringing out his best for this dinner, and Lind put down the goblet with a smile, little dreaming that his host might have more than one intent in setting forth these treasures.

There were two doors to the dining-room—one opening into the reception room, the other into the butler's pantry and kitchen.

Slowly the hours wore away toward evening. Lind, who had hoped for Solomon's arrival with every passing moment, finally sought his room at six o'clock and started to dress. Ali appeared, and, despite the protests of Lind, insisted on shaving him and acting the part of valet generally. Lind had to admit that the man proved wonderfully deft in the task.

Barely had Ali patted down his white bow when one of the

other Arabs appeared and summoned Lind to the telephone. The caller proved to be no other than Solomon.

"I'm at me office, sir," said the Cockney, in what appeared to be a state of breathless haste. "I'll 'ave to change me clothes 'ere, and I may be a bit late. Will you be so good as to receive—"

"Sure," broke in Lind. "I'll take care of 'em. Did you find Dubois?"

"No, sir, but I 'as me 'opes. Mr. Lind, I wants you to promise me one thing, and werry important it is."

"Consider it done, John. What is it?"

"Why, sir, if so be as there's a row, or if anything 'appens, so to speak, you sit tight and let me act first."

"What do you expect to happen?"

"I don't know, sir. Nothin' at all may 'appen. But it's the things you don't expect what makes it 'ard for you, as the old gent said when 'e found the butler 'uggin' of the 'ousemaid. Then you'll keep werry quiet, sir?"

"I'll not stir a muscle till you start the scrap," laughed Lind. Solomon rang off abruptly.

Did the little Cockney expect to have an actual fight of any kind? Lind rather thought not. He considered that Solomon was anticipating, as usual, anything that might happen, and that in case Bogard was tempted to use force, Solomon had some card up his sleeve. This, after a fashion, was correct. Lind failed to consider, however, that even John Solomon was not infallible.

When Lind sought the reception-room to await the guests, he found the Arab servants decked out in full native costume— kamis, *burnous*, scarlet head-dress and all. They were picturesque certainly, and quite carried out Solomon's scheme of Oriental grandeur.

Abruptly, Ali ushered Jack Brune into the room. Solomon's silent door-bell was a remarkable item of his establishment.

Lind soon found that his friend had not seen John since the latter's return from New York, and knew nothing of any developments. Accordingly, he displayed the dragon rug and related what he had gathered from his two conversations with Solomon that day, and had barely finished when Ali bowed in Diana and Lucius Bogard.

If Lind had expected a dramatic meeting, he was disappointed. He caught one swift flicker of surprise sweeping over Bogard's florid powerful features; then, reflecting that he was playing the role of host, he held out his hand and met a firm grip. For an instant the two men looked into each other's eyes, and in that instant Lind read vivid and unveiled hatred in his enemy's look. Then Bogard had bowed slightly, acknowledging his introduction to Brune.

"A beastly rainy night," remarked the importer, with his affable smile. "Oh, so here is our famous dragon rug, eh? By Jove, what a collection this man Solomon has!"

With unfeigned eagerness he inspected the rugs and weapons about the room, and Lind could find no nervousness or anxiety in his bearing. Plainly, Bogard was quite unconscious of any impending disaster. The voice of Ali broke in upon his fluent admiration:

"John Solomon!"

Ali turned. Lind could scarcely repress a smile, for Solomon was arrayed in the full glory of evening clothes, which hardly suited his pudgy figure. The little man advanced and shook hands with Diana, then turned to Bogard, hand extended.

"Ah, this is Mr. Bogard, eh? Werry 'appy I am to see you in me own 'ouse, sir."

If there were a veiled threat under those words, it was hardly apparent.

"And I'm glad to meet the famous John Solomon," smiled Bogard, white teeth flashing through his neat beard. They shook hands, and Solomon turned to Ali.

"Let's 'ave them 'ere cocktails, Ali! I'm mortal 'ungry, and Miss Diana 'ere is main faint for food! Werry sorry I am to 'ave detained you, sirs and miss."

While Diana expressed her unashamed rapture over the

Arabs and the place in general, Ali brought in cocktails; another of the Arabs held open the door of the dining-room, and with a stately salaam announced that dinner was served.

Lind observed with some amusement that Solomon had gone to the extent of setting place cards—but there was method in that madness, as he was soon to find. He and Brune sat together, facing the buffet and the diamond-studded scimitar; Solomon and Diana took opposite places, while Bogard sat facing the outside wall and two windows.

"I have seldom seen finer rugs than yours, Mr. Solomon," said Bogard, who seemed quite at his ease. "And this silver, if I may remark, is magnificent. Old German workmanship, is it not?"

"Yes, sir," returned Solomon, blinking apologetically. Lind noted that Bogard flung the little Cockney one swift glance that spelled covert contempt, not unmixed with wonder. "Yes, sir. A present to me, it was. Most o' these things was presents, it 'appens."

Lind felt tense, strained. Diana, too, seemed to divine something unusual, for Lind detected a puzzled inquiry in her eyes. But Solomon's face was devoid of all expression, and the cheerful energy of Jack Brune kept the conversational barometer high.

Whoever had planned that dinner, reflected Lind, had done good work, save in one detail of using the silver goblets for the rich, sparkling Burgundy that was served. Solomon seemed rather hasty in emptying his own goblet, though Ali also seemed to neglect refilling it.

After the preliminary courses, a great silver salver bearing a half-dozen roast guinea hens was set before Solomon, who set about his task of carving with beaming good-humour suddenly apparent on his placid features.

"I ain't a rug expert, Mr. Bogard," he observed negligently, "though I 've some werry good rugs, if I do say it as shouldn't. I'd be werry glad to know, sir, just 'ow it is that some folks make new rugs look old, if so be as you could tell me."

"Why, certainly," laughed Bogard. "There's no secret about it, you know. Often a rug is dipped in a coffee solution, and more often it is immersed in a very weak solution of sulphuric acid. Ironing will give it the gloss of an old rug, too."

Sulphuric acid! Lind started suddenly and looked at Solomon, who was very busy with his carving. Then the Cockney gave Bogard a look of mild interest.

"But don't that hurt the rug, sir?"

"Not a bit, Mr. Solomon. Of course it softens and gives a rug the appearance of age, but it really improves the piece. I don't sell such specimens myself. A rug treated in that way is called 'washed', and eighty per cent of the rugs in the market to-day are washed, but I make a point of avoiding such things."

"That's werry interesting," murmured Solomon. "Thank you, sir."

Lind eyed Bogard, who had evidently treated Solomon's queries very lightly. Was the importer a liar? Lind could swear that he had detected sulphuric acid on the person of the packer in Bogard's basement on that eventful Monday, yet Bogard now stated that he never treated his rugs with the fluid. Of course, he might have used it for other purposes.

"This 'ere subject o' making new rugs look old is werry interesting to me," observed Solomon after a space. "Mebbe you wouldn't think it, Mr. Bogard, but that 'ere Imperial Dragon rug 'as been washed, as you call it."

"Eh?" Bogard's face seemed to tense suddenly, his dark eyes gleamed with a deep flare as he turned to Solomon. "Surely not, Mr. Solomon?"

"Yes, sir. As you say, it ain't 'urt none. You see, I 'ad me men soak a corner of it in water yesterday. I took the water to a chemist, who obtained a barrium sulphate precipitate. Ali! Bring in that 'ere rug."

The casual, utterly apologetic manner of Solomon caused the flare to die from Bogard's eyes.

"That is a surprise to me," he answered, with evident concern. "Of course, it does not hurt the rug—was probably done by some

Chinese scoundrel before it came to me. As I sold it to Mr. Everingham, I'll gladly take it off your hands in case you don't want a
doctored rug, Mr. Solomon. I guarantee such things, you know,
and I should have seen—"

"No, sir; thank you werry much," returned Solomon, watching
the two Arabs who were carrying in the rug. "I'm werry glad to
'ave that 'ere rug, washed or not."

Lind caught a savage nudge from the knee of Jack Brune, but
had no need of the hint. He, too, had perceived that something
lay beneath these placid queries of Solomon.

Surely Bogard had not doctored the rug before selling it to
Everingham? Lind dismissed the thought at once. Such a thing
was not a crime, and it was too absurd and petty a deed to be
the point of John Solomon's elaborate preparations. There was
something else—something which had caused that swift flare
of suspicion in Bogard's dark eyes.

The rug was brought in. It was thrown loosely over a chair
just behind Brune, against the wall which Bogard faced. Beside
it and behind Lind stood another chair. Why Solomon had
ordered it brought in was something of a mystery, for no further
reference was made to the rug. The little Cockney had other
questions to put, however.

"I've often wondered, Mr. Bogard," he said, while the salver
was being taken away, "if there was differences in wool, so to
speak. Like this, sir—take a Keshan rug and a Kazak rug. The
wool on each one is sheep's wool, o' course, but are the two kinds
o' wool different? Mebbe you could tell me that, sir."

Bogard had been chatting with Diana. Lind saw his face tense
again as he directed a level gaze at Solomon.

"Yes," he nodded. "The Keshan is very fine, while the Kazak
wool is taken from rough, mountain-bred sheep. Every rug has
a different kind of wool naturally."

"Well, then, sir," and Solomon's blue eyes widened a little as
if in earnest bewilderment, "take a Chinese rug, now. I s'pose

there ain't no difference between the old Chinese rugs and the new ones, in that 'ere way?"

Bogard seemed to hesitate, his dark eyes resting steadily on Solomon.

"Yes, there is," he returned after a moment. "Antique Chinese pieces were all made in northern China, and the wool in them is exceptionally fine. The modern ones are made in southern China, and the wool is coarse, as a rule. Of course the difference could only be told by an expert. Your imperial Dragon rug over there, for example, is about four hundred years old and is very finely made."

Into the man's rich voice had crept a deeper more aggressive tone, as though he were deliberately venturing on risky ground, and he eyed Solomon as if he expected the little Cockney to dispute his final assertion. Lind thrilled to the scene as Brune again nudged him. The net was being drawn, imperceptibly, but surely! Yet what was the object of it all?

"Well, sir," and Solomon leaned forward, his eyes wide, "I was in New York the other day, and I picked up a werry nice Chinese piece, Mr. Bogard. It looked to me like summat werry good indeed, it did that! But what's good to one ain't good to another, I says; if so be as you'd look at it, sir, I'd be werry 'appy—"

"Why, I'd be glad to," smiled Bogard, and relief came into his face.

"Bring in that 'ere rug I got in New York, Ali," said Solomon, fingering his wine goblet. "Set it over them 'ere chairs."

Two men appeared, carrying a rug that was evidently both large and heavy. They passed behind Lind and Brune, and spread the piece out over the two chairs, covering the dragon rug below completely from sight. Lind, who was eyeing Bogard, saw the man suddenly clutch at the tablecloth, staring at the rug with distended eyes. Then he caught a little cry from Diana, and turned in his seat.

He saw, spread across the two chairs, an exact replica of the Imperial Dragon rug!

BOGARD WAS the first to break that startled silence. "Why—why, where did you—" he began. Solomon broke in ruthlessly, a sudden firmness leaping into his wheezy voice.

"You sit werry still, Mr. Bogard! Ali, stand be'ind Mr. Bogard's chair."

Lind, looking at Bogard, saw the man compose his features with an effort that was obvious; great drops of sweat stood out on his brow.

Now Solomon directed his wide-eyed stare at Diana, who had half-risen.

"Miss Everingham, I told you this 'ere dinner-party was business, and so it is, and werry bad business it is, so to speak. Let me—"

"But—what does it mean?" cried the girl, gazing from face to face with astonished eyes. "Mr. Bogard—are you ill?"

"If you was 'im you'd be ill, miss," returned Solomon, with the faintest hint of a smile on his pudgy face. "Now, miss, let me ask you to sit werry quiet and just listen, like Mr. Bogard is a-going to do."

At this, Bogard made a convulsive start as if to rise, but Ali touched him on the shoulder, and he shrank back.

Slowly Diana obeyed the little man. Brune chuckled, but said nothing, and Lind looked from Solomon to the rug in blank amazement.

"John, is that a duplicate rug or what?" he asked.

"Mr. Lind, when that 'ere rug was fetched to Mr. Evering-ham's 'ouse, you saw a tag on the back.

"The day after Mr. Everingham was killed, you found the tag missing, just like that. I bought the rug from Miss Diana 'ere, and mebbe you looked at it when it came?"

"Yes," said Lind quickly. "The tag wasn't on it."

"You take a look at this 'ere duplicate rug," said Solomon calmly, still toying with his empty wine goblet.

Lind rose and turned back the rug. So far as he could tell, it was an exact duplicate of the first rug—then an exclamation broke from him, and he straightened up, amazed.

"There's the tag!"

"Yes, sir, that's it. That 'ere rug is the original piece, and I found it in the 'ands of Jeremiah V. Gillam—"

"Gillam!"

The cry broke from Bogard like a snarl. With the rapidity of light his hand flew to his breast and he started up. Then Ali, from behind, seized his wrist in both hands and forced him back, cursing—and a revolver dropped on the table.

So swiftly did the whole thing occur that Bogard was back in his seat, one arm doubled behind his back in Ali's grip, before anyone else could move.

"Werry sorry I am, miss," exclaimed Solomon, unperturbed, "that you should 'ave to witness this scene.

"But it 'ad to be done, miss, 'cause why, you trusted this 'ere man and thought 'im a werry good friend. It was 'im as caused your father's death, miss."

Lind turned to Diana, pitying her in that moment. She sat as though frozen, her black eyes fastened on Solomon.

"What—do you—mean?" she asked in a dull lifeless voice. "Mr. Bogard is a gentleman—"

"Beggin' your pardon, miss, 'e's a thief," broke in Solomon, with more heat in his voice than Lind had ever before heard.

"For a long time 'e's been workin' to where 'e could make the biggest 'aul ever a man took out o' Chicago, just like that. And 'e's been an' done it, too! Only, it was these 'ere what tripped 'im up."

From his pocket Solomon extracted an envelope and tore it open. From the envelope he took two tiny tufts of yellow wool.

"These 'ere bits o' wool, miss, is what I found outside your 'ouse the day after your father's murder.

"They came from this 'ere rug wi' the tag. Dubois 'ad brought the duplicate rug, 'ad put it in its place, and 'ad thrown the real rug out the window, when your father caught 'im. 'E stabbed your father and fled, draggin' the real rug after 'im for to 'ide 'is tracks. 'E got away in a motor car."

"Look here, John!" And Brune squared around determinedly. "I don't understand this rug business at all. I thought there'd be no sale for such a rug if stolen? I thought there was no duplicate of such a rug? I thought the duplicate itself would be immensely valuable?"

"All werry true, sir," nodded Solomon. "I'm a-coming to that. Everything in its turn, says I, and there's a turn for everything, if so be as you give it time."

He paused, and regarded Bogard calmly. The importer, sitting very quiet under Ali's restraining grip, looked back at him from a livid face, and said nothing.

"Them 'ere bits o' wool, miss, is werry fine. That 'ere rug what Dubois left is werry coarse wool. 'Cause why? 'Cause that rug ain't five year old, miss, just like that! Each one o' them fine rugs as your father took such pride in, miss, is imitation. Each one o' them is doctored. This 'ere Chinese rug was made in Shanghai last year—"

"That's hardly possible, John," broke in the girl very quietly.

Lind saw that she was exerting a tremendous effort to keep her poise. "Father knew too much to buy any imitations. Besides, other people examined them—"

"Yes, miss. What's more, your father didn't buy no imitations. Now, wi' Mr. Bogard's kind permission, I'll tell you what

'appened. Suppose, so to speak, that I was in Mr. Bogard's shoes.
I gets in a werry fine Oriental rug, worth thousands o' dollars,
and I gets it from an agent in Constantinople mebbe.

"That 'ere agent 'as 'ad 'is orders, miss. Before 'e sends that 'ere
rug on to me, 'e sends it to Smyrna. At Smyrna there's a factory
where they duplicate any rug as was ever made—making a new
rug, o' course. Me agent tells 'em to take extra care to duplicate
that 'ere wallyble rug. They make a copy that's as like as two peas
in the colour, size, an' length o' wool. Shanghai factory does the
same by Chinese rugs—"

Here Lind could contain himself no longer. He began to see
light at last, and in high excitement he broke into the explanation.

"But, John! No factory can make such rugs; they have to be
made by hand—"

"I know that werry well, Mr. Lind—And them 'ere rugs is
made by 'and. A factory don't 'ave to use machines, sir. Well, I
sells me wallyble rug, and me duplicate comes in from Smyrna—
thanks to you, Mr. Brune, I got that 'ere fact well established
from the custom-house books. I takes the copy, and I goes into
the basement o' me store, and I works on that 'ere copy for mebbe
a month—"

"I see, I see!" cried Brune excitedly. "Say, Bogard, you're some
high-class crook! Oh, what a story I'll turn in on this thing! And
that's where Bogard used Dubois, eh? Got hold of the burglar-
alarm systems, destroyed them at odd times when he was at the
different houses installing rugs, and sent Dubois to sneak away
the originals! How about it, Bogard?"

The importer was still watching Solomon, his dark eyes lurid
with hatred.

"I think," he said slowly, "that you'll have a hard time proving
this cock-and-bull story, my friend."

"Beggin' your pardon, sir, we'll not," returned Solomon placidly, still fingering his wine goblet. "You see, sir, Mr. Lind 'ere
'ad a look around your basement. 'E smelled sulphuric acid, and

'e seen a box addressed to Gillam. So I went to New York and looked up that 'ere Mr. Gillam."

"Yes?" Bogard smiled—a ghastly dangerous smile that showed his teeth like the snarl of a wolf.

"Yes, sir," nodded Solomon, and looked at Diana. "You see, miss, that there Gillam was a clerk who ran a store for Mr. Bogard in New York, all innocent. Mr. Bogard, after stealing 'is wallyble rugs back again and replacing 'em with the counterfeits, sent the real ones to Gillam. Gillam sent 'em to England and sold 'em there.

"Now, miss, in the basement o' Gillam's store we found every blessed rug what your father 'ad bought from Mr. Bogard. What's in your 'ouse now is imitation—prob'ly the finest imitations ever made, miss. Your father never examined a rug after 'e'd 'ad it a few months, and them 'ere imitations—"

"All right, Solomon, I give in," announced Bogard quietly—too quietly, thought Lind, who was watching him closely. "You've got me. Anything you want to know?"

To Lind there was something terrible in all this, for it is an awful thing to have a gentleman sit down to dinner with one, and to break that gentleman and turn him into a thief and murderer before dinner is out.

Bogard's confession brought Lind little exultation. Rather, it sobered him, steadied him, and rather sickened him. Diana must have felt something of the same description, for now, she came to her feet with a little cry that was a half sob.

"Oh, I—I can't stand any more of this, Mr. Solomon! Harve—take me away from here—"

"Mr. Lind, sit werry still!" commanded Solomon sharply as Lind rose.

"Ali, you can leave go o' Mr. Bogard's arm. Take Miss Diana upstairs and stand guard at 'er door. Miss, you'll find a room all ready, and mebbe you'd like a touch o' powder or summat o' that kind. If you'll 'ave the kindness to wait, miss, Mr. Lind will take you 'ome after a bit. We ain't through 'ere yet."

To this dictum Lind would have protested, but he caught one sharp biting look from Solomon that warned him something was afoot.

But Diana forced a smile to her pale lips as she turned to the door.

"John," she said, "I don't believe you ever overlook anything, do you?"

"No, miss, I try 'ard not to."

Bogard, though no longer held down by Ali, did not rise with the others as Diana left. He sat slumped down in his chair, moodily plucking at his beard with one hand. On the table lay the revolver he had tried to draw, but it was well out of his reach.

At the reply of Solomon, however, he looked up suddenly, and in the dark eyes Lind fancied that he caught a swift mocking gleam, as if Bogard had thought of something which Solomon had indeed overlooked. But the gleam was gone instantly.

The little Cockney quite dominated the situation.

Lind, habitually silent, was sitting, watching Bogard, his ice-blue eyes cold and steady. Jack Brune, visualizing the tremendous story he was going to turn in at the city desk later, was conning the facts mentally and letting the other fellows talk.

Solomon fingered his empty goblet and eyed Bogard.

With the going of Ali the four men were left alone, the other Arab servants not making their appearance.

"So you're not through yet, Solomon?" asked Bogard, heaving himself up a bit in his chair.

"No, sir." And Solomon reached out toward the revolver and knocked it from the table. "There's summat I want to know werry much."

"Why not ask Mr. Lind?" Now, for the first time, Bogard looked squarely at Lind. Despite those mocking words, Lind read a terrible fury in the lurid eyes of the man—a venomous, virile savagery that struck him like a blow.

"I owe you a very pretty debt, Lind. Take care that I don't settle it!"

"Beggin' your pardon, sir, but you're dealing wi' me," said Solomon quickly. "Where's that 'ere murderer—John Francis Dubois?"

Bogard laughed again mirthlessly.

"Why didn't you search the basement of my store?"

"I did," said Solomon placidly. "I was there at six o'clock to-night, sir, with a search warrant. I found that 'ere 'idden room where you 'ad the acid bath for them rugs, but I didn't find Dubois."

With this, Lind had the last link. Solomon's trip to New York had netted him the stolen rugs and the understudy—Gillam—who must have made a frank statement of his innocent share in Bogard's crafty work. Finding that Dubois had vanished, Solomon had gone to Bogard's store that evening after closing time and had discovered some secret nook in the basement where the rugs were doctored, completing his evidence.

"I'm a-going to turn you over to the police, Mr. Bogard," went on the Cockney gravely. "'Ow many rugs you've been an' stole from them other collectors I can't say. Just now I want Dubois."

"You won't get him," retorted Bogard. "If this European War hadn't held up my shipments you'd never have found those rugs in Gillam's place, either."

"Mr. Bogard," said Solomon, gripping his wine goblet, "I want that 'ere man Dubois. Where is 'e?"

A sudden sound startled Lind—a sound like a sharp *"twang!"* as if a piano string had snapped somewhere in the house. Bogard leaned forward over the table.

"You want to know where Dubois is?" he asked, smiling his evil smile.

"Yes, sir, and look sharp about it," said Solomon.

"Then I'll tell you. My friend, I suspected that you had something up you sleeve when I received your invitation, though I must say I never suspected that you had so nearly trapped me. Also, I knew that Lind, having escaped from Dubois, was a dangerous person. So I made my own little plans in case they were needed, as they prove to be.

"Shall I tell you where I sent Dubois to hide with some of his men?"

Solomon, his face suddenly white and aged, licked his lips nervously.

"Yes, sir, if you'll be so good."

There was an instant of silence. Bogard laughed. Then—

"Much obliged, Bogard, but I'll speak for myself," came the cool voice of the murderer. "Hands on the table, gentlemen!"

Lind sprang to his feet, then sank back, helpless.

At the kitchen door stood Dubois, with levelled revolver, and the revolver was lengthened by a Maxim silencer.

At the other door stood a second man, a ragged, grimy, burly-jawed fellow, all too evidently a denizen of the underworld, with another such weapon.

"Very thoughtful of Bogard to hide me in your own house, wasn't it, Solomon?" sneered Dubois, with a thin smile. "We came in last night, three of us—had a job lying hidden all this time, I can tell you! Careful there, Lind! These silencers don't make much noise, though you may have heard me shoot one of Solomon's Arabs a moment ago."

"Well, Solomon," drawled Bogard, "I guess we win, eh?"

"**D**ANG IT!" exclaimed Solomon slowly. "Dang it, Mr. Dubois! If I 'adn't clean forgot that you was a werry clever man!"

White-faced, desperate, the little Cockney stared up into the clean-cut face of Dubois, whose closely set eyes seemed to twinkle with the merriment of hell.

"Yes," nodded Bogard, rising. "And you're going to die, Solomon."

Lind and Brune sat motionless, hands on the table before them. Neither was armed.

To Lind, at least, the infernal craftiness of Bogard and Dubois was terribly apparent, and he knew that no mercy could be expected from these men. In a flash the whole scheme of John Solomon seemed to have toppled over like a house of cards. Bitterest of all must have been the fact that Dubois had been hiding here in this very house for the better part of twenty-four hours!

"Think we'll settle our score now, Lind?" asked Bogard, with a laugh.

"I suppose you will," said Lind steadily, his blue eyes flaming as he looked at his enemy. "How do you expect to close our mouths, you scoundrel?"

Bogard shrugged his shoulders.

"Dead men tell no tales," he said simply. "Here are you, Solomon, and Brune, the three men who could expose me. I expected to catch Solomon, and I've caught you all. That's what I call neat work, eh, Dubois?"

"Very neat," assented the murderer.

"Who's this gentle gunman in the corner?" inquired Brune, nodding toward the ruffian guarding the door.

"One of two friends I enlisted," smiled Dubois. "Are you going to stay, or depart with the young lady, Bogard?"

"Oh, I'll stay. I can't run any chances—have to be sure you do the work right."

"Never fear—I don't intend to hang by a long shot!"

Watching the two partners in crime, Lind saw clearly that Bogard's threat of death had been uttered in terrible earnest. Indeed, there was no choice in the matter. Incredible as it seemed, utterly unreal and fantastic as it might appear, Bogard and Dubois either had to slay or be slain.

Did Lind, Brune, or Solomon leave that house alive the two plotters would most assuredly suffer for the murder of Evering-ham and for the theft of the rugs. On these two counts, Dubois would hang and Bogard would get jail for life beyond question.

Wondering a little at the reporter's silence, Lind glanced at him. He saw Brune, while gazing straight up at Bogard, tracing his forefinger across the tablecloth. Lind felt a sudden thrill. Brune's apparently aimless finger was tracing words in short-hand—words plainer than English to Harvey Lind:

"You—take—gunman—I'll—take—Dubois!"

"If it comes to the worst, yes," muttered Lind.

Bogard caught that mutter, but failed to interpret it aright. He looked down at Lind with a sneering laugh.

"So you expect the worst, eh? Well, you'll get it, Lind. It's your life or ours. I've spent too many years working up this game of mine to fall down at the last minute. I've lost these Everingham rugs, of course, as I can't take them with me, but we made a rich haul off those other chaps—Garvel, Hardinge, and Larsen. I guess we can skip to Canada and get away, eh, Dubois?"

"Easily," nodded the other coolly. "Once in Europe now and this war will prevent extradition should we be even suspected."

"Where's Miss Everingham, Dubois?" asked Lind sharply, pierced by a sudden misgiving. "You've not disturbed her?"

"No gentleman would disturb a lady," mocked the other. "No. Solomon's man was at her door so we knocked him on the head and left him. The rest of those Arabs are locked in the kitchen, with my second man holding a gun on 'em. We were hidden upstairs, you see, and came down at the opportune moment. Going to silence the girl, Bogard?"

The impostor looked at Lind, his white teeth flashing.

"Oh, yes, I'll silence her, my dear Dubois! She shall go away with us, in fact."

The rising fury in Lind's heart choked him. Not so long ago he had believed this man a gentleman! Now he saw only too clearly how Bogard's long careful scheme of thievery had rotted out the man heart and soul; he saw how Bogard had painstakingly built up a reputation as connoisseur and gentleman while in reality he was nursing and fostering this incredibly crafty method of looting his friends and customers.

"I'd have skipped out in another week," said Bogard, favouring Solomon with a black look, "if you hadn't stepped into this game, damn you. Yes, by the eternal, I'd have won the girl and stepped out with my loot—you damned, sneaking little Cockney!"

His poise turning to a swift cold rage, he glared at Solomon with the same hatred he had loosed on Lind.

"What business had you nosing into my affairs, eh?" he continued furiously. "I don't blame Lind so much, for we were after the same girl. But I'm going to make you pay first, you—"

With that he flung a burst of epithets at the shrinking Solomon, his pose of polished gentleman vanishing completely before the consuming anger which had gripped him.

Under the blast, Solomon seemed to wither in abject fright. His hands, trembling visibly, wandered over the tablecloth before him, while his mild blue eyes had become shot with fear and horror. So obviously was he cowed that Bogard's rage blew itself out with the same swiftness it had arisen.

"But, Mr. Bogard, sir," spoke up Solomon wheezily, "you ain't a-going for to—to murder me, sir?"

"He isn't—I am," said Dubois, that same devilish humour in his face. "Anything to say before I plug you?"

"Yes—yes!" cried Solomon, turning a white face to Lind. "Mr. Lind, you remember your promise, sir, just like that! You remember your promise!"

And in a flash Lind remembered, urged thereto by one swift flicker of the little man's eyelids. A thrill shot through him—why did Solomon want him to wait? Was it possible that Solomon had some desperate counterblow ready to strike?

But Bogard had caught at that word, and he swung on Solomon with an oath.

"What promise? None of your slick work, you damned Cockney! What promise?"

"Why, sir," and Solomon positively shivered in his fear, "Mr. Lind, 'e promised that if so be as anything 'appened to me, 'e—'e would look after me things and take care o' me papers and such."

The very audacity of that lie, which drew a laugh from Dubois and Bogard, indicated to Lind that Solomon was not so frightened as he seemed.

"Lind will need an executor himself," grinned Dubois cheerfully. "Well, Bogard, there's no sense in wasting time. If I'm to kill these three men, I'd better do it, for it's a nasty job to say the best."

"Don't sir! Don't!" cried out Solomon, his fingers wandering nervously over the tablecloth, "Don't do it yet—"

Bogard gazed at him in mingled hatred and contempt.

"Well, got anything you want to say?"

Solomon stared down at the table. One of his nervous hands came to rest on his empty wine goblet, and as if in abstracted thought he moved the massive piece of silver slowly across the cloth, halted it, and set his thumb on the blazing ruby in the pedestal. Then he looked up at Bogard, wide-eyed.

"Yes, sir, I've an offer to make. Mebbe you know, sir, as I've money in the bank—quite a tidy bit, so to speak. If I was to give you a 'alf million dollars, just like that, and promise not to say a bloomin' word about this 'ere—"

Bogard broke in with a shrill laugh.

"You poor fool—I wouldn't trust you five minutes! No, you can't bribe us worth a curse, Solomon. We're going to loot your place to-night, anyhow, as I've taken quite a fancy to some of these jewel-studded relics. Shoot him, Dubois!"

Lind felt a convulsive jerk of Brune's leg as the reporter gathered himself together. But he touched the other with his knee, and shook his head slightly. Something about that massive silver goblet under Solomon's thumb fascinated him.

"Just one minute, sir," and Solomon looked squarely into the revolver which the murderer levelled. "I 'ave another offer you might be werry much interested in 'earing—you especially, Mr. Dubois."

"Let's have it, then," snarled Dubois, with a vicious twist of his lips that spelled murder as plainly as did his shifty, close-set eyes. "Quick about it!"

Solomon's face changed. As if by magic the shrinking, frightened look was gone, and in its place was the old, placid, mild-eyed stare.

"Why gentlemen," he said wheezily, "it's a werry good offer, as the old gent said when 'e kissed the 'ousemaid! Now you listen 'ere just a minute."

His stubby thumb pressed down, and the ruby seemed to sink into the pedestal of the silver wine goblet. At the same instant a loud hammering echoed through the house.

"That's the bobbies," said Solomon calmly. "Jump quick, Mr. Lind!"

With that, his hand swept the massive goblet off the table squarely into the face of Dubois.

Lind saw the revolver spit fire, saw Solomon reel and fall with one choking cry ringing from his lips—then he had plunged over the table full at Bogard, all the smouldering fury of his heart unleashed into a mad craving for vengeance.

THE ROOM leaped into pandemonium.

Lind had flung himself headlong over the table, gripping Bogard and dragging him down amid a wild tangle of dishes. Jarred apart by the violence of the fall, the two men rose together; Lind drove into Bogard with a savage fury.

He was met by a crashing blow in the mouth, and laughed at the sting of it. Still laughing, he sent his fist smash into Bogard's jaw, and saw the man plunge down. The whole thing had passed like a flash.

A sudden cry from Brune caused Lind to whirl. The reporter had Dubois by wrist and throat, and was bending the murderer back across the table, blood from Dubois's cut face staining the cloth, but the gunman from the farther door was leaping in from one side, his weapon spitting fire, and Lind was barely in time to meet the assault and protect Brune.

Another spat of flame and a sharp *"twang!"* and Lind had a swift vision of Brune sinking down across the body of Dubois. Before the gunman could fire again, Lind was upon him like an avenging fury, quite forgetful of the fallen Bogard.

As Lind caught him, exerting all his terrible strength in mad fury, the burly gunman screamed horribly—for Lind had caught his revolver arm and twisted it in a quick jerk, whirling him about and lifting. The gunman screamed again—his arm had snapped. Then he went up, swung clean over the table in that iron embrace, and fell into one of the opposite windows with a crash that shook the building. He lay there motionless.

Lind, recovering from that tremendous effort, heard shots and loud voices ringing through the house. Knowing that the police had entered, he remembered Diana, but he had no chance to act. Brune had slipped to the floor, limp. Dubois, staggering up with ghastly features, locked his fingers about Lind's throat and clung like a leech.

Then, almost at his side, Lind heard a revolver's crashing explosion. A shock, a blinding stab of pain, and he reeled back against the wall with Dubois hanging to him grimly. Somewhere in the red mist before him he saw Bogard, and too late remembered the revolver which Solomon had knocked to the floor.

That murderous bullet had barely grazed his head, however. He saw Bogard in the act of firing again, and, like a flash, swung the body of Dubois around. Another explosion, and Dubois shrieked hoarsely as the bullet tore into him, but Lind felt the clinging fingers loosen, and his fist sent the murderer down under the table.

Then he plunged at Bogard, knocked the revolver away, and the two men closed in deadly embrace—a brutal desperate battle for life in which neither man dared let the other draw free for a blow.

The sheer physical power of Bogard amazed Lind. Back and forth reeled the two men with furious infighting that knew neither rules nor laws. Lind got his elbow under Bogard's chin and thrust back until the other gasped—then a knee drove into his stomach and sent him back groaning. Bogard drew in, snarling like a wild animal, sending a thumb to Lind's eye—in a horror of rage Lind caught the reaching thumb, bent it back—snapped it, put a choppy blow to Bogard's jaw that rocked the man's head—and felt something catch his foot.

Unable to stop himself, he knew that the dragging tablecloth had caught him, and loosed Bogard in a vain effort to get clear. Too late! Bogard plunged at him bodily, and Lind toppled back.

His last memory was the sneering laugh of his enemy—then the wall seemed to reach out and hit him, and he knew no more.

Slowly a dream came upon him—a very pleasant dream of peace and quiet, through which pierced the voices of men. He recognized those voices, too. One was that of Jack Brune, another that of Solomon. Then he heard the gruff tones of the chief of police, and opened his eyes in swift fear.

The horrible reality of the battle leaped in upon him instantly. Then he knew that he was lying on a divan in Solomon's reception room, and Solomon was standing at his side, upheld by the big chief of police himself. Other policemen were crowding around.

"Hello, John!" he exclaimed wonderingly. "Thought they'd killed you?"

Lind sat up, and was suddenly conscious of a severe pain in his left arm. He glanced down to see his coat off and a bandage about his shoulder. His shirt sleeve was red with blood also.

"Dubois smashed me wooden peg, sir," chuckled Solomon. "You 'ave a nasty-lookin' 'ole in your shoulder, Mr. Lind, but no great 'arm done, and 'appy I am to say it!"

"Eh?" Lind looked around suddenly at the policeman. "Where's Brune? I saw him go down—good God, John, they didn't kill him?"

"No, sir. A bullet nicked 'is 'ead, but 'e's upstairs this blessed minute, sir, a-talkin' wi' Miss Diana."

"Lind, you're a holy terror, man!" The chief of police spoke out, frank admiration in his powerful features. "Dubois is dying, and Bogard's in the wagon outside. We got to him just as you went down. Here, get outside, you men!"

Lind got to his feet, found himself badly shaken, but able to walk, and looked at the grinning policemen as they filed out. When the room was empty, the chief took something from his pocket and passed it to Solomon.

"There's your blasted cheque; say, I never thought you'd do it!"

"No sir!" And the Cockney chuckled again. "You 'ad 'opes of resigning, eh? Werry worry I am to disappoint you, sir!"

The chief laughed rumblingly, and nodded at the questioning look of Lind.

"Dubois has confessed to the murder. Bogard's bullet took him in the lungs."

"Of course," muttered Lind, and then his face cleared. "Well, I guess I'll go upstairs, John."

"Better go outside, sir. Ali is waitin' wi' the limousine, and I'd be werry glad if you'd see Miss Diana safe 'ome."

So Lind, with some what unsteady steps, was helped out to the limousine, where the grinning and bandaged Ali stowed him inside. The patrol wagon clanged away, and as Lind stretched out on the cushions he smiled slightly to himself. A moment later he saw Diana appear on the steps of the house, with Brune at her side.

"A hundred a week," he muttered, watching her approach. "A hundred a week—why, sure? What was that question she asked me—why should such a man want her? Well, I guess I'll tell her why!"

SOLOMON'S SUBMARINE

CHAPTER I

AT THE CHICAGO OFFICE

H ARVEY LIND caught up the receiver.
"Hello! Yes, chief, this is Lind speaking. No, Solomon's not here yet. Eh? What name? Wait a minute and I'll see."

Setting down the receiver on the desk, Lind left the inner office and proceeded to the larger room outside. Here he began a quick search through an immense cabinet, one of many which lined the walls; a moment later he returned to the telephone.

"Nothing doing, chief. We haven't a word about any such man— Eh?" Lind's face became serious. "Secret service, you say? Military or— Whew? Say, send him over. Solomon will be here any minute, and may know something that I don't. Yes, right away." Barely had Lind swung around in his chair, when John Solomon entered the office.

"Chief of police just called up, John. Wanted data on a fellow named Rezek by the name, a German Pole. Nothing in the files. The chief is sending a man right over to see you—secret-service chap, military branch. Looks serious."

Solomon, who was a pudgy little man, said nothing, but went to the window and looked out over Michigan Boulevard and the lake front.

As a person who dared not revisit his old haunts in the Levant, and as a detective who had made Chicago famous, John Solomon was distinctly a disappointment. His round, moonlike face was devoid of expression, and his wide blue eyes were perpetually innocent. He was short, possessed a wooden leg, and was at present smoking a vilely old clay pipe.

"Do you know anything about this Rezek?" asked Lind, who was Solomon's assistant, and a very proficient helper.

"Not a blessed thing, Mr. Lind," responded Solomon, without turning. "But I'll wenture to say, sir, as 'ow I'm a-going west this werry night."

"Eh? Not on account of Case—"

"Yes, sir."

Lind said no more. After a moment Solomon sighed wheezily, and settled into his easy-chair. Thus he was found ten minutes later by the secret-service operative, a square-shouldered, incisive man named Lang.

"Set down, Mr. Lang," and Solomon fingered the card handed him. "Werry 'appy I am to see you 'ere, sir. Quite a rumpus we're 'aving down in California!"

Mr. Lang shrewd eyes narrowed.

"Mr. Solomon, the chief of police has so fully recommended you, and has told me such apparently incredible details of your work, including the case of Solomon's Carpet, that I have no hesitation in coming to you."

"Werry good; and there's ain't no 'arm done, as the old gent said when 'e kissed the 'ousemaid," observed Solomon wheezily. "Fire away, sir!"

"Do you know anything of a man named Jan or John Rezek?"

"Not a blessed thing, sir."

"Thank you. Then I'll not trouble you further."

Mr. Lang rose. Solomon looked up at him, wide-eyed.

"I'm werry much afraid, sir, as 'ow you won't find no trace of them 'ere submarine* plans."

---

* *The submarine described in this story is no product of the imagination. It has been invented, built, tested fully, and very possibly may go into use by the United States government. Those who desire further information are referred to the files of the United States patent office, it being for the purposes of this story only that the invention is described as being unpatented.—H.B.-J.*

Mr. Lang sat down abruptly, staring.

"Good God!" he exploded. "What do you know?"

"Nothin', sir," said Solomon placidly. "Only I see by the paper as 'ow that 'ere Case died of apoplexy in Los Angeles yesterday. I 'appen to know as Mr. Case 'ad interested the government in 'is submarine—"

SOLOMON'S SUBMARINE

"My Lord! How on earth do you know so much?" demanded Lang, bewildered.

"Very simple, Mr. Lang." Harvey Lind came forward, laughing. "You see, when Case was turned down by the government last year, he was negotiating with other countries, also, and Mr. Solomon was looking into the plans on behalf of Turkey. Turkey got into the war and went broke. Then our own government was prodded into action by the public clamor over national defense, and Case made certain improvements in his plans. As a matter of fact, Mr. Solomon helped to finance the trial submarine which Case had been building, and which was lost or sunk after her first trip, three days ago. Further, we sent out Jack Brune to act as Case's secretary and assistant—"

"Brune was arrested last night for theft of the plans," interjected Lang.

"What?" Solomon sat up suddenly. "Of all the danged fools as I ever seen—but where did you 'ear tell o' this man Rezek. Mr. Lang?"

"We know only his name." Lang wiped his brow nervously. "It was written on a paper found clenched in Case's hand. I happened to be in Chicago, and was summoned to Los Angeles at once to handle the case. If you'll go with me—"

"No, sir." Solomon picked up his clay pipe. "I'll not."

"Eh?" Lang stared at the little man. "Why not? I have reservations for to-day's train—"

"Mr. Lang, if so be as I takes the case, I want 'ands off, just like that! Secret service is all werry well in its place, says I, but John Solomon ain't secret service, I says. If you'll be so good as to 'ave Mr. Brune set free, and put this 'ere matter in me own 'ands, I'll do me best. If not, I'll stay 'ere. If you 'as your doubts about me, wire the Turkish or British or French ambassadors, at Washington—"

At six o'clock that evening, John Solomon was on his way west, alone. Mr. Lang had wired, had argued, had pleaded— and had capitulated. Jack Brune, in Los Angeles, had been set at liberty. The United States government was trusting Solomon.

The intrigue, known in diplomatic circles as that of Solomon's submarine—which is now for the first time made public—had begun. John Solomon, cockney, servant and enemy of the Porte, man of mystery, string puller of the Orient, decorated by emir, king, and kaiser—this man, who had now become a citizen of the United States, had set forth to save his country.

Neither he nor his country suspected that fact, however.

CHAPTER II

MISS MILNE

JACK BRUNE, sitting in the Santa Fe station and awaiting the arrival of the train bearing John Solomon, was unwontedly despondent as he reviewed the events of the past few weeks.

Jolly, good-natured, pugnacious—Jack and his black-rimmed spectacles had been beloved of his brother newspaper men in Chicago. At Solomon's advice and prompting he had come West to be secretary and manager for Milton Case, the California inventor.

From the start he had had unflagging faith in Case's submarine and its under-water engine. While Case constructed his trial undersea boat, Brune had handled negotiations, and had done his part well. When the submarine was finished, Brune had gone down with Case; he had felt the boat ram herself into mud thirty feet under water, had felt her lifted and extricated: he had seen her twenty periscopes automatically replace each other as they were presumably shot away from above—and a dozen other such things.

Then had come the trouble.

With the plans practically accepted by the government, and almost completed for delivery, the trial submarine had been sunk at her moorings off San Pedro, and had apparently been swept out to sea by the backwash of the tide. Two days later, Case had died, supposedly from apoplexy, on discovering that his perfected and improved plans had been stolen from his desk.

No one had seen him die, but the plans were gone, and his body was found.

Wakening too late to the chance it had lost, the government had promptly arrested Brune—and had as promptly released him on the demand of John Solomon. More than this, Brune knew nothing.

"The whole blamed thing swept away like mist!" he reflected gloomily, frowning at the passing crowd. "Boat gone, plans gone. Case dead! I guess you fall down hard this trip, John—Hello! There's a peach— Oh, my! Do I wake or dream, Adolphus? Zowie!"

Mr. Jack Brune sat up and squared his massive shoulders, trying hard not to stare. Directly before him were pausing two people, a man whom he did not observe and a young woman whose fresh, clear beauty, combined with fashionable but well-chosen tailoring, to smite the ex-journalist's attention.

The girl, facing him, touched upon him with casual eyes, and Brune hastily glanced away. But he caught the harsh, metallic voice of the man in a few drifted words.

"—arrives Monday. Huggenheim Motion Picture Company, remember—thank you, Miss Milne. The gentlemen from Japan will arrive to-morrow."

A silvery query from the girl:

"And my father?"

The two passed on, the crowd closing around them. But Jack Brune sat very still, as though he had been stiffened by a blow. For, like an echo, he caught one word coming in the man's peculiarly metallic voice—a single word: "Rezek!"

"*Rezek!*"

Brune leaped up and darted toward the entrance.

That word, that name, had been totally unknown until Case had been found dead. In the inventor's hand, written in Case's own writing, had been a scrap of paper bearing the name "Jan Rezek." Case had apparently scribbled it almost as he died.

This had been the only clew to the identity of the thief.

"Rezek!" muttered Brune, as he pressed through the crowd in pursuit of the girl and man. "How did that chap know the name? If he can give us a hint as to who this mysterious Rezek is—"

He caught a glimpse of the girl's blue corded silk and wide hat, out on the sidewalk, far ahead of him. Blocked momentarily by a swirl of the crowd, Brune made no headway. He emerged at last, only to see the girl step into a limousine, the man after her.

"Hello, there—wait!"

With the shout, Brune leaped down the colonnade to the street. Too late! The limousine sped away. He had a brief vision of the man's face, looking back from the car window—a lean, swarthy face. Then it was gone.

"Damn!"

Jack Brune pulled up with a single savage word, and turned back. Already his mind was resolving into component parts the few words which he had heard.

"Somebody" would arrive Monday—this was Friday. The girl's name was Miss Milne; the man was evidently no relation to her. They were connected in some way with the Huggenheim Motion Picture Company, a concern of which Brune had never heard. Who were the "gentlemen from Japan"?

"Possibly some actors engaged for a special film," thought Brune rapidly. "Now, this isn't so bad, after all! We can trace that film company, look up the girl and the man, and put that fellow through a quiz. Sure! Miss Milne, eh? Wonder what her first name is!"

He found the limited already pulling in. Five minutes later, he was shaking hands with pudgy John Solomon.

"Werry 'appy I am to see you, Mr. Brune," said the little cockney, with his half-apologetic air.

"Any of your Arab men along?" queried Brune. The other dissented.

"No, sir, not yet. Come a bit sudden, I did. But they'll be along all shipshape! Time enough for all things, as the old gent said when 'e buried 'is third."

Jack Brune grinned, knowing well that Solomon's "old gent" was invariably a sign of complacent satisfaction; a weather token, as it were, of "all bright and fair."

It was late afternoon, and Solomon expressed a desire for dinner, so Jack said nothing of the case in hand. When their taxi dropped them at the *Angelus,* and they were comfortably settled in the suite which Solomon had ordered ahead, the card of a Mr. Evan Hartley was brought up.

"Hartley's the secret-service man on the case out here," explained Brune. "Shall we have him up, or—"

"Yes, sir, 'ave 'im up, an' dinner with 'im," nodded Solomon. "I'm mortal 'ungry, I am that! We can talk at dinner."

Half an hour later, their private meal was being served. Hartley was an efficient, dark, quiet man, who eyed Solomon in frank astonishment and wonder, and who still regarded Brune with suspicion. But Solomon had taken a swift dislike to the operative.

As Solomon knew only the general outlines of the case, Hartley now set forth the details—which were meager enough, as he regretfully admitted.

"'Ave they 'ad an autopsy over Mr. Case?" asked Solomon suddenly.

"No. It was apoplexy, plain enough. The body was absolutely unmarked, and Case had just come to his office, which was a sun parlor adjoining his library. The plans had simply vanished, that was all. The thief had broken the lock of the desk, but he had left no finger prints. He was absolutely clew-proof. We tried everything from dogs to microscopes, and Brune was finally gathered in on suspicion. The thief was an expert—"

"Beggin' your pardon, sir, 'e wasn't nothing of the kind," said Solomon gravely.

"Eh? He was no expert?"

"No, sir; 'cause why, 'e done 'is job too well. Also, 'e broke the lock o' the desk; a thief would 'ave unlocked it. The job was so bloomin' good that it must 'ave been done by a man what 'ad never pulled off such work before—a man what 'ad thought about it a werry long time, a man what 'ad concentrated on that one job."

Hartley bit at a cigar, and nodded, with more respect in his gaze.

"Right!" he said curtly. "Case had no servants. He lived alone, with Brune, here. By the way, you'll want to see the premises?"

Solomon shook his head. "Why was the plans stole, Mr. 'Artley?"

"Ah, you're getting to the point!" Hartley cast a sidelong glance at Brune, who grinned back complacently. "Imagine a submarine which could replace its conning tower and periscope a dozen times, as fast as they were shot away; with a submerged speed of twenty-five knots; her engine a gasoline type, able to run full speed under water, and with a cruising radius of ten thousand miles—that boat could sweep the seas!"

"I 'elped to build 'er," chuckled Solomon. To the amazement of Hartley, he related how he had financed Case. Then he turned to Brune:

"What 'appened when that boat was lost?"

What had happened, no one knew. The submarine, a small trial vessel barely large enough for her purpose, had been moored to a wharf at San Pedro, the port of Los Angeles. Her mooring lines had been broken, and, since she had not been found at the bottom of the harbor, it seemed that some miscreant had opened her cocks, and that the tide rip had swept the water-filled boat out to sea. This had happened two days before the death of Case.

"Still, her loss has nothing to do with the theft of the plans," said Hartley. "Mr. Solomon, we *must* have those plans! Case had not patented his engine, meaning to sell the whole thing at one crack. Consequently, the government is up against it. If we had either the boat or the plans, we could go to work, but both are lost—"

"The boat ain't lost," said Solomon placidly.

"Not lost!" The words broke from Hartley and Brune alike.

"Not a bit of it. S'posing as you was the thief, Mr. 'Artley. You knew as 'ow Case kept them 'ere plans in 'is 'ead. You knew as 'ow 'e was making a set o' drawings for the government. You knew as 'ow there was only one way to get sole possession o' them 'ere plans. That way was to steal the drawings, steal the bloody boat, an' kill Case. That's what was done, just like that. And 'e done it up to the mark."

"Who did?" gasped Hartley.

"Jan Rezek, whoever 'e is. Polish name—"

"But Case wasn't murdered!" protested the operative. Solomon chuckled.

"Yes, sir, 'e was. There's poisons as'll kill a man an' leave no trace for an autopsy to find. But more like, 'e breathed poison—"

"Breathed it?"

"Yes, sir. Cyanogen or its derivatives. Rezek was waitin' for Mr. Case, and 'eld a bottle o' prussic acid, say, under 'is nose. Then 'e took the plans an' fled. Mr. Case, 'e scrawled Rezek's name, then 'e up an' died."

"But," broke out the operative impatiently, "if Case had breathed prussic acid it would have been discovered, man! No one observed any peach-kernel odor—"

"No one was lookin' for it, sir. A cyanogen poison causes death by arrested breathin', just like that. It's werry 'ard to make sure of, an' passes for apoplexy—"

"Then, an autopsy would show it," exclaimed Hartley. "The silver-nitrate test would soon establish your theory, or else demolish it."

"Too late now, sir," wheezed Solomon. "Mr. Case, 'e's been dead too long, 'cause why, when decomposition sets in the black silver sulphide masks the white cyanide. O' course, Jacquemin's process might be used—but it don't matter now, sir. The main thing is to find them 'ere plans, or else the boat. And it's a-goin' to be a mortal 'ard job."

Silence fell upon the three, while Solomon sucked noisily at his pipe.

To Brune, the startling statements of Solomon appeared quite logical—though they had occurred to no one else so far. Instead of a mere theft of plans, there now stood forth a well-designed, well-executed plot which included the destruction or capture of the submarine, the theft of the drawings, and the death of the inventor.

Thus, in the possession of the plotter remained the secrets of the Case submarine, proven a perfect invention by the one trial trip made by Brune and Case. The over cautiousness of the inventor had been his own ruin, while the United States was even a greater loser—loser of a wonderful deep-sea boat, loser of the next war, loser of ocean domination.

"Does any one know who this man Rezek is?" asked Brune suddenly.

"Not unless you do," was Hartley's tart response. "Probably an agent for some foreign government—"

"Not likely," said Solomon.

"Why not? It looks very likely to us, after the hyphenated-American activity over here."

"All right, sir; 'ave it your own way. But as to this 'ere Rezek, no one knows anything about 'im—"

"I do," said Brune, with a grin of exultation.

Solomon's rotund features changed not a whit. A sharp oath broke from the operative.

"If you'll step to the phone, Mr. Hartley," said Brune, who thoroughly enjoyed keeping the secret-service man in the dark as long as possible, "and have the chief of detectives give you all the information possible on the Huggenheim Motion Picture Company, and also on a man named Milne, who has a daughter—then I'll be glad to tell what I know."

Hartley met Brune's laughing, hazel eyes, and, swearing beneath his breath, stepped to the telephone. Getting the detective bureau, he requested that the desired information be phoned him as soon as it could be obtained.

"Well?" he snapped, returning.

Brune leisurely filled his pipe, lighted it, and then told of the two persons whom he had that afternoon encountered, and the scrap of conversation which he had overheard. At the close. Hartley sniffed in open disgust.

"You're not even certain that the man mentioned Rezek's name? Perhaps you imagined it, eh?"

"If it were to hang any one, I wouldn't swear to it," said Brune, flushing a little. "But for our present purposes, I *would* swear to it."

The telephone rang, and Hartley responded. After a moment, he rejoined them.

"The Huggenheim concern is a tenth-rate film company, located at Long Beach. No one seems to know much about it, except that a man named Huggenheim is the boss. As for Milne, no one of that name is listed in the rogues' gallery—"

"Who said anything about the gallery?" snorted Brune hotly. "You seem to think—"

He subsided before Hartley's half-malicious look.

"I was going to say," continued the operative coolly, "that there is a Captain J. Harrod Milne, of the navy, who is now stopping at the *Hotel Virginia*, Long Beach. He has a daughter, also."

"Is he retired?" queried Brune.

"No. He's on special duty. As a matter of fact, he's an engineer, and one of the naval advisory board. He came here from San Francisco a couple of days ago, in order to see Case—"

"Eh?" Brune's eyes narrowed. "Mr. Case trusted me fully, and I knew nothing of Milne."

"Case himself knew nothing," smiled Hartley. "Milne came on short orders, to see if Case's engine could be adapted to the M type of submarine, now building for the navy. He arrived the day after Case's death—or murder, as Mr. Solomon seems to call it."

Solomon cleared his throat wheezily.

"Mr. 'Artley, can you get that 'ere Wirginia 'Otel on the wire?"

"By long distance, certainly."

"I'd be werry much obliged if you'd get 'old o' that there Cap'n Milne, sir."

Hartley nodded half contemptuously. He went to the instrument and put in the call. A moment later he picked up the receiver.

"Yes, this is Hartley—eh? What's that? Since when? And Miss Milne—"

For a few seconds he listened, but over the telephone his startled eyes were staring at the other two men. He hooked up the receiver savagely.

"By the Lord Harry!" he burst forth. "Milne has been gone since yesterday, and his daughter has not been heard from since this morning. The hotel people are worried—"

"I thought so," nodded Solomon, looking very much like a blinking blue-eyed owl. The operative turned on him furiously.

"You thought so!" Hartley fairly howled. "Why the devil didn't you say so, then? Confound it, I'd like to know who put a fathead like you on this case—"

Solomon laid down his pipe and rose. His wheezy voice snapped out with sudden force:

"Mr. 'Artley, get out o' this 'ere room! Don't you never come around me again, mind! You've 'ad your orders from Washington—now get out o' ere prompt! I don't want you nor no one else a-nosing into me business—get out! Get out!"

Knowing quite well that Solomon had been put in charge of the case, the secret-service man spluttered apologies—but he went. When he had departed, Solomon drew forth a handkerchief and mopped his brow.

"Mr. Brune," he said to the chuckling ex-journalist, "you get out early tomorrow mornin' an' buy me the werry biggest, blackest, strongest motor car as you can find in Los Angeles. 'Ave it 'ere by nine o'clock sharp."

"But you—what?" Brune's jaw dropped. "Where's the money? What are you planning?"

"You and me is a-going to 'ave the biggest fight ever was, sir," said Solomon gravely. "More'n that I can't say, 'cause why, I don't know. But summat mortal big is bein' pulled off, Mr. Brune—summat as scares me to think of! You get that car, mind! Wait—'ere's a check for ten thousand dollars, sir."

"Who'll run the car?" demanded Brune, wondering why the pudgy little man was so terribly agitated. He had never until this evening seen John Solomon so unnerved.

"You will, sir, till me men gets 'ere—a matter of a day or so. Now, tell me, what did that 'ere Miss Milne look like?"

"Like a dream!" sighed Brune, pocketing the check.

HAVING KNOWN Solomon in Chicago, and remembering that the pudgy little man took an unaffected delight in this one form of extravagance, Jack Brune was on hand promptly at nine the next morning, with the largest, blackest, most expensive touring car that could be obtained. Solomon inspected it, wheezed satisfied assent, and settled back in the tonneau.

Brune took the Long Beach Boulevard, and was complimented on his perspicacity. Then, as they whirled down the great valley toward the sea, Solomon lowered one of the extra seats behind Brune, and began summing up the case in hand.

So far as the loss of the trial submarine, the death of Case, and the theft of the drawings were concerned, the mysterious Jan Rezek was undoubtedly to blame. But the disappearance of Captain Milne, coupled with the scrap of conversation overheard by Jack Brune, was most puzzling. At least, it was so to Brune himself, although Solomon made no comment on the matter.

"Why don't you open up a bit?" demanded the ex-journalist at length. "What's back of this affair, John? Surely you have some notion—is it a foreign government?"

Solomon tamped at his clay pipe, his face quite blank.

"I knows nothing and I says nothing, sir, just like that! It ain't every man as can keep 'is mouth shut when 'e ain't got nothing to say, as the Good Book says. We'd better go to that 'ere Wirginia place and 'unt up Miss Milne."

Brune thought back swiftly. He remembered that the girl had asked after her father; somewhere in the man's answer had come the word "Rezek."

"Melodrama—secret service—spy systems!" he commented aloud. "John, you don't imagine that Miss Milne has been kidnaped, and her father, as well?"

"I don't imagine nothing, sir," was the blank response. "We're a-going to find out, as the old gent said when 'e married 'is third."

The powerful car hummed along beneath Brune's touch, and soon they were past Los Cerritos, and sweeping down into Long Beach itself. Five minutes later, the magnificent ocean front opened out before them, and Brune drew up at the entrance of the *Virginia*—the one splendid building of the beach city, its sunken gardens, walks, and colonnades overlooking the sparkling Pacific, with the rugged lines of the Catalina Islands showing against the horizon.

"Do you want to go in, or shall I inquire?"

"If you'll be so good, sir."

Brune leaped out and strode into the hotel. He had several times stopped here with Case, and caught the eye of the passing manager.

"Hello, Mr. Nestor! Any word from Captain Milne?"

Nestor, a small, polite, smiling man, gave Brune a keen glance. "No, Mr. Brune. He hasn't returned—"

"How about Miss Milne, then? Is she in?"

Nestor beckoned him beyond earshot of a group of tourists, and turned to him with evident anxiety.

"See here, Brune, what the devil's going on? Miss Milne left yesterday morning, and has not returned. She was worried over her father's absence."

"So are other people," rejoined Brune grimly. "Did she leave by herself, or with any one?"

"She took the interurban into Los Angeles, alone. Do you know anything about this affair?"

"I know enough to advise you to keep the business out of the newspapers." Brune took his spectacles from their case and began to polish them fervently. "Hold the rooms occupied by the Milnes, and allow no one access, unless it happens to be a government man. Now, can you lend me a bell hop for an hour? I need a local guide."

"Certainly." Nestor beckoned a blue-clad boy. "Seriously, Brune, has anything happened? Remember, I'm in a responsible position here—"

"You're all right," and Brune forced a smile. "Say, I don't suppose you ever heard of any one named Rezek. Jan Rezek?"

To his astounded surprise, the other nodded casually.

"Oh, yes! Rezek is the little comedy man with the Huggenheim people—they use the hotel occasionally for ball-room scenes, you know."

Brune gasped. Then, conquering his stupefaction, he donned his black-rimmed spectacles and nodded his thanks as he turned away.

Rezek—the mysterious Jan Rezek—a member of a motion-picture company! Brune's amazement was unbounded at the way he had stumbled upon this fact, which seemed unknown to detectives, secret-service men, or any one else. His brain was busy with the problem, as he strode back to the car with the bell boy following.

"John," he exclaimed guardedly, leaning over the door of the tonneau. "Rezek is a member of the Huggenheim film company!"

Solomon's round eyes opened a little wider.

"Where's Miss Milne?" he wheezed.

"Eh? Oh—she's been gone since yesterday morning. I brought the boy along to show us the way around town. Jump in, son!"

If Jack Brune had expected congratulations on his placing of Rezek—which he had—he met with disappointment. Solomon merely produced a plug of black tobacco and proceeded to whittle some shavings into his clay pipe.

"I suppose you want to run out and look over that film bunch?" said Brune curtly, waiting for the other to light his pipe. "It certainly looks as if there were some connection established between—"

"'Old 'ard!" exclaimed Solomon. "Let me think a bit, sir."

As another car approached, Brune ran from the entrance and drew up at the curb farther on. This indecision was a trifle puzzling. Since they were now certain who the mysterious Rezek was, and where he could be found, it seemed to Brune that the most logical course would be to go and find him.

Yet Solomon, lighting his pipe and puffing placidly, seemed to think otherwise. Why, Brune could not determine. It did not occur to him that he and Solomon might be pondering two very different things. At the moment, he himself was thinking of Miss Milne as he had seen her the previous afternoon.

Brune had been long enough on the coast to know that, with all its hastily applied veneer of refinement and its freak law, it still had an understratum of cave-man ethics and acts. Despite the automobiles and wonderful tourist hotels, men died of thirst on the desert and men were wrecked on the coastal rocks; despite the miles of boulevards and the influx of Easterners, men still fought over homesteads in the hills and men still smuggled forbidden fruit into the cities. Here one could find action or ease, smoothly flowing time or rugged battling with men, nature, or elements; deferential servants or reckless footpads. It was all according to the circle in which one lived, moved, and had one's being. This was the ideal country for treason, stratagems, and spoils.

And, Miss Milne having evidently been lured or forced into some circle other than her own, the result was very apt to be unhappy—for her. That Captain Milne seemed to be in the same predicament was no alleviation.

"It's a werry bad thing to be in a 'urry," observed Solomon

at length, and turned to the bell boy: "Young man, could you drive this 'ere car?"

"Sure," grinned the youngster happily. "But they're kinda strict on minors drivin' in this town, mister."

"Werry good. If you'll be so good as to 'op out, Mr. Brune, me an' this young gent will take a little ride. You see, sir, it might be best for me not to be seen along o' you, as the old gent said when 'e kissed the 'ousemaid in the back pantry."

Brune comprehended, and turned over the steering wheel to the boy, with a nod of assent. If this fellow Rezek had really killed Case and stolen the plans—as seemed improbable, considering Rezek's position—then Jack knew that he himself would doubtless be watched, as having been Case's confidential secretary. In that case, it might prove wiser for Solomon to avoid being seen in company with him, for Solomon's activities must remain unsuspected.

Watching the big car thrum off up Ocean Avenue, Brune turned back inside the hotel and found Nestor behind the desk.

"What kind of a fellow is this Rezek, anyway? What does he look like?"

"Oh, the actor?" Nestor smiled fleetingly. "He's a fat, jolly guy—haven't you ever seen him in the pictures?"

"Never saw any of this firm's output," grunted Brune. "How long have they been in business?"

"About a year, I guess. Huggenheim sells to one or two of the big companies, who send out the films as of their own make. That's probably why you never noticed the name advertised. Who was that in the car outside with you? A government man?"

Brune nodded, and turned away.

Strolling through the lobby to the seaward side of the hotel, he emerged on the broad veranda, drew a chair to the railing, and settled himself with his pipe. As he gazed out at the white sails of the flitting yachts, however, he was thinking hard.

"After all," he muttered, "it seems as if we're on a false scent.

This fellow Rezek—is he modeled on the pattern of a villain, a murderer, and thief? Rats!"

Indeed, it seemed to the rather disgusted Brune that Solomon's veiled hints regarding plot and intrigue and murder were sheer nonsense.

While Rezek had been enveloped in the mystery of the unknown, anything had seemed possible and plausible. Now that the cloak had been stripped away, and Rezek revealed as a merry, fat man, an actor for a small movie company—the heretofore plausible seemed absurd to Brune.

How the name of Jan Rezek had come to be found on a scrap of paper clutched in the dead hand of Milton Case might be explained in a dozen ways. That Case might have been murdered, the submarine destroyed, and the drawings stolen, all by a fat, twenty-per-week mountebank, was the height of absurdity. Brune could not well conceive a jolly Falstaff in such a role. Like Mr. C.J. Caesar of old, Jack Brune connected fat men with nothing more involved than beer and skittles.

He quite overlooked the fact that John Solomon was by no means skinny.

"Well," concluded Brune, chuckling to himself, "John made up a highfalutin theory—and it'll collapse like a pricked balloon when he sees friend Rezek! Honest, I never thought that John Solomon would fall down so hard. Poor chap! He looks pretty old, and I suppose age is telling on him!"

Still, the thought of Miss Milne troubled him. And, also, he had noted one rather peculiar coincidence. It was a little over a year since Case had attracted attention with his submarine plans; and it was about a year since the Huggenheim Motion Picture Company had been running. The coincidence meant nothing, Brune promptly decided.

Looking out at the long walk below, which led down to the sea wall, Brune idly noted a figure approaching the steps leading up to the veranda. Something oddly familiar in the man's appearance caught his eye; but, being a trifle short-sighted,

Brune could not make out the face below. Instead of turning to the stairs, however, the man kept on and vanished beneath the basement entrance leading to elevators and billiard rooms.

Ten minutes later, as Brune contemplated ordering luncheon for himself and John Solomon, to be ready against the latter's return, the hotel manager emerged on the veranda, and came over to Brune's chair hastily.

"Oh, there you are! We've just had word from Captain Milne."

"Eh?" Brune whirled. "You have?"

"Yep." Nestor rubbed his hands, beaming. "He phoned in to say that he was all right, and that his rooms were to be held."

"Where is he?"

"At San Pedro, and Miss Milne is with him. He's taking the boat for San Diego this afternoon, and expects to be back in two weeks or so."

"Sure it was Captain Milne speaking?"

"Why—naturally it was he! The desk clerk got the message—"

"Did he know Milne's voice?" snapped Brune.

"What's on your nerves, Brune? No, I don't suppose I'd have recognized the captain's voice myself over long distance, considering that I've hardly spoken with him; but—"

"When does his boat leave? What's her name?"

"In an hour, I believe. She's the *Beaver.*"

Brune reflected hurriedly. Here was an excellent chance to demolish Solomon's theory at one blow. If he could get over to San Pedro, see Milne, and make sure that everything was all right, he would have a nice bit of news for John. If, as now seemed most improbable, the message were faked, it would be well to ascertain the fact at once.

"When does the next car leave for San Pedro, Nestor?"

The hotel man glanced at his watch.

"Just leaving the station now—it'll pass here in about two minutes—"

"If any one asks for me, tell 'em where I've gone," exclaimed Brune, and dashed away.

He gained Ocean Avenue barely in time to stop the San Pedro interurban, and climbed aboard in all haste.

Then he paused to consider his action.

One or two other men had swung aboard the car at the hotel, but Brune had been in too great haste to observe them. Paying his fare, he dropped into a seat, and felt very well pleased with the latest twist of chance.

It would be easy to see if Milne's name were on the passenger list of the *Beaver*, which by now would be at her dock. A few words with the naval engineer would serve to adjust matters, so far as his presumed kidnaping was concerned. Moreover, it was very likely that Miss Milne and her companion, on the previous afternoon, had mentioned the name of Rezek in connection with a proposed visit to the Huggenheim film establishment.

"It's ridiculously simple!" reflected Brune, watching the giant swinging bridge of the ship-building works as the car whirled past. "And we exaggerated a little thing into an absurdly big affair. I'd like to have seen John Solomon when he reached the film studios and interviewed Jan Rezek! Still, however—"

Brune frowned. There was undoubtedly a good deal of explanation required—first and foremost, as to why the dying Case had scrawled Rezek's name. That Solomon's theory was quite absurd. Brune had by this time decided fully.

As they left Wilmington and started on the last lap of the short ride, a man came past Brune and strode forward to the smoking section, where he sank into a seat out of Brune's sight. The ex-journalist started, and a frown crossed his strong features.

Was he dreaming? Or was that the same man whom he had observed coming into the *Virginia*—the man whose figure had struck him as being vaguely familiar? When he could see the man no longer, he found that dim resemblance troubling him; whom the figure resembled he could not tell.

"Well, it may be some one I've met and forgotten," he

concluded. "If it's the same chap I saw at the *Virginia*, he must have gotten aboard there just ahead of me, and I was in too big a hurry to observe him. No matter. Since he didn't recognize me, it's some one I don't know very well, that's sure!"

Brune forgot the matter. San Pedro harbor was now opening up before them as the car swept around the mud flats—otherwise "valuable harbor tracts." The days of square-riggers has almost passed, even on this coast; but here and there Brune could make out spars of a bark or brig still in the lumber trade, while one three-master lay, in all her glory of yards and rigging, a protest against the noisy, puffing steamers around her.

A stranger at San Pedro, Brune left the car at the station, opposite the docks, and inquired his way to the *Beaver.* By the time he had found the right wharf, and was approaching the object of his search, a few moments had elapsed. The *Beaver* was one of the smaller coastwise ships, and as yet her passengers had not begun to crowd aboard.

Consequently. Brune had no trouble in gaining access to the purser's desk.

"Have you a Captain Milne on your passenger list?" he asked. "If so, I want a word with him before you pull out."

The purser searched his sheet, then nodded.

"Yes—upper deck, stateroom No. 134. The gentleman came aboard a few moments ago. Steward!"

With the white-clad guide leading the way, Brune followed to the upper deck, and so to the stateroom in question. Handing the steward a quarter, he knocked.

"Well? What is it?" snapped a voice from within—a harsh, metallic voice, which brought a wondering frown to Brune's face.

"Captain Milne?" he inquired. "I'd like a word with you, if you please?"

"Come in!"

The steward had departed. Brune opened the door. He had a brief glimpse of a man before him, and recognized the man at once.

It was the same person whom he had seen at the Hotel *Virginia* and on the car—the lean, swarthy face leaped into his remembrance now, too late, as that of the man whom he had observed with Miss Milne at the Santa Fe station, on the previous afternoon!

Barely had he comprehended it, when something crashed into him. Brune staggered, and instinctively struck out. His fist landed. Then the ceiling seemed to fall on him, and all was blotted out; Brune had a faint vision of that dark, saturnine face smiling into his, and after that he knew nothing more.

The trap had been sprung.

CHAPTER IV

TRAPPED!

BRUNE RECOVERED to find himself in a horrible situation.

He found himself lying upon the lower bunk of the stateroom, whose wooden curtain had been drawn, half darkening the interior. His head was aching in a thousand places, it seemed, and he thought at first that this pain came from the knock-out which had been administered to him. But in this he was wrong.

Sitting in a chair beside him, and gazing into his eyes with a sardonic smile, was the lean, swarthy man who had trapped him. Brune tried to spring up, tried to call out, tried to dash his fist into that sneering, leering face. But he could not. He was quite powerless to move.

Still that sneering visage peered down, as if watching in cynical amusement the struggling of its victim. Brune felt his breath coming hard; indeed, his respiration was so difficult that for one terrible instant he fancied that he had been strangled and was dying. The stateroom seemed filled with a disagreeable, animallike odor.

Now the sitting demon, as Brune mentally described him, pushed back his chair and picked from the washstand a flat case. Opening it, he took out a hypodermic syringe and tested this, then from his hip pocket produced a flask of whisky. The rank breath of the liquor seemed to clear Brune's nostrils, although he remained unable to move or speak. Carefully his captor filled the syringe with a few drops of whisky.

Brune realized quite clearly that he had been trapped in some devilish manner—that the message to Nestor had been a blind, that this man had seen him at the hotel, had gotten him aboard the *Beaver* with diabolical ingenuity, had there downed him and poisoned or injured him. But how? The agony of the thought was torture. Brune wondered if his back had been broken—and why. Why? Who was this devil?

"Poor Mr. Brune!" The evil, swarthy visage leaned over Brune in sardonic mirth. "Such an athletic, handsome young man! Such a muscular young man! And so eager to see Captain Milne! Well, he shall see the worthy captain—but now a little whisky in the blood, for I must not kill the worthy young man."

Brune felt the needle jab into his arm, but he could not feel the strong fingers that kneaded at his flesh. His paralysis frightened him; his labored breathing, the leering face above him, his whole terrible situation was agonizing. Gradually, however, his breath came more easily as the whisky began to work. Again that harsh, metallic voice addressed him:

"Mr. Brune knows nothing of toxicology, eh? Now he has solved a great secret—the secret of how Socrates met his death! Is it not interesting? Such a gentle thing is conine, the simplest of alkaloids yet the least known! And all the while the intellect remains clear. Is it not beautiful? Ah, Mr. Brune appreciates it fully!"

Brune tried vainly to speak. The other leered devilishly.

"Quite useless! A drop or two upon the tongue, and the beautiful hemlock does the rest. Two grains, only two grains, would prove fatal; but you will not die! No. It is a pity, but I have been ordered to keep you alive. Now we had better leave the boat, for we do not wish to go to San Diego."

The man rose, threw open the door, and vanished. A moment later he appeared, with one of the ship's officers at his side. The sardonic deviltry had now been tamed down into a suave, calm poise. Further, Brune soon found that the man was playing a role which was bound to confuse Solomon or any one trailing the vanished Jack Brune.

"As you see," said the swarthy man, in an excellent professional manner, "my friend is under a slight paralytic stroke. Here is my card—you will note that I am a physician as well as a naval officer."

The inconsistency of a ship's surgeon ranking as "captain" apparently did not strike the ship's officer, who glanced at the card, nodded, and looked down at the helpless figure of Brune with evident concern.

"Is he in bad shape, Captain Milne?"

"No; but I shall give up my trip to San Diego. If you will have a stretcher brought here, I will take him ashore and attend to him. Poor fellow! He often has these attacks—a constitutional failing. Better hurry with that stretcher so as not to arouse comment or attract attention from the crowd."

Evidently anxious about the reputation of the boat, the ship's officer assented, and strode from the stateroom. The false "Captain Milne" looked down at Brune, with a harsh chuckle.

"Poor Mr. Brune! How awful it must be to discover that one is a paralytic! Now a little strychnine, I think—Mr. Brune's eyes appear much dilated, and he received a stiff dose of conine, so we must keep his lungs going. How the gentlemen from Japan will be interested in his case!"

Producing the hypodermic again, the speaker swiftly dissolved a white tablet and shot the liquid into Brune's arm.

This was the second reference which Brune had heard to the mysterious "gentlemen from Japan." The repetition impressed the phrase on his mind. Who were these gentlemen, or was the phrase some kind of devilish jest? This man had used the words to Miss Milne at the railroad station—and what had become of the girl?

As the thought flashed through Brune's mind, he saw his captor hastily wash out the hypodermic, fill it with a liquid from a small tube, and hastily turn to the bunk. Again the needle

pricked, and almost instantly Brune felt a delicious repose stealing over him—delicious, even were it the repose of death.

Gradually his eyes closed and his senses were dimmed. He
vaguely comprehended that he was lifted and carried out to a
stretcher—but that was all.

How long this coma lasted, he could not tell. This infernally
clever poisoner, this latter-day Borgia, had not quite put Brune
to sleep, for the coma was pierced by dim visions which later
resolved themselves into coherent memories. They were sensa-
tions rather than visions.

He sensed faces and voices—the harsh, metallic voice and the
Mephistophelian visage of the false Milne, and others. He knew
that he was being tossed about, as if in a small boat. An odor of
fish permeated everything. Gradually the daylight passed into
darkness—all sense of time was lost, but Brune knew later that
the afternoon had passed and gone while he was still gripped
in that partial coma. And the night came. With it, the nausea of
seasickness—a fearful sickness, in the midst of which came the
poisoner bringing his hypodermic; and after that Brune slept.

Whatever might have been the intention in thus pumping
dose and antidote of poison into Brune, the result was a fever-
ish illness of two days, from which he passed into a dreamless
sleep. Awakening from this on the following morning, he was
himself again, save for a natural weakness, But—where was he?

Brune was utterly bewildered. At first he thought himself
crazed.

It was one of the mornings, common to California, when
everything is shrouded in fog until noon. Looking around,
Brune found himself lying on a stretch of dry, sandy beach;
behind him were what appeared to be great rock masses, dimly
visible through the mist. At his feet the ocean was flooding up
in long, sullen breakers.

Dazed, Jack Brune stared about him, wondering if this were
some weird poison dream, some fantasy induced by his illness.

But, no—he felt perfectly well, undeniable hunger was gnaw-
ing at him, and, except for the weakness, he was quite himself.

"Where am I—on the beach near San Pedro?" he muttered.
"By George, I'd like to get a crack at that fellow—just one good,
square crack!"

Scrambling to his feet, albeit somewhat shakily, Brune gradually found himself gaining coherent realization of his position.

Beyond a doubt, he had been left on the shore—where and
why he had no idea. He could detect no sign of life around him,
no smoke of factory or loom of building. While quite certain
that he had been carried aboard a boat, probably a fishing craft,
he could see no boat upon the fog-inclosed waters. Nor were
there footprints in the sand.

"Marooned on a desert island!" and Brune half grinned as
he tried to penetrate the fog with his eyes. "Knocked on the
head, twenty-first-century style, shanghaied, and marooned, by
George! Or, if not by George, then by that dark-faced Mephisto.
All right, friend Mephisto—just you wait till I land on your
frame when we meet again!"

Who the poisoner could be he had no idea. It was not Rezek,
certainly—unless there were two Rezeks. But Brune had no
doubt that his captor was the same who had slain Case. And very
probably Case had been poisoned, just as Solomon had thought.

He promptly sat down again to think it over. The more he
thought, the graver seemed the situation.

He saw now that Solomon's theory must, to some extent, have
been correct, whether or not Jan Rezek were the plotter. The
poisoner had spoken of having "orders," therefore was not alone
in the plot; Brune knew that his own kidnaping had been carried
through with a consummate, diabolical cleverness, and that the
false Captain Milne was a tremendously dangerous person.

"They left my pipe and tobacco and money," reflected Brune,
searching his clothes, "so the object was not robbery. No, it looks
as if they had been watching me since the death of Case, and

decided that I would be better out of the way for a while. Though why the deuce they picked on *me*—"

He grimaced at the thought. Then he started suddenly and came to his feet as a cry pierced the mist from behind:

"Hello there! Hello!"

Amazement gripped Brune's heart, amazement and bewildered incredulity. The thing was starkly impossible! For a long moment he stared, flung into doubting of his own senses, for the person who had hailed him, and whose figure loomed out through the mist of the rocks behind, was no other than Miss Milne!

Moreover, she was dressed as he had last seen her, except that now she lacked the hat; her gown of shimmering blue-corded silk, trimmed with old Chinese embroideries of gold and fawn, seemed sadly torn and rumpled. But her face was the same—to Brune's eyes glorious in its beauty, delicate of outline, each feature clearly chiseled, with something of the transparent beauty of an onyx cameo.

"You!" gasped Brune, startled out of himself. "You!"

At his words, the eager light died out of her face; it was replaced by a swift frown that was even more bewildering to him—a frown of suspicion, of fear, of anger.

"Yes, I." Her voice rang to him clear as a silvern bell. "Since you seem to know me, I presume that you are one of those who brought me here. I thought that you—"

"Hold on!" cried Brune. "For Heaven's sake, go slow, Miss Milne! Where am I?"

Contempt shone in her dark-blue eyes.

"You should know that perfectly well, sir. Pray do not attempt to carry through any further trickery. Where is your friend Carlisle?"

"Carlisle?" repeated Brune. "Never heard of him, Miss Milne. My name is Jack Brune, and I assure you I haven't the faintest notion of where I am or how I got here, except—except for that devil who poisoned me—"

He halted, wondering what to say, wondering what was in the girl's mind. She laughed coldly.

"Very clever, sir. So you claim to be Mr. Brune, and I suppose you will also claim to have been private secretary to Mr. Case?"

"I—well, I thought that was my position, but I'll not argue about it if you'd prefer something else," returned Brune, groping for some straw, some pointer, to show him how the wind blew with this energetic young woman. "May I inquire if your father is in the vicinity?"

A flush, unmistakably a flush of anger, suffused the girl's face.

"Oh—I would like to *kill* you—and your whole gang!" she flashed. "How dare you mock me! How dare you! After all you have done to us!"

"Proud lady, have your way," quoted Brune, with an attempt at singing which made him feel suddenly lightheaded and giddy. "Have you ever heard 'Pinafore'? Very possibly. As I say, have your own way about it. I'm very ready to oblige a young and charming lady, and I only wish that you'd tell me where I am, and where I can find a quick-lunch counter and a cup of hot coffee. Although it may strike you as absurd and unusual that a scoundrel should have need for food, still I do protest that I can't help it. If—"

"You look as if you'd been on a week's debauch," she interjected. "I don't—"

"Worse than that—far worse!" Brune felt a warning spasm, a trembling of the knees, but he forced a shaky laugh. "I've been on a poison debauch. Miss Milne—fact! That leering devil fed me every kind of dope on the menu, and topped it off with seasickness and stale-fish smells. Pray tell me where I can obtain a cup of coffee, at least—"

"Will you get out of here?"

The girl came a step toward him, her fists clenched, anger flashing in her deep blue eyes. Yet, with the anger, was a trace of tears.

"I don't want you around here—as if I didn't have enough on

my hands already! Oh, you're a fine actor, all right! Now get out of here—understand? Go back to your precious friend Carlisle, and leave us alone! I won't have you here—I won't! You can't bully me, just because your thugs have shot poor dad—"

Brune flung up his hands, literally and figuratively. To his eyes the form of the girl was swaying about in the swirls of mist, and all things were growing remarkably vague and dim. But he essayed another and more shaky laugh, with the half-conscious conviction that something must be wrong with the girl's brain.

"All right, all right," he muttered, taking a staggering step on the sand. "If it will make you happy, Miss Milne, I'll go some-where else. Anything to oblige. Only, I wish I had—a cup—of coffee—"

With a sudden deep sign, he collapsed and fell in a heap, unconscious.

The girl stood motionless for a long moment, gazing at his recumbent figure with suspicion frankly written in her face. Brune lay with his face upturned, and the deathly pallor of his features was beyond any man's assumption.

Evidently realizing this, and with a swift, startled surmise creeping into her eyes, the girl stepped forward slowly. She came to Brune's side and leaned over him. Her hand went to his breast pocket, and drew forth some papers. Glancing at them, she replaced them and stared at his face again.

Then, with a little, gasping cry, she leaped up, ran to the water's edge, and returned with her cupped hands full of water. Dashing this into Brune's face, she forced him to sit up.

Thus, opening his eyes, he found her arm supporting him, her hand wet on his brow, her tear-wet cheeks almost against his. Brune did the most natural thing—for Jack Brune—under the circumstances. He kissed her cheek, and then fainted again.

When he came to himself, he found her pouring hot coffee into his mouth. He drank greedily, feeling new life course through his veins at every swallow. When the coffee was gone, Brune gripped the hand she held out to him and rose. He felt exceedingly foolish, and wondered if that kiss would mean disaster. But apparently the girl had forgotten it. As he staggered, she caught him by the shoulder—and there was surprising strength in her arm.

"All right, thanks," said Brune, with the ghost of his old smile. "I fancy I was just weak from hunger, Miss Milne. By George, that coffee was fine! Is there any more around?"

"Come!" she answered.

Being, most emphatically, not a fool, Jack Brune was not sure just what to say, and, therefore, held his peace.

With her arm twined in his, they turned from the beach and approached the frowning rocks behind. Brune was glad of her help, for his own weakness, on trying to walk, was amazing. The coffee had helped him tremendously, however.

"We were just having our own breakfast," volunteered the girl suddenly. "I came down to the shore, for dad thought he heard a boat engine—"

"Good thing you did," nodded Brune. "This fog is a confounded nuisance!"

Five minutes later, they came to a sheltered nook among the rocks, overhung and guarded against wind and rain by the huge cliff masses. Two khaki dog tents were pitched in the niche, a little fire of driftwood burning at one side. Stretched out on a blanket by the fire was a man, who tried to sit up at their approach, but fell back again.

"Father," said the girl, pausing, "this is Mr. Brune, formerly secretary to Mr. Case."

"Very glad to meet you, Captain Milne," said Brune, but his eyes wandered to the coffeepot and the frying pan beside the fire. "Sorry I horned into your camp like this—"

Milne snorted. He was a rather small man, grizzled, with the stubborn, combative eyes of the born fighter.

"Don't mention it, sir, don't mention it! What the devil's wrong with you?"

"Hunger, mostly," and Brune lowered himself to the ground, with a sigh. "Also, I'm lost. Where am I?"

"If you don't know," sniffed Captain Milne, staring at him, "you're either a confounded fool or else you're in the same fix we are."

"And what's that, if I may inquire?"

"Marooned on a desert island—damn it!" exploded the other. "I beg your pardon. Marge. Oh, this cursed leg!"

Brune stared, agape. He began to think that he was quite mad.

CHAPTER V

MAROONED

HAVING ABSORBED a pint of coffee, four eggs, a dozen slices of bacon, and an unknown quantity of other things, Jack Brune lighted his pipe at the fire, with a huge sigh of repletion, and sat back to get the tangle untwisted.

He knew by this time that at least he was not crazy.

Since the business of explaining was first up to him, and since the obvious method was to begin at the beginning, he started with the death of Case and related his own misadventures since then. Knowing that Captain Milne was one to be trusted fully, he made no secret of John Solomon's activities.

"After what happened at San Pedro," he concluded, "I'm a bit hazy as to details. That fiend drugged and doped me, right enough. I think I was aboard a boat, for certainly I was seasick. Then he gave me more hypodermics, and I woke up, to find myself on the beach down there. That's all I can tell, but there's a whole lot I'd be glad to know. Where am I—or, rather, where are we?"

The naval engineer's explosive tendencies having been allayed by Marge—which Brune rightly took to be short for Margaret—the position of father and daughter was soon made clear. Already Brune, while eating, had found that they were actually marooned on a desert island; nor was the statement so mad, impossible, and fantastic as seemed on the face of it.

"I believe, sir, that we are on one of the channel islands," said Milne. "To be more exact, San Nicolas or Santa Barbara. I'm inclined to think this island is San Nicolas. As you see, Brune, I'm unable to move—that dashed scoundrel Rezek put a bullet through my leg!"

The girl rose, extending her hand to Brune.

"I'll run down and collect some driftwood—I know dad is dying to swear freely! And let me say, Mr. Brune, that I'm very sorry for what I said upon meeting you."

"To judge from what I've been through myself," and Brune rose, smiling, "you were quite justified, Miss Milne! And since I had to be marooned somewhere, I'm very glad indeed that I was brought into such happy company."

She had been correct. Upon her departure, Captain Milne proceeded to swear, not only volubly but emphatically, until he was purple in the face.

"Confound it all!" he concluded, having exhausted his vocabulary. "Brune, do you know what's happened? Do you know that our country is in a devil of a fix?"

"Hold on—hold on!" protested Brune. "I don't know anything at all—not even how you got here. Since I've emptied myself pretty well, suppose you spin your yarn, and give me an idea of what's happened? Did you come directly here from Long Beach?"

The other growled assent.

"Your poisoner, Brune, is a fellow named Carlisle—I know that much about him. He called on me at the hotel, the evening I disappeared, and represented himself as being one of a syndicate engaged in some development work down the coast. He asked me, purely as a personal favor, to meet the others that evening and to lend them my advice.

"Naturally, I consented. An automobile arrived for me just after dinner, and I went to the meeting, as I supposed. As a matter of fact, the car took me to the docks at Wilmington, where Carlisle met me with damned profuse apologies. He conducted me aboard a boat warped to the dock, and we found his precious companions in her cabin.

"There were three of them—a Japanese, who bowed and scraped like a Frenchman, an ugly fellow named Huggenheim, and a little fat scoundrel named Rezek—"

"By George!" interrupted Brune. "Excuse me—go ahead."

Settling back, Brune puffed at his pipe, excitement working strongly within him. But with the excitement was a great and compellent admiration for John Solomon.

The little cockney had been right, after all! The flagrant absurdity of connecting Rezek with this affair was not lessened, to Brune's mind; yet Solomon had been right.

"Those four cutthroats," continued Milne, "showed me a set of submarine plans—and by the eternal! They were the very drawings stolen from Case! I recognized them at once, as I had passed favorably on Case's invention last year, when I was in the minority and was given the cold shoulder for my pains. The fat man, Rezek, stated that my candid opinion was desired as to whether Case's gas engine was practicable."

"Just a moment," broke in Brune, frowning. "You mean they had the nerve to show you those drawings, knowing that you'd recognize them and—"

"Nerve?" glared Milne. "It was damned insolence, and I told 'em so! Rezek, who seemed to be the head of things, only grinned and asked again for my opinion. I rolled up the plans and put 'em in my pocket and started off. Carlisle tried to stick a hypodermic needle into me, and I smashed his dirty jaw. Then the others piled on to me and got me down.

"When they had me in a chair, Rezek offered me five thousand cash for my opinion of the drawings. I told him where to go. Then the little Jap butted in and offered me five thousand additional. I got one foot free and kicked that damned Jap so hard in the stomach that he took the count; then I tore loose and waded into 'em. I cursed near made it, too—got to the companionway, when Rezek dropped me with a bullet. Then Carlisle jumped on me and put a hypodermic into my leg. Next thing I knew, I was here—"

Captain Milne tailed off with a volley of curses, not particularly profane, but surprisingly heartfelt.

"And Miss Milne?" inquired Brune, who was gradually getting order out of chaos.

"She started raising heaven and earth to find me. Carlisle called at the hotel next morning, with a fine cock-and-bull story, got her into Los Angeles under pretense of meeting me, where you saw them—and doped her. She joined me here next morning. They've marooned us, with plenty of provisions, but without a chance to get clear. That's why they got you, too—because you were looking me up."

"Why?" queried Brune. "Why are they so worried over you?"

Milne gave a snort of disgust.

"Don't you see—good Heaven, man, where are your brains? Those damned scoundrels stole the submarine drawings and sunk the submarine, and now they're trying to sell the plans to Japan! They had the colossal nerve to try to get my O.K. on the plans in the presence of that cursed Jap!"

As a hypothesis, it was extremely plausible.

Brune puffed at his pipe, his rather square face set in a frown. For the moment he abruptly dismissed the puzzle of the Huggenheim Motion Picture Company, and went down to basic facts.

Milne had been neatly kidnaped, in order that his approval or disapproval of the submarine plans might be learned at first-hand, presumably for the benefit of the Japanese gentleman in question. His daughter had also been kidnaped, because she was raising too much trouble over his disappearance. Also, Jack Brune. With no one else left on the ground, the astute Carlisle could easily allay all apprehension over the absence of the Milnes—in fact, had done so on the day of Brune's mishap.

"The question is," reflected Brune, "does the gang know anything about John Solomon? If not, there's still a chance; and it's very unlikely that they do. I wonder what happened when he visited Huggenheim's studio? Well, while there's Solomon there's hope!"

Aloud, however, he contented himself with backing up Milne's theory—despite a still small doubt lurking at the back of his head.

"If you're right, Captain Milne, those chaps have put across something mighty big. You know, perhaps, that Huggenheim and Rezek have established themselves locally—in Long Beach, I mean?"

Milne knew nothing of them, so Brune proceeded to expound what he had learned.

"Thus," he went on, "this moving-picture concern has been working for a year in Long Beach—where it could keep its eye on Milton Case and his experiments. Beyond a doubt he knew something of them, or rather of Rezek, whose name he scribbled as he died. This Carlisle may have been associated with them. If Rezek—"

"Let me tell you this, Brune," interrupted Milne earnestly. "If that submarine is lost to this country, there'll be the devil to pay! Now, I'm knocked out—the wound is all right, but I don't dare get it inflamed. I can't do a blasted thing. Marge is only a girl, but she's a damned sight better to have in a pinch than most girls— God bless her! It's up to you. Get off this cursed island if you have to swim—you and Marge must do something—you *must!*"

"All right" nodded Brune, and rose. "I'll go look her up. You quiet down and keep your mind off things, or you'll have that wound in bad shape before you know it."

Turning away abruptly, he strode toward the shore. The mist was already lightening, and as he emerged from the masses of rock, Brune saw the girl's figure a quarter mile down the shore. She was presumably gathering driftwood.

Jack Brune was more sobered down than he had been in many a long day; not by his recent experience, but by the aim and end of the whole thing. Even so, it was hard for him to realize that the fate of the Case submarine might mean everything to his country—and that its fate lay, for the moment, in his own hands.

Could he get back to the mainland, could he put his newly gained knowledge in the hands of John Solomon, there was still hope. Otherwise, the stolen drawings would be purchased and on their way to Japan before anything would be learned about them. Solomon might suspect and theorize, but he would get nowhere—unless he drew the attention of the conspirators and was brought to San Nicolas Island, to keep Milne company.

Further, Brune knew that time was short.

In telephoning the Hotel *Virginia* under the name of Milne, Carlisle had arranged to lull all suspicion for two weeks—no more. By that time, the plotters no doubt figured that nothing much would matter, for the drawings would have been disposed of to Japan and the birds would have flown.

"Well, I'm finding quite a little firewood!" smiled Miss Milne, as Brune strode up. "I think—what's the matter? You didn't have a row with dad?"

Her face changed swiftly at sight of his brooding eyes.

"No," and Brune met her look squarely. "No. But your father put it up to me to get away from here and have our kidnapers rounded up. How to do it, I can't see."

"Oh!" She searched his face with incisive eyes. "You agree with dad that we're on San Nicolas?"

"Agree? I don't know anything about it! Where *is* San Nicolas?"

"It's a desolate little island, seventy miles off the mainland—the farthest of the channel group. Personally, I think we're on one of the others, because I could see the tip of Catalina when the fog lifted yesterday. As a rule, however, it's just like to-day, and nothing in sight."

Brune followed her pointing finger, due east. The fog had indeed lifted, and the sun-smitten, bleak, rocky island lay clear in the warmth of noon. The horizon was unbroken, however.

Questioning the girl, Brune found that Catalina was fifty

miles distant, but on an unusually clear day the rocky tip of the latter island could be made out. Beyond a doubt, however, the light-lying mist would inclose San Nicolas from view, and the only hope of rescue lay in a passing boat.

"But we're far off the traffic lanes," said Margaret Milne, gazing wistfully over the blue waters, "and even if this were the fishing season, which it isn't, San Nicolas is very rarely visited. We've not seen a sign of any living thing."

"How about a signal fire?" suggested Brune. She pointed to the beach.

"All our wood is here—driftwood, and little enough of it. Carlisle left us no lack of supplies and several casks of drinking water, so that I suppose no harm will come to us—"

"Oh, I'm not thinking of that!" exclaimed Brune. "I'm thinking of the submarine! Don't you see, girl, that unless we get that bunch of crooks rounded up, our country will lose the biggest thing ever?"

"I know," and her eyes rested on his, calmly. "But why get excited over it, when we can do nothing? Besides, if the government had acted on dad's advice last year, Mr. Case's invention would have been accepted. It's the same old story of turning down everything until there comes a crash of public clamor, and then—"

"And then being left at the post," nodded Brune. "You're right, Miss Milne. If we had a few of the inventions which have been grabbed by other countries after we refused them we'd be in better shape to-day. But, as to getting away from here—I can't very well swim fifty miles. If I could, I would."

"I believe you would," and she looked again at his wide hazel eyes, his square features, his half-smiling mouth. To her own lips crept a slow smile, as if in answer. "If there's anything that I can do, Mr. Brune, please don't hesitate to call upon me—no matter what it is. I realize fully what is involved, and if I can in any way serve my country, it will be a privilege."

The common-sense manner of the girl, her absolute freedom

from any pose, her evident sincerity, surprised and delighted Brune. There was depth to her. He wondered if she had noticed that kiss—"

"We'll manage it some way," he found himself saying, with more show of confidence than he felt in his heart. "I'll carry in this driftwood while I'm about it."

Of course, there were larger problems which his escape to the mainland might not affect. No one knew where the conspirators had their headquarters, for one thing. But, if Solomon once received warning of what was afoot and had grounds for arresting those who could be taken in hand, the luck might yet break even.

Hour after hour, Brune thought the situation over as he sat on the sand that afternoon and watched the seemingly limitless ocean outspread before him. How to get away? The more he considered it, the more impossible it looked—and was.

"There's only one thing to hope for," he reflected at last, seeking a secluded nook along the shore where he could take a dip in the cool surf, "and that's chance. If some kind of luck happens along and favors us, all right. If not, we stay here."

The afternoon was wearing away when he returned to camp, intending to find Margaret Milne and do a bit of exploring. For some time she had been gone on the same errand, said her father, and directed Brune after her, toward the western lip of the island.

He strode along the beach, still busied with his problem. The island was treeless, and all that day he had seen no boat on the horizon. Unless he could make the solid rocks float, it looked as if he were to stay.

"Mr. Brune!"

Brune glanced up. He had come perhaps two miles along the shore, and now, a half mile ahead, saw Miss Milne running over the sand toward him. He waved his hand, and she halted. Brune at once broke into a run.

"What's the matter?" he called, as he approached.

"Don't run—it's all right!" she responded. "I have something to show you!"

As he joined her, he was surprised by the eager animation that fired her whole being—she seemed as though transfigured by some virile happiness.

"What is it?" he demanded again. She only laughed and sped on before him. Then, as they turned a corner of rocks a moment later, she flung out her hand.

"This! Do you understand?"

Brune looked at the little indentation amid the rocks and sand. There, half buried in sand by the retreating tide, was a great square of wood—a hatch cover, battered, but solid, blown off some ship, smashed from some moorings on the other side the world, and drifted here.

"Chance!" laughed Brune. "I thought so! Well, what about it, Miss Milne?"

His words brought a little puzzled frown to her face, but it was gone instantly.

"Don't you see?" she cried. "Won't that be a splendid raft? You can fix up a mast, and we can make a sail from one of the tents—I can spare mine easily—and you can get off by sunset! By to-morrow morning you'll be near Catalina, at least, and some tourist launch or passing boat will be sure to pick you up!"

Brune eyed that battered hatch speculatively. He saw that it was large enough to support him, at least. Then he glanced out to sea. Fifty or sixty miles of waves, with wind that might take him anywhere, on a crazy craft, without more food and water than he could take with him—

"It's a chance, as you said," the girl continued hastily, misinterpreting his word of a moment previous. "But really, not so much as you'd think, for the wind always blows from the west, and you're sure to land somewhere on the coast, even if you're not picked up! Will you try it? I'll run back to camp and get some supplies and the tent while you go on along the shore and try to find something that'll serve as a mast. Will you?"

"George, what a girl!" thought Brune; looking at her, marveling at the clear freshness of her beauty, heightened by the excitement that was upon her.

Under his silence, her face changed while she watched him.

"You're not afraid?" she asked slowly. "You're not afraid—"

"I am," and Brune smiled a little. "I'd sooner cut off my leg than make that trip, or try it. I'm scared clear through! Just the same, you run back and get the stuff, and I'll rig up some kind of a mast on that—that infantile raft."

"You'll—you'll try it?"

"Oh, sure!" nodded Brune, white-lipped. "I'll try it, of course. And you tell your dad to whistle that the wind won't change to-night!"

CHAPTER VI

SOLOMON TAKES A WALK

JOHN SOLOMON, ensconced in his suite of rooms at the *Angelus,* was making life miserable for every one in the vicinity.

Three neatly dressed gentlemen wearing fezzes had located him and were installed in his apartments—one acting as his chauffeur, and the other two serving as valets, though every one wondered why such an unassuming, fat little Britisher should use valets. The blank smiles, the imperturbable calm, the magnificent courtesy of these befezzed gentlemen had driven the hotel wild with curiosity and baffled interest.

Disregarding Solomon's previous warning, Mr. Hartley had called and had attempted to force his way into the suite. Result: Mr. Hartley, bruised and sore, rushed to the wires and sent frantic messages to Washington, the replies to which made him swear violently and seek the Mexican border in search of opium smugglers. He was eliminated.

Mr. Lang, having come on from Chicago, also arrived and was closeted with John Solomon for an entire evening. The next morning he returned east—also eliminated. Meantime, it seemed that John Solomon did nothing but smoke his vile clay pipe and ride about in his big black car.

The newspapers heard of him, and he met the reporters with perfect aplomb. The only thing which seemed to interest him was the tuna-canning industry. He learned that no tuna was canned, albacore being cheaper, more plentiful, and quite as satisfying to the Eastern palate. He learned that there were one or two Japanese tuna-canning factories, one of which was located near San Pedro, but that no stock was allowed to be sold to white men, under California law.

The newspapers quoted him in flowing eulogies of the California climate, although in private John Solomon had said something else. Beyond this, they said very little, for they had learned very little. After that, the newspapers forgot him.

Suddenly, one morning, Solomon visited the Federal building and asked so many irrelevant questions about the Chinese and Japanese colonies that relieved sighs went up when he departed. But he obtained his information—under instructions from Washington.

That same afternoon, Solomon hired a bell boy from the hotel to serve as guide, and the twain sallied forth afoot. Solomon's chief interest seemed to be centered in the plaza, whither they bent their way.

He did not care to enter the ancient church of the Angels, but seemed to find vast satisfaction in the crowds of loafing Cholos, the Mexican and Italian signs and shops, and in the very atmosphere of the place itself.

"Young man, this 'ere ain't werry far from a foreign country!" he observed.

"That's right, mister," grinned the bell boy—all bell boys grinned when Solomon was in the offing. "See that dobe store yonder? Gen'ral Fremont lived there once."

"It seems to be a feed an' grain store now," said Solomon, peering across the plaza. "Young man, don't this 'ere town 'ave no reverence for suchlike things?"

"Not a darn bit," said the youngster cheerfully. "We ain't got time to waste on old shacks an' things. Why, only the other day they cut down an old tree out here, so's to make the street better, and a hull crowd o' Cholos an' oldtimers hung around an' shed tears. Huh! Can you beat it?"

Solomon puffed at his pipe, his blue eyes very blank.

"This 'ere is a queer world, young man, as the old gent said when 'e got took up for bigamy. Now, where I come from, them 'ere things would be kept all shipshape—"

"Where'd you come from, mister?"

"Egypt, young man. Egypt—and I ain't never goin' back no more."

"Gosh!"

Solomon heaved a wheezy sigh, while the bell boy stared at him in awe. Suddenly the pudgy little man pointed to a five-barred flag above a building opposite.

"What's them 'ere buildings across the plaza, young man?"

"Them? Oh, that's Chinatown! Want to see her? Ain't much to it—mostly faked up for tourists, but they got a fine joss house. Say, the chinks an' Japs have some scrap on right now, ain't they?"

"Oh, 'ave they?"

"You're darn right! Ever since the Japs jumped on China an' bluffed her cold, these here chinks are so darn sore on the Japs that they won't be seen talking to a Jap in the street. That's right, too. Them darned Japs ought to be run out o' the country, but you take a chink, now, and he's the squarest, straightest guy you ever seen."

"Werry interesting," murmured Solomon, fishing a coin from his pocket and tendering it to his guide. "Now, young man, if so be as you'll run back 'ome I'll sit an' rest a bit. I can find me way back all shipshape an' Bristol fashion."

"Thanks, mister!" The boy darted away with a salute.

For a moment Solomon stood motionless, looking around. Then, instead of sitting down, he walked across the plaza toward the Chinese quarter. He paused, meditatively slicing tobacco from his black plug into his horny palm.

"It's werry singular," he observed half audibly. "It is that! Them 'ere gov'ment men, they'd say as I was a plain fool. Mebbe I am, just like that! But it's better to be a fool along o' doin' summat than a fool along o' doin' nothing, as the old gent said when 'e kissed the 'ousekeeper. An' I'm blessed if Arabs an' Chinese ain't werry much alike, in spite o' bein' different."

Now, be it borne in mind that John Solomon knew the Orient from A to Zed, and never was misled by appearances—in the Orient. Consequently, when he left the busy streets of the American city behind him and entered the streets of Chinatown, he felt very much at home.

He had not the slightest idea of whom he was going to see, but he had a very definite idea of the kind of person he wished to see.

Ambling slowly along, he paid no attention to the ornate joss house, but peered with keen interest into the shop windows. The queer strings of dried oysters, dried fish, and dried fruits fascinated him. The odd bamboo and steel pipes, the dirty little shops, the strange Chinese tobacco, the crowds of glowering Celestials, the wicker workers, all drew his undisguised interest and admiration.

"It's werry strange," he observed anew, "'ow Providence works! It is that!"

With this remark, he came to a pause before a window full of curios. But he did not glance at the window. Across the street was a dark, dirty shop, with absolutely blank windows—as if they had been glazed and over-spread with dirt. Over the door was a faded gilt sign, bearing ideographs and the English words "Hip Sun, Importer."

Solomon knocked out his pipe and crossed the street. He pushed open the door of the dirty little shop and entered.

Solomon was, in vulgar parlance, following a blind lead. He had knocked about in most of the back alleys of hither Asia, and was quite at home in every hell hole from Port Said to Calcutta. Consequently he had—by birth and by experience—the invaluable quality of instinct. He was in totally strange surroundings, but he knew the soul of Asia.

He found facing him a blear-eyed, wrinkled old Chinaman of evil aspect, who sat writing with brush and ink at a long roll of red paper. Save for a narrow lane leading to the Chinaman, the place was stacked to the ceiling with chairs and other objects wrapped in matting—evidently articles of importation.

"How do," observed the old Chinaman impartially.

"Werry glad to meet you," nodded Solomon, blinking. He extended a small bit of pasteboard. "If you'll be so good as to take me card to Mr. 'Ip Sun, I'll thank'ee kindly."

The old Chinaman gravely donned a pair of horn spectacles, held Solomon's card upside down, and inspected it for a moment. Then he nodded in turn.

"Velly good. Wantee me?"

"I said as I was wanting of Mr. 'Ip Sun," repeated Solomon.

The other blinked, grinned, and finally frowned. He flung out his skinny yellow hands in an abrupt gesture.

"Me him! You no savvy? Me him!"

"Werry good, sir." Solomon turned, shut the door behind him—and shot the bolt. Then he pulled out one of the square objects wrapped in matting and sat down upon it.

The old Chinaman began to chatter in shrill rage. Solomon eyed him blankly, pulled forth his plug, knife, and pipe, and proceeded to make himself comfortable.

"Now, me friend," he said—and the old Celestial listened—"when so be as you're ready to get Mr. 'Ip Sun, why werry good! I've 'ad me lunch, and I ain't in no 'urry, none whatever. I 'ates to be a-scratchin' of matches with all this 'ere flimsy around, but 'ere goes."

To tell the honest truth. Solomon was taking long chances. He knew it, but the ancient Oriental did not know that he knew it. That round, blank face and those blue, wide-open eyes were Solomon's great stock in trade.

The old Chinaman chattered again, then grunted and continued his writing. Solomon puffed away placidly. Some one rattled the front door; Solomon shot back the bolt and opened it. A Chinaman entered, exchanged voluble chatter with the old chap at the desk, and went out again. Solomon went to the door, knocked out his pipe, and reseated himself. Then he calmly began to whittle more plug into his pipe.

At this, the old Celestial swept Solomon's card into his sleeve, dived toward the rear of the place, and vanished. A moment later he reappeared, holding open a door, and beckoned. Solomon sighed wheezily, rose, and followed through a narrow passage.

At the end of this passage was a large, well-lighted room fitted in American style with flat-topped desk and chairs. On the floor was a Ming rug which, ten blocks away, would have brought as many thousands of dollars. Seated at the desk was a rather small Chinaman, impeccably tailored, who rose and came forward with outstretched hand.

"Mr. Solomon, you honor me," he said, shaking hands. "I am sorry you were kept outside, but my servants are rather careful—"

"Werry 'appy to meet you, Mr. 'Ip Sun," said Solomon, seating himself.

"I never thought to see Mr. John Solomon in my humble office," and Hip Sun smiled. Only when he smiled could one tell that he was not a young man. "You see, I have been in the East, where I have heard that the name of Solomon is the keystone that covers truth."

Solomon started perceptibly. His blue eyes opened a trifle.

"Eh? You don't mean as 'ow—"

Hip Sun laughed heartily. "When I finished my course at Oxford, I spent many years in Cairo and Alexandria. The firm with whom I was connected had certain dealings with you, in the matter of a certain bronze statuette of the then empress, which you managed to recover for—"

"'Old on, 'old on!" broke out Solomon, mopping at his brow. "You was with the Leong Sing people?"

"I am now in the West for them," and Hip Sun smiled again. "But I also have a house of my own, as you see. Curious how things happen, eh?"

Solomon wheezed something inarticulate. It sounded like "Well, I'll be danged!"

Hip Sun seemed hugely to enjoy the pudgy little man's discomfiture, but he was too polite to take further advantage of it. Instead, he put Solomon at ease by casual questions anent California in general, and the United States as a whole, and sundry other topics to which Solomon wheezed out answers at random.

"At home—for I still call China home, though I see it only at long intervals," said Hip Sun, "things are in a bad way just now. The concessions forced from us by Japan are humiliating, and our people are storing up trouble for the Japs."

"That's what I come to see you about, sir," remarked Solomon. "To see if there was any truth in that 'ere boycott story."

Hip Sun smiled thinly. "It costs," he returned, "each Chinaman five dollars to be seen in company with a Jap, or to do business with a Jap. May I ask who directed you to me, sir?"

"No one," said Solomon blankly.

Hip Sun's eyes narrowed slightly. A mask seemed to drop over his face.

"Your pardon, Mr. Solomon, but it seems a trifle odd that you should have come so directly to me unless you had some reason for it—"

Solomon told the truth. He could do nothing else. At his conclusion, Mr. Hip Sun broke into a hearty laugh, tapped a bronze gong, and told the resulting attendant to bring tea. Then, turning, he administered to Solomon the worst shock of all.

"You have come to see me, I presume, about the murder of Mr. Case and the theft of his submarine drawings?"

Solomon sat quite motionless. His china-blue eyes opened a trifle wider.

"Yes," he said, in a choked voice. "But—but 'ow in 'ell did *you* know it?"

Hip Sun leaned forward, his ivory-carven features grave.

"Mr. Solomon, there has been hatred between Japs and Chinese for hundreds of years. You may know that much of the market gardening, fruit picking, and fishing up this west coast is done by Japs; they are active in business, in all walks of life—but so are we Chinese, we who, once every year, clean every debt off our books! And, Mr. Solomon, not the Japs, nor your former friends the Senussiyeh, nor any other race in the world, are so well organized as the Chinese."

Hip Sun paused. His servant shuffled forward with a tray and set it on a light wicker table between Solomon and the host. But Solomon hardly noticed the delicate thimble-cups, filled with tea whose bouquet was like an exquisite scent from a Moroccan perfume shop.

"We cannot fight the Japs openly, Mr. Solomon," said Hip Sun, a hint of sadness in his voice. "What we can do for Mother Asia, we do. For a long time we have known that the Japanese government has been after the submarine invented by Mr. Case. They tried vainly to buy his submarine engine—vainly, because Mr. Case had not give up hope that the United States would take it over. When, at the last moment, they had failed in everything else, they murdered him and stole the drawings."

"You 'ave proof o' this?" demanded Solomon. The other made a delicate shrug of negation.

"Not what a Western court would term proof. We do not know the details. We do not know exactly who is concerned. But—we know what has been done. If we could block the Japanese in this, we would do it gladly—at any cost."

Silence ensued. Solomon applied himself to his tea, refused the cigarette offered him, and abstractedly began to fill his pipe. He sighed wheezily.

"Mr. 'Ip Sun, them 'ere Japs ain't alone in this."

Something very like a gleam of rage lightened the Chinaman's face.

"No!" he snapped. "But—shall I tell you why we hate them—why men in my position hate the Japs in this country, and the white men associated with them? Because they make thousands, hundreds of thousands, a year by running opium into this country and selling it to my countrymen! What are these Jap colonies doing in Mexico? Bah!"

Solomon leaned forward, puffing earnestly at his pipe.

"Well, sir, let's you an' me 'ave an understanding. I ain't able to fight these 'ere Japs alone, and white men ain't a mortal bit o' good against 'em. If so be as I'm a-goin' to do anything. I'll 'ave to 'ave 'elp, just like that. Now, Mr. 'Ip Sun, if you'll be so good as to put me where I can 'ave plenty o' men to work with, men what'll do just as I tell 'em an no more, we'll bust them 'ere Japs wide open, just like that!"

Hip Sun, fingering his cigarette, eyed Solomon for a long moment. Then he smiled.

"My dear sir, if you were any one but John Solomon, and if I did not personally know a good deal of you, and how you were intrusted with the most delicate of missions in the old days, what you ask would be quite impossible. But, as it is—"

Turning, Hip Sun tapped his bronze gong.

The servant entered, and Hip Sun said a few rapid words in Chinese. Bowing, the servant withdrew. A moment later there entered another Celestial, clad in flowing silk robes, who bowed low to Hip Sun. Coming forward, he produced from his sleeve a lacquered box, which he handed to his master reverently.

Hip Sun took a key ring from his pocket and opened the box with a small key. From the box he took a ring and extended it to Solomon. It was a flat, oblong piece of soapy-gray jade, set in silver; on the face of the jade was cut a single ideograph, which had no meaning to Solomon.

"Keep that, Mr. Solomon," said Hip Sun, "and wear it constantly. As you leave my office my chief men and aids will see you and will know you hereafter. Any Chinaman you see will obey your orders at sight of that ring—no matter who he is. Every morning and evening one of my lieutenants will telephone you for orders."

"Thank you werry much, sir." Solomon slipped the ring on his pudgy finger and sighed in wheezy relief. "Prowidence is a werry strange thing—it is that!"

CHAPTER VII

FROM FRYING PAN TO FIRE

DESPITE HIS fears, Jack Brune did not even get his feet wet.

When the islet was a mile behind him, the wind died out. The sea went down into a long, sweeping ground swell, on which his impromptu raft floated a good inch high. At dawn the island was a scant five miles distant, and Brune sighted a launch to the south, in which direction he had drifted with the current.

At his frantic signals the launch headed for him, and ten minutes later he was aboard the *Ichi Hondo*, of San Pedro, fishing boat—her captain, crew, and engine-room squad consisting of two wiry little Japanese men, who grinned and chattered volubly.

Brune hauled his little packet of supplies aboard, chuckling over the contrast between his anticipations and the reality of that journey. He had suffered not a whit.

"Where you come from?" inquired the Japanese skipper, when Brune was standing beside him in the pilot house. The other slant-eyed man had disappeared below.

"Back yonder," and Brune pointed at the islet, half concealed by morning fog. "Is that San Nicolas?"

"No, Santa Ba'b'ra."

"Oh, Santa Barbara!" Brune knew nothing about the channel islands. "Where's San Nicolas?"

The smiling brown face darkened suddenly—a flash which spelled danger to the watchful Brune. But the skipper pointed to the southwest, where all was obscured by the morning fog.

"Twenty-fi' mile that-a way."

"All right, captain." Brune nodded, and felt in his pocket. His money was secure, and be pulled forth the roll of bills and passed it to the other. "Here's a symptom of my gratitude for rescuing me. You can earn that much more by heading back for Santa Barbara and picking up a couple of friends of mine there."

The little brown man pocketed the money and grinned.

"No go Santa Ba'b'ra."

"Eh?" Brune frowned, thinking that he had been misunderstood. "I said, captain, to run back to Santa Barbara and pick up two friends of mine—one is a lady. Understand?"

Brune, upon coming aboard, had decided instantly that the best plan would be to run back, pick up the Milnes, and land them in safety. Nothing would be gained by going ahead and leaving them to suffer.

"Get me?" he continued. "Pick up my friends—at Santa Barbara. Land us at San Pedro, and you'll be well paid."

The Japanese nodded. His narrow, jetlike eyes flitted over the waters ahead.

Brune stood at the man's shoulder, waiting. He saw by the compass that the *Ichi Hondo* was heading out to the westward of Santa Barbara, but he took for granted that the skipper was holding that course for some definite reason—to avoid some sunken reef or other such peril. Since the launch gave no sign of heading in to the island, he finally demanded an explanation.

"Say, captain, when are you going to get in to the island over there? I want to get right back to Pedro, and I'm in a hurry—"

The leathery, brown face turned suddenly to Brune. In that snarling grin, in those black slitted eyes, the American read a sudden vicious tensity—a deadly ferocity which smote him into a terrible realization of danger.

"You' name Brune?" snapped the skipper, and laughed again silently.

Thunderstruck, Brune stared. How did this brown man know his name—which he himself had not uttered?

His exultation died away swiftly. His exuberance over his rescue was dissipated like mist by that evilly smiling brown visage. Like many another man before him, Jack Brune found himself abruptly staggered, bewildered, before the mystery of the Oriental. The skipper's grinning insolence was like a slap in the face.

Suddenly there came to him the remembrance of what Rezek had said—something about "gentlemen from Japan." Could it be that he had stumbled upon two members of the conspiring group—

"Han's up, Mr. Brune! Quick, plees!"

At the soft voice, Brune turned. Standing just outside the door of the pilot house was the second Japanese, grinning and extending a wicked-looking automatic revolver at Brune.

The American promptly stuck up his hands, backing as he did so until he stood behind the skipper, who had remained at the wheel.

"What the devil do you chaps mean by this?" he demanded hotly.

There the brown skipper made a very bad mistake. He turned toward Brune with his evil grin, one hand resting on the wheel, and taunted his captive.

"You vary foolish man," he declared exultantly. "Mabbe you not know Nippon men, eh? You think all same, eh? Mabbe you not know Nippon gent'men like me are got vary good nose? Common men are got flat nose—"

The skipper's dissertation upon the subject of noses and ancestry, while perfectly correct and undeniably interesting, was brought to an abrupt conclusion.

Brune had realized at last that these seeming fishermen were in reality members of Rezek's mysterious conspiracy—and that they seemed to know exactly who he was and who was upon Santa Barbara Island.

While he considered that his chief debt was to Carlisle, Brune was quite willing to make payment to any one in general—and he was promptly in a furious rage. When angry, Jack Brune was a surprisingly agile young man.

With a very proper respect both for the automatic revolver and for the mysteries of jujutsu, Brune made one quick side-step that took him behind the skipper, bringing that individual in front of the revolver. At the same instant, Brune drove up his knee and sent the brown man hurtling through the starboard door, slap into the second Jap.

Before the latter could get free of the gasping skipper's clutch, Brune was upon them in one leap. The automatic spat fire, but the bullet went into the sky, for Brune's hand had closed on the man's revolver wrist.

As he wrenched the weapon away. Brune found the skipper at his throat, catlike, and a thrill of pain shot through him when the brown thumbs drove into his neck. But the skipper was a fraction of a second too slow. Desperate, Brune smashed the revolver into the brown, snarling face, and the skipper fell back with a groan. The second Jap was in the very act of leaping.

The American leaped back out of reach and leveled the automatic. The man from Nippon stood motionless, his brown features working in diabolic rage.

"Stand by the rail and put up your hands!" commanded Brune coldly. The man obeyed.

The skipper, dazed and bleeding from the impact of the heavy automatic, was dragging himself up. He poured forth a flood of Nipponese, which Brune halted abruptly.

"Cap'n, come up forward here and put your hands around this mast!" and Brune indicated the stumpy mast of the boat, up in the point of the bow. "You, engineer, take that coil of line off the life buoy there and tie the skipper's hands! Move lively, you yellow dogs!"

In no slight fear lest the two rush him, Brune threw down the revolver and sent a bullet smacking between the feet of the skipper, who came forward on the jump and put his hands around the mast as ordered. The scowling, cursing engineer tied

his captain's wrists, effectually anchoring the skipper in place.
Brune saw that the knots were securely tied.

Brune then sent the engineer to the port stay—a tautly
strung wire line that ran from masthead to rail. Here, wary and
extremely watchful against a kick or blow, he managed to tether
the engineer in the same fashion. With a deep breath of relief,
he stepped back and surveyed his two prisoners. A cheerful grin
overspread his features as he eyed them.

"Now, my friends, you can count noses all you damned please.
Don't forget that this gun still holds one or two bullets, and I'd
have no compunction whatever about puncturing your yellow
hides. Cuss all you want to, gents!"

Retiring into the wheelhouse, he spun the helm about and
pointed the *Ichi Hondo* for the fog-wreathed Santa Barbara.
The sun was now up, and Brune was able to make out the island
plainly enough, although Catalina was hidden from him. The
engines of the launch were kicking along steadily, and Brune
was surprised at her speed.

With the island dead ahead, he slipped a loop over a wheel
spoke and, confident that his captives were secure, set about
exploring the vessel. His search brought little to light. Forward
was a cabin, which produced nothing more suspicious than
an empty shotgun, and nothing at all in the way of papers or
documents.

The engines were of the usual gasoline type, and Brune
decided that he could handle the vessel very well by himself;
he was too wary to loose the Nippon engineer unless it should
prove absolutely necessary.

Returning to the helm he took a pair of binoculars from their
case on the wall and focused on the island. The southern end
consisted of cliff and rock scarp, but on the eastern side, where he
had himself been landed, he made out a slim blue figure standing on the shore. Undoubtedly Marge had discerned the launch;
Brune put away the glasses, with a little smile twisting his lips.

"What a girl—what a girl!" he muttered. "By George, she has

spirit! I wonder if her mother's dead—very probably is. Well, when I get my hands on Mr. Carlisle, I'm sure going to teach him to leave girls alone after this! I will say, however, that she didn't complain of any mistreatment—she's not the complaining kind. Not a whine out of her, and most girls would be in hysterics if they were in her boots!"

As the *Ichi Hondo* drew up toward the eastern side of the island, where a landing appeared possible, if not exactly easy, Brune stepped out and waved his arms. The blue-clad figure returned the greeting, and he knew that he was recognized.

"I wonder why that skipper was heading out to the southwest? He wasn't going after fish, that's sure—and the only land out that way would be another island. Well, no matter now. I'm going to have a job getting ashore without making a mess of things."

The launch came in a hundred yards from shore, and as there seemed to be no outlying rocks, Brune lashed the helm, ran below, and threw off the engines. He leaped back to the helm and allowed the craft to run in closer to the beach under her dying momentum. Margaret Milne was already waiting to receive him.

"What's happened?" she called. "Who are those men—"

"You get ready to catch a line," shouted Brune. "These two Japs are lashed to the mast, and you keep out of their way."

As he could find no coil of rope at hand, he caught up another life preserver with its attached line and stood ready. The launch was drifting to the swells, twenty feet from shore, and Brune tossed the belt to the girl, who picked it up.

"Draw in on the line—slowly! Pull us ahead to those rocks."

She nodded, and, with obvious effort, slowly managed to pull in the launch, close to a natural jetty of shore rocks. Brune feared at each moment that the craft would ground, but without mishap the launch drew alongside the rocks.

"Fine!" cried Brune, leaping ashore and shaking hands exultantly with the wondering girl. "Can we lift your father aboard, you and I? Can he be moved?"

"Why, yes—we can do it, I suppose—"

"All right, then! Hold on a moment till I get this line fast and make sure that my yellow beauties are safe—"

Once certain that the line was well secured. Brune approached his scowling captives and assured himself that they were in no danger of immediate escape. Then he rejoined the girl and set forth at once.

As they hurried over the rocks, now blazing hot under the morning sun, Brune gave a brief sketch of what had taken place.

"It's quite evident that your father was right," he concluded, "in thinking that this submarine affair was a Japanese plot. At the same time, there's one thing I can't reconcile with that theory."

"What is it?" she asked.

"The part taken by the Huggenheim movie concern, of which Rezek is a prominent member, and Carlisle, also, I expect. They've been located in Long Beach for nearly a year, evidently watching and waiting. When they finally secured the plans and destroyed the submarine, or stole it, why should they linger around this locality any further? Their work is done—why not turn over the loot to Japan and skip out?"

"The Japanese agents," suggested Marge, "may have interposed difficulties—you know, they seemed anxious for father's opinions of the drawings."

"Doesn't stand to reason." Brune lighted his pipe, frowning. "Unless they had gone pretty well into the matter, they wouldn't have wasted a year in making preparations. And besides, Rezek seems to have stolen the submarine—he could demonstrate with that. Well, I expect we'll solve the whole thing when we arrest the bunch. Hello, Captain Milne!"

The surprised naval engineer was quite able to be moved, it proved. While Marge made hasty explanations, Brune prepared a pair of blankets, into which Milne was then lifted; they raised and carried him without great difficulty, although it was not exactly a pleasant experience for the wounded man.

However, they gained the *Ichi Hondo* and got him aboard in safety, while the helpless skipper and engineer glared their hatred. Milne was placed on the forward deck, near the wheelhouse; when the launch had drifted a few feet from shore, Brune managed to start the engines and get headed away from the island without trouble.

"I'll depend on you for guidance. Captain Milne," he called, the girl standing at the helm beside him. "These Japs said that our island was not San Nicolas, but Santa Barbara. Which way shall I steer to hit San Pedro?"

"Due northeast ought to fetch Point Firmin," returned Milne promptly. "Catalina is southeast of us, if this is San Nicolas."

"Then, Miss Milne, if you'll take the wheel, I'll rustle up some breakfast," and Brune turned over the helm to her. "Have you had anything to eat this morning?"

"Yes—we had breakfast a half hour before I sighted you," she nodded. "Run along, and I'll manage to steer safely!"

Brune gave a last glance around the horizon. All was clear. To the southeast lay a bluish line on the horizon, which was presumably Catalina Island. There was no sign of a boat in sight.

Having previously observed a locker of provisions in the cabin. Brune dropped below. He lighted the tiny alcohol stove, set water boiling for a cup of tea, and opened a package of bread and smoked barracuda. Things were moving, he reflected, in a highly satisfactory manner.

The first shock of amazed unbelief had long since passed, leaving his brain clear and ready to grapple with whatever turned up. The seeming impossibility of finding himself drawn into what might prove an international tangle, the stunning incredibility of the whole thing, had been resolved into cold, hard fact.

"What a newspaper story it'd be!" he reflected, with a fleeting grin at the very thought. "Where I'm coming out on salary and expenses, I don't quite see—but I guess that can safely be left to Solomon. If I can pull into San Pedro with the information we have aboard, I should worry! In any case, I can always get my old Chicago job back."

He was just swallowing his tea, when a sudden cry from above, in the voice of Marge Milne, caused him to leap for the companionway:

"Mr. Brune! Mr. Brune!"

Up dashed Brune, his first thought being that the Japs had gotten free of their lashing. But upon reaching the deck, he saw that they occupied their former positions.

"Eh? What's the matter?" he exclaimed hastily, as he came to the wheelhouse.

"Look to our right—about a hundred yards behind us!" she cried, pointing to the water.

Brune frowned as he looked. The sea was slightly choppy, but there was no evidence of any boat in sight.

"By George!" the cry broke from him.

Breaking the surface of the water, he detected a round, saucer-capped object, which seemed to be approaching them fast. Even as he cried out, the object became a slender tube, and this in turn merged into a solid steel surface as the conning tower of a submarine emerged from the water.

"It's Case's boat!" Brune drew out his automatic, then dropped it with a groan of helplessness. "No use, girl—we're gone. They can go three knots to our one, and could ram us in a moment."

"What's that, sir?" exploded Captain Milne, writhing to one elbow. "You're not going to give up? Damme, sir, hand me that revolver—"

"If anything could be gained, Captain Milne, I would fight. But we can do nothing, and with Miss Milne aboard we must think first of her."

The hood of the conning tower opened, and the head of a man appeared, looking over a leveled rifle.

"Hands up. Mr. Brune!" cried a strangely piercing, whistling voice. "Loose those Japs, please, Miss Milne!"

"Do it!" groaned Brune, putting up his hands.

CHAPTER VIII

THE MASTER MIND

FROM THE furious ejaculations of Captain Milne, and from what he already knew, Brune realized that their captor was no other than the mysterious Jan Rezek himself.

The two craft lay side by side, the Japs flinging Rezek a line and drawing him alongside. He caught at the launch's rail and drew himself up to her deck. Inspecting the man, Brune wondered.

Undoubtedly Jan Rezek was something of a comedian—his very construction was at first glance comic. A squat, ugly body, excessively long arms, and a fat face which seemed mere rolls of flesh, contributed to this appearance, as did his small mouth and uptilted nose. But the eyes of the man betrayed him. Deep, glowing bronze they were, hard and richly yellow as the eyes of a bronze Buddha; grotesque, remarkable, striking.

"Your health, Miss Milne," and Rezek bowed to the girl, who was now standing at her father's side, watching him with fascinated eyes. He spoke English which was very slightly accented, with the precise intonation of a foreigner.

"Mr. Brune," and the fat man chuckled, bending those glowing yellow eyes on Brune, "kindly step over the side into my submarine."

Brune regarded him steadily, unswervingly.

"I shall do nothing of the sort, Mr. Rezek—if that's your name. I want to know what you propose to do with Miss Milne and her father."

The bronze eyes contracted a little. Rezek's chuckle was like a shrill whistle of devilish mirth.

"You are quite in a position to demand, eh? Well, I will ease your mind, sir. Since it appears not so hard as we thought to escape from Santa Barbara, Captain Milne and his daughter shall be taken to San Nicolas Island, where we will join them to-night. Meantime, I would advise you to accede to my commands, unless you wish to die very sharply. Over the side, at once! No harm shall come to this lady—you have my word upon it."

Brune sneered, but his sneer died away. This man was no mere moving-picture actor. Behind those bronze eyes, behind that odd whistling voice, was a consciousness of power which was not assumed, a keen smiting strength which bespoke character. Brune remembered that the two Japanese had said not a word since their release.

And, remembering what manner of man Carlisle had been, and that according to Milne this Rezek was the chief of the plotters, Brune swiftly realized that he was dealing with some one very much out of the ordinary. Then, while he still clinched with those lurid bronze eyes, he felt the girl's hand on his arm.

"Please go, Mr. Brune," she said quietly. "Please—"

Brune bowed and stepped to the rail. Rezek's chuckle followed him.

"Very wise of you, sir! Thank you, Miss Milne."

With an effort, Brune held himself in check and climbed over to the submarine. He was helpless in the grip of this fat man; he felt that his own strength was as nothing compared with the mental and physical force which this grotesquerie in human form seemed to exert.

Brune lowered himself down the steel ladder, and was in another world.

He had been over this trial boat time and time again, although he had made only one descent in her. She was little more than a miniature of the inventor's dream—able to accommodate five men at most—yet she embodied to the last detail the epochal features which Case had perfected. She had never received a name, by some odd chance or mischance.

As Brune stood at the foot of the ladder and glanced around, he realized as never before how the exclusive possession of this submarine by any one nation would effectually insure peace for years to come—or might insure a destructive war of conquest.

The craft was impervious to shell fire, since her periscope could be replaced as fast as shot away—even while she was submerged. She could dive at a few seconds' notice, the conning-tower hatch closing automatically. Only a battle cruiser could outstrip her in speed, or a destroyer; and at top speed, submerged, she could half circle the world. Amid half a dozen other such improvements, the greatest was her gasoline engine, the first whose automatic exhaust enabled it to run beneath the surface of the ocean. The dangers and the unreliability of the storage-battery type were eliminated.

Brune found a suave, frock-coated Japanese bowing to him.

"Will you follow me, please, Mr. Brune?"

He obeyed mechanically, and was ushered into the electrical-control room, where a tall, red-headed, broken-nosed man clad in overalls met them.

"Mr. Brune, this is my friend, Mr. Huggenheim," said the suave Oriental. "My own name, by the way, is Tokuhara."

The speaker's smile told that this last was a nom de guerre. But before the American recovered from the dose of politeness, Huggenheim beckoned and spoke in a harsh, nasal voice:

"Brune, you'll have to show me one or two things about the electrical control—"

"I certainly do admire the nerve of you crooks!" exclaimed Brune heatedly. "You can go to the devil, as far as I'm concerned."

Tokuhara smiled. In the electric light, Huggenheim's evil face contracted—then it changed swiftly. Brune caught a light step, and turned to face Rezek.

"Sit down, gentlemen, sit down!" and the fat man grimaced.

"There is no hurry, none whatever, because no mistake must be made. Huggenheim, for your own sake I must caution you to make no mistakes."

The words were easily spoken, but there was in them something that bit; something that caused Brune to shiver slightly. The acute deliberation, the terrible catlike poise, the blazing bronze eyes of this fat horror—ugh! Yet he sensed the man's power also.

"Sit down, Mr. Brune!"

Brune took the camp stool indicated, and all four settled down as if they were not seated in a compartment of a submarine that was half awash, open to the sky above, apt to be sunk by any chance wave.

Whoever and whatever the fat man was, it was clear that Huggenheim was an American—a tall, wiry, powerful man of much the same type as Carlisle. But Rezek was in command; and a terrible man was Jan Rezek, as Brune was later to learn.

"Now we will talk." The bronze eyes, like those of a sleepy cat, wandered from face to face, dwelling at last upon Brune, who met the gaze steadily. "Let us have an understanding, Mr. Brune. We know you very intimately, and we propose that you should also know us. I want to know just how much of our little scheme you are aware of."

"Your little scheme? I wish I knew more of it," smiled Brune scornfully.

"Do not deceive us, please. There is no necessity for it—speak freely, by all means! We know that you have been arrested and freed again, and I think you have formed various ideas about us—especially since meeting Captain Milne. But have no fear—no matter how dangerous you are, you will not be dangerous to us in the future. I pride myself on being a neat workman, Mr. Brune, and—well, I promise that no harm shall come to you if all goes well."

"What do you mean by all that?" demanded Brune, puzzled by the man's cryptic words.

"Ah! I mean that I wish to know exactly what you know, then I shall put a proposition before you. We must make no mistakes—we must work together, you and I, for I do not wish to kill you if it can be avoided."

Brune held himself impassive.

"Who are you—all of you?" he inquired curtly.

"I am—well, I am Jan Rezek, a motion-picture actor." Rezek's small mouth was smiling, fishlike. "Mr. Huggenheim is a mechanical genius, who falls a trifle short on the complicated electrical problem of this craft. Mr. Tokuhara is one of several gentlemen investigating my submarine on behalf of, let us say, the Peruvian empire," and Rezek chuckled, while the Japanese smiled blandly.

Brune settled himself more comfortably on his stool, thinking swiftly. It would be dangerous to tell this man what he knew and guessed—yet why not? It might be infinitely worse to let the conspirators know anything about John Solomon. It would be best, he decided, to play the game as it was set before him—taking upon his own shoulders the burden of knowledge and theory, and protecting Solomon by silence.

He was not deceived. He knew that Tokuhara was a snake, ready at any instant to strike; he knew that Huggenheim disliked him and was inclined to brutality; he knew that Rezek, beneath the smile and the chuckle and the bronze-flaming eyes, concealed the sharpest, most ruthless claws of them all. He knew that the more information he gave and took, the more precarious was his ground; and he put no faith in promises. But he must protect John Solomon—he must keep them in ignorance that the little cockney was at work, somewhere, as Brune hoped against hope was the case.

"You're a fine little bunch of crooks," he smiled cheerfully. "Conceded! Well?"

"Just what do you know about our—ah—endeavors?" Rezek cocked his fat head on one side, the yellow eyes narrowing to thin slits.

"I can make a pretty straight guess at a few things," returned Brune lightly.

"Make it."

"Well, you've had your eye on this submarine for some time—I've been looking up your record, you see! The Huggenheim Motion Picture Company was brought into being for that purpose, I imagine. Then, your precious scoundrel Carlisle murdered Case."

The shot told. A snarling oath broke from Huggenheim.

"How do you know that?" queried Rezek, his whistling voice very soft.

"I don't—I merely guess at it," and Brune laughed complacently. "You stole this model submarine, and the drawings as well. You kidnaped Captain Milne and his daughter—a dirty piece of work, and to my notion rather useless. Now you're trying to sell your loot to Japan, but you seem to be doing it in a very bungling fashion."

Huggenheim broke in with a sudden outburst of profanity:

"—it, that's my say, too! Rezek, what in hell are you fooling around for? Let these blamed Japs take it or leave it, and we can skip. What the hell do we want to go after more money for, when we can get enough out of the drawings—"

Rezek looked at his partner. Under the ominous, perfectly poised flare of those bronze eyes, Huggenheim fell into sullen, frightened silence; his evil face flushed and then paled.

"I think," observed Rezek slowly, "that I would like to hear how we have bungled, Mr. Brune. Perhaps you will enlighten me?"

"With pleasure. You should have gotten rid of the stuff and skipped out. Instead of that, you're hanging around this vicinity day after day, and when Uncle Sam drops on you—"

"Uncle Sam—pouf!" Rezek snapped his fat fingers. "He is in his dotage, my dear Brune. I gather from your late outburst, Huggenheim, that you do not care to stay for the ultimate game?"

"Oh, I'm staying!" growled the broken-nosed one. Rezek chuckled.

"I thought so! Well, Mr. Brune, you are quite off the track—quite! As a matter of fact, we do not propose to sell this submarine to any one, having need of it ourselves; for motion-picture purposes, let us say. We are selling the drawings, however, and our visitors are making quite certain that this working model proves all details of the plans to be absolutely perfect. Now do you understand more clearly?"

Brune nodded.

The problem was being rapidly simplified. Setting aside the fact that the submarine itself was being retained by Rezek for ulterior purposes, Brune saw that the wary Japanese were making quite certain that they were getting full value before they paid over any money. Rezek, having failed in the endeavor to get Milne's O.K. on the plans, had put Milne out of the way for two weeks, by which time the gentlemen from Nippon would in all probability be thoroughly satisfied that the submarine and the drawings correspond in every detail.

"Yes, I begin to comprehend," said Brune slowly. "But why, if I may inquire, did you not hold up the United States for a good round sum, instead of dragging in our friend, Mr. Tokuhara, as he calls himself?"

"For the best of reasons," chuckled Rezek. "First, because your pork-barrel diplomats could not spare us enough money to compensate us. Secondly, because Mr. Tokuhara and his friends have been interested in the project for a long time past. Thirdly, because in the future we expect to make a good deal more money with the aid of Mr. Tokuhara's friends than we will get out of the plans alone. Excellent reasons, all!"

"I presume so," and Brune smiled genially. "To come to the point, why am I here?"

Rezek glanced at Huggenheim, who leaned forward and spoke:

"Brune, you're no fool—we know that. Now it's up to you to

be a sport! We've got the boat, and we've got the drawings. The scheme will go through with or without you, but you might as well salt away ten thousand easy money. You can do this by showing me some of the electrical kinks aboard here. Case didn't have his drawings as far along as we thought he had—in fact, he had just begun on the electric apparatus. I'm no electrician, and we daren't bring one into the game, see? But you're on the inside, and in half an hour you can put me wise to what I want to know—I've busted two or three jiggers now, fooling along by myself. Inside of a week we set you free with ten thousand bucks. You're not doing any harm by helping us out, not a mite, and you're doing yourself a lot of good."

Brune's hazel eyes hardened as he listened.

"Well," he replied, "I suppose I'm in your power, eh?"

"Sure!" nodded Huggenheim. "You can't help yourself, see?"

"I see," and Brune smiled. "I can only say one thing, Huggenheim."

"Then you'll do it?"

"Oh, pardon me! I can only say one thing—and it's this. You're a dirty, low-down dog," and Brune still smiled sweetly. "You're so dirty I could get big damages for personal contact with you! Why, you damned cur, do you think I'm in *your* class? Not much!"

Huggenheim, his ugly face suffused with rage, half started from his chair. But a single low, tense word from Rezek sent him back again:

"*Careful!*"

To the surprise of Brune, he found the fat man gazing at him in unassumed mirth. Tokuhara was also smiling.

"Mr. Brune, you confirm me excellently in my judgment of you!" said Rezek. "I told Huggenheim that he was a fool to think you could be bribed. Still, it is now my turn to set forth a proposal."

At the fishy smile and the half-hidden, complacent yellow eyes. Brune felt a chill run up his spine.

"As you have just said, you are absolutely in our power. Now, there are several things which we wish to know about this wonderful undersea boat, owing to the failure of Mr. Case to incorporate them in his plans, before his unfortunate demise. We could learn these by taking this model to pieces, but we are extremely anxious to preserve this boat in every detail—for our own use.

"I want you to explain these electrical details to us. I do not offer you a bribe, Mr. Brune, for I am no fool. However, you must realize that human life means very little either to me or to Mr. Carlisle. Give us the information which we desire, and you will not be betraying your country in any sense. Give it, and we will answer for the safety and ultimate freedom of you and our other two prisoners.

"But," and Rezek leaned forward, his bronze eyes narrowed, "refuse to do this, and you shall die within two minutes; also, Captain Milne and Miss Milne shall suffer the same fate, this same day. With the three of you out of my way, I shall go ahead. Yes or no, Mr. Brune—I have little time to waste."

In the man's fat, inhuman face, in those devilish eyes, Brune read an inflexible purpose, a calm poise that was far more terrible than any mere anger. The very coldness of the man bespoke his purpose, and was more to be feared than the brutal hatred of Huggenheim or the crafty, cynical smile of Tokuhara.

Yet Brune hesitated. Not his own fate, nor that of the Milnes, threatened his decision; his only query was whether or not the imparting of such information would be traitorous and dastardly. He decided that it would not. Were he to live, he might accomplish something against these men, and he could tell them nothing that they could not find out for themselves ultimately.

"Yes," he nodded, white-faced. "Yes. I accept your offer."

"Very well." Rezek leaned back. "In proof, kindly describe to us the workings of this engine."

Desperately, Brune strove to recall what he knew of Case's invention; he must make no slip now!

"It is a six-cycle, three-phase engine, absolutely silent," he said slowly. "There are three charges of gas in each cylinder at once, and six strokes complete the action on any one charge."

Rezek nodded. "Go on. Any fool could see that."

"On the fourth stroke, as I remember it, the burned gases are discharged into a space containing a partial vacuum, and this vacuum cleans the burned gas from the working cylinder. The fifth stroke utilizes all the heat in this exhaust, which in other engines is a pure loss of efficiency; it is like the intake stroke of a vacuum pump, producing the partial vacuum and passing on the heat of the exhaust, while the last stroke sends out the burned gas, or exhaust. This exhaust is absolutely cold. The engine has only one sleeve valve, free from all heat, while the Knight motor, for instance, has two; yet this one valve is mechanically more efficient. In other words, the engine does not require an eccentric shaft; it accomplishes double the result of any other engine with less than half the moving parts; the sound of the exhaust is eliminated, while the exhaust heat is put to use; and the highest possible mean effective pressure is obtained—"

"That is quite enough," and Rezek came to his feet. "As you know, this boat utilizes electricity for cooking, lighting, heating, replacing the periscope and ventilator if shot away, and operating the motors for handling torpedoes. Further, they can operate the boat itself in case the gasoline gives out. Well, Huggenheim has not been able to connect these motors, and from what we can see, Mr. Case must have purposely left the electric units out of order. We can make the electric lights work, but nothing else."

"Any boy mechanic should be able to do the work," said Brune, frowning.

"I can get no power at all, and I can't find the batteries!" explained Huggenheim. "Where the devil are the batteries?"

Brune's frown leaped into a quick grin of comprehension.

"Oh, I see! Case had done away with the chlorine-gas danger by putting most of the batteries into a waterproof box, not an integral part of the hull. Didn't you find it?"

The conspirators exchanged glances of chagrin.

"I found the cursed box and hove it overboard," growled Huggenheim. "It was empty."

"Quite possibly," laughed Brune. "All you need to do is to get some batteries and connect them up! I'm afraid you're a mechanical genius with reverse English, Huggenheim. If you don't mind, Rezek, I'm going to have a good, long sleep. I think I've earned it."

And Rezek only nodded, in helpless amazement.

CHAPTER IX

INSULT AND INJURY

THE ISLAND of San Nicolas is a desolate spot, the most remote and sterile of the channel islands.

Brune's first glimpse of the place was toward sunset, when the submarine reached in for the low, sandy point at the south end of the island. Eight miles long and a trifle over three in width, the island rose six hundred feet in height, with bold, precipitous sides. The flat top fell away toward the southern end, the sandstone cliffs becoming a low beach where the surf cut in at an acute angle.

Off this beach, the best anchorage afforded by the island, the *Ichi Hondo* lay at anchor, and beside her were two other large launches. As the submarine came in, on the surface, Brune saw that one of the other craft possessed a wireless. Up on the shore, where the crumbling plateau broke down to the low point, were half a dozen brown, almost invisible, tents.

"Do you see that?"

Rezek, standing beside Brune on the superstructure, pointed off to the westward. There, etched in blackness against the sunset, Brune saw the clearcut outlines of a sailing ship, a large brig; she was about three miles off.

"That," and Rezek chuckled, "is the old whaler *Narwhale*, which has the Huggenheim Motion Picture Company aboard— they've been making some first-class sea pictures. Before the *Narwhale* gets in here, my submarine will be gone for the night. Really, Mr. Brune, we are making some very fine moving pictures! I myself have attained some reputation as a comedian."

"Then your picture actors are quite innocent in the submarine affair?" queried Brune.

"Of course. Huggenheim, I, and our friend Carlisle are the only interested parties, and we have plenty of Nipponese to aid us. By the way, all our Japanese friends are taking part in the present film, so that Huggenheim and I are making money both ways. Very neat, eh? We stand to lose nothing at all, you see."

Brune merely nodded. He felt very much afraid of Jan Rezek; the man invariably reminded him of a huge cat, and he knew very well that he himself was the mouse, with no more chance than a mouse's of escape. For he had not given up the fight, by any means.

Ahead of him, Brune saw just one thing—self sacrifice. He knew perfectly well that, with Japan in exclusive possession of the Case submarine, the United States would be the first nation to suffer, and to suffer terrible losses. Therefore, Brune had assented to the demand of Rezek; not to save his own life, but to lose it.

Sooner or later his chance would come. He could have sunk the submarine that same afternoon, and himself with her, but the drawings would remain in Japanese hands. He must get the plans—either destroy them, or place them in hiding. After that, he could destroy the submarine. There was nothing melodramatic about it, to his mind; nothing heroic or noble. It was simply the only thing that he could do to save his country. Since he could by no possibility win, he must see that Rezek did not win. That was all.

Huggenheim remaining aboard the submarine, Brune, Rezek, and Mr. Tokuhara went ashore in a whaleboat rowed by two Japanese. The submarine sank out of sight.

Brune had wondered how these amazing conspirators would manage to keep him and the Milnes out of contact with the movie actors, who knew nothing of the intrigue behind their picnic party on San Nicolas. Did the actors learn what was going forward, trouble might ensue for Rezek.

This had been well guarded against, however, for instead of going to the tents in view, Brune found himself marched toward the western side of the island. Here, under a crag of sandstone and well sheltered from sight, he found a second camp, in charge of the poisoner, Carlisle, who advanced to meet them with a leering grin at sight of Brune. The figure of Margaret Milne showed at the door of a tent for a moment, and she waved her hand, then vanished. The rapid southern darkness was falling.

By the light of gasoline flares, small brown men were bustling about, and two frock-coated Japanese came forth to meet Mr. Tokuhara. The party went direct to the mess tent, where the brown men were already setting forth dinner about the long table. Brune was introduced to the other two Japanese, but did not get their names; it was clear, however, that Tokuhara was their leader, and that all were prominent men traveling under false names.

Rezek sat at the head of the board, around which were gathered the three Japanese, Carlisle, and Brune. Margaret Milne joined them a few moments later, being greeted with respectful courtesy by all the men. She shook hands with Brune, exchanged a silent look, and took her seat at the right of Rezek, beside Brune. Half an hour afterward entered Mr. Huggenheim, clad now in gorgeous raiment and flashing with jewelry. Where he had left the submarine did not appear.

As the meal progressed, Jack Brune became more and more amazed; it was as if he sat in a circle of friends. Rezek asked after the health of Captain Milne, assuring the girl that her father should have every comfort, and a physician, if necessary. Beyond this, no reference was made to the matter in hand; but the table talk, which courteously included Brune and Miss Milne, was of a very surprising nature.

Except for the broken-nosed, flashy Huggenheim, who ate and glowered around in sullen ill humor, the conspirators showed themselves men of no mean education and knowledge. Rezek engaged in argument with Mr. Tokuhara regarding the *bushido* or knightly code of old Nippon, and not only cornered the visitor, but utterly routed him. Carlisle, suavely Mephistophelian as ever, held Margaret Milne in frank interest with a dissertation on fraudulent Sheffield silver. He, too, knew his subject through and through.

After a space, Huggenheim rose and left the tent, growling to himself. With his departure, the slight constraint of the others vanished, and Brune had rarely spent a more enjoyable hour than this. Not only the Japanese, but Rezek and Carlisle proved to be polished, cosmopolitan, studious men of affairs.

When at length Miss Milne rose. Brune accompanied her outside, and to her own tent. They stood together in silence for a moment.

"I am sorry," said the girl softly. "We so nearly succeeded!"

"It's all right," returned Brune, under his breath. "If I manage to block their game as I hope to do, and if I don't come out alive, please go to a man named John Solomon, at the *Angelus,* Los Angeles, and tell him all that's happened. He's handling this for the government. Will you do so?"

"Yes. But what—"

"You've met with good treatment to-day, I hope?"

"Yes," she nodded. In the starlight, he saw that her face was troubled. "But there's one man—Huggenheim—whose look frightens me—I can't help it! Did you see how he stared during dinner?"

"I didn't, but I'll take notice," said Brune. He paused and turned at sound of a soft footfall on the sand behind, and saw Carlisle coming toward them.

"I beg your pardon," said the poisoner, with the same curious indirectness of speech which he had formerly used toward Brune. "If Mr. Brune is ready to retire, I am to share my tent with him."

"All right!" snapped Brune, and turned to the girl. "Good night, Miss Milne! God take care of you."

"And you," she breathed, her fingers resting for a moment in his before she vanished in her tent.

Brune followed Carlisle to a near-by tent, where the poisoner lighted a candle and displayed two cots.

"Mr. Brune may take his choice, and I trust that he will sleep better than when we last met—"

"See here, Carlisle," and Brune turned on the man, a tug of hatred at his heart. "I don't want any more words with you. If there's one thing you can do to avoid trouble, it's to keep your mouth shut around me, understand?"

The other gazed at him, a sardonic smile lighting the lean, swarthy features. Then Carlisle nodded and calmly began to undress. No more was said.

As he fell asleep, Brune was still thinking of Margaret Milne's words concerning Huggenheim. The broken-nosed mechanician, who was the head of the film concern, was in Brune's opinion the weak link in the triangle of conspiracy, in that he lacked the smooth poise of the other two. Neither was he in complete accord with, although afraid of, Rezek, as Brune had that morning noted, aboard the submarine.

"If he does try any funny business with—with Marge," thought the American, "I'm very much afraid that he'll feel something drop mighty hard. The flashy bum! I'd just as soon take out some of my debt on his hide as on Carlisle's."

He slept lightly, and wakened with the sunrise. As he lay with his eyes closed, the sound of voices pierced to him, and he looked up to see Carlisle standing at the flap of the tent, talking with some one outside. The soft, whistling tones of Rezek drifted in:

"No, I'm going to take the submarine out myself to-day—I have the hang of her pretty well, and Huggenheim must stay here to get his scenario into shape and keep those actors busied. He's going to make arrangements with Tokuhara, also, about the ultimate game. I want you to go with—"

"Why carry on the farce further?" broke in Carlisle. "We could dispense with these actors and let the company drop, as we must do in another week or so."

"Ah, but this is not next week, my excellent Carlisle!" purred Rezek. "If a cruiser came nosing around here, or any party of tourists, we would need our mask very badly. No, come with me, and we'll take the other two Japs, leaving Tokuhara here with Huggenheim. Our actors are already putting out to sea with the *Narwhale*. We will make a final examination of the drawings to-night and endeavor to get an answer from Mr. Tokuhara. If he remains obdurate, you had better use a little conine to shake him out of his scheming deviltry."

"Begin pressing the screws, eh?" and Carlisle laughed in his silky, diabolic way. "Oh, he'll come across with the money, all right! Run along—I'll join you in a moment."

Brune closed his eyes as the poisoner reentered the tent and dressed.

What was the "ultimate game" to which Rezek had referred, both now and on the day previous—the "ultimate game" for which he was retaining the stolen submarine himself? This was mysterious enough to Brune, but he saw nothing mysterious in the final words of Rezek and Carlisle, master minds of evil if ever such mastery existed!

Beyond a doubt the conspirators were growing exasperated by the delay—as Huggenheim had plainly shown during the talk aboard the submarine. Tokuhara, wary and subtle, was perhaps preparing a double cross on his own account; it was the Japanese way, reflected Brune, to let some one else pull the chestnuts from the fire. Rezek, who must be quite aware of the danger, was now putting Carlisle to work on the Nipponese; and, Tokuhara was undoubtedly a man of such position as to insure the payment of the money involved, or else to hold it up.

"That's the play, all right," and Brune chuckled as he rose, Carlisle having departed. "Rezek suspects that the Japs are double-crossing him, which is quite possible, and he's going to put some of that devilish conine into Tokuhara. Hm! From what I learned of Mr. Carlisle's methods, the hint will produce the money in a hurry! Tokuhara will cough up and take his drawings home, and Rezek will go on with—with what? What the deuce is that 'ultimate game,' anyway? Surely, the man will have to drop out of sight! He can't go on making films unless he murders me and the Milnes!"

When Brune issued forth, he found one of the Japanese fishermen ready with breakfast, no one else being in sight. Having breakfasted, Brune strolled to the camp of the moving-picture people, where he found Huggenheim working at a typewriter, but he did not address the broken-nosed man.

The submarine had vanished, the *Ichi Hondo* and her two consorts lying at anchor. Off to the east Brune made out the *Narwhale* standing over under a stiff breeze. Since there were only brown men in sight. Brune returned to his own camp, to find Margaret Milne and Mr. Tokuhara breakfasting together with much laughter and jollity. Indeed, so openly did Tokuhara admire the girl, yet with such refinement and courtesy in his words and actions, that Brune felt confirmed in his estimate of the man as one of high rank.

The morning passed without incident, Brune sitting with Captain Milne for an hour, and taking a stroll along the shore with Margaret. He told them what he had learned of the whole conspiracy, and related Solomon's activities in the case, but said nothing as to his own intentions. Neither Milne nor the girl could throw any light on the nature of the "ultimate game."

Toward noon Huggenheim returned and strolled down the beach with Tokuhara. At mess call they came back, Huggenheim evidently in an ugly mood, although the gentleman from Japan seemed quite cheerful and urbane.

The four lunched together. Brune, watching Huggenheim, saw that the man was covertly eying Margaret Milne.

The ex-journalist knew that Huggenheim bore him no love for his words of the previous morning aboard the submarine, and he determined to bring matters to a crisis before Rezek returned, largely for the sake of his own cause. If he could discredit Huggenheim in Rezek's eyes, or cause a breach between the two, so much the better. He was saved the trouble, however.

Finishing her luncheon, the girl went to her father's tent, then walked down to the beach to wash out a handkerchief. Huggenheim left the mess tent, and Brune promptly followed. Without looking back, Huggenheim strode directly down to the shore and stopped to speak with Miss Milne.

Brune, his hazel eyes watching closely, strolled toward them. He had nearly reached the two when he saw Huggenheim put out a hand to the girl's wrist; she pulled away, flashing Brune a startled, appealing look.

"That's plenty from you, my friend," said Brune evenly, striding up, unheard, on the soft sand and swinging Huggenheim around by the shoulder. "Beat it!"

With a scowling snarl of fury, Huggenheim struck—so swiftly that the blow took Brune squarely under the ear, staggering him for the moment. Huggenheim was in on the instant with a storm of hard, snappy jolts, thinking to finish Brune on the spot.

Therein he was deceived. Brune side-stepped the rush, contented himself with covering up until he had recovered from that first lightning jolt, and then waded into his opponent with savage joy. It was his first opportunity to repay something of what he had gone through, and since from the corner of his eye he saw Tokuhara summoning the brown fishermen, he lost no time.

In vain did Huggenheim attempt to guard; Brune's quickness and weight far overmatched him, and he went staggering under blow after blow. Brune planted each drive with methodical force, fighting not to sting, but to hurt, and he alternated between smashing jolts to the heart and heavy right swings to the jaw.

The result, as the sporting writers say, was never in doubt. Brune's last blow was a straight left to the heart, sent home with all his weight behind it. He saw Huggenheim go reeling and staggering away, utterly done up, and was leaping after for the knock-out when Tokuhara's little brown men swarmed over him.

Caught by two of them in jujutsu holds that wrenched him with agony, Brune gave in at once and allowed himself to be bound firmly. Huggenheim, gasping, staggered up, and, with a vicious curse, drew back his fist. It was caught and held by Tokuhara, who faced the broken-nosed one with his usual urbane smile.

"My dear Mr. Huggenheim," he said sweetly, "let me point out to you that if you again molest this young lady, or obtrude yourself in any fashion upon my notice, Mr. Rezek will miss a very good mechanic."

Lending point to this remark, the two Japanese nearest Huggenheim grinned and displayed revolvers. With a single sullen curse, the man turned and strode away. Tokuhara bowed to Margaret Milne.

"Pray excuse this man's insolence. Miss Milne. I must keep Mr. Brune in safety until the return of Mr. Rezek, but I assure you that neither you nor he may expect further molestation."

"Good for you, Tokuhara!" exclaimed Brune, and chuckled. "For that, I'll give you a tip. Watch out for Carlisle to-night! He may try to slip something over on you."

Tokuhara's jet eyes searched him gravely. Then the other smiled.

"Thank you, sir. I regret that I must keep you bound."

"Then give me my pipe and tobacco," smiled Brune.

Ten minutes later he sat in his tent, his wrists bound, but his pipe between his teeth, while a rifle-armed fisherman stood sentry at the door.

The hours passed slowly and painfully. Despite his aching arms, Brune managed to stretch out and sleep during the heat of the day. No one came near him until nearly dark, when a Japanese entered with a tray of food and painstakingly fed him. Had it not been for the pain of his wrists, Brune would have found good store of humor in this careful guardianship.

He heard the voices of Huggenheim, Rezek, and Tokuhara from the mess tent, then silence ensued. Brune was just begging his guard to fill up his pipe and light it, when the Japanese was abruptly ordered back, and Rezek entered the tent with Carlisle, the latter striking a match.

"How long do you propose to leave me here tied up?" demanded Brune.

"Oh, I'd forgotten you!" chuckled Rezek, pulling out a knife and stooping. The next moment, Brune was free. "You stay here under guard, however. I would advise you not to try to leave until dawn. Mr. Carlisle and I are going to make a little expedition to-night, eh?"

Carlisle, having lighted the candle, bent over his own cot and got out the same flat case which brought back such unkindly memories to Jack Brune.

"Yes," he muttered. "Do you want it strong?"

"Pretty stiff," nodded Rezek. Brune knew that Carlisle was preparing the conine for Tokuhara, under the very eyes of the fisherman guard.

"If it's too stiff," rejoined the poisoner, "I'll have to keep things moving with strychnine and whisky."

"All right, make it the limit," and Rezek chuckled. "We'll take him with us on the boat, and you can make it interesting for him, eh? Now, Mr. Brune, your guard will have orders from Mr. Tokuhara to shoot if you try to leave. I'd advise you to stay quiet."

Carlisle blew out the candle, and the two departed. The Japanese guard settled into place just outside the flap of the tent, which remained open.

Brune smiled grimly. It mattered little to him whether or not Tokuhara heeded his warning, for his game had been to sow dissension in the ranks. If Carlisle succeeded in his devilish work, and Tokuhara was taken aboard one of the boats or the submarine on the trip mentioned by Rezek, the Nipponese might listen to proposals of revenge within a day or so. If Carlisle failed, open war might result.

An hour passed, and no outcry broke the deepening silence of the night. Brune kicked off his shoes, lighted his pipe: and stretched out on his cot, listening. He could hear nothing, however. Apparently the camp had settled down for the night.

At length he made up his mind that Tokuhara had been gathered in. After all, the man was no more than man: he would have to be a devil to escape the infernal cunning of that poison fiend, thought Brune. It was not hard to picture what had happened: Rezek, with his gorillalike arms, holding Tokuhara helpless while Carlisle inserted the needle and leered—

From before the tent came a slight scuffling sound, as though the guard had wearied of one position and had arisen to his feet. All was silent again. Brune was just finishing his pipe, and had determined to roll in for the night, when he suddenly sat up on the cot, listening.

A quiet, wheezy voice was sounding from just outside the tent flap, a voice that left him utterly astounded:

"If so be as you'll come outside, Mr. Brune, I'll 'ave some werry interestin' fireworks to show you, just like that, sir!"

Brune started up, gasping with incoherent amazement. John Solomon, of all men!

CHAPTER X

SOLOMON STRIKES

"**D**ON'T MAKE no noise, sir—just take it easy, as the old gent said when 'e kissed the curate's wife by mistake."

Solomon's hand caught Brune's arm, pressing the latter down to the sand at the door of the tent. A motionless, huddled figure lay six feet away, and Brune took it for that of his guard. The night was foggy and cold.

"By George!" he whispered. "Where did you spring from, John? How on earth—"

"Let's 'ave a light, sir, then we can talk a bit."

Brune passed over a match, and the little man lighted his pipe.

"But, man," broke out the ex-journalist suddenly, "do you know that there are two camps here—that Rezek has a bunch of Jap fishermen—"

"You set werry tight, sir."

Solomon puffed wheezily at his clay pipe, and finally sighed.

"Mr. Brune, I've 'ad a mortal lot o' work lately, just like that! What's more, I ain't got time for talk, 'cause why, them 'ere men o' mine are a-waitin' for me signal. Yes, sir, I knows all about this 'ere place, an' about Miss Milne, an' about other things. But what I'm a-wantin' to know, sir, is just this: where's that danged submarine?"

"I don't know," responded Brune, in helpless wonder. "It must be somewhere near at hand, though. Have you some secret-service men here, then?"

"I 'ave, and I ain't," and the other chuckled again. "That was a werry pretty go you 'ad wi' that 'ere 'Uggenheim this morning."

Brune swallowed hard, staring at the pudgy little figure beside him. Solomon spoke as an eyewitness of the encounter—a thing which seemed absurd and incredible.

"Loosen up!" demanded Brune curtly, and a bit angrily. Solomon chuckled.

"Well, sir, we found at Long Beach as 'ow the 'ole bloomin' picture company was off somewheres makin' pictures, wi' the *Narwhale*. There's one or two colonies o' Chinese fishermen, an' they was good enough to tip me off—"

"Chinese?" interjected Brune. "Are your men here Chinese, too?"

"Yes, sir, and werry fine men they are, sir. As I was sayin', we guessed as 'ow San Nicolas was a werry interestin' spot, so last night we landed an' lay 'id up on the cliffs yonder, and to-night 'ere we be, just like that!"

"What's the idea?" queried the puzzled Brune. "Are you going to drop on the whole bunch and wipe 'em out?"

This, it appeared, was precisely Solomon's intention. The *Narwhale* had been observed from afar by some Chinese fishermen, and from her course it was conjectured that she was heading for San Nicolas. So, with a party of Chinese followers, Solomon had landed at the north end of San Nicolas during the preceding night and had remained hidden on the plateau in order to get a line on the situation.

Helplessly bewildered as he was by Solomon's appearing on the scene with Chinese at his back instead of secret-service men, Brune was compelled to admiration of the way in which the pudgy little man had guessed straight to the mark time and again, and had backed up his guesses without hesitation. But now Solomon briefly informed him that there was no further time to talk, and demanded information as to Rezek's whereabouts.

Brune, in a few words, told of the plan to carry off Tokuhara, and indicated the tent occupied by Rezek. This, which stood nearest the beach, was dark like the rest: but from time to time a tiny flicker of light appeared upon the canvas, showing that its occupants had not yet departed. Further, it showed that Tokuhara had succumbed without a struggle, and that Carlisle and Rezek were working over him, presumably by the light of a pocket electric torch.

The remainder of the camp was in darkness. Except for the huddled form of his Japanese guard, Brune had no evidence that Solomon was not absolutely alone; the fogginess of the night, in contrast with the sharp clarity of the night previous, was sufficient to blot out all detail.

"Now, sir, set werry tight," and Solomon removed his pipe from his mouth. "An' kindly remember, sir, as 'ow you're not to question me orders."

Brune wondered what those final words meant, but said nothing. Indeed, he was given no time for speech. Solomon knocked the pipe against his palm and sent a little burst of sparks flitting to the sand.

As if this had been a signal, the misty night suddenly became filled with noises, and Brune discerned flitting figures around the tents. The light in Rezek's tent went out; then the harsh, metallic voice of Carlisle lifted in a curse, followed instantly by a shot, and another. The spaces between the tents seemed filled with struggling shapes.

From across the island came a third shot, and Brune knew that Solomon must have sent some men to take care of the other camp. Glancing at the tent of the Milnes, he saw two dark figures standing before the door, evidently guarding it.

The ensuing events were like portions of a nightmare, to Brune at least; while through it all sat Solomon at his side, watching in silence.

To determine what took place was not easy, owing to the confusion caused by the darkness and the fog. Solomon's dozen Chinese were not quite equal in numbers to the men under

Tokuhara—but Tokuhara was helpless, and his men were divided and caught by surprise. A moment later, also, the nature of Solomon's orders became evident.

A little swirl of men had centered about Rezek's tent, but the canvas went down as though blown flat, and the rattling explosions of automatic revolvers spat fire on the night. What took place could not be seen distinctly, as there seemed to be an outburst of shooting in all directions.

A half-clad figure which Brune recognized as that of one of the two Japanese with Tokuhara came running past Brune and Solomon, shouting something indistinguishable amid the uproar. The two Chinese guarding the Milne tent stepped forward, two shots cracked out, and the Japanese gentleman fell in a heap.

Other shots sounded from across the island. Magnified and distorted by the mist and darkness, the shouting, struggling, shooting figures of men turned the little group of tents around Brune into an inferno. Then order began to come out of the chaos, as two tall Chinese came rushing up, bearing a bound and helpless Japanese between them, and flung the latter down before Solomon. As they rushed away, another prisoner was likewise brought up; this one Brune recognized as the second of Tokuhara's aids.

One or two more scattered shots cracked out, but no other prisoners came in. Brune, standing now beside Solomon, made the suggestion that the gasoline flares be lighted; the pudgy little man assented, in an agitated voice.

"Dang it!" he broke out suddenly. "What's become o' that 'ere Rezek?"

"Probably he's under his tent, there," said Brune grimly. "There was enough lead flying to kill a regiment."

Before the other could reply, a tall, slender figure appeared before them, tendered Solomon a military salute, and spoke in a slightly accented voice:

"All are disposed of and the boats are captured, sir. The white people at the other camp are unharmed, but prisoners."

"Werry good," wheezed Solomon. "I'll go over there an' see as they keep quiet. Mr. Sin Woo, this 'ere is Mr. Brune. You'll take orders from 'im till I get back 'ere."

Sin Woo saluted and stood motionless. Solomon turned and caught Brune's arm in a quick grasp, and even in the darkness his agitation was evident.

"Mr. Brune, I 'as to 'andle them actor people, an' do it smart. You get them flares to goin' an' find that 'ere Rezek. Find 'im, mind! If 'e ain't 'ere, if 'e's got away, I'll 'ave to know it. Dang it! Dang it!"

Solomon stumped away, muttering to himself.

Being no less anxious over the fate of Rezek and Carlisle, Brune turned to Sin Woo and ordered the gasoline flares brought from the mess tent and lighted. Then he hurried over to the tent of the Milnes, pausing outside.

"Miss Milne! Captain! Are you all right?"

"All right," responded the brusque voice of the naval engineer. "What the devil's burst loose? Is that you, Brune?"

"Yes. Keep Miss Milne in there until I come back."

Brune hastened on to Rezek's tent. As he reached it, Sin Woo ran up with one of the flares and lighted it promptly, the Chinese clustering around.

The canvas was hauled away by eager hands, and a sharp cry of disappointment broke from Brune. The only body revealed was that of Tokuhara, who had evidently caught a chance bullet through the head, and was quite dead. At sight of the yellow, convulsed face, however, murmurs of amazement arose from the Chinese, and it was plain that Tokuhara was recognized by some of them. Brune whirled on their leader.

"Send out some of your men along the shore at once—Rezek and Carlisle must have broken through!"

Sin Woo crackled out an order, and the group of Chinese melted. The Celestial touched Brune's arm.

"They might be among the dead, excellency."

"Then I'd better make sure at once. You don't mean to say that you've killed all the Japs except those two prisoners?"

The Chinaman's bony face, doubly yellow under the flaring light, contracted in a swift grin of cruelty.

"All are dead, excellency."

"Collect the bodies outside the camp—hurry up! Set two men to work making a trench ready to receive them before Miss Milne sees them."

Brune turned away from the man, horror tugging at his heart. He was just beginning to realize, so swiftly had it all occurred, that this band of Celestials had descended on the camp with the intent of ruthless slaughter—and had carried out that intent.

Blood was not a novelty to Jack Brune. As a newspaper man in Chicago, he had perforce rubbed elbows with squalid crime, with open murder, with battle, accident, and sudden death. He had sat at table with Solomon, Harvey Lind, and two desperate criminals, and still bore a scar beneath his hair from the death struggle that had ensued. But he had never participated in a raid whose object had been the deliberate slaughter of fifteen men. He felt a little sick as he followed to where Sin Woo was at work with the remainder of his force.

Beyond the tent of Rezek, the ghastly row was laid out upon the sand, under the flare of the light. First of all, Brune saw Huggenheim, who had twice been shot; besides Tokuhara and his aid, seven other Japanese were here, but neither Rezek nor Carlisle.

As Sin Woo suggested, they might have fallen at the camp of the actors, where the Japanese in charge of the boats were domiciled. Only two of the Chinese had fallen, and their bodies were already being sewed up in canvas by two of their comrades. Repressing a shudder, Brune turned from the scene.

"Cover these bodies at once. Get your wounded men out of sight—"

"Did you find 'em, Mr. Brune?"

Solomon's voice wheezed through the gloom, followed by the pudgy little man himself. Brune shook his head.

"Huggenheim is here, but not the other two. No sign of them at the other camp?"

"No, and I 'ad mortal 'ard work convincing them 'ere actors as I was workin' for the government, without givin' away the 'ole thing." Solomon mopped his brow, his wide blue eyes roving from face to face.

"Then you've lost them, I guess," said Brune, frowning. "They have the submarine laid up somewhere near here at night, so that the moving-picture bunch would not see anything of her. They're probably aboard of her and gone by now."

"Dang it!" muttered Solomon. "Fix a light in that 'ere big tent. Mr. Sin Woo."

Brune led the way toward the mess tent. As he passed the one where he himself had been confined, he stopped suddenly. The two prisoners were being raised and marched off by four Chinese. Brune strode forward and halted them brusquely.

"Here—where are you fellows going with these men?"

The Chinese scowled. Tokuhara's aid, however, made answer, with a smile:

"They intend to kill us, Mr. Brune—so we have been informed."

"Solomon, call your damned murderers off!" exclaimed Brune, whirling. "This thing is more—"

"Mr. Brune, you listen 'ere." Solomon laid a hand on Brune's arm and looked up. In the aged, expressionless face Brune saw a look of indescribable feeling—pity, sorrow, determination.

"Them Japs are spies, Mr. Brune. If they was to be let free, none of our lives would be safe after this 'ere doings, an' besides, they know too much about that 'ere submarine. We can't chuck 'em into quod, 'cause why, there'd 'ave to be a trial, and this story ain't for the public, not yet. For the sake of—"

Brune nodded. Then he looked at the aid and broke into Solomon's speech:

"See here, my friend, if you'll tell us what game Rezek intended to play with the submarine, after your return home,

I'll promise you life. Don't think you have to stand by Rezek. He poisoned Tokuhara to-night—look at the body if you don't believe me. Tell us what the 'ultimate game' was of which he spoke to me, and I give you my word that you shall go free, if I have to fight for you myself!"

Solomon stood silent, staring questioningly at Brune. The Japanese, however, said nothing for a moment. His slant eyes narrowed to slits at Brune's mention of poisoning, but at last he smiled and made answer:

"Thank you, Mr. Brune, for your offer. But I assure you that I could never return alone to Nippon, after what has happened here. Therefore, it is better that I die—and take my secrets with me. *Sayonara*—farewell!"

And, like the brave man that he was, the gentleman of Japan marched away to his death, smiling. Brune growled a curse and strode into the mess tent. Even Solomon seemed white and silent as the flare was set upon the table.

"Now we'll 'ave a bit o' talk," observed Solomon, with a sigh, "when Cap'n Milne can be fetched in—eh? You found 'em?"

Sin Woo entered, with a salute. For a moment Brune imagined that Rezek and Carlisle had been located, until the Chinese leader advanced and laid something on the table.

"They were among Rezek's effects, excellency. Are they the ones?"

Solomon pushed the long roll which lay before him across to Brune.

"'Ow about it, Mr. Brune?"

With a glitter of excitement threading through him. Brune opened the roll and glanced at the blue prints and drawings it contained. He looked up swiftly.

"Yes—they are Case's drawings! Then, by George, we've won!"

To his wonder, Solomon quietly produced tobacco plug and knife and shook his head.

"No, Sir. I'm werry much afraid as we ain't done nothin' of the sort, sir."

CHAPTER XI

LOST — JAN REZEK!

TEN MINUTES later, Solomon's "council" was assembled in the mess tent.

Captain Milne was brought in on a stretcher constructed by the Chinese, and at his side sat Margaret, white-faced and grave-eyed. Across the table sat Sin Woo, high of cheek bone and nose, evidently a northern Chinaman. Brune and Solomon completed the circle.

In his trip to the other camp, Solomon had effectually disposed of an annoying element in the situation—the moving-picture people. Their manager had been placed under arrest for further investigation, and the others had been bundled aboard the *Narwhale,* with instructions to return to their Long Beach studio and keep their mouths shut, under penalty of arrest. The crew of the *Narwhale* consisting of a few old seamen from San Pedro, men who beyond a doubt had nothing in common with Rezek's plot, Solomon considered that he was well rid of the whole crowd.

Brune further satisfied him that, since the company's manager was innocent also, he had better be sent with the others; and orders were given to that effect.

"Now, sir," said Solomon, when the Milnes had entered, "give me a line on what you've been an' learned. And make it brief, sir."

Accordingly Brune related briefly what had happened to him after he had parted with Solomon at the Hotel *Virginia.*

Between Captain Milne and Margaret, the tale was soon completed.

"And you've seen nothin' o' that 'ere submarine since comin' to the island?"

"Not a thing," assented Brune. "Rezek was careful to keep her out of sight of the actors, whom he proposed to use as a blind in case visitors came to the island. But she was not far from here, and I'll bet he's cleared off in her, with Carlisle."

"And a werry bad job it is," nodded Solomon, puffing gloomily at his pipe.

"Didn't you take any of those Japs prisoners?" queried Milne.

"Two of 'em, sir. But they was werry 'earty men, they was that! They knowed as Rezek 'ad poisoned Tokuhara, but they wouldn't tell."

"Where are they?"

"I'm werry sorry to say as 'ow they're dead, sir."

"Dead!" The word broke from Margaret Milne. With a sweep of color surging into her face, she gazed at Solomon in startled horror. "You didn't murder them?"

"No, miss. They was executed." Solomon winced slightly.

"Oh!" The girl drew away, her eyes dilating. "You murdered them—oh, it can't be true! Mr. Brune, you didn't allow this thing done?"

"Yes." Brune nodded gravely, his eyes steady on hers. "They were spies in our country, enemies in disguise. They met the fate of spies."

"Nonsense, Marge!" broke in Captain Milne, reaching up and catching the girl's hand. "Don't be a fool. Those cursed Japs would have murdered us all had they had the chance, and they simply staked their own lives and lost. You did exactly right, Mr. Solomon, and I would do the same thing in your place."

Solomon merely nodded. In his eyes rested that same fleeting expression of half pity, half determination, which Brune had noted previously. Margaret Milne said no more, but she avoided John Solomon for many a day thereafter.

"Well," exclaimed Brune impatiently, "we have the drawings, and Tokuhara is eliminated, so what does there remain to do? Even if Rezek has escaped in the submarine, he can't get far without more gasoline, and he's practically harmless to us."

Captain Milne snorted.

"Harmless? Can't he run that submarine to Japan and turn her over there? Can't he lay her up somewhere along the coast and wait—"

"No, sir," broke in Solomon. "That ain't 'is game."

"What is it, then?"

"Werry 'ard to say, sir. It's me own notion as 'ow 'im and that 'ere Carlisle is werry much in need o' ready money. This 'ere game o' theirs must ha' cost a pretty penny. Mr. Brune 'as some idea o' what Rezek plans, mebbe."

"No idea at all," dissented Brune. "He and Carlisle twice mentioned an 'ultimate game,' and Huggenheim vainly tried to make some arrangements with Tokuhara about it. More than that, I can't say."

"But I can make a werry good guess, sir—or Mr. Sin Woo can," and Solomon waved his pipe at the Celestial, who smiled slightly.

"What are these Chinamen doing in the business?" demanded Captain Milne sharply, before Sin Woo could speak. "You claim to be a secret-service man, Solomon, but I want to say that it looks fishy to me."

Solomon chuckled and held up the jade ring upon his finger.

"Quite right, cap'n." Without mentioning the name of Hip Sun, he explained briefly that he was fighting Orientals with Orientals, mentioning the present feud between Nipponese and Chinese. Then, with a calm disregard of Captain Milne which left that gentleman furious, but silent, he requested Sin Woo to give his theory of Rezek's proposed "game."

This, in his carefully cultivated English, the Celestial did.

It seemed that for some time past the chiefs of the Chinese colony in Los Angeles had been aware of an influx of opium up and down the coast. Their belief was that this was smuggled by a well-organized Japanese ring, and after having been run up from Lower California, was sold to the various Chinese distributors through one or more white agents. Not even the opium users, it appeared, would deal directly with Japanese.

As Sin Woo showed, nothing more safe and lucrative than opium running could be done with the stolen submarine. Rezek could bring in huge quantities of the drug; by means of his silent engine and his diving abilities, he could land the stuff literally under the noses of the customs men, without detection. His profits would be vast, and a few loads of hundred-tael cans would not only set him on his feet financially, but would place him in a position to treat anew with Japan or some other government.

"It is quite as much to our interest as to yours," concluded Sin Woo, "to check him at the start, for we Chinese of the better class are sparing no efforts to stamp out the opium habit, both here and in China. That is one reason, Mr. Solomon, you were given the ring which you wear, and the power which goes with it."

Solomon's blue eyes widened; then he chuckled, as though surprised and amused.

Sin Woo's theory was highly plausible. Rezek could obtain gasoline from any Japanese fishing boat, and could also turn over the smuggled goods to those boats while they were at sea, or could bring opium into San Pedro itself if he so wished. But, provided that this hypothesis were correct, how was Rezek to be run down?

"It looks to me," observed Brune slowly, "as though the execution of those Japs, unavoidable as it was, would have a boomerang effect. Had we let them go free, with the story of Tokuhara's poisoning, every Japanese on the coast would have been out for Rezek's scalp. As it now is, they will all aid him."

The others nodded assent.

"It looks bad," said Captain Milne. "How are you going to get those fellows, Solomon?"

"What's to be 'ad can be got, as the old gent said when 'e married 'is third, sir. If you was that 'ere Rezek, what would you do?"

"I'd run for Mexico and put over a big cargo of dope. Wouldn't you?"

"No, sir, not me," and Solomon's blue eyes twinkled through the smoke.

"Well, what would you do, then?" snapped the other crustily.

"I'd go werry careful like, after what 'appened to-night, sir. I'd want to know who it was as killed them Japs—Rezek, 'e never 'eard o' me. I'd be werry apt to send Mr. Carlisle to poison Mr. Brune, out o' revenge like, an' to make arrangements about takin' care of the opium when so be as I got it landed."

Brune shivered slightly at the thought suggested by Solomon's words. The remembrance of Rezek, perfectly poised, catlike, bronze-eyed, was not pleasant; defeated or not, the man was terribly potential of evil. And Carlisle—

"Then you're going after Rezek still?" broke out Brune hoarsely.

"O' course, Mr. Brune! Don't 'e know the details o' them 'ere plans? Ain't 'e got that model submarine to sell when 'e gets a chance? Ain't 'im an' Mr. Carlisle two o' the most dangerous, 'orrible scoundrels as ever was?"

Solomon mopped his streaming brow, something like fear in his own face. Then he continued more composedly:

"No, Cap'n Milne, if I was Rezek I wouldn't make no mistakes." At this, Brune gave a start of surprise, remembering Rezek's own words; the amazing keenness of Solomon was never better illustrated. "That's 'is kind, sir. 'E don't make no mistakes. But mark me words, sir, 'e's goin' to make a werry big mistake one o' these days!"

"Eh?" Milne caught at the sudden eagerness in Solomon's voice. "You've thought of something?"

"Yes, sir, I 'ave that. Beggin' your pardon, sir, no one ain't to know it but me an' Mr. Sin Woo—an' Mr. Brune, if so be as 'e's in with us."

"Of course," nodded Brune quietly. Captain Milne sighed.

"You're right, naturally—but if it weren't for this blasted leg I'd be with you! Well, what now?"

"I'll ask you to be so kind as to stay at the Wirginia 'Otel until you 'ears from me again, sir an' miss. I'm a-goin' back to Long Beach with you to-night, but must get on to Los Angeles—"

"What? To-night, you say?"

"Yes, sir. Mr. Brune an' me 'as werry important business in Los Angeles. What I wants to do must be done in a 'urry, as the old gent said when 'e saw the new—"

What Solomon's "old gent" saw remained forever a mystery. Something nicked through the seaward wall of the tent, plowed a neat furrow in the table board, sang between Brune and Solomon, and left a round hole in the opposite canvas wall. From somewhere followed a whiplike crack.

Like a flash, Sin Woo leaped to the gasoline flare and extinguished it.

"Down!" cried Brune, realizing swiftly what had happened. "Rezek is shooting—down low, every one!"

With the words, he sprang up, caught the hand of Margaret Milne, and pressed her to the sand at the side of her father's stretcher.

From the Chinese outside came a scattered crack of rifles, then silence. Sin Woo called out something, and received a hasty reply. He translated at once:

"That was a rifle shot from the sea, excellency! The flash came from two hundred yards off shore."

"Werry good," sounded Solomon's wheezy tones. "If so be as you'll light the flare, Mr. Sin Woo, we won't 'ave no more bullets."

"Hold on, there!" exclaimed Milne sharply. "How do you know that, Solomon?"

"That was a partin' token o' farewell, sir," and the little cockney chuckled. "They was in the submarine, and now they're off. There ain't no more use o' your men a-keepin' out, Mr. Sin Woo."

It was palpable enough that Rezek and Carlisle had escaped. Sin Woo called in the men who were still out, searching the shores below the cliffs; the fog was now lifting fast, and since there was no boat visible on the night-rimmed sea whence the shot had come, the correctness of Solomon's guess was evident.

It was decided that the whole party should return direct to Long Beach, after which the Chinese could take the launches to San Pedro and leave them. The *Ichi Hondo* being the largest of the three. Captain Milne was taken aboard her and placed in the cabin, Margaret with him.

"Make yourselves at home," smiled Brune, who accompanied the girl down. "We'll be at the Long Beach pier shortly after daybreak, and you can get to the hotel without being observed."

"Then we'll say good-by in the morning." Margaret extended him her hand. "Good night!"

"Good night," returned Brune quietly. "Allow me to say that we'll *not* say good-by in the morning, Miss Milne—that is, not unless it is your wish."

For a moment her eyes dwelt on his, and then she smiled.

"Perhaps we would better obey the scriptural injunction, Mr. Brune—and take no thought to the morrow!"

Brune climbed to the deck, smiling cheerfully despite his weariness; he came slap upon Solomon and Sin Woo, who were talking together beside the wheelhouse.

"About officers, now," Solomon was saying. "If so be as you can get Chinese as 'as the proper tickets, all well an' good!"

"It is possible," responded Sin Woo. "Our men would not have American board-of-trade licenses—"

"Werry good—we'll put 'er under Chinese ownership, just like that!"

"What's all this?" queried Brune, holding up his lantern. "What are you cooking up?"

Solomon chuckled.

"A werry 'ot pot o' broth for that 'ere Rezek, sir—if so be as 'e falls into it!"

On the second morning thereafter, Jack Brune, who was once more comfortably domiciled in the suite occupied by Solomon at the *Angelus*, came to their private breakfast table with a copy of the *Times* folded in his hand. He grinned cheerfully at Solomon.

"Well, we got her over! Your friend Hip Sun must be a wonder to make the newspaper boys swallow this stuff—but it's dressed up pretty well. Front-page stuff, too!"

"Read it out, sir, if you'll be so good. Me eyes ain't what they might be."

Brune nodded good morning to the Arab who served them, and read aloud the news feature which had drawn his remark. It was a boxed story, on the front page, and was headed "The Passing of the *Narwhale*."

> "San Pedro, Aug. 10.—The whaling brig *Narwhale*, last of the old Frisco whaling fleet, is soon to be only a memory. In her time she brought in millions of dollars' worth of oil and bone, but having been forced from the business by the steam fleets, she was last year sold to a film company for use in moving pictures.
>
> She was again sold to-day, this time to the Leong Sing Company, of Los Angeles and Shanghai. Her name is to be changed to the *Kut Sun*, and as soon as her cargo of gasoline is stowed she is to set forth under a Chinese crew, her destination being given as Mazatlan. Whether her cargo is destined for use by Chinese colonies along the west coast of Mexico, as her new owners declare, or whether it is to be delivered to the Carranzistas, is conjectural."

"Conjectural," laughed Brune, "is correct! John, I'll bet my busted black-rimmed spectacles against your old clay pipe that we reach Mazatlan without a hitch."

"Done!" exclaimed Solomon, and chuckled delightedly. "Mr. Brune, I'll be werry sorry to deprive you o' them 'ere spectacles, but that's what I'm a-goin' to do, just like that! 'Cause why, Mr. Carlisle is a-goin' to see that 'ere newspaper."

Brune only smiled. He had no faith whatever in the mission of the *Kut Sun*.

CHAPTER XII

THE KUT SUN SAILS

WERE THIS a tale of sheer fiction, instead of being a chronicle compiled from the notebooks of John Solomon, and therefore much stranger than fiction, one might expect to find a thrilling love story entwined with the voyage of the *Kut Sun*.

While quite true that Jack Brune fell in love with Margaret Milne from his first sight of her, and fell more deeply in love at each subsequent meeting, it must be regretfully stated that Solomon did not invite Miss Milne aboard his whaling ship. In fact, Solomon never invited any woman anywhere, if he could help it.

In his past experience his chosen friends had more than once mingled work with love. The results, thanks to Solomon himself, had been satisfactory enough, but Solomon had wearied of it, as he frankly stated to Brune on the morning of their last day together at the *Angelus*. It came through Brune's remark that he intended to stop at Long Beach that afternoon, on his way to San Pedro.

"Mr. Brune, beggin' your pardon, sir," returned Solomon, "you step werry careful around that 'ere 'Otel Wirginia. When so be as we puts Mr. Rezek where 'e'd ought to be, I'll 'ave a bit o' work for you an' Mr. Lind, and I don't want no womenfolks spoilin' me plans."

"Eh?" Brune looked up keenly. "Aren't you a bit previous with your advice?"

Solomon looked at him with impervious blankness. Brune regretted his words instantly.

"No, sir, I'm not, 'cause why, I like you werry much. What's more, Miss Milne is a extry-fine young lady, an' proud I am as 'ow you and 'er is friends, just like that. But mind this, Mr. Brune— she's run a lot o' danger on this 'ere job so far, and I don't want 'er in it no more, nor no other female! So you be werry careful, sir."

Realizing that a good deal might underlie Solomon's scheme, of which he himself knew little, Brune nodded and said no more. Had he known the plans which Solomon was then making regarding the capture of Rezek and Carlisle, Brune would have cheerfully admitted that the *Kut Sun* would be no place for a lady.

However, Solomon might have spared his worry on the subject, for all went well.

That afternoon Brune took his way to Long Beach and the *Virginia.* He was not to show himself in San Pedro until after dark, the whaler sailing at midnight; for if Solomon's guess were correct and Carlisle had been set ashore to make the arrangements necessary to the safe smuggling of an opium cargo, Brune must not be seen in connection with the *Kut Sun.* Were the hook to show, the fish would not nibble at the bait. Nor indeed did Brune have more than a general idea of Solomon's scheme, for the pudgy little man had a habit of keeping essential details to himself.

Brune found Captain Milne fuming in the depths of a wheeled chair on the hotel veranda. A moment later, Margaret joined them, her slender beauty well set off by white duck and a gay silk sweater-coat.

"No news of our friends yet?" growled the naval engineer.

"None," smiled Brune. "I'm leaving to-night on a little trip, however, and I may not be back for some time. Sorry I can't say more about it—"

"Tut, tut—don't mention it. Brune, why didn't you tell me this confounded town was dry as a last year's bone? Deuce take

it, sir, one can't obtain a drop of liquor here even as medicine!
Blast these Iowa farmers and their blue laws!"

"I'll telephone up to Solomon—I think he's at the hotel,"
laughed Brune. "If you'll nominate your preference, I can promise you a special-delivery package this evening, Captain Milne."

"Gad, sir, if you will, I'll—I'll send you two young folks off
to the Pike in freedom! And Brune, you'll dine with us this
evening, of course."

Brune stepped to the telephone booths, found Solomon still
at the hotel, and made his request, to which the little cockney
assented with a chuckle.

The remainder of the afternoon Brune spent on the sands and
on the Pike with Margaret Milne. He found her a different girl
from the one whom he had known on the islands—a trifle grave,
perhaps, beneath her light-hearted gayety, yet wholly responsive
to his own cheerful optimism. Only when they paused before
the seaward approach to the hotel on their return did a deeper
word pass between them.

"You'll be here when I get back from my trip?" asked Brune
quietly.

"Father can't travel for a week or two, at least," she returned.
"You'll be back by then?"

"I trust so. One can never say definitely, of course, as the
circumstances are—er—somewhat unusual. I believe Solomon
has requested you to remain here until the conclusion of his
work, has he not? He spoke of needing your testimony to turn
in with his report, when the case is finished."

"Oh, I believe he did mention it!" and she smiled on meeting
Brune's level eyes. "I think that you'll find us here, Mr. Brune.
And—and truly I hope that you will come back in safety—both
of you!"

"Thank you, Miss Milne. Such is me earnest intention, as the
old gent said when 'e kissed the 'ousemaid!"

His imitation of Solomon's tone was perfect.

Laughing together, they went on to dinner. When Brune

caught his San Pedro car later that evening, he felt in uncommonly high spirits. Upon reviewing all that had passed, he could see no reason for such exhilaration other than, as he cheerfully admitted to himself, "the general nature of things." Which, it may be, was reason enough.

Without difficulty, Brune located the *Kut Sun,* for she was about the liveliest object in San Pedro that night. Solomon had placed her sailing date at the earliest possible moment her cargo would be aboard, and gangs of half-naked Chinese were working by the light of high flares, sending aboard mammoth pipes, or butts, of gasoline.

On the outskirts of the wharf space was gathered a goodly crowd, and Brune passed into it unostentatiously, seeking some propitious moment for getting to the ship unobserved. On every hand he heard mutters of contempt, for the Pedro "dock-wallopers" were amazed both by the presence of so many Chinese and by the industry of the yellow men.

"Ain't that a chink for ye?" demanded one burly loafer indignantly. "Why didn't they charter a tank ship, hey? But, no—they has to take an old windjammer an' load her up with butts! Huh! It's about time the chinks was run out o' this country. And a chink skipper, too! Huh! I'd like to be surveyor of this port for about ten minutes!"

Brune listened, smiling at the comments. If Solomon were trying to get free advertising for the gasoline ship, it was certainly being obtained in good measure, he reflected. At the same time, he could see no way of getting across that well-lighted space without being observed by the crowd; and Solomon had expressly cautioned him against being seen.

Still considering this problem, Brune found himself at the edge of the watching throng, when suddenly his sleeve was tugged. He turned, to find at his side a Chinaman, and the man's sibilant whisper came clearly to him:

"Mistel Blune! Mistel Solomon say go to customhouse velly quick!"

The speaker glided away and disappeared. Brune turned and made his way back along the water front until he reached the ferry landing, and crossed to the customhouse—a small, square building across the railroad tracks. At the doorway, he was halted by three dark figures, who proved to be Solomon and two indistinct white men—port officers.

"Ah, 'ere's Mr. Brune now!" wheezed the little cockney. "All ready, sir?"

"All ready," nodded Brune. "Your chink sent me here."

"Yes, sir. If you'll just come along wi' me an' these 'ere gents, we'll lay aboard our boat."

Brune followed down the ferry steps, where a small rowboat was lying. Dropping into this, two oars were put out and the boat dropped slowly along the wharves and lumber docks to where the flaring lights denoted the ex-whaler. Without incident, they reached her side.

Solomon and Brune ascended the ladder which was out ready for them, and the rowboat dropped away.

"Best get below at once, sir," said Solomon. "I'll go for'ard. When we cast off, then come on deck."

With a softly padding Chinaman guiding him, Brune passed aft, hidden from the wharf by the deck house and try-works, and a moment later was in a very comfortable cabin; his own suit case lay on one of the bunks. He closed the door and dropped into a chair.

"Whew!" he observed whimsically, filling his pipe. "For secrecy, dark-mantled plotters, and treading the shaded ways of night, John certainly has the old school of melodrama faded a dozen ways from Sunday! But if Carlisle is anywhere around here, he certainly knows about this ship. Whether or not he'll figure that the gods are sending gasoline to Rezek is another matter. I'll bet he smells a rat."

Not daring to go on deck, and the cabin being absolutely bare of entertainment, Brune hauled forth pencil and paper and fell to inditing sonnets. An hour later, he was still writing, with neither rhyme nor reason, when the door opened and a yellow head appeared, with a few hasty words in pidgin English:

"Mistel Solomon say get leady come topside!"

While still puzzling over this cryptic message, Brune suddenly realized that the thumping and smashing had ceased, and that a singsong voice was bawling out orders from overhead, while bare feet pattered on the deck above him. Laughing at his own obtuseness, he strode to the door and so to the companionway. The ship was lurching gently, and without hesitation he climbed the steps to the deck.

The *Kut Sun* was moving out to the open sea, on the line of a puffing tug which crawled a hundred yards ahead of her. The night was clear, starry, moonless; on either hand were the riding lights of fish boats and small craft, while the soft clang-clang of the bell buoy off Dead Man's Island lifted across the harbor like an undying requiem.

The shouted orders had ceased. Brune, standing with Solomon beside the helm, looked up to see spectral figures lining the yards, while up at the fore and main royals, eighty feet above the deck, a single dark shape topped the whole; the sails were hanging half stopped, bellowing rolls of darkness against the stars. Over all was an air of expectancy, of stillness, of almost ominous waiting, transformed by the darkness and touched with the mystic romance that has ever hovered upon the men who go down to the sea in ships.

Then, like a whip crack, all was changed.

As the revolving light at the end of the long breakwater drew in on the starboard bow, there came a shout from the tug. A small Chinaman standing near Solomon gave a weird, shrill order, which was repeated from forward and was echoed back from the masts above. The hawser was cast off with a resounding splash: the dark figures overhead passed into quick action; the canvas began to flit into dim clouds of white, and with a quick stamping of feet men tailed on to braces and sheets. The helmsman spun his wheel, slant eyes frowning upon the binnacle light, and slowly the *Kut Sun* leaned over and over farther, until there was a white scud of water foaming past her port scuppers.

"Well, we're off!" came the wheezy sigh of Solomon. "Mr. Brune, meet Cap'n Wun Sing."

Brune shook hands with the small Chinaman near by, and was then bluntly ordered by Solomon to go below and sleep, the pudgy little man promising to join him in a moment. Brune obeyed, and had barely undressed when Solomon, who was sharing the cabin, entered and made ready for bed also.

"Don't tell me," was Solomon's parting word for the night, "as them 'ere chinks ain't up to the mark when it comes to makin' sail! It's a werry strange world, as the—the old gent said—when—"

The rest was lost in a snore. John Solomon was a weary man that night.

When Brune went on deck next morning, he found to his surprise that the twin heads of Santiago Mountain were not yet abaft of them—the *Kut Sun* had only come a trifle over twenty miles! She was no yacht-built craft, true, with her snub nose and wide beam: but even a whaleboat with her tiny leg-o'-mutton sail would travel twenty miles between midnight and eight bells in the morning watch.

This slow rate of speed, however, proved to be the result of skill and not mischance. The transmuted *Narwhale,* reeking now of gasoline where once she had reeked of sperm oil, and once again of grease paint, was no more than a bait; a royal bait, a costly bait, for her voyage meant that some one was paying untold thousands of dollars.

When it comes to settling old scores, when it comes to exacting eye for eye and tooth for tooth and huge interest besides, the Chinese have dollars and the will to spend them. The far-fabled memory of the red Indian is dwarfed beside that of the Mongol, from whom he obtained it. Further, no one knew the abstruse genius of John Solomon better than the Leong Sing Company.

"Well, we ought to be 'earing summat afore night," observed

Solomon, as they messed that noon with the skipper and the second mate. "You'll keep a good lookout, cap'n?"

"Two man topside allee time," nodded the wrinkled Wun Sing. "Mebbeso catch 'urn, mebbeso not. Keep first-chop look-see."

The crow's nest, a heavy box of canvas on a wooden frame, which had been rigged on the crosstrees abaft the foremast by the motion-picture people, was now utilized by the lookouts. It was also to be utilized for something else, which Brune did not yet suspect.

"Where's your destination—where are we bound for?" he asked the mate, upon returning to the deck. The yellow man only grinned faintly.

"Mazatlan, Mistel Blune! Mebbeso we stop along Colona-dos."

"Colon—oh, Coronado!" Brune frowned. "Coronado is at San Diego, though—we're not putting in there?"

"Mebbeso you ask Mistul Solomon."

Brune promptly did so, received a cryptic "Them as asks questions gets less'n they asks, I says," and upon that he retired to the lee shelter of the tryworks, where a game of fan-tan was in progress.

"I'll ask no more blamed questions," he resolved. "But if we put in at San Diego after drawing papers for Mazatlan, even Rezek will think there's something wrong."

For lack of better employment, he sat in at the fan-tan game with varying success, and about four o'clock challenged the bank—which in this case was no other than the second mate. Card after card began to come true, and Brune, quite as excited as the rest, was seeing visions of making a record haul, when there came a sudden hail from aloft.

Like a flash, the game dissolved, the cards went overboard, and the players scattered. At first Brune, half angry, thought that a clever "game" had been put over to check his winning; but as he followed the running men forward, he was stopped by a sharp call in Solomon's voice:

"Mr. Brune! Lay aft 'ere, an' be bloody quick about it!"

Apprised by the tone that something had happened—possibly the submarine had been sighted, he thought—Brune raced back along the port side and joined Solomon at the companionway. The little cockney beckoned him below frantically. The men in sight were all staring off to starboard, but Brune darted obediently down the ladder.

Solomon stumped hastily to the stern cabins, opened a port, and beckoned. Joining him, Brune looked out to sea. A thrill of disappointment passed over him.

"Huh—a fish boat!" he exclaimed. "I thought you'd raised Rezek at least. Say, this nervousness of yours cost me a—"

"Look at 'im!" cried Solomon excitedly, passing Brune a pair of binoculars. "Look at 'im! If 'e ain't been an' took the bait—"

Brune focused on the fish boat, which was a good four miles distant, but coming up fast from the southeast.

In her bow he could make out a tall, erect figure which was apparently inspecting the *Kut Sun* through a telescope. Its familiar aspect made Brune's pulses leap—it was the figure of the poisoner, Carlisle, beyond a doubt!

"You think Rezek is with him, John?"

Solomon shook his head in negation.

"No, sir, werry sorry to say as I don't. You see, sir, it ain't a werry easy job for Rezek to get gasoline for that 'ere submarine, but gasoline 'e 'as to 'ave. So 'e puts Carlisle ashore to get 'im a big stock o' gas, while 'e goes off wi' the submarine to lay up somewheres an' wait—"

"Where?" interjected Brune hastily.

"That's what we want to know from Carlisle, sir. 'E'll come aboard to buy our gasoline, 'aving 'eard o' this ship and 'er crew. If so be as the chinks won't sell, 'e means to force 'em to sell."

"But how? He couldn't expect to force—"

"You look steady at that 'ere launch, sir. See that pile o' canwas in 'er bow? That's a gun, I'll take my davy, sir, wi' canwas thrown over it!"

Brune nodded, as he peered through the glasses.

"You may be right, John, but it's a mighty queer thing that fishing boats along this coast could carry guns and get away with it! I tell you—"

"All werry good, Sir, but them 'ere Japs is main sharp ones. It's a werry good thing, Mr. Brune, as there ain't no foreign warships around this 'ere coast right now, 'cause why, we're a-goin' to commit a crime for which we'd be 'ung mortal quick if we was caught."

"A crime?" echoed Brune, staring at the little man. "A crime? What crime?"

"Piracy on the 'igh seas, sir," and Solomon chuckled. "And a werry odd crime it is, as the old gent said when 'e was took up for bigamy."

CHAPTER XIII

PIRACY

T O IMAGINE the *Narwhale-Kut Sun* as a pirate, especially against a launch which was presumably armed with a gun, at first drew a smile from Brune.

The fish boat was now drawing up close, however. At half a mile, Carlisle, distinctly recognizable, turned and gave an order; a Japanese came to the bow and ran up two flags to the launch's stumpy mast—a blue-and-white checkered flag, and beneath it a red-circled white pennant.

"International signal NC!" exclaimed Solomon, who had obtained a second pair of binoculars. "Distress, that is—'e's a-trying to stop us!"

"Will our chinks know the signal?" queried Brune.

"Trust 'em—they was raised in Shanghai waters!" chuckled the other.

Almost at once, indeed, it became evident that they had understood Carlisle's message. The *Kut Sun*, which had been bowling along with a stiff breeze on her quarter, was brought up into the wind, and there was a great chattering and shouting as the after yards were braced up and sail was shortened.

It was soon plain that the Chinese were putting as much lubberly work into the operation of heaving to as they possibly could. Aboard the fish boat, the figures of two Japanese were now in sight, one being forward beside Carlisle, the other at the helm. The launch ran in rapidly toward the brig, Carlisle examining the old whaler critically as he drew nearer. Solomon promptly drew back from the open port, Brune doing likewise.

The launch's puffing engine sounded beneath them, then ceased. Brune quivered as the harsh, metallic voice of Carlisle pierced to him:

"Where's your captain, *Kut Sun?* I want to speak with him."

"Me cap'n," came the tones of Captain Wun Sing. "Mebbeso you wantee help?"

"I want gasoline—your whole cargo," returned Carlisle. "I'll make you a better price than you can get at Mazatlan, and you can deliver it within a half day's sail of here. Will you sell?"

Solomon looked at Brune with a significant nod.

"Rezek's 'iding place ain't werry far off, sir!"

The shrill tones of Wun Sing, in reply to Carlisle, came down to them:

"Mebbeso can do. You stop along one time. Me see."

A moment later the wrinkled skipper pattered down before them, with an inquiring glance at Solomon.

"Mebbeso you sell?"

"Yes," and Solomon chuckled wheezily. "We'll sell, cap'n. All's ready in the crow's nest?"

The other nodded and pattered away. Solomon beckoned Brune into the mess cabin and took his place at the table, facing the door.

"If you'll be so good as to go into that cabin o' the skipper's, Mr. Brune, you'll be out o' Mr. Carlisle's sight. We'll give 'im a bit of a surprise, just like that."

Brune obeyed silently. For all the lightness of Solomon's words, the pudgy little man was tense with anxiety; he began to fill his clay pipe, and when he lighted the match his fingers were trembling.

Inside Wun Sing's room, where he had a view of the mess cabin through the door crack, Brune stood watching and waiting. He wondered if Solomon had planned this very thing all the time—the capture of Carlisle, and the possible discovery of Rezek's lair. How that discovery was to come about, Brune could not quite see; he was certain that Carlisle would not be a traitor to the fat man.

He could tell nothing of what was passing alongside, for the captain's cabin lay on the port side of the ship. But, after a few moments, there came the shuffle of feet on the companion stairs, and then Carlisle strode into the mess cabin—alone.

At sight of the pudgy figure of Solomon, seated at the table and puffing at the old clay pipe, Carlisle stiffened, one hand resting in his coat pocket. His lean, swarthy face was cruel with suspicion, baffled surmise; his powerful figure was alert, tensed, ready for whatever might befall.

Brune felt a thrill of hatred as he gazed at the man. He still had his own score to settle with Carlisle—but the settling was to come after a far different fashion from that which he now anticipated.

"Well?" snapped Carlisle harshly. "Who are you?"

"Me name's Solomon, sir—John Solomon. I'm partners wi' the Leong Sing people in this 'ere cargo."

"Oh!" The response was more grunt than word.

For a long moment Carlisle stood, still gazing at Solomon. Evidently he had never heard the name before, and did not suspect that it was this man who was hounding down Rezek to ruin. His hand did not budge from his coat pocket, but the suspicion slowly died from his swarthy features, to be replaced by something like contempt as he looked down at the seated figure.

"Cap'n Wun Sing was tellin' me as you wanted to buy some gasoline, sir," went on Solomon placidly. "For your launch, if I may make so bold as to ask?"

Carlisle's white teeth showed in big leering smile.

"No. I'd heard of the *Kut Sun,* and I came out expressly to intercept her. I'll take your whole cargo off your hands, if you'll sell."

"I don't 'ardly see as it could be done, sir," returned Solomon, puffing forth a cloud of white smoke, with a regretful shake of his head. "You see, we've been an' took a contract from them 'ere Carranzistas at Mazatlan, and we've posted a five-'undred dollar forfeit, just like that."

Carlisle made a gesture of irritation.

"Nonsense—I'll cover that bet, Mr. Solomon. What price will you take for the entire cargo of gasoline, with the five hundred extra?"

"Well, sir. I don't rightly know. These 'ere Chinamen are werry 'ard men to do business with, as you may know, sir, an' they're expectin' to go to Mazatlan, just like that. It all depends where you wants the stuff delivered."

So bland, so innocent were Solomon's wide blue eyes and pudgy, expressionless face, that Carlisle's swift flash of suspicion passed instantly.

Brune chuckled to himself. At last he comprehended the strategy afoot, and he marveled at the clever acting displayed by Solomon.

"Well, that's not unreasonable," said Carlisle slowly. "I'll tell you this much—the gasoline is to be unshipped not fifty miles from here, Mr. Solomon. I trust that will be satisfactory?"

"I'm werry sorry to say as it won't, sir. It ain't me, mind you—it's them 'ere blessed Chinamen! You'd never dream 'ow 'ard they was to get along with, sir. What's more, this secret destination ain't to me liking, 'cause why, I'm werry anxious to keep on good terms wi' the law, just like that. Now, if so be as you'll say downright just where you wants this 'ere cargo delivered, why, I'll name me price. If that's all shipshape, I'll do me best wi' the skipper. More'n that, sir, I can't do."

Solomon leaned back with an air of calm finality—to every appearance a cautious, obstinate Britisher who had stated his position and would cling to it. And so, evidently, Carlisle considered him.

"Very well. You'll know where the Coronados are?"

"Never 'eard o' them, sir," lied Solomon placidly. "I ain't no seaman, you see."

"They're seven miles off the coast, fifteen miles south of San Diego. In Mexican waters. The gasoline is to be put ashore on the smallest of the three islands."

"Thank you werry much, sir. Now, that 'ere gasoline cost us eight cents in Los Angeles, and we was to get fifteen in Mazatlan. If so be as you'll make that eighteen, wi' the five 'undred extra, an' sign a paper to that effect, all well an' good."

"Done!" nodded Carlisle.

"Then 'ave a seat, sir, an' I'll call the skipper 'ere."

Carlisle, his last suspicion removed, took a seat across the table from Solomon, who clapped his hands. A yellow face appeared at the door.

"Ask Cap'n Wun Sing to step 'ere, right away."

Surely an innocent message, if there ever were one! But it spelled death to two men.

"Mebbe you noticed that 'ere crow's nest on our crosstrees, sir?" asked Solomon, turning to Carlisle and picking up his pipe with fingers that were quite steady.

"Yes. Why?"

"I s'pose, sir, it didn't occur to you as that crow's nest would be a werry good place to put a couple o' men wi' rifles—"

Carlisle sprang up, his hand flying to his coat pocket. But not swiftly enough. Through the door behind him leaped two sinewy, half-naked yellow men, who seized him by wrist and shoulder and held him helpless.

At the same instant there came a rifle crack from above, followed swiftly by a second. Solomon, who had not budged an inch, looked at the writhing, cursing Carlisle and nodded quietly.

"It was a werry sorry day for them 'ere Japs when they tied up wi' you and Rezek," he observed. "That's two more on 'em as just died. Mr. Brune, you might come out an' pass the time o' day wi' this 'ere gent."

Realizing now what that mention of the crow's nest had meant, and that the two Japanese with Carlisle must have been shot down, Brune came into the mess cabin. He remembered that the Chinese helmsman had mentioned the Coronados, and while at the time he had not connected them with the better-known Coronado Beach at San Diego, he now saw his mistake.

"Very cleverly done, John," he said quietly, while Carlisle snarled at him in vain fury. "Kind of our poisoning friend to tell us where to find Rezek, wasn't it?"

"Yes, 'e's a werry benewolent gentleman, though you'd 'ardly think it to see 'im now," chuckled Solomon.

"I wish you'd let him free for about ten minutes," went on Brune. "I owe him for quite a bit of suffering, and I'd like nothing better than a good chance to give him a trimming with bare knuckles. Will you do it?"

"No, sir—Mr. Carlisle, 'e's aiming to get 'ung for the murder o' Mr. Case. I'm a-goin' to put 'im in irons, sir, just like that."

And Carlisle was dragged away, cursing like a fiend, by the yellow men. Solomon promptly went on deck with Brune, in high exultation over the success of their ruse.

They were met by Wun Sing, who stated that nothing had been found aboard the launch save a flat case, which he handed them. Brune recognized it, with a shudder, as Carlisle's poison case. Solomon nodded and retained it for future evidence.

"Just the same, sir," he said soberly, "we ain't won yet. It's werry easy to slip up, an' that 'ere Rezek is a-going to be watching out sharp, so don't you go an' imagine as 'ow we got a clear road ahead, 'cause we ain't."

Two of the Chinamen were sent over the side, and after a few ax blows scrambled aboard the *Kut Sun* again. The yards were braced around, the old whaler leaned over on her girders, and drew away under the foaming breeze; behind her, the fishing launch went lurching and sinking into the wave hollows with her two dead men. The object in her bow had been a small machine gun, loaded and ready for use. Carlisle had been ready to adopt other measures if the Chinese had refused to sell their gasoline; so at least it appeared.

As Solomon and Brune reasoned it out at mess that evening, the lure of that gasoline cargo had been too much for the plotters. They could obtain the essence in comparatively small quantities by means of Japanese fishermen, of course; but with a big cache stored away on one of the deserted Coronados, Rezek would be secure for some time to come.

"There's not a warship out here that could catch him," said Brune, "while submerged he would have a clear field. It's a mighty lucky thing that Case never fitted up the boat with real torpedoes, John! That fellow would hold up anything going, and he could get away with it clean."

"Well, we ain't got 'im yet," responded the cockney gloomily. "Nor 'e ain't got the gasoline yet. But we've got Mr. Carlisle down in the fore 'old, and 'e stays there."

Brune ascertained that Los Coronados were barren rocks sticking out of the ocean, within sight of San Diego, and used for nothing except target practice by the United States ships. The smallest island, according to Wun Sing, was only a bare rock, fifty feet high and a half mile long, and there was no landing on the island.

"There's landings on some o' them there islands?" queried Solomon.

Wun Sing got out his "North Pacific Pilot" and proved to the satisfaction of all concerned that there was but one landing place, and that this was upon the largest of the three islands, and was not easy of access.

"Then why did Carlisle direct us to the smallest island?" inquired Brune.

"To throw us off the track, sir," declared Solomon. "Mr. Wun Sing, you'll lay your course for that 'ere big island and mind it lays south eleven east from Point Loma. We ought to reach there about midnight, mebbe?"

"Six bells, mebbeso," corrected the skipper. "Plenty first-chop wind."

"Why not wait till morning to reach there?" queried Brune, frowning. "There'd be no mistake by daylight, and you've failed already at night—"

"Mr. Brune, me plans is made, and I won't change 'em," said Solomon, with dignity. It seemed that he did not care to be reminded of his late coup. "If so be as we gets there by eleven to-night, well an' good. I thought all along as Rezek would lay up at them 'ere Coronados, 'cause why, they're the werry best place for 'im."

"You thought so all along?" repeated Brune. "Say, I'd like to know whether you're a crystal gazer or just a plain medium, John! How on earth do you do it?"

"Well, sir, there's a 'ole lot in putting yourself in the other bloke's boots," chuckled Solomon, mollified completely by Brune's candid amazement. "Also, them as trusts in Prowidence ain't werry far mistook in their guess, as the Good Book says. Well, I'm a-goin' to get a bit o' sleep, and I'd adwise you to do the same, sir."

Brune turned in readily enough, but he could not cease wondering at the marvelous brain of John Solomon.

Even did Solomon possess an intimate knowledge of the Pacific coast, which he did not, by what reasoning could he have selected the Coronados as the hiding place of Rezek, when there were plenty of other desolate spots? Solomon was usually inclined to attribute his successes to "Prowidence," but Brune knew that Providence alone was not directly responsible for the little cockney's amazingly correct forecasts.

"Perhaps it's intuition," thought the ex-journalist, as he rolled in for the watch, below. "More likely, however, it's an infernally clever knowledge of human nature. And I'm inclined to think that Solomon is able to discount the law of chances pretty safely; no matter what turns up against him, he seems to have foreseen it!"

Brune's faith in this particular ability, however, was destined to receive a very rude shock before many more hours.

He wakened in darkness, to find Solomon urging him from sleep. As he sprang out of his bunk and felt for his clothes, he heard the ship's bell striking six—eleven o'clock at night.

Solomon left the cabin and went on deck, and Brune followed in five minutes. He found the night perfectly clear of fog, for a wonder; as he emerged from the companionway, the sea ahead was hidden from him. Astern, and to port, he saw the alternating red and white light of Point Loma, with the glare of San Diego on the horizon.

Then, as he went over to the rail and gazed ahead, a cry of admiration broke from him.

Towering out of the water to a height of six hundred feet, and so close that the *Kut Sun* seemed directly upon its surf-pounded cliffs, was a huge, wedge-shaped mass of rock a mile and a half in length.

It rose abruptly from the water, massive and yet clear cut in the delicate starlight, with the surf sending long streamers of phosphorescence along its length. Grim and great it was, ominous in its towering grandeur, threateningly somber as the long Pacific surges thundered and boomed upon its seaward cliffs.

"Well, we're 'ere," sighed Solomon, at Brune's elbow. "We're 'ere, and there ain't no sign o' Rezek in sight."

The *Kut Sun* was making no effort at concealment. A man was in the chains taking flying soundings and shouting back the results; besides her regular white lights, a lantern had been run up to the crow's nest; half of her crew were in the rigging, taking in sail in lubberly fashion. It seemed that she was rather seeking to attract attention than to escape it.

Slowly they forged in under the eastern side of the island, and within its lee the wind dropped away, while over them towered the massive rock, dark and terrible. Watching it, Brune started suddenly; from the Chinese broke a guttural cry. A swift-darting flash of light had appeared and vanished, halfway down the eastern shore of the rock.

"An' that'll be Rezek," said Solomon and mopped at his brow.

Brune did not reply. Like every one aboard the *Kut Sun,* he felt that this night-brooding mass of rock was ominous, mysterious, menacing. He wished that they had reached the place by daylight.

The soft bell at the mast forward struck seven bells. It was a half hour to midnight.

CHAPTER XIV

REZEK

BRUNE HAD never been quite sure just how many Chinamen the *Kut Sun* carried.

To him, the yellow men all looked alike. Owing to this confusion, and to the division of the crew into watches above and below, his impression at San Pedro that they carried an extra large crew had remained as nothing more than an impression.

Now, however, when he heard Solomon ask the skipper if all hands had been called, and Wun Sing nodded. Brune glanced along the lantern-lit deck and found that his impression must have been incorrect. Including the skipper, he counted just fifteen yellow men. All bore rifles, and all were on deck.

"Going to send any one to the crow's nest?" he asked Solomon.

"No, sir, I ain't. I 'opes as it won't be necessary. If so be as you'll stand back out o' the light, I'll 'ave a bit o' talk wi' that 'ere Rezek."

Brune stepped into the shadow of the try works and waited.

Another chattering cry broke from the grouped crew at the rail. With sudden excitement leaping through him, Brune looked—and caught a long V-shaped trail through the faintly phosphorescent water between the brig and the island. At the tip of the V was a tiny object, barely visible in the starlight.

It was the periscope of the stolen submarine!

Swiftly, Brune wondered how Solomon could hope to tempt Rezek aboard without the presence and voice of Carlisle to allay any suspicion. He knew that Solomon wanted Rezek alive, if possible, and wanted to recapture the submarine—otherwise, it would have been simple to let Rezek show himself, then riddle him with bullets.

Now Solomon went to the starboard rail, while two Chinamen brought lanterns and stood on the rail above, so that the little cockney was excellently lighted. As this was being done, the periscope, now a hundred feet away, rose and became the conning tower of the submarine. Then it came to rest. A moment later the hood of the tower slid back, and the dark shape of a man's head and shoulders protruded.

"Aboard the *Kut Sun!*" came the piercing, whistling voice of Rezek. "Are you there, Carlisle?"

"No, sir, 'e ain't," responded Solomon promptly. "Mr. Carlisle, 'e made arrangements wi' me, an' then 'e went off in 'is launch to San Diego after givin' me sailin' directions. Where's your danged anchorage?"

"Who the devil are you?" demanded Rezek's startled voice.

"Solomon's me name, sir. I'm on shares wi' the Leong Sing people in this 'ere boat. Mr. Carlisle come aboard about two bells in the first dogwatch, sir."

"Was he alone?" Rezek evidently wanted to make quite sure.

"Two Japs in 'is launch, sir. 'E signed an agreement to purchase our cargo at eighteen cents a gallon, but we'd be werry glad to touch a bit o' the money afore we breaks out any cargo, sir. It's in butts, and werry mean to 'andle, it is."

Brune could hear the chuckle of Rezek at this speech.

Solomon was playing his little part of stolid British seaman, and was playing it well. But, for that matter, no one would have suspected the pudgy little man of playing any part at all.

"Are you ready to unload cargo right now, to-night?" demanded Rezek.

"All ready if you be, sir."

"Then you'd better anchor where you are. It's good enough ground in this wind."

"Werry good, sir."

Evidently Solomon's tone had quelled any suspicion which might have arisen in the mind of Rezek. Wun Sing sent men bustling forward and aloft: the sails were clewed up, and the anchor went overboard with a resounding splash and rattle as the chain ran out. Solomon stayed where he was.

The torso of Rezek disappeared, and an instant later the submarine came gliding in to the brig like a ghostly thing, so silent were her engines. Presently, as she drew alongside, Brune could see her no longer without going to the rail; but he could see John Solomon mopping his brow, and knew that the cockney was struggling against temptation to drop a couple of Chinamen into the submarine and finish Rezek.

But Solomon, it seemed, preferred a safer and more theatrical finish, and so resisted the temptation.

"Pass me down a line, will you?" sounded Rezek's voice. "Tow this craft up forward so the drift of the current won't bang her against you. I'll come aboard and make you a first payment, after which we'll see about getting the casks ashore."

"Werry good, sir," responded Solomon, giving Wun Sing a nod.

The crew quietly laid their rifles out of sight, and waited, half a dozen of them tailing on to the line and towing Rezek to the bow. That plausible statement about the drift of the current quite escaped the notice of every one; but Brune remembered, later, the smoothness of that request.

Solomon turned inboard. The Chinese seamen clustered aft, also, the lantern light making every portion of the quarter-deck clear; Brune drew back closer into the shadow of the try-works, as he heard the firm tread of Rezek coming down the deck. Then the man himself came into the circle of light.

He was smiling that same pursy, fishlike smile which Brune remembered so well. In the yellow light, his bronze eyes blazed at the circle of men with the same sleepy, feline expression; his long, gorilla arms hung at his sides. He strode forward, fat, confident, terrible. With his coming, something of his great force of character seemed to be felt by every man there—aye, though they knew that he was coming into the trap unarmed, they shrank from him!

Jan Rezek, with all his faults, was a man.

"Werry 'appy to meet you, sir," observed Solomon, with an inane smile.

He replaced his clay pipe in his mouth, and stared at Rezek, who in turn stared at him. Under that baleful stare, perhaps even John Solomon lost his nerve, for he abandoned all further pretense, and plunged straight to the point.

"Mr. Rezek, put up your 'ands werry quick!"

There was a little movement among the Chinese standing around. Rezek looked from side to side, and found rifles leveled at him. His fat face never changed.

"I am unarmed," he said slowly, raising his hands.

Captain Wun Sing stepped forward and confirmed this statement.

"Tie 'is wrists—be'ind 'im," wheezed Solomon.

Rezek submitted to the operation without a word. But still he stared at the little cockney, until Brune, hardly able to realize that their man was captured without a fight, stepped forward into the radiance of the lanterns. Then Rezek looked at him and smiled.

"Good evening, Mr. Brune," he said quietly. "Do I have you or Mr. Solomon to thank for this neat little trap?"

"I'm afraid I can't claim the credit," and Brune forced a smile. He still felt fear of this man, he scarcely knew why. "Mr. Solomon has genius a trifle better than your own, Rezek."

"So?" Rezek smiled, though there was a blaze of fury in his bronze eyes. "Were that so, it would indeed be a compliment to Solomon. Where, may I ask, is Carlisle?"

"Down in the 'old," answered Solomon, mopping his brow in evident relief. "Down in the 'old, in irons. And 'e's a-goin' back wi' you, Mr. Rezek, to answer for the murder o' Mr. Case."

"Very interesting, I'm sure. You're an interesting person, too, Solomon! You must have guessed that I wanted gasoline very badly indeed."

Still Rezek was smiling. Despite his bound wrists, he looked anything but a beaten, desperate man who was destined to the penitentiary or worse; only by the furious, yellow eyes could one know the fires raging within him.

The Chinese crowded around, staring. Like true Mongols, they admired a good gambler, and certainly Rezek appeared to be losing with excellent grace. Moreover, the terrible catlike poise of the man was fascinating. Leaning on their rifles, they watched him with intent eyes.

In their intentness was cold cruelty, and not a little fear mingled with perplexity. Rezek's attitude impressed them, puzzled them. They would have shot him without compunction at the slightest danger sign, yet they could not understand his impassive acceptance of defeat. He awed them. Even Brune, whose fear of the man was not a physical fear so much as an uneasiness, a mental uncertainty as to what lay behind those glowering, bronze eyes—even Jack Brune sensed that Rezek was laughing at them all. So, at least, it seemed.

"Well," and Solomon sighed wheezily as he filled his pipe, "you'd best take 'im below with 'is chum, cap'n. Then we can 'ead for San Diego—"

"Wait a minute," put in Rezek, rather in demand than request. "Was it you. Solomon, who jumped us at San Nicolas Island, and murdered my men?"

"Yes, sir, it were," responded Solomon, with some asperity. "And a werry good job, if I do say it as shouldn't! If we 'adn't gone an' slipped up on you an' Carlisle—"

Rezek interposed his whistling chuckle. He seemed quite at his ease.

"You may call it a good job, but I don't—you made a bad slip when you let the two of us get away! If I were you, I wouldn't be so proud of a murderous piece of work like that—wiping out men as if they were flies!"

Solomon lighted his pipe.

"'Oo killed Mr. Case?" he asked placidly.

"Carlisle, of course. What of it? We only killed one man in our whole campaign. Yet we came within an ace of winning a tremendous stake, Solomon. It seems to me that one would call that neat work, very neat work! And what do you do? You come in with a splurge of bullets, with wholesale murder, and then call it good work—even when you miss your biggest game! Bah!"

The scorn in Rezek's voice stung the little cockney. He gazed at Rezek, puffing clouds of smoke from his old clay pipe.

"That's all werry fine," he responded, with evident restraint. "But your men was spies—"

"Are you working for the United States, then?"

"Yes, sir," nodded Solomon.

At that, Rezek laughed suddenly, and drew himself erect; his piercing voice held a new ring, as of sudden exultation.

"Solomon, you might be very much surprised to know where I was about this time last night! I was in San Pedro harbor, alongside this old tub of yours, and I saw you and Brune go aboard with the port officers. What do you make of that?"

A startled exclamation broke from Brune, as he realized what the man's words must mean. Solomon stared—then from the Chinese broke a sudden, shrill word, a cry of alarm.

"Quiet!" Rezek's voice lifted in wild triumph. "Quiet! The first man to move is dead!"

Brune turned with the others. On either side the try-works he saw a shadowy figure with leveled rifle; and on the brick try-works, in complete command of the quarterdeck, were two others. He knew them at once for Japs.

Amazed, incredulous, Brune stared, with the Chinese. Solomon stood motionless; but from his nerveless fingers dropped his pipe, and shattered on the deck.

"Shoot the first man to lift a rifle!" commanded Rezek swiftly. "Solomon, kindly loose my wrists."

Turning, he backed to Solomon, being careful not to cover the little man's figure with his own. Solomon, looking suddenly aged and worn, stooped and loosened the rope that bound Rezek's wrists together.

The fat man glanced around, chuckling horribly. Not one of the Chinese dared to move, although Solomon eyed them in mute and agonized appeal. Brune himself, full in the light, knew well that a single motion meant swift and merciless death.

"Now, gentlemen, I will collect your rifles," said Rezek, and suited action to word. "Mr. Brune, kindly pick up one of these lanterns and go forward into the extreme bow. The rest of you follow him in single file. Solomon, go last."

The rifles flung down on the deck, the Chinamen disarmed without any attempt at fight. Brune had no choice but to obey. Rezek's startling turning of the tables seemed to have paralyzed them all alike. The man was inhuman—supernatural.

As Brune took up a lantern and started forward, quite conscious that one of the Japs on the try-works was training a rifle on him, he heard Rezek's chuckling explanation, directed at Solomon behind:

"You see, my dear Solomon, you overlooked one thing—the genius of Jan Rezek, if I do say it as shouldn't!" The mockery was bitter. "Yes, I vaguely suspected your little scheme and was in San Pedro last night. I sent Carlisle to you, as you wished, to lure you here. I will pay you the honor of saying that you are too dangerous a man to leave alive, Mr. John Solomon. Therefore, you must die—presently, presently! You see, I really have need of the gasoline you so kindly brought me, and I took pains to assure myself at San Pedro that you were really putting gasoline aboard here."

Brune groaned as he stumbled forward.

Rezek possessed genius, indeed—infernal, diabolical genius! Worse than all must have been the realization to Solomon of how he himself had been tricked, both by Rezek and by Carlisle—how the latter had come aboard in full expectation of being made prisoner. He had doubtless sacrificed his two Japs in cold-blooded calculation.

"John has met his match at last," thought Brune miserably. "And now that devil means to kill him—confound it, we're absolutely helpless!"

How Rezek's four Japs had come aboard was only too clear. The submarine had been towed to the bows of the brig; while Rezek had come aft, with the whole crew closed in around him, the four Japs had stolen aboard from the submarine and had posted themselves. Instead of taking warning from the two men with Carlisle, Solomon had evidently taken for granted, just as Brune had done, that Rezek was alone with the stolen submarine. The ironical climax of the whole thing was that Solomon had brought the gasoline which Rezek needed.

Forward into the bow went Brune, and after him trailed the crestfallen Chinese, all fifteen of them. They bore the rest of the lanterns which had illuminated the after deck, so that, what with those in the rigging, the bows of the ship had no dark places. Up around the heel of the bowsprit clustered the Chinese in a frightened, herded mass; Brune stood a little apart from them, watching.

Last of all came Solomon, with Rezek at his heels. The pudgy little man seemed quite crushed. Without a word, he obeyed Rezek's orders, and seated himself on the edge of the forecastle head, just beyond Brune. Thus, Solomon, Brune, and the Chinese sailors were crowded into the angle of the bows, facing Rezek and directly under the fire of the four Japanese, and consequently unable to make a move without detection.

The hogsheads had been lowered into the hold by means of a single spar derrick, fitted with pennant purchase topping lift, and winch. It still stood in place above the fore hatch, and Rezek looked up at it with critical eye. Then he kicked at the hatch cover and beckoned to the Chinese.

"Two of you men step out here. Take off this cover, and bring up Mr. Carlisle."

Wun Sing chattered an order, and two of his men obeyed sullenly. The hatch off, they dropped into the hold, while one of the Japanese, at the open hatchway, watched them, with rifle ready. A moment later they reappeared with Carlisle in train.

"I'll trouble you for the key of those handcuffs, Mr. Solomon," said Rezek.

Solomon handed over the key in silence. Carlisle was released, and for a moment he stood glaring at Solomon in an evil, leering silence, while he rubbed his chafed wrists. Then he smiled the Mephisto smile which brought back to Brune such memories of suffering.

"I think," he said metallically, "that Mr. Solomon will enjoy having known me. He will be paid a great compliment. He will be a subject on which I may experiment with my mixture of conine and strychnine—the result will be fatal, of course, but think how interesting! The action of two such opposite drugs on the worthy Mr. Solomon will be a delightful thing to watch!"

"You devil!" cried out Brune hoarsely. "Rezek, you're not going to let this fiend do his will—"

"Why not, Mr. Brune?" Rezek laughed slightly, his yellow eyes flaring out at Brune. "According to your own testimony, Solomon is the man whom I should regard as dangerous—and not you. Therefore, Solomon must die. Be very careful, sir, that I do not give you to Carlisle, also! Another word from you, and I will do so!"

The final words cracked out piercingly. Brune clenched his lips and said no more. But his heart smote him on catching Solomon's look of entreaty, of hopeless despair; the little man was white-lipped, bowed down, crushed.

Rezek, however, turned on Carlisle.

"Your case is somewhere aboard."

"I imagine it is," nodded the poisoner. "Solomon seemed to cherish it."

His malevolent leer smote the little man.

"Well, go and find it!" snapped Rezek. "Then get back and help us. We'll have to get as much of this gasoline ashore as we can, and the yellow men can work."

"I've been thinking of it," nodded Carlisle. "You'd best rig a tailed block to the topmast, send a hawser ashore, and lay up the hogsheads among the rocks."

Rezek nodded comprehension and Carlisle strode away aft—doubtless in search of his deadly flat case.

Now, with a swift alertness which showed that his fat was not all extra tissue, Rezek walked up to the huddled Chinese, hauled Captain Wun Sing forth by the neck, and issued his orders—with the four Japs in the background to enforce them. The yellow seamen leaped to obey; and it soon became evident that the mysterious Rezek knew exactly what was to be done.

A whaleboat was lowered, and two Chinese set off for shore with a hawser and whip, in charge of a Jap. Two other seamen went aloft to the foretop. Then, with one Jap down in the hold to oversee the breaking out, and the other two remaining above to keep the captives in hand, Rezek set his prisoners to work at the derrick and cargo.

The huge butts, or pipes, each containing a hundred and a quarter of gallons, required careful handling. They were stowed in three tiers below, and to get one of the huge butts securely lashed, broken out from its bed and quoins, and hoisted to the deck above, was no light task; in fact, Brune was pressed into service at the winch, together with the sweating Celestials, before the first butt was safely landed on deck.

At this juncture, it was discovered that the two men aloft were having trouble with the tailing block—whereupon, Rezek sent Carlisle, who had returned with his flat case from somewhere below, to set matters right. This was barely done, when it appeared that the whipline, which had been taken ashore, had been partly hauled in by mistake, and lost between shore and ship. This necessitated the whaleboat returning for its recovery, and between the angry chattering of Chinese and Japanese a goodly amount of time was lost.

In the meantime, butt after butt came up from the hold. They were placed along the rails—perhaps a dozen in all. At that, Rezek called a halt on operations until the lines ashore could be made ready to sling the butts to the beach. A moment later, a hail from ashore gave word that all was right there, and Rezek gave orders to lash the first butt to the running block for the shore trip.

Carlisle, however, stopped him. The swarthy poisoner had opened his flat cast atop of the capstan, and seemed hugely gratified over finding its contents intact.

"Let us first remove our friend Solomon, Rezek," he said. "My experiment will require several hours, and it might do no harm to have Mr. Solomon on his beam ends in case anything went wrong with the work."

"Have it your own way," nodded Rezek. "We will knock off work until you have—ah—eliminated our very kind friend. I trust you will appreciate, Mr. Solomon, the absolute neatness and efficiency of the kind of work *we* do! A werry good job, I calls it."

Again the mockery stung deeply. Solomon lifted a weary, aged face.

"Mr. Rezek, you ain't a-goin' to 'ave me killed?"

"Too brutal a word," and Rezek laughed in his pursy manner. "You are to become a martyr, let us say, to the cause of Carlisle's science."

Solomon dropped his head again, in hopeless despondency. Brune felt a thrill of pity for the little man, whose carefully planned scheme had proven so futile, so puerile, against the infernal cunning of Jan Rezek.

Carlisle, holding up a hypodermic in the lantern light, carefully tried the tiny instrument again and again. Like Rezek, he seemed to enjoy playing with his victim. As he filled the syringe from a small vial, he looked at Solomon and smiled.

"Conine is a very interesting alkaloid, Mr. Solomon," he observed. "As our mutual friend, Mr. Brune, has perhaps told you, its results are quite opposite to those of strychnine. What, then, would a combination of strychnine and conine effect?"

He paused, leering down at the pudgy little man.

"With strychnine producing convulsions and rigor, with extremely rapid heart action, we find conine producing paralysis and lack of respiration—in fact, the two toxic qualities are somewhat of an offset to each other. You can well imagine that the combination of the two, in sufficient quantity to be vital, must have very startling results, eh? Now, Mr. Solomon, kindly stretch out your arm, unless you would prefer to be forced."

Solomon seemed dazed, stupid.

Slowly he bared his arm, while Carlisle stood over him. Then, as the blank blue eyes passed from face to face, Brune could have sworn that he caught a swift wink; but almost instantly the pudgy little man was gazing at Rezek.

"One minute, sir," he said. "Might I 'ave the liberty of askin' you one thing, Mr. Rezek?"

CHAPTER XV

THE GENIUS OF SOLOMON

R EZEK'S BRONZE eyes glowered steadily at Solomon.

"What is it?"

"Well, sir, I was wantin' to ask you if you'd ever 'eard o' them 'ere Maxim silencers bein' used on revolvers—automatics?"

Very blank, very expressionless was Solomon's upturned face. At that inane, pointless query, even Brune's heart sank; it seemed that the little man had given way beneath the strain.

Perhaps Rezek had the same idea. He stared at Solomon, then laughed slightly.

"Why, it's very possible. The silencer can be used on a single-shot pistol, but not on a revolver, owing to the backfire of the gases. An automatic, with a long recoil chamber, however, would find the thing very practicable."

Solomon nodded gravely.

"I've thought so meself, sir. Would you mind lettin' me 'ave a whiff o' baccy afore Mr. Carlisle jabs that 'ere needle into me?"

Rezek nodded in contempt. Brune, knowing that Solomon's pipe had broken some time before, took out his own and filled it, handing it to Carlisle. He could not speak.

"Thank'ee, Mr. Brune," said Solomon. "If you'll be so good as to light it, Mr. Carlisle, I'll be werry much obliged. Mr. Rezek, did you ever 'ear of a book called the *Arabian Nights?* Werry interesting wolume it is, sir."

"Yes, I've read it," nodded Rezek, while Carlisle searched his pockets for a match, and at last produced one. "Why?"

"Well, sir," went on Solomon, taking the lighted match and holding it over his pipe, "did you ever read that 'ere story about 'ow a girl went an' found forty thieves a-lying 'id inside o' big jars?"

Rezek's eyes narrowed suddenly. But, with the words, Solomon had expelled a cloud of smoke from his mouth.

As if that had been a signal, from somewhere came a sharp "ping-g-g!"

Carlisle took a backward step. With a look of intense surprise on his face, he suddenly threw out his arms and slumped to the deck—shot between the eyes! A spat of flame seemed to leap from one of the huge butts standing by the rail, and one of the Japanese fell, with a choked cry.

Through Brune's brain flashed the connection between Solomon's final words and that wink. In one or two of these huge butts were concealed Chinese, armed with silenced automatics!

With the realization, Brune saw Rezek's hand go to his pocket. Instantly he flung himself forward and struck the fat man bodily, in a flying tackle that carried them both headlong into the scuppers.

The *Kut Sun* leaped into pandemonium.

Though he dimly realized that the Chinese had flung themselves on the remaining two Japs, Brune had no chance to divide his energies. He found himself fully occupied in handling Jan Rezek.

In that first moment, he was amazed at the tremendous power in those long, gorillalike arms. Gripping Rezek's fat throat, he tried to fling the man's head against the rail as they went down; but he could not. Those long arms had wrapped about him with fearful pressure, and now they began to tighten remorselessly.

It was no fight of science or skill, but a mad, merciless struggle, while above them the other two Japanese were dying, exacting a life apiece from their rifles as they went down. Still the long arms tightened, tightened about Brune's ribs; desperate, he loosed his grip on Rezek's throat and drove in blows as best he could to the man's face.

He could put no force into those blows—he had no purchase. In his ears sounded a horrible, whistling chuckle, and his ribs were cracking under the death hug. Brune lashed out wildly, trying to break that hold with a fierce savagery; as the two men thrashed about the deck, their bodies interlocked, the watching Chinese leaped away. There was no chance for a blow that would help Brune. The fighters were weaving about swiftly, and Rezek managed to keep underneath, Brune's body shielding him from those around.

Whatever might be his opponent's ultimate object, Brune felt that terrific grip crushing the resistance from him. He had been a fool to jump in! With desperate, spasmodic struggles, he tried to writhe clear of that deadly embrace. The terrible arms only closed about him more tightly, until he could have screamed with the sheer agony of that constricting clutch about his waist. He felt ringed with fire.

A gasp broke from him—he was failing fast, and knew it. Still he strove to batter his way clear, but a red haze obscured everything about him, now.

Then, as from a great distance, he heard the voice of Solomon:

" 'Old werry still, sir!"

Brune stiffened, instinctively obeying the mandate. A sudden choking cry burst from Rezek. The awful arms loosened their grip, and Brune rolled away. Half senseless, frantic with pain, he could only hang to the Chinese who caught him, and gasp for air.

A moment later, the pain of his body finding relief, he straightened up as the red mist cleared from his eyes. On the deck before him he saw Rezek, arms and legs held out by four Chinese; his fat face horribly contracted, the man was staring up at the figure of Solomon. The latter was speaking calmly, holding up a small, glittering object.

"Werry sorry I am to 'ave to say it. Mr. Rezek, but I can't recommend your kind o' work—no, sir. I can't! You ain't got a werry neat manner o' doin' things, as the old gent said when 'e kissed the new 'ousemaid."

"You damned mountebank!" snarled the prostrate Rezek. "You—you shot that into me—"

"Yes, sir, I did, and a werry good job it was! As for bein' damned, why, that ain't neither 'ere nor there, as the Good Book says."

Brune stared at the glittering object held in Solomon's fingers. His eyes dilated with horrified recognition. It was the hypodermic which Carlisle had charged with poison.

An hour later, Brune, feeling acutely conscious of his two broken ribs, stiffly descended the companionway of the *Kut Sun*.

Brune found Solomon in the cabin, where beneath the swinging lamp lay Jan Rezek on the mess table. The man was quite motionless, but his great, yellow eyes blazed in mute hatred at sight of Brune.

"Well, how is he? According to what Carlisle said, he should be slated for the Great Divide."

Solomon chuckled, and motioned toward the case that lay at his side.

"Well, sir, some men ain't a-goin' to die afore their time. Mr. Rezek, 'e's making werry 'ard weather of it, so to speak, but I'm a-dosing 'im with every blessed thing 'ere. There ain't no danger of 'is dying afore we gets to port."

Brune lowered himself carefully to a seat.

"John, you're a wonderful man," he said gravely, "but I'm through with you. Why, you infernal scoundrel, up to the very last minute I was pitying you and figuring on making a jump at Carlisle! And all the time you had those men in the butts, waiting!"

"Yes, sir," chuckled Solomon. "Werry neat work it was, if I do say it as shouldn't."

"Well, I'm through with you!" exclaimed Brune. "I have every respect for you—I like you up to the hilt—I'd do anything on earth for you; except to work with you again! I'd not go through another half hour like that for a million dollars, flat. You worked the same trick when we handled those rug thieves, and it nearly gave me heart failure then. This time I'm done."

"Well, sir, I'm werry sorry to 'ear it," said Solomon, gazing at him placidly. "You see, sir, one o' me friends as is werry influential in Los Angeles—Mr. 'Ip Sun is 'is name—'e's been and asked me if I knowed a level-'eaded young American gent as could take care o' some business deals in Chicago and New York. I've been an' fixed it all up, and werry sorry I'd be to 'ave you go back on me now."

"Eh?" Brune stared in amazement. "You mean—"

"Yes, sir, just like that. It ain't only a matter o' five thousand a year wages, but a commission, to boot. Werry good proposition it is, sir."

Brune said nothing for a long moment. Then he laughed suddenly.

"John, I'll not go back on you if you'll tell me one thing," he said slowly. "Did you actually set out from San Pedro with the intention of catching Rezek and Carlisle on a gasoline bait—or did you all along have a trap within a trap? By George! It doesn't seem possible that any one would take such chances—"

"Mr. Brune," interposed the little cockney earnestly, "this 'ere Rezek, 'e never made no mistakes. Prowidence don't never make no mistakes, neither. But man ain't Prowidence, I says. When so be as a man thinks 'e's in the shoes o' Prowidence, 'e's liable to get 'is foot pinched. Now, this 'ere Rezek is a-goin' to prison for a werry long time, and the United States 'as got the Case submarine. There's only one thing as I'm werry sorry for."

"What's that? The death of Carlisle?"

"No, sir. It's that old pipe o' mine as got bust."

Brune's involuntary laughter was cut short by a stab of pain. He caught himself up with a groan.

"John, these ribs of mine need attention! I'll have to have a week's rest, too."

"You might come along o' me to Los Angeles—"

"Sure I might—but I have another idea. What's the quickest way to get to Long Beach from San Diego?"

ABOUT THE AUTHOR

H. BEDFORD-JONES is a Canadian by birth, but not by profession, having removed to the United States at the age of one year. For over twenty years he has been more or less profitably engaged in writing and traveling. As he has seldom resided in one place longer than a year or so and is a person of retiring habits, he is somewhat a man of mystery; more than once he has suffered from unscrupulous gentlemen who impersonated him—one of whom murdered a wife and was subsequently shot by the police, luckily after losing his alias.

The real Bedford-Jones is an elderly man, whose gray hair and precise attire give him rather the appearance of a retired foreign diplomat. His hobby is stamp collecting, and his collection of Japan is said to be one of the finest in existence. At present writing he is en route to Morocco, and when this appears in print he will probably be somewhere on the Mojave Desert in company with Erle Stanley Gardner.

Questioned as to the main facts in his life, he declared there was only one main fact, but it was not for publication; that his life had been uneventful except for numerous financial losses, and that his only adventures lay in evading adventurers. In his younger years he was something of an athlete, but the encroachments of age preclude any active pursuits except that of motoring. He is usually to be found poring over his stamps, working at his typewriter, or laboring in his California rose garden, which is one of the sights of Cathedral Cañon, near Palm Springs.

www.ingramcontent.com/pod-product-compliance
Lightning Source LLC
Chambersburg PA
CBHW020433030726
47495CB00006B/1781